C000003204

Above All C

Book Three of Above all Others:
The Lady Anne

By G. Lawrence

Copyright © Gemma Lawrence 2017
All Rights Reserved.
No part of this manuscript may be reproduced without
Gemma Lawrence's express consent

This book is dedicated to Brooke Aldrich, my Editor.
For helping me to achieve my dreams,
And for always being a friend.

No coward soul is mine
No trembler in the world's storm-troubled sphere
I see Heaven's glory shine
And Faith shines equal arming me from Fear

O God within my breast
Almighty ever-present Deity
Life, that in me hath rest,
As I Undying Life, have power in Thee

Vain are the thousand creeds
That move men's hearts, unutterably vain,
Worthless as withered weeds
Or idlest froth amid the boundless main

To waken doubt in one
Holding so fast by Thy infinity,
So surely anchored on
The steadfast rock of Immortality,

With wide-embracing love
Thy spirit animates eternal years
Pervades and broods above
Changes, sustains, dissolves, creates and rears

Though earth and moon were gone
And suns and universes ceased to be
And Thou wert left alone
Every Existence would exist in thee

There is not room for Death
Nor atom that his might could render void
Since Thou art Being and Breath
And what Thou art may never be destroyed.

Emily Bronte
No Coward Soul is Mine

Prologue

The Tower of London
The Morning of the 18th May 1536

I thought I was to die today.

I was ready... eager, even... I was prepared for the end of life; ready to take the skeletal hand of Death and step into the light of Heaven. I had steeled myself to face the crowds who would come to watch me die. I welcomed the thought of seeing my brother once again. I thought by now I would be free of my mortal pain and fear. At dawn, I took the Sacrament and made my last confession. I called Master Kingston, the Lieutenant of the Tower, to hear my confession. I swore, upon my soul, before witnesses and before God that I had never offended the King with my body, that I had never betrayed him with another.

But they did not come for me... I sat upon my stool. I waited.

The women about me, these horrors in the pay of Cromwell and Chapuys, they tell me Henry is already engaged, although I am not yet dead. Their words strike deep into my heart. My mind whispers, reminding me he did such once before... with me... with Katherine.

Their eyes gleam, bright and happy, to see the pain they inflict... How much more can they maim me? I have already lost everything. Only my immortal soul is left to me now. My husband has chosen another; my daughter will be declared a bastard by my own words; my brother and friends are dead and soon I will follow them to the coldness of the grave. I think on my poor mother and sister... what are they thinking now? Hiding at Hever, hoping this tempest will pass them by. On my father, I try not to think. I know he will scrabble about in the dirt that stains my name for a chance at redemption.

He will try to put the loss of his heir, George, from his mind. But I cannot. The empty hole my brother's death has left is a gaping wound in my heart; raw and bloody, it tears, it rends, it rips when I think of him.

His smile... his laugh... the way we used to talk... walks promised, now never to be taken. His soft friendship armed me against a hard world. I cannot forget him. My brother... He was my courage and my best friend.

I had thought that by now I would feel his hand, soft and warm, curled about my own. I had thought by this hour I would see them all again, all the innocents who have died for my sake, as we stood before the Almighty, in the soft light of Heaven. But it was not to be. My execution was delayed. The small hope I had left, to leave this life and enter the next, was ripped from my hands.

What do they hope to achieve with this delay? Is it a sign that the King relents? I think not. Were I to believe the worst, I would consider my enemies wished to offer me false hope. They would offer me this just so they could snatch it away, so I might understand their power over me. Hope... it can become a weapon, when it is used well.

When Master Kingston told me my execution was postponed, I gazed at him with glassy eyes brimming with disbelief. I had been in thought and prayer all morning, thinking of the past, and praying to God for strength. I rose unsteadily from my stool, my legs numb. My mind swam with the knowledge that I must wait another day, another night, for the blessed release of death. My courage faltered. My face fell. I must linger yet, in this pain and horror. Outside the Tower, the wind blew strong and fast, whipping about the walls. Its scream of despair echoed in my frail heart.

But even then I could not quite bring myself to believe that this delay meant that I would live. Events have gone too far now. My enemies would fear that Henry might agree to see me, if I lived, and might come to forgive me. They feared the remnants of my power over him. They worried that, even now, I might be able to reach into his heart and find mercy there. To allow me to live would only endanger them, as well I know from the lessons of the past. They would not make those mistakes, my clever enemies who had bested me at my own game. No… I knew that this delay was not my salvation. It was but another punishment.

I turned to Kingston, regarding him with my weary, red-rimmed eyes and tired mind. "Master Kingston," I murmured. "You say I shall not die afore noon and I am very sorry therefore, for I thought to be dead and past my pain."

"I am sorry, my lady," he said, not conferring upon me the title of Queen that I had so long worked for, and yet held for so small a time. The title is mine no longer. I gave it up in the last hope that it might buy my life, might save my daughter from persecution by my enemies. It was a fool's hope, but I had done as they asked; for Elizabeth even more so than for myself. I agreed I was never married to the King, both for my long ago dismissed contract with Henry Percy, and for my husband's past affair with my sister. "Your execution will come on the morrow, at nine o' clock, my lady," Kingston continued, glancing at me with troubled eyes.

His words sparked something of my old humour. I chuckled, strange emotions were bubbling within my breast. "I have heard the executioner is very good." My lips quivered with eerie mirth. "And I have a little neck."

I put my hands about the slim contours of my throat and pressed them into the soft skin there. Once, Katherine had called me a swan for the elegance of my bearing… Many times, Henry had kissed me here, his warm lips lingering on my flesh as he muttered words of love and devotion. It all seemed so far away now… as though that person were another Anne, one who was loved so deeply by her King that she could never fall from grace. I wondered where that Anne was, now. She was lost to me. I started to laugh louder. The sheer ridiculousness of my present fate overtook me.

Master Kingston stared at me as mirth spilled out over my lips, over my form, bouncing from the walls. It sounded unearthly… unnatural. I was nearing the edge of my capacity for calmness. I forced the laugh to end, shutting my lips over it, and turned my feral, dark eyes away. "I will return to my prayers, for the rest of the day, Master Kingston," I whispered, seeking to claim control over myself again. "If you would be so good as to leave me with my almoner."

Poor man… What was he to do for me? What was anyone? Did he remember when he faced one of my enemies in a situation so similar to this? When I brought down the great Cardinal Wolsey and Kingston was sent to bring him to this same Tower? How history enjoys circles. How fate likes to play games. Should I have known then that one day I would face the same destiny as the foe I crushed on my path to the throne? Should I have known that one day I would be a pawn in this game, when I had always thought myself a queen?

I returned to my prayers; that is the only love I have left within me now… for God… for my faith… But amongst the words I offered to God, the past beckons to me, still my memories cry out.

My memories… They call to me. They speak of the years that passed after I ran through my family's lands, crying out for joy that I was loved… that Henry, the man I had adored from afar for so long, had offered me his hand, and a place on the throne of England. What dreams for a young maid to be offered! What riches! What promise life held for me then! We thought it would only be a matter of months until Katherine could be prevailed upon to take the veil. It would not be long until we were joined as man and wife. Perhaps within a year, I would hold Henry's son in my arms. How very wrong, how very arrogant we were…

I bow my head in prayer as Kingston leaves. But amongst my pleading words to God, memories rise, reminding me of all I did, all that I achieved, all that I fought for... All that I became. I had thought that merely holding the heart of the King of England in my hands would be enough to secure my future and my happiness. I was wrong. It took more, so much more... so much of my wit and intelligence, so much of my guile, strength and allure... I had to use all the weapons at my disposal to achieve what I wanted.

The past does not want to be forgotten. It calls out for its tales to be told.

Chapter One

Hever Castle
Summer 1527

Nine Years Earlier...

The night after Henry left me to ride for London I could not sleep. I lay, wide awake in my bed of soft eiderdown, with the covers bunched about my waist. I stared at the hangings about my bed and ran a hand through my thick, dark hair. Strands of it stuck to my skin. It was a sultry night. The light rain which had fallen earlier in the day had passed over, heading to London... following the same path as my King...

My King... *My* Henry! He loved me as I loved him. Our love had been made truth by our words. It was done. We were promised to each other. One day soon he would be mine, as I would be his.

I remembered his forceful words of destiny and duty... I remembered his soft eyes... the way he had looked at me when he told me of his love. No longer was Anne Boleyn considered suitable as the mere *mistress* of the King of England... No, he wanted me as his own, his love, his wife, his Queen. Henry had said this was decreed by God; that I had been sent to Henry *by* God to make him understand the sin within his marriage. Was Henry right? I wondered on the manner in which Henry talked of God. It was as though the two of them were equals, allies, friends, even. Was that the usual way, for kings? To feel so close to the Almighty that they could sense His thoughts? That they could know His will? Kings were chosen by God... Was it indeed God's will that I become Queen in the place of Katherine? Even as I welcomed the thought, I was made uncomfortable by it. It seemed arrogant... And yet, somehow, when Henry said those words, they had made perfect and beautiful sense.

I thought of the past. How swiftly had life changed for me! Thoughts and recollections of my life swam before my eyes, knotting my thoughts into confusion. I remembered shaking before I met the Archduchess Margaret in Mechelen. I remembered Henry's blue eyes watching me as I danced at his court and the sight of him riding through London on the eve of his coronation. I recalled how his hands had burned when he touched me. I remembered the day he had fallen from his horse… the day I thought I had lost him. I remembered him saying he loved me, that he wanted me, that he would make me his wife…

It must come to pass! I thought. Katherine *must* be prevailed upon to see the sense and reason in Henry's arguments. Theirs was no true marriage. Being so good and pious a woman as she was, she must come to understand she had been living sinfully with Henry all this time… she must…

But there was another part of me that was not as sure… *She is proud*, it said. *She will not suffer to be set aside, as she was once before, when Arthur died. She has known abandonment and poverty; she will not willingly choose that path again… She will not look on the King's arguments with an eye of favour…*

"What of her, then?" I said aloud, to myself, willing that troublesome voice to cease its prattling. "If she will not see reason, then she will be *made* to… The King has decided that this is how it will be, and so it will!"

Bess rolled over in her pallet bed on the floor and blinked sleepily, roused by the words that had tumbled from my lips. "Mistress…?" she asked, rubbing a hand over her eyes and gazing up at me blearily. "Did you need something?"

I shook my head and felt my cheeks ignite. "It is nothing, Bess," I murmured. "I must have been talking in my dreams… Please, go back to sleep."

My tired maid hardly needed telling twice. She put her head to her hay-stuffed pillow and was asleep before I ceased to speak. It had been a long few days for her. Standing at my side as Henry had laid out his plans to leave Katherine, annul their marriage and marry me was quite enough excitement for my young maid to merely witness. I, who had been part of these plans and events, was even more exhausted. And yet, slumber would not come for me.

I lay awake. I listened to the quiet sound of Bess breathing, her nose burrowed deep into her covers of thick, warm English wool. In the depths of the night, the sticky heat of the day retreated and coldness grew. I pulled my covers over my slim shoulders, ruffling into them, thinking that nesting like a harvest mouse amongst the barley stalks might lull me to sleep. But it did not.

Late that night I heard the screech of an owl, and climbed from my bed to go to the window. Through the fine panes of glass I saw her; a ghost winging through the black-blue skies. She floated, white and silent through the air like a lost soul seeking rest. I watched her until she was out of sight, and only then noticed how cold I was. My bare feet padded eagerly across the floor and I climbed back into bed.

I had thought I would never sleep, but eventually I must have, for I found myself within a dream; a dream so familiar that for a moment I looked around with wide and astonished eyes. *I have been here before*, I thought, *I know this place…* I stood on a barren and open hill, surrounded by scrubby, half-dead plants dotted here and there, resting on red-brown earth baked by the brilliant red-yellow sun above. Fragments of earth skittered, dry dust flying along, pushed by a small breeze. The wind lifted my hair from my hot neck. I stood before a tower built of great grey stones, so tall I could not see the top… and from the walls and stones of the tower, there flowed blood.

This was why I knew this place… I had dreamed of it before, when I was but a girl and journeyed to Mechelen to become a part of the Archduchess' household. I gazed at the tower. It bled. Blood seeped from the walls and the stones, from the cracks and oozed up from under its foundations… It burbled like a busy brook, seeping over the parched soil. I stared at the tower in fascinated horror and then I reached out and touched the stones. The blood spilled over my hands, under my nails, over my palms, down my wrists. I could feel it… warm and sticky, its sickly sweet, iron-stench rising from the heat of my skin. I shuddered and pulled my hand back, but blood continued to flow, as if from nowhere, over my hands. I held them out before me, shaking, and saw a drop of blood fall from my chin to join the swirling mess upon my hands.

Putting my bloody hands to my face, I found there was no skin there, but only raw, red and pink flesh… muscle, sinew, bone… I looked up at the tower, and its walls and stones had disappeared, concealed under the flow of blood. It fell, as though from a vast waterfall above me, pouring over the dry land, soaking into the parched earth. The scrubby plants shuddered, their roots lifted. They drifted away, carried by the river of blood.

As I stood staring, a wave of blood rose and washed me away. I went to cry out, but the wave lashed over my head. My feet lifted from the ground. I was carried into the surging river. I struggled to keep my head, my mouth, from the soft yet insistent power of the blood-river, but I could not. I cried out weakly for help, gulping in mouthfuls of the tepid blood and spitting them out. But there was no one there to help me. As my head disappeared under the crimson waves, I awoke with a scream, which sent Bess reeling to my side, half-tripping, stumbling, her legs half-tangled in her covers. She crushed her toes painfully on the edge of my bed and with a pale face, biting her lip hard to stop from cursing with pain, she scrambled to my side.

"My lady!" she exclaimed, grabbing hold of me, her eyes white-wild. "What is it?"

Seeing Bess made me realise I was no longer in that awful dream. I shook my head, falling back upon my pillows, unable to speak for a moment. I shuddered, but assured Bess it was but a bad dream. I tried to lie down again, but the cloying sensation of my own sweat on the covers made me rise. It felt like the sticky blood. I did not care if the room was cold, or that it was still an hour before dawn. I wanted to be out of this bed, and away from the horrific dreams that had visited me on what should have been the happiest night of my life.

Bess helped me to dress and I went outside, ordering her to stay within the castle. She looked confused, but did not seek to accompany me. I walked quietly through the empty, shadowed corridors, down the stairs and into the courtyard. The cool, fresh air was soothing against my heated skin. My soft shoes made little noise on the cobblestones. I wandered the paths of my mother's gardens until the dawn began to emerge on the horizon, unwilling to return to bed. I could not shake the dream from my mind. My skin felt dirty; soiled by my nightmare. Where had that dream come from? Should I not have dreamt of happiness and joy? I had just been promised all I wanted, and more. Why now had this nightmare struck? Was it a warning? A portent?

I shook my head angrily. I did not believe in such things. Visions were for the blessed of God… holy men and women… and even then they were rare, and often faked for profit and acclaim. No… this had not come from God… but if not He, then whom? The Devil? My imagination? My fears of the future?

I had gone to bed happy, yes, but another part of me had questioned the girlish joy that had been mine that day. Another part of me had whispered warnings before I slept. *Perhaps it is as simple as that*, I thought. My own suppressed fears had intruded upon my dreams, since I had not allowed them a voice when I was awake. My fears were trying to be heard.

I glanced up at the sky. Dawn was coming. Streaks of orange, pink and white flitted through the darkness on the horizon. Dew was as silver upon the grass. At the edge of the woodlands, heads of graceful columbines bobbed in the light breeze, their petals like grey-blue eagle claws. Woody nightshade fluttered, reaching up to stroke the shadows, the dim light of dawn revealing its dark red berries. Bitter rue whispered as I passed it in my mother's physic garden. I could see the tiny yellow tufts of flowers upon stalks of silver-green. I rubbed a hand over my gritty eyes and smoothed my dress. I should go in and await the arrival of my father and mother. They knew Henry had come to Hever, and they would have guessed at his purpose. Soon enough all of my family would know I was Henry's intended wife and future Queen. Soon, all of the world would know too… although for now, Henry and I had agreed secrecy was of the utmost importance. But we knew it would not be long… Not long until he could leave Katherine, and I could take her place…

I gazed up at Hever. Her bright stone sides had started to glimmer with the distant light of the dawn. I would need to give orders to the kitchens and to the servants to prepare my parent's room anew after Henry had slept there. But right now, the thought of going back to the castle was too much for me. I needed time to clear my mind of all the horrors I had dreamt of last night. I needed to leave those visions behind.

I turned on my heel and made for the stables. The lads there would be rising. They would not mind if I came for my palfrey and took a ride before dawn turned to day.

Chapter Two

Hever Castle
Summer 1527

That afternoon my parents returned to Hever, finding me dazzled and somewhat bemused by the prospect of my glittering future. My night of but little sleep, and my strange dreams, had left me with a haunted mind. I sought to dismiss the eerie feeling, and look instead to the future Henry had promised me. This was not a time for worries and fears! I should be rejoicing, for all I had and all that had been promised to me. I did not speak of my dreams to my parents. I did not wish to trouble them with such foolishness.

My father grinned widely at me as he leapt from his horse. His questioning, hopeful glance was mirrored by that of my mother, and quickly he ushered us into their chambers, so that we might talk in private.

"Well?" my father asked, pouring himself wine from the leathern jug that Henry had touched only the night before. My father smirked at me. He seemed to be treating me less like a *tool* and more like an ally these days. He did not want to relinquish the power he had over me as a father, but now, there was a subtle change in his manner. Perhaps he respected me now, or perhaps he simply saw me as more useful than I had ever been before…

"Henry has asked me to be his queen…" I nodded slowly. "He proposes that the Pope should annul the marriage between Katherine and him, and he and I will marry within the year. He has gone to court to take the counsel of his advisors…" I lifted an eyebrow at my father. "I trust my uncle Norfolk will advise him rightly on the course that he should take?"

My father laughed heartily. "Aye!" he exclaimed. "I have no doubt that your uncle will advise him on the best course for our family."

"Should you not also be there, father?"

"I return almost immediately," he replied. "I will stay here tonight, and return to London in the morning. I just wanted to hear what occurred from your own mouth first." He looked jubilant. I don't believe I had ever seen him so happy. "You have done well, Anne. I am delighted… Finally! We have the outcome we desired! My daughter will be the Queen of England, and my grandsons will become kings!"

My father's crowing tone gnawed at my frayed spirits. He thought only of what this meant to *him*, rather than all it meant to me. But I did not attempt to reproach him; there would have been small point. My mother was quiet but she, too, smiled to hear Henry's intentions. She was happy that, unlike Mary, I would not have to whore myself to win the man I loved. My father may have been the wiliest in our family, but it was my mother who read people better. She knew I loved Henry. She knew I was concealing the depths of my feelings from my father. She was happy for me. After all, I was to be married most advantageously to a man who truly loved me, and whom I loved in return. What more can a mother ask than happiness for her children?

My father, true to his word, stayed the night and left before first light the next morning. He promised to send word, as soon as he was able, on the progress of the King's secret *Great Matter*; the process and proceedings of the annulment of his marriage. My father seemed almost impatient that I was so eager for news to be sent to me… as though, now that I had secured Henry, I would, in truth, have little to do with what followed. My father believed now was the time for men to take control. I was to sit back and wait, fulfilling my role as a woman. I was to be the placid girl hiding behind these men of action and decision. I did not like it, but if they could get our *Matter* decided quickly, I would not complain.

Before my father left, he gave me a book. It was to remain a secret, for it was a banned text in England, and many other countries. It was an English translation of the New Testament, by a scholar and reformist named Master William Tyndale, and it was a work of brilliance. Working from Cologne, Tyndale had managed to get his translation of the New Testament printed, and copies had started to trickle into England in the year just passed. It was illegal to translate the Bible into English, but Tyndale believed, as I did, that the common man had the right to hear the Word of God in his own language, to better understand his faith. Tyndale was an exile, banished from England for what the Church called heretical beliefs. But no matter this dangerous condemnation, he continued to work for the good of the faith.

Working from the original Greek, rather than the Latin translations of the Bible, Tyndale's text contained many revolutionary elements; one being the use of the word 'congregation' rather than 'Church'. The different choice of words showed that the authority the Church had long professed over spiritual matters was erroneous, and demonstrated that all of God's children were the representatives of Christ on earth. He also used 'elder' rather than 'priest', thus again nullifying the power of the Church. This work questioned the tyranny of the Church, and showed that each soul was responsible alone for their goodness, and faith. It was no wonder the Church had been scared by this text. Last year, Sir Thomas More, Henry's good friend and advisor, had led a raid with armed men upon merchants suspected of supplying Lutheran works. A procession of condemned men had been led through London after the raid. They had been bound in St Paul's, with symbolic faggots tied on their backs, as Cardinal Wolsey conducted a Mass over them. Forced to publicly recant, confess and beg forgiveness, the men had been pardoned for their 'sins', and baskets filled with seized works the Church considered heretical were taken outside to the rood, and had been burned on huge bonfires.

I have always thought that those who choose to burn books are those who fear the knowledge they contain.

More and Wolsey worked together, hunting down the banned Tyndales which were now flooding into England, along with other works of 'heresy', as they saw it. Last summer, the influx of Tyndale's work had caused the Church to set up a special meeting. Henry, ever a conservative in religious matters, and intensely proud of the title *Defender of the Faith*, conferred upon him by the Pope, had supported Wolsey. A proclamation had gone out banning Tyndale's New Testament and threatening arrest, and death, if any were found in possession of it. Bishop Tunstall had preached a passionate sermon against Tyndale's translation, and hundreds of copies had already been burned. Many, such as I, thought it was more disrespectful to God that His own words had been burned, than that they had been translated....

Thomas More set himself up in opposition to Tyndale, and the two men hated each other with a passion. Tyndale saw More as an enemy of God, and More saw Tyndale as a heretic. But the experience of reading the Bible in English was not one many forgot. It was exciting, and since the Church was so zealous in its attempts to have the book wiped from the face of the earth, many came to read it.

It was a dangerous, revolutionary book to have in one's possession. Banned by the King, banned by the Church, and should More have found my father had a copy, dangerous to our position at court. But Tyndale's book was beautiful. Tyndale might have been a poet for the glory of the language he used. It was lyrical, pretty, clever and sweet to the tongue. I had never read anything like it. I was captivated. Never had I been so inspired by an author before. Not even the reformists whose works I had read in

France had expressed themselves so beautifully. I treasured the book, and I kept it safe. It would not do to have it fall into unfriendly hands. And neither could I share this with my love, for he would see my possession of such a text as scandalous.

It was the one thing I was saddened about, in Henry. He was a fierce defender of the Church, even in matters where he should not be. His devotion to the Pope, and to the institutions of the Church as a whole, was passionate and intense. He would not understand my opinions. He would see them as heretical.

But that book helped me a great deal in those days of waiting. For a few hours each day, I could lose myself in it. Give myself up to the power and poetry of Tyndale, and hear the Word of God resounding in my head and my heart.

As I tarried restlessly at Hever, waiting on news, I had something made for Henry; a novelty that I thought would please him and allow him to understand my feelings. Henry loved games and riddles, and so I sent him one. A rather expensive riddle. It was a ship made crafted from pewter with a single woman standing on its bow. The woman held a diamond, tiny, but perfect, in her hands. Pewter waves crashed at the side of the ship. The jewel-makers did a fine job and I had it sent to Henry. The ship was to symbolise his protection over the lady from the storms of the sea, and the lady was, of course, meant to represent myself. The diamond was to signify my purity, my virginity, which I had now placed in his hands as my future husband. Henry wrote to tell me he was overjoyed with the gift. *"For so beautiful a gift and so exceeding, I thank you right cordially; not alone for the fair diamond and the ship in which the solitary damsel is tossed about, but chiefly for the good intent and too-humble submission vouchsafed in this your kindness..."*

I smiled as I read; he understood my meaning then. Henry continued, *"...ensuring you that henceforth my heart shall be dedicate to you alone, greatly desirous that so my body could be as well, as God can bring to pass if it pleaseth Him, whom I entreat once each day for the accomplishment thereof, trusting that at length my prayer will be heard, wishing for the time brief, and thinking it but long until we shall see each other again,*

Written with the hand of that secretary who in heart, body and will is

Your loyal and most ensured servant

H aultre AB ne cherse R "

Henry despised the task of writing. It was a mark of his devotion that he took on the office of scribe in writing to me. I kept every one of the letters Henry sent to me in a small chest in my rooms. When I missed him I would take them out and read them over and over, until I knew them by heart. Henry sent not only declarations of his love, but also some news on our *Matter*. He would soon speak to Wolsey, he wrote, and they would convene learned men to put together the case for his separation from Katherine. He assured me it would not be long until we were together, and soon, we would never again have cause to part.

His words brought me comfort, but I felt isolated at Hever. Even though I understood the sense in keeping me away from the proceedings, it still irked me. I did not like to be so far from Henry, so far from court, which was the only place I felt truly myself. The days went on, and I found myself staring out with a troubled brow at the beautiful countryside, wishing I was in London.

I tried to distract myself. Tried to fill the dragging, lonely hours. I read my Tyndale. I rode and I walked in the summer sun, wearing a plain mask of linen, strengthened with smooth bone so that my skin would not darken. Purple and russet butterflies flew to the tops of the tall trees, fluttering to the ground to sip water from small puddles left by the rain. Every now and then, as dusk fell, I would see the slinking shapes of black-striped badgers or russet foxes moving in the undergrowth. Maids from the village were out in the woods during the day, gathering wild herbs to dry and save for winter medicines. I heard their chatter as I rode with my father's servants through the country, and saw them emerge from the dark woodland with baskets full of wild mint, feverfew, tansy and hawthorn leaves.

There was a sense of happiness in the countryside at such times. Nature gave to her people bountifully in the summer, and none had to worry for the cold or the rain. There was enough for all… In the summer months, only sickness was a worry, for plagues spread more rapidly and with great vigour in the heat. But that summer at Hever, nothing came to threaten us. But even with the peace and beauty of Hever's lands surrounding me, I was restless.

The next letter from Henry arrived as I returned from one of these rides, and it came with another gift; a portrait, a miniature of Henry's handsome face set into a bracelet. It was beautiful… made of gold with our initials twinned in love knots on either side of his image. Whenever I missed him I would wear it. Soon enough, as the waiting wore on, I wore it every day.

Chapter Three

Hever Castle
Summer 1527

After two weeks, George came riding home to Hever. As he arrived I ran into the courtyard. "What news, brother?" I demanded, grasping at his reins and staring up at him with eager, desperate eyes.

He smiled and cocked his head. "May a man not climb off his horse and be greeted by a loving sister before he is bombarded with questions?" He swung gamely from his mount and threw the reins into the hands of a waiting servant. He pulled me into his arms. There was something calming about the comfort of his strong body and the smell of his fresh sweat.

"I *am* pleased to see you, George," I said, drawing back from his embrace. "Of course I am! It is just so frustrating... being left here to wallow in the country, not knowing what is occurring in London.... How is Henry? Have you seen him? Does our father send word? He promised he would write, but I have heard naught from him since he left."

"George!" came our mother's voice as she emerged from the house.

George put a hand on my shoulder. "I will tell you all I know, Anne," he promised, "but first let me get into the castle and change my clothes... then, I am yours." He marched to our mother and took her in his arms, lifting her slight form from the cobbled courtyard with ease. She giggled as he swung her around, as though she were a child. She beamed at George as he set her down again.

"Your father is well?" she asked.

George lifted his eyebrows. "Busy," he said in a dry tone. "Since his return to court, he has been running more errands for the King than I have ever known him to do before. Wolsey is *most* confused that our father has suddenly become the King's messenger... The Cardinal thirsts to discover what secret has brought them so close."

"But the Cardinal does not know about me, does he?" I asked.

George shook his head. "He knows nothing of the King's offer to you, Anne, but he knows of the King's *Great Matter*, of course... Wolsey believes you are Henry's new mistress, but thinks the King wants an annulment of his marriage in order to marry a fabulous French princess... neither Henry nor our father have enlightened Wolsey. Nor do they intend to, yet."

I breathed out. "Good," I said. "I little believe the Cardinal would be my friend, or would support the idea of the King marrying me. He has always detested our family."

George made a short, comical grin of frustration. "May I get into the house now, ladies, and remove the dust of the road before I am pecked to death by your questions?"

My mother giggled, leading George into the castle. I stood for a while in the courtyard, wondering on his words. The Cardinal knew nothing of me, then... Or, at least, he believed I was only Henry's mistress. That was good, even thought it annoyed me that the paunchy rodent should think so little of me to believe I would fall with ease into the place my sister had recently occupied in the King's bed... But still... it *was* better that Wolsey knew nothing of Henry's offer. It was safer that way, at least for now. I wanted to be in a secure position, and preferably at Henry's side, when the Cardinal found out. That way I could ensure the slippery eel did not pour words of poison into Henry's ear. I knew how convincing Wolsey could be, and Henry loved him, leaned upon him, doted upon him and listened to his counsel. I did not want Wolsey tainting Henry's thoughts or feelings for me if I was not there to contradict him. Wolsey hated and feared my family; not only for the power and influence we were gaining at court, but for his suspicion that we harboured reformist leanings. Both elements were a threat to his various powers.

When George had changed, washed and eaten, he was ready to tell us more. We strolled together, all three of us, through the grounds. In the walled gardens, where the warmth of the sun radiated back at us from the patterned red-bricked walls, we sat. My mother on a seat made for the garden from good oak, George and I lounging on the grass. The herbs and sallat plants of my mother's gardens were lush and bonny. Prickly thyme and rosemary were flush with purple and white flowers. Yellow rue and the pink-topped marjoram my mother had grown from imported seeds stood basking in the sun. Betony grew tall and sweet in the garden beds, and comfrey hung her purple flowers like sodden bells over her scratchy leaves. My mother's roses were in full and glorious bloom. I remembered our games here when I was but a child. I could almost see myself hunting for her through the leaves and bushes... almost hear her laugh as it echoed through my memories and into the present day.

My scarlet skirts spread out about me, I leaned back to feel the sun on my face for a moment. I listened to the sound of the breeze as it whistled through the nearby marshlands, making reeds whisper secrets and the trees sound like the oceans. I lifted a hand and unpinned my hood from my head, throwing it carelessly to one side.

"Anne!" scolded my mother, snatching the hood from the floor, handing it back to me and gazing at me with scandalised eyes. "What if someone were to see you?"

"Since I am a maiden still, there would likely be little comment, my lady mother," I said lightly, placing the hood on the grass at my side. "Besides, I am here with you and my brother alone. I promise, if the Pope turns up unexpectedly, I shall put it back on at once!"

"Anne…" My mother laughed, shaking her head. I looked to George.

"So tell us, brother… what else has been going on at court?"

George twirled a sharp twig of hawthorn in his fingertips, playing with the spikes by bouncing the tops of his fingers off them. "The King went direct to Katherine when he left you, sister, and told her that their marriage was unlawful." His brown eyes narrowed against the glaring sun. "Henry told her many scholars and members of the clergy had raised the problem with him over the years, and now his conscience was too troubled to let it be. He told her he was having their marriage investigated, and it was likely to lead to an annulment."

I stared at George. "And what said Katherine?" I frowned, and went on before he could open his mouth. "I thought the idea was to proceed carefully and secretly… Why did Henry go straight to Katherine?"

George shrugged. "Perhaps he wanted to give the lady fair warning of what was about to happen… Remember, Anne, they have been married for a long time, and she loves him. Perhaps he simply thought it was fairer this way."

I pursed my lips, but said nothing. I was unsure that Henry had acted rightly; not so much for Katherine, for I understood the sense in my brother's words, but for us.

George took my silence as assent to continue. "The King has enlisted Wolsey to work on the *Great Matter*, and obviously our father is helping too. Norfolk knows about the

King's proposal, Anne..." George trailed off and cast a wolfish grin at me. "Oh yes, dear sister!" he added with mocking glee. "Our uncle sends his *utmost* congratulations on your soon-to-be marriage. He even said that you had done *well*... High praise from a man like Norfolk!"

I snorted. "I am nothing more to my uncle of Norfolk than a means to an end, George. I am well aware of that, I assure you."

"Anne!" My mother was shocked. "My brother is not the warmest of men, I know, but he is still your uncle and your elder. You should respect him. He has done much to aid us."

"I will respect him for holding the same blood as *you* within his veins, my lady mother," I turned to her. "But I know he has no love for me. He loves only what I am able to bring him and his family. You know that as well as I."

"There is nothing wrong with family loyalty, Anne," my mother reproved.

"I know that." I reached up and squeezed her cold hand. "I *am* loyal to my family, mother... it is just I choose to be *most* loyal to those who are closest to me, and love me best... that is all."

"Katherine did not take kindly to Henry's arguments," George cut in, perhaps to distract us from arguing about Norfolk. "She said she was his *true* wife. She said she and his brother had never lain together whilst they were married and if there were anything sinful in her union with Henry then she would have known instinctually... being as devoted and pious in her faith as she is."

A shiver ran its finger down my spine. "And what said the King?"

"That *he* was not convinced, and therefore Katherine could not possibly be either. He insisted that many learned men believed their marriage was a sinful union in the eyes of God, and that the investigation would go ahead." George paused, throwing the hawthorn twig aside. "They are still seen in public with each other, of course," he continued, his busy fingers plucking now at the grass. "At court functions, entertainments... and they dine with one another, but the servers in the Privy Chambers say when they are together, they barely speak. They are awkward and drift readily into silence. It is for duty alone that they appear together now, sister, so if you hear about this from another source, do not be troubled by it."

"Another source!" I snorted. "What other source would that be? *Yours* is the first proper news I have had since Henry and our father left. Henry sends me messages, it is true, but he told me nothing of confronting Katherine. And our father sends nothing at all!" I sighed at George. "Why did Henry not tell me he had gone to Katherine, George? He is keeping things from me, trying to protect me, no doubt, but I need to know what is going on, brother. You must understand this. I cannot simply sit here, wondering, fearing and hoping... I need to *know*!"

"Hence why I came." George beamed at my surprised face and waggled a finger, stained green by the grass, at me. "I know you better than you know yourself, sister," he teased. "I knew you would be simmering to a boil here in the country. You were never one for patience, my sister *spirit*."

I laughed. "Fine!" I cried, throwing my hands into the air. "You have me! Now, tell me all else that you know!"

"Katherine has called the Spanish ambassador, Mendoza, to her chambers even more often than usual," said George. "Wolsey has women placed aside the Queen in her household, and they try to discover what it is she and Mendoza say to one another, but they whisper in Spanish, which makes gathering intelligence harder. There are some fears that she may try and contact her nephew, the Emperor Charles, even though the King has forbidden her to do so."

George noted my worried eyes and shook his head. "Wolsey has Katherine's correspondence under control, Anne, fear not," he consoled. "Every letter Katherine writes is taken to the Cardinal before it is sent. Apparently, the Cardinal has been doing this for a long time... not that he had revealed such to the King... Henry was surprised and not best pleased when Wolsey disclosed this, but he cannot deny it is useful to us now. Mendoza's dispatches are also being checked, secretly, of course, since he is supposed to be free to contact his master. News of this will not get out of England until we are ready, sister."

"I hope you are right, George," I said, my heart and my mind swimming with worries. Much was being kept from me. It made me uneasy. "I hope you are right."

Chapter Four

Wiltshire
Summer 1527

George rode for court again after two days with us, leaving me to return to my increasingly frustrated fog of annoyance... I wanted *news*! And I did not want to wait for it! My mother kept me company as best she could, but even she was eventually driven away by my scowling face and fragile temper. All that had passed between Henry and me seemed to be almost a dream, as though it had never happened. I began to fear that if I did not see him soon, then he would think the same. His letters were passionate and intense, but I could not help but worry that if we were kept apart for too long, would his passion for me wane? If Wolsey was offering him French princesses, would Henry find one that was pleasing to the eye and forget me? Would he decide all of this was too much, and return to Katherine?

We are all fools when we fall in love, and I was no exception. I dreaded losing Henry, but I also feared to lose the future he had offered me. This sparkling, magical, perfect future. Long had I been schooled by my father to aim for the highest match, and here was the highest of all being offered to me. To lose it now would be unbearable... It would have tried anyone's patience to wait for such a gift as I had been offered... And even at the best of times, I was not a patient woman.

After another week, Henry wrote, urging my return to court. Although I worried about the need to preserve my reputation, I felt that I should be there. I was supposed to be in service to the Queen. I had been recently elevated, at Henry's request, to the post of lady-in-waiting, and my absence had been noted. I felt, too, that I needed to be near Henry at this delicate time. He had made me an offer, but I needed to make sure it actually came to be... But there was something I had to do before I returned. I had a family matter to attend to. I wrote to Henry, and told him I would be back at court soon. I travelled with servants to the small Carey estates in Wiltshire, stewardship of which had been granted by Henry to my brother-in-law, Will, as a demonstration of his love for the young gentleman of his Privy Chamber. I needed to speak to my sister.

Mary and I had not always agreed on everything, but she was my sister and now her former lover had proposed marriage to me. I was concerned that Mary would not understand and this happy event could cause a rift between us. She had assisted me thus far, but I needed to be sure of her support in the future. I also wanted, I think, to assure myself that she still loved me, despite the odd situation we were now in. I was afraid of what she might say, in truth, but however this turned out I had to see her face to face. We rode out that day, and stopped at an inn on the roadside that night. Riding fast and changing horses regularly, we reached the small estate the Careys now managed on behalf of the King two days later.

I found Mary in the orchard with little Catherine and young Henry in tow. Both children had the red-gold hair of their mother... *and of their possible father*, I thought. I started when I remembered that these children were likely to be the bastards of the man I had just agreed to marry. And they were the children of my own sister! I felt God was watching me closely that day and hoped He did not disapprove. If God had frowned on Katherine and Henry's marriage because Katherine had lain with his brother, then why should it be any different for Henry and me? Mary was my sister, and she had been his mistress. But I assured myself that Henry had not been *married* to my sister, and the union between Henry and me, once a proper papal dispensation was arranged to nullify this past sin, would be lawful in the eyes of God. Mary and Henry had been together to satisfy lust, but he and I would be married in the sight of God for honourable reasons;

for love, for children. But despite my silent reassurances, I was uneasy as I walked towards my sweet sister and her children sitting under a blossoming apple tree in the orchard.

The sun was shining brightly on the three golden-red heads as Mary read to her daughter from a book of fables. Catherine was giggling at the voices Mary created for each character. Henry's small head nestled at Mary's breast, nodding in his sleep. They sat under the twisted and gnarled tree, with tiny, infant-apples hanging from the branches over their heads. Beside Mary, a nursemaid sat mending shirts, listening to her mistress as her needle flashed in and out of the linen, catching the sun. The late blossom of the tree, white with an inner shadow of pink, bobbed in the wind. Leaves whispered above them. They made a pretty picture.

As I approached, Mary looked up, saw me, and smiled. She whispered to Catherine, who turned her little head my way, her eyes opening wide as I walked towards them in my fine gown of expensive black damask, with sleeves slashed with grey silk and my riding cloak of deep green velvet billowing behind me. Mary handed Henry to the nursemaid, and told Catherine to stay and look over the book. She walked towards me. "Anne," Mary called with affection as she approached across the grass. "It seems so long since I saw you."

There was nothing of the distance and coolness I had feared apparent in her speech or face. There was nothing but welcome and gladness. We went into the house where for an hour or so we talked of nothing but the babies and the lands Will managed for his King. I played with my niece and her dolls and little Catherine was rapt with admiration for my fine gown and my French hood decorated with pearls. Her chubby, small hands reached out to touch the pearls as I dipped my head towards her. When she had stroked at their milky surfaces, she snatched her hands back, looking shy and awed. Mary laughed at her daughter's blushes.

"She has never seen a lady so grand, sister," she said with a chuckle. "For I wear more simple attire at home." Mary indicated to her plain gown of red. It was true that she wore few adornments. She looked a simpler lady here than she had done at court, and told me it was a relief to not have to be dressed so grandly all the time.

Eventually, Mary signalled for her woman to take the children for some food and suggested we two walk and view the park lands that she thought I would try some day. They were fine grounds for flying falcons, with which she knew I loved to hunt. Little Catherine left with a whimper of protest and Mary grinned. "You do know that in no time all her dolls will *have* to have gowns like yours, don't you, sister? Your visit has condemned me to many hours of miniature dress-making. But do not think I am not pleased to see you."

We set out through the gardens, through the gate, and into the park. Mary's manservant followed at a respectful distance, to ensure our safety. We strolled along the edges of great fields rich with silver-gold crops of wheat and barley, starting to crackle and crack with ripening promise. High, wiry grasses heavy with seed heads stood proud between billowing green grass and flowers along the edge of the path. Mary pulled at the grass as she walked, stripping out white, fluffy seeds and sprinkling them along the path. We wandered past purple-blue flowering hound's tongue with hairy green-silver leaves, past vervain with russet fronds and tiny white flowers, and paused to smell chamomile flowers as we crushed them in our hands. In the distance we could hear men in the lanes herding sheep to new pastures, cursing at them when they would not move past an obstruction. The summer sun burned above us in the bright blue, cloudless sky, and for a while we were both lost in our thoughts and in our appreciation of a warm, pretty day in England.

Mary pointed down to the bottom of the park where there were long, flat marshlands; good ground for hunting with falcons. She pointed out the small patches of woodland that remained, the rest having been removed to make ships for the King's navy, and said she had seen wild deer here, and believed they would make fine hunting if the King permitted it.

Eventually, as we walked quietly, I turned to her before my courage could flee, and spoke rapidly, gabbling at her. "Mary... the King has asked me to be his wife."

There was no surprise on her face, but a small sad smile flitted across it briefly and she stopped walking. She faced me, weaving a long, tough strand of grass through her fingers. "You were afraid I would hate you," she said, her face calm. There was no question in her words. It was what my heart had feared, in truth.

"Yes..." I answered honestly and looked at her, biting my lip. "Do you?"

She slowly drew breath through her nose and puckered her lips in thought. She drew the white-cream seed head of the grass stem through her fingers again, lingering over it as though it were a bolt of finest silk. "I had thought I might," she admitted. "It is not easy, Anne, to be a man's lover, to bear his children... And then to be cast off. Politely... yes... but still, cast off, so that the same man might chase your younger sister and offer her what he never thought to offer you." She paused. "Yes," she said, her keen eyes upon my face. "It is a difficult. To find yourself replaced, so easily, as easily as first you were taken, as first you were loved..." She paused and my heart tripped over its own beats. Sweat pearled on my brow and my fingers were cold despite the heat of the day. "Do you love him, Anne?" she asked.

I hesitated. I could lie, as I had hidden the depths of my emotions from my father and uncle... But I knew Mary would see through me where they could not. "Yes," I replied simply.

I had no true wish or want to lie to my sister. Perhaps for the first time, I had someone I could confide in.

"I have had little experience of love, Mary. I have had none of the lovers that you and George have had. I know not much of the ways of love. There was a time when I believed I loved Henry Percy, but it was not love, not really. I placed all my desires and ambitions within his form... I made a construction of my fantasies and pushed them into his skin. But it was a lie. And he... he thought I was unworthy of him, as the Cardinal told him I was. If a man will not fight for love, then it is not love at all. I see so clearly now.... All that was once between Percy and I was false. There was a time when I thought I could love Tom Wyatt, but I never allowed my heart to open to him. But with the King, with Henry..."

I paused and stared into her deep brown eyes, like pools of dark honey they shone back at me. "With Henry... when he is near me there are such emotions in my breast, in my blood... Sometimes I believe I will drown in their intensity. I am drawn to him, excited by him, challenged by him. In some ways, I feel he is but another part of my soul, one I never knew was separate from me. What is this, if not love? When I am with him, there is nothing missing in my life. He is all the company I should ever need or want... I do not deny there is a part of me that loves all he has offered. It is a dazzling future... to become a queen. But I would love him even if he were a pauper. I would love him even if it meant my own destruction." I breathed in. "I love him, sister. He is my friend, he is my passion. He is my calm rest and my excited hope. He is my past, my future and my present. I want for nothing when I have him. I have found where I was supposed to be. As though I have found my home, in him. Yes, Mary, I do love him."

Mary regarded me steadily. I could almost see her mind thrashing away like a waterwheel. Then she smiled and shook her head. "I never felt that way about him," she said. "When I first saw him, I thought of him as a great man. I admired his handsome face and fine form, and as we came together I adored our embraces," she paused. "But I never loved him, Anne. It is a giddy experience to have someone as noble and as widely desired as Henry of England turn to you and beckon. I could not resist it."

Mary tilted her head to one side. "I thought that I would feel more jealousy than I do, if I am honest with you, sister... but my affair with the King is long gone. I am not unhappy with my lot. I have my children and I have Will. I cannot be sad for losing Henry, when I have gained so much. I love my family and I would not have them if not for the King, but I do not mourn that I have his affection no longer."

She breathed in deeply. "Anna, you are my sister and I will support you. If you love Henry, then you should be with him. I will see you married. I will drink your health without rancour even though you are to wed the man who may be the father of my children. I bear you no ill-will... No one chooses to whom they give their hearts. You love him, and so it is done. You have your path and I have mine, and you will always have my love and support; that I swear to you. If you love him, Anne, you must do all you can to have him." Mary put her hands on the sides of my arms. "But heed my warning on one matter."

"What is it?"

"That until you are sure this marriage will take place, you will not share his bed." Her face turned grave. "Remember, I have known him longer than you. I am sure his present promises to you are real and that he means them, but Henry is a *boy* at heart, Anne. He tires easily of his toys. If you do not hold out until you are married or have some firm assurance that the marriage will come to pass, you will regret it. I am sure he loves you, sister. But his love can be fickle." She looked at me closely. "Do not let your desire for him blind you to his nature. Understand where your own power lies. He wants to possess you entirely... He wants you as his own. Do you understand? If you give yourself to him, you could lose all that you so desire. If I am right, Henry will respect you more for not giving in, even if it does frustrate him."

She was so serious and so grave that I nodded dumbly. Her advice was sound and echoed my own thoughts. It was not as though I wished to believe ill of Henry, but I had been raised to think thusly of the passions of all men. I had to keep Henry. I had to hold his interest. Before marriage, I would be the prize he was aiming for, the prey he would chase. And once we were married, I would be the one to give him the sons for which he so longed. In such ways, my position would always be secure.

"Come now." She grinned suddenly, a smile breaking through her seriousness. "We should not be so grave. Just think…" She dropped the stem of grass and held her hands out. She held me at arms' length, running her eyes over me. "My little horse-haired sister is to become Queen of England! What a fine mare you will be wearing a crown!"

She giggled as I aimed a cuff at her for this old insult of our youth and she danced out of the way. Although child-bearing had given her some thickness of waist, she was as nimble and light on her feet as she ever had been when we were girls. To my eyes, her generous curves gave her a new kind of beauty.

"You will stay a few days, Anne? At least?" She entwined her arm with mine. "Will is here, and will be happy to see you. He has just as many plans as father does for how you may further advance us at court." Mary lifted her eyebrows playfully and laughed throatily as I groaned, but I knew she was teasing me. Will was doing well enough at court without help. Henry was fond of him, and unlike my brother, Will had not lost his place in the Privy Chamber as a result of Wolsey's ordinances. Clearly, Wolsey believed George was a greater threat than Will. The Cardinal feared any who might steal the King's love away from him.

"And I should like to share some days with you," she went on. "It has been long since we had much time together, and now you are on such a great path, I feel that these family visits shall be much interrupted. For a while, at least, it will be nice to have you as my sister, before I must mark every meeting with you by bowing to my Queen."

"I am no Queen yet," I sighed.

"It will not be long, I think," Mary said as she led me into the great hall.

It was one of the few occasions when Mary was wrong.

Chapter Five

Wiltshire
Summer 1527

Whilst I was still with the Careys, my mother sent on a letter from Henry. He wrote that Wolsey was to go to overseas to gain support from François de Valois, King of France, for the annulment. Wolsey would convince François to help Henry restore Pope Clement to full power, taking him from the clutches of Katherine's nephew, Charles, King of Spain and Holy Roman Emperor, who had been occupying the Pope's lands for some years now. Spain and France were still at war over Italy, and it was hoped, by England and France, that French forces would break through and remove the Emperor's troops from the Pope's lands. Cardinal Wolsey was to entice François with promises that Henry would wed a princess of France once freed from his marriage to Katherine.

"It is, of course, sweetheart, not so," Henry wrote, his words scribbled rapidly upon the parchment as he sought to reassure me he was not about to abandon me for a foreign bride. *"But suggestions of marriage here will allow us to bargain more effectively with the French King, and bring about our wishes with more speed. Be ever assured of my love for you, and my impatience to look upon your face once more. To find myself in your loving arms, and kiss the lips I dream of every night.*

Written with the hand and the heart that is ever yours, I remain

Your loving servant,

Henry R."

I passed the letter to Mary to read and she nodded at it a few times. She handed it back and frowned at my worried face. "He *loves* you, Anne," she consoled, squeezing my shoulder. "And see? He does not keep anything from you. That is a good sign."

Mary had heard often during my short visit about my frustration at being left without information. She had listened with patience, and sought now to reassure me. I did not feel so at ease. "I should be there," I said fretfully. "I am sorry, sister, but I will leave on the morrow with the first light. No matter what is written here, I fear what Wolsey may convince Henry of… That snake could convince anyone of anything."

"No one can convince another person who is in love that they are *not* in love," replied my wise sister. "There is no tongue in all the world that has such power. Calm your fears, Anne… Henry loves you."

I agreed with her. I tried to heed her. But still, I worried.

The next morning, before we were to ride out, my mother sent word from Hever that I was unlikely now to catch the King and his party before they left London for summer progress. Realising this, Henry had sent word that he would instead meet me at Beaulieu Palace, in Essex. Katherine was to accompany Henry on progress, but when he came to Beaulieu, he was to come without her. My mother wrote that I should return to Hever and meet her; she would come to Beaulieu with me as my chaperone, for the sake of appearances. When I got back to Hever, there was another letter waiting for me from Henry.

"Soon you and I shall be man and wife in truth, my dearest love; once Wolsey returns from France we shall have the support of François to help our cause in the eyes of the Pope. But until then, you must not be seen to be the reason

why all this should come about. I will not have your reputation tarnished, my beloved. But the thought of a whole summer without you is unbearable, so I have arranged that you and your mother shall take up residence at Beaulieu and there shall I come to you, in secret."

I wrote back, telling him I loved him, and of my impatience to see him again. "*We have been too long apart, my love,*" I wrote. *"I fear every day that some chance event will take me from you; that you will turn your eyes from me and love me no more. Do not let us be parted for so long a time again. I cannot bear this separation."*

When his reply came, I was struck by the force and intensity of his words. He was grieved, he wrote, more grieved than he could express that I would fear such a thing, but so happy to hear I loved him as he loved me. *"I hope soon to have you in my arms, where I will convince you with the force of my love that there is no cause to fear or be troubled, even when we are apart. When we are once more together I shall kiss your lips, and lean my head against your pretty breasts and tell you of my love for you. Soon there will come a time when we are parted no more, and will be joined together, forever, in the eyes of God and man. My heart is yours. Trust in me and in our love.*

Written with the hand and heart that is yours alone,

Your servant

HR."

God in Heaven! How I wanted to see him again! I went to Beaulieu, with my mother and tried to wait patiently for Henry to come to me.

Chapter Six

Beaulieu Palace
Summer 1527

Beaulieu was as beautiful as its name; a quiet palace situated in a great park. I knew the place well, of course; Will had been the warden of this palace for Henry in days passed, and Mary had given birth here. But I came to it this time with new eyes that saw not the past, but the glorious future I would have.

I was impatient to see Henry. I spent my days trying to be occupied, but every day willing him to get there faster. I wanted to know that my fears and frustrations were groundless. I wanted to feel his body close to mine. I wanted to know the touch of his lips. I wanted to know that all of this was not a dream.

In the days before Henry arrived, I filled my time by inspecting and choosing falcons with which to hunt. I talked to Beaulieu's Master of Game to find the best and most secluded hunting grounds. I left it to my more than able mother to instruct the kitchens. She had grand feasts planned, and intimate suppers, too, for Henry and me to enjoy in the private chambers. I wondered how well I would be able to resist my ardent suitor here in this secluded place. I wondered also how much I *wanted* to resist him. Everything in me was calling for him. I felt myself overcome with desire imagining him on me, his hands upon my body, his lips on my skin… No woman has burned as I did then, thinking of a lover I wanted, who wanted me… a lover I could not take.

Eventually, Henry and his party swept into the courtyard in a flurry of clattering hooves and loud shouting. I raced down to meet them and there he was, his eyes searching the crowds of servants, looking only for me. His golden-red hair shone in the sunlight from under his dark cap. His beard had been trimmed anew, and his eyes were blue and bold as the sea. I ran forwards, suddenly weak at seeing him after our weeks of separation. He caught me in his arms and laughed heartily. His eyes sparkled and his kisses were those of a man dying for thirst of me. Much of my fear melted away. I could feel his eagerness, his desire, his love, in every kiss.

"How I have missed you, my Anne!" he crowed as he kissed me again and again; on the lips, on the cheek, on the throat. His travelling party excused themselves swiftly and made for the kitchens to take ale and bread. My mother hovered at the edge of the courtyard, her back to us as she inspected the stones of the red-bricked walls with much interest as Henry held me to him.

"I have missed you too, Henry," I laughed, trying to pry him from my body as his eager hands roamed over me.

"I love this neck," he whispered, burrowing his head into my white skin and breathing in the scent of my rose perfume. "I have dreamed of this neck…" His lips stumbled across my skin, over my throat and down to my chest.

"Release me, my lord!" I giggled, my own senses excited by his closeness. There were such sensations flowing through me, wild and untamed… If I did not stop him now, I would be unable to stop myself at all. "Come," I struggled free of his embrace, earning a lustful glare from Henry for having escaping his clutches. "My *mother*, my lord," I inclined my head to the distant figure at his back, "…has made great preparation for your arrival."

At that, his face flamed and I giggled. He whipped around to see my mother who was still turned resolutely from us, gazing up at the beautiful windows as though she had never seen one before. Henry glanced back ruefully at me, his cheeks delightfully pink. He looked like a boy caught stealing soft honey tarts from under the kitchen maid's nose.

"Elizabeth!" he cried warmly, covering his embarrassment by marching brisk and merrily towards her. He embraced her with affection, refusing to allow her to bow to him. Henry kissed her on the lips and put her arm through his. Walking towards me, he stopped and offered his free arm to me, and together we walked into the house as servants rushed to bring us ale and wine.

We stayed there for a month; a perfect month together with my mother acting as a distant and often easily-distracted chaperone. Henry had told the court and Katherine he was hunting with his close friends. As he so often took off with a small party, it was an easy rendezvous to arrange. Since I was supposed to be at court also, word had been sent to Katherine I was unwell, and would re-join her household when recovered. There were many of Henry's advisors and close friends happy to keep his favour by covering his visit to Beaulieu. They had done so many times before, when Henry wanted to spend time with a mistress without his wife knowing. They did not know, however, that I was no ordinary mistress.

We rode out at dawn each day and spent the daylight hours in the woods hunting and talking together. We spent evenings either in the hall with his small band of friends, dancing and playing cards, or in his private chambers, supping on tasty treats and talking of architecture, literature and works of art that we had seen and loved. In all tastes we seemed to agree, and with every shared interest found, we became more certain that we were meant for each other, made for each other.

As we hunted and as we walked together, Henry would take opportunities to touch and caress me. On horseback he would put me in front of him and as he adjusted me to suit his frame, his thumb would gently, as though by accident, caress my breast and nipple, making that soft skin hard by his touch. To be touched so, so intimate and yet so freely, made me shiver with a kind of pleasure I did not fully understand. It frustrated me, too, for I knew he was teasing me.

When I sat in front of him, I would often feel him hard behind me, and, in retaliation for his teasing, I would shuffle mischievously against him making him sharply draw in breath and pull me closer. In the evenings, when my mother left to go to bed, he would kiss me, drawing my body into his lap where he could run his hands over my breasts and my face. We danced together each night, our bodies slipping close to each other and then prancing away. It was as though those dances showed our present relationship... wanting, touching, coming so close to each other, and then having to draw back. It was as exciting as it was infuriating.

There was desire in every touch that we gave each other, and at times it was difficult to bear. But in every touch I allowed, and all those I did not, I heard the warning words of my sister in my head. Touch and look and graze of flesh were all there could be between us... for now. There must be no more; there must be some prize left for him to strive for. I would not be cast aside, as he had done with my sister and so many others. No... no matter what the temptation to give in, I must remain a virgin until our marriage was assured. But Henry did not seek to take more from me than I was willing to offer. Our embraces, our kisses... the stroking weight of his hand upon my skin... they went no further than that. Henry wanted me, of that I had no doubt, but I was also assured, perhaps more so than ever before, that he wanted me as his wife before he would bed me.

Whilst we were at Beaulieu, Henry held an entertainment to which he invited most of my family, including my uncle Norfolk and his wife Elizabeth. Since so many of my family were to be there, Henry hoped it would not appear as though I had been with him at Beaulieu all along. Suffolk and his Duchess, Mary Tudor, were also present, as were a select group of other guests, all nobles of court. My dear friends

Margaret and Bridget came, happy to be reunited with me again, but Tom Wyatt was not present. The Queen, too, was absent, nor was my sister invited. Henry seemed to find Mary's presence embarrassing now, and he did not want her close.

Henry presented me with a new gown for the event, made of rich, black velvet, with huge over-sleeves of russet fur, and a stunning black French hood with two lines of pearls cascading over its rim. It was beautiful. The furs were soft and warm over my arms, and the ends of the sleeves had been made in the style that I had made famous at court. At the same time, Henry gave me a long chain of golden links, which could be doubled up to wear about the throat, and a tablet inset with an enamel cross. There were ear-rings made of pearls that looked like droplets of milk, and rings of gold with which to adorn my hands. He chuckled like a happy lad on a bright spring day when I thanked him, and insisted on seeing the gown upon me immediately. When I came to him, he took my hands and ran his eyes up and down me, pausing and lingering on certain parts of my body.

"There was never a beauty to match you, my dark-haired love," he murmured, drawing me to him and kissing my lips.

At the Beaulieu gathering, despite his words advising caution in front of others, Henry could not keep his hands from me. He could not help himself. We danced together, and at the feast he insisted I sit beside him in the place his Queen would have taken had she been there. Throughout the feast, he stroked and pampered me, feeding me titbits and stroking my hand. Henry felt safe enough, with the select group of courtiers he had invited, to show his love for me more publicly than he had ever done before. He was seeking to find out whom he could rely on for support, when the time came to announce our love. There was another gift; a beautiful emerald set in a ring of gold, to add to my growing collection of jewels… Henry presented me with this before all of the guests. I was flushed and pleased, for it was as though I were already Queen that night; as though this were my court.

He told me quietly I could consider it an engagement ring. "Since the one I first gave you at Hever hardly fits," he said with a smirk.

As I took the ring and thanked Henry, slipping it upon my delicate finger, I saw his sister Mary, regarding me with disgust. She ate her meal delicately and it was delicious fare, so I knew that the twist of distaste on her lips was naught to do with the food. She did not like the idea that I was the King's mistress, and had stopped speaking to me socially when she was able to. Mary of Suffolk loved her sister-in-law Katherine, and was greatly attached to her. She saw me as a whore, and, with the evidence of the ring, as a money-grabbing jade... She liked not her brother's outward affection for me. The place of a King's mistress in England was to be demure and quiet, a sultry shadow on the edge of court, and yet here we were flaunting our love for one another in public. She scowled at me, obviously thinking I had overstepped the bounds of my position. Every attention her brother paid to me she saw as an insult to her friend Katherine.

I wondered if it was a mistake for Henry to have invited his sister, for I was sure Katherine would hear of this through Mary... But it would have been hard to invite Suffolk and not his wife, and the Duke of Suffolk was another matter. Suffolk was watching me with speculative care. He was to be a part of the circle of support that my uncle Norfolk was carefully constructing for our cause. Suffolk was well-beloved of Henry and if we Howards and Boleyns could capture him for our side then we would be more powerful at court than we had ever been before.

I smiled at Suffolk, and lifted my glass goblet to him. Fine malmsey wine shone blood-red in the King's expensive Venetian glass, twinkling in the candle-light. Suffolk responded and drank to my health, much to his wife's disgust, but the Duke earned a joyous smile from Henry for honouring me in public. Henry was happy to see that his oldest friend and I could get along so well, and he ignored his sister's obvious displeasure.

When the feast was done and after I had engaged in some dancing, my brother's wife, Jane, appeared next to me. "Sister," she greeted me warmly. "It seems that you are in high favour! I hear much of you and the King from my husband, and I am pleased for you."

"Thank you, sister… although you know there is much that may not be spoken of such things, in such company as this."

Jane's smile was as wicked as it was pretty. "But of course, sister." She put a finger to her lips, her golden rings sparkling in the candle-light. "Your secrets are safe with me."

I did not doubt Jane had talent at concealing secrets. She took delight in them, which made her an able and formidable courtier. I had grown to like Jane more as I grew to know her better, but I still always had the sense there was something unknown under what she allowed me to see. *Perhaps it is only natural, for she was raised in the court,* I thought. *She is like a female version of father… Like a veil which when lifted reveals only another veil...*

Jane handed me a goblet of sweet, chilled white wine. I drank deeply for I had danced with vigour and Henry was an able and energetic partner. I was giddy and not just from the wine coursing in my blood, but from Henry's adoring attentions before all of these people. *Soon all will know that I am the object of the King's affections*, I thought, smiling at Jane a little unsteadily. *I and no other.* I was flighty with wine and pride and love. God forgive me my arrogance… I was young and silly then.

"It seems to me," Jane continued smoothly, "that at this time, all our family should be together as one." She ran a hand over her russet gown. The scarlet of her sleeve reflected across golden candlesticks and the gilding on the chairs, making them flash red; like blood and gold mingled into one. "You know, sister, I have long been at court... I grew up here, almost."

She gazed at me steadily, her stunning green eyes glowing. "George would have me stay in the country," she continued in a mocking tone, "so I might tend to all the children we *do not* have...." Her tone was bitter. Acid. Jane trailed off and sipped from her goblet, her lips thin against its pewter rim. Despite her beauty, this expression made her ugly to my eyes.

She turned her face to me again and her smile was sour. I could not return it. Jane and George had been married a long time now, and there was still no sign of an heir. Jane may appear to try to make light of it, but her jests were belied by her expression. There was deep sorrow there, hiding under her courtly mask. I wondered why they had no children. Was Jane barren, or was George simply not spending enough time with his wife?

"But I feel I could be of better use to you and the family if I *were* at court..." Jane continued. "I have been a good supporter of my sister thus far, have I not? And, as I said, I *know* the court, and how it works, very well. You have many supporters now, and their numbers will grow, but how will you know who is true to you and who is not? I could help you with that. I have ever had a talent for discovering secrets, and you know that you can depend on a *sister's* loyalty."

I agreed, hearing sense in her words, even though I disliked her sly tone. "Perhaps it would be as well that you did join the family when we return to court," I murmured. "I need those around me that I can trust, as you say. There can be no office for you in the country. I will speak to George. I cannot think why he wants you there instead of court."

She gazed at me with glee. Her black pupils, dark and glorious against the emerald of her eyes, met my own gaze. "I shall look forward to returning, sister." She curtseyed, and wandered off through the milling crowds. I sighed. Whatever reason George had for keeping his wife from court, I had just interfered with it. This was unlikely to make my brother happy. I guessed that he had a new mistress, and wanted Jane to remain unaware of her identity. He had mentioned before that she had reproached him indignantly for his infidelity. But Jane was right; I needed friends and allies... George would just have to take more care with his adventures, or consider spending his time with his wife rather than bedding other women.

I watched Jane return to George and firmly take his arm. He smiled at her with an absent expression and continued his conversation with Suffolk. I looked on with unhappy eyes. Jane watched George with rapt attention, while he seemed almost unaware she was there at all. There was as much pain in her green eyes as there was love. She adored him, of that I was sure. Who would not love my brother? He was affable, witty, strong and learned. He was also handsome, virile and well-built. He wrote poetry and songs, jousted like a true knight and could converse on many interesting topics. He was a woman's dream... and more often than not, he set out to make their dreams of him come true...

This was what pained my sister-in-law. George was a man of the court, a man of the world. He was not about to be faithful to Jane, no matter her love for him. With every dalliance her sorrow deepened. Yet she clung to the hope that he would one day love her as she loved him. It was awful to look on. Unrequited love is painful to watch, and even worse to experience.

I breathed in and exhaled through my nose, feeling intense, writhing pity for Jane. She could chase and chase, and never catch him. George wanted to be the hunter, not the hunted. It was not her looks that put him off her, but the very love she held for him. He found her cloying and distasteful in her desperation for his affections.

Soon enough I would have to explain to my brother why I had ruined his chances for secrecy with his latest mistress. I was sure Jane would inform him of my interference with some relish. No matter how warm her words to me, she did not like the place I held in George's heart. She did not, in truth, like that he should show affection to *any* but her... but then, perhaps she was right to be jealous of the care he showed to others, for he showed little enough to her. That thought made me cold for a moment. Would that happen to me, when I married Henry? Would he find me less interesting because I belonged to him and he could do as he wanted with me by law? I shook the thought from my mind... of course not! It was not the same situation and we were not the same people. Whatever problems of compatibility Jane and George had, Henry and I clearly would not have the same.

I watched them until I felt a pressure on my arm. I went to turn around, but a great hand closed over my eyes. I gasped in shock, but I knew who it was. A breath escaped my lips. I heard a soft rumble of laughter and felt boyish happiness radiate from my Henry as he took hold of me. "Come, lady," Henry whispered. "This bandit would steal you away."

I giggled at his game. "I would ask only that you take care of my honour as a lady, sir." My body melted backwards into his arms as his lips grazed my throat.

"Your honour will be safe with me, my lady," he said gruffly.

I allowed myself to be stolen out into the courtyard and led into a garden. The sounds of the dance were behind us and the servants were far off. I shivered in the sudden cold. "What brigand are you, sir, to kidnap a lady and bring her to the cold without hope for warmth?"

Henry chuckled, placing his lips on my cheek. For a moment he did not allow me to see, and kept one hand over my eyes as he kissed me. I could hear from the quickness of his breath that he found this exciting. It was a foreign sensation for me too. My heart quickened and my breath escaped in short gasps to be kissed so... to know not what was about to happen. It was exciting... *too* exciting.

"My lord," I whispered, "I beg of you to release me..."

My eyes were uncovered even as a cloak fell about my shoulders and two hot hands grabbed my waist. "I'll warm you, my lady." Henry pulled my body into his embrace.

I felt his hard, muscular strength against me and wrapped myself eagerly to his touch. His mouth tasted of wine, sweet and rich. Flickers of excitement coursed through me as he pushed me softly but insistently up against a garden wall. The wine in my blood and the thrill of this stolen moment made me reckless. His hands moved down my body, to my thighs, where he grasped at them through the thick folds of my gown, and moved himself between them. He rocked gently forward, pressing himself into me. Each movement caused parts of me to tingle. But he did not seek to do more; my skirts and his clothes remained as a barrier between us as we moved against each other. The weight of our bodies gently crushed the delicate wild honeysuckle flowers that lay between my back and the cool stone wall. As we moved, as we kissed, the heady scent of the flowers was released into the night air. Eventually, from behind a fog of longing, I heard him groan. He became still and leant his head on my shoulder, loosening his embrace. I drew a shaky breath, dizzied from the wine I had drunk and the passion I had felt. I kissed his cheek gently and he shuddered with the pain of self-control as he moved his body from mine.

"This waiting… it is excruciating …" He smiled ruefully, his blue eyes dancing in the moonlight, his handsome face bathed in the light of the burning torches about the palace walls. "But wait we shall. I shall have you on the night we marry and by God, Anne, what a night that will be!"

He kissed me. It was supposed to be a kiss of release, I believe, but all it did was to re-kindle the fire between us. We threw ourselves together again. He pushed himself against me again, lifting one of my legs so that it was hooked about his waist. Sweet Christ in Heaven! What temptation was mine then! But again Henry stopped. He stepped back, his chest rising and falling with rapid speed. One hand lingered on me, as though its owner was not in command of it. His finger traced a line from my lips, down my throat, between and over the curves of my breasts. He watched its slow progress with hungry eyes.

He gazed down at me. My eyes were glassy, dazed with the sensations he had roused in me. I was glad that he had stopped, for I was not sure I had the strength to do so. He looked on my face with satisfaction, liking well the effect he had had on me, and then took his hand from my body. He breathed in deeply. "Come, Anne," he said. "Let us walk around the gardens a little, that I might walk off this lust that drives me to kidnap an honourable lady." He smiled. "Calm my thoughts with your presence, my love… as you always do."

We walked the paths, talking quietly. We remarked on the fine moonlight, silver-grey, dappled on the still surface of the ponds. We watched the starlight dance over the beautiful knot gardens, catching flowers hidden in the darkness and radiating them with hoary brilliance. Jasmine flowers sent their night-blooming scents to mingle with the honeysuckle on the cool air. We walked and talked together as friends. Desire for Henry burnt in my body like fire, but we assured each other it would not be long now until we could be together.

Chapter Seven

Greenwich Palace
Summer's End 1527

I returned to the court a week later with my mother and re-entered the service of Katherine; the woman I now saw as the obstacle in the way of all my hopes and dreams. Once Katherine stepped aside, I could take her place as Henry's wife and queen. I hoped that time would be soon. Surely, such a wise princess would see the truth in the arguments against her marriage and bow out with grace? It was not the first time that such an event had happened, after all. *It cannot not be long*, I told myself.

The Queen, however, was now aware that Henry was investigating their union. She brought the Spanish ambassador, Diego Hurtado de Mendoza, to her often to talk in private. Mendoza had been sent to clear the foul air that lingered between Henry and the Emperor Charles after their alliance had faltered, but I doubt he found much ease in his task, particularly when he became aware, through Katherine, that the King was considering casting off his master's aunt. Katherine clung to Mendoza, seeking solace in his friendship and in the fact that he was a man of her native country.

When I came to her chambers, her countenance was sad and solemn even more often than usual. She would stare out of the window, looking at nothing, but I knew where her thoughts took her. Her heart was broken and although she showed nothing of it in public, we all knew that at night she cried and prayed to the Virgin to fill her barren womb. In the evening, when we combed her auburn hair, still thick and lovely, she would stare into her polished steel mirror, her dark blue eyes far away, lost in the past.

It was not without some sense of guilt that I re-entered her service that year. I had nothing against the Queen, not then at least. And yet, here I was, waiting to take her place. I knew that she loved Henry and was a good Queen. But I rationalised my actions, telling myself Henry loved Katherine no more and her position stood in the way of greater good for England. These were the things I told myself to ease my guilt. But, being human, I had to include the wishes of my own heart. I loved Henry and he loved me. We needed to be together, we *should* be together, for the satisfaction of our love *and* to produce heirs for England... and in order for that to happen, Katherine needed to understand that her time with Henry was done.

I was playing a game with high stakes but I was ever a keen gambler. I was playing to win Katherine's place and I could not afford to be sentimental about her poor situation. I steeled my heart, telling it Katherine could give neither the King nor the country what each needed to be secure. Katherine had failed in fulfilling a queen's most sacred duty; to provide an heir. Now it was time for another to take up her mantle. That other *must* be me.

Katherine was unaware that I was anything more than the King's new plaything. She assumed I was his mistress, as most did, and treated me with the reserve and respect with which she always approached his mistresses. There was nothing in her outward attitude towards me but polite indifference. But there were times when I would feel her eyes hot upon my back, and I wondered if she suspected what had passed between her husband and me. There were times when a cuff on my arm or hand, a rebuff common from masters to servants, was not deserved. There were times when I believed she hated me, for even if she was unaware that Henry had proposed marriage to me, she was still aware his love waned for her, even as it waxed for me. She knew he was investigating their marriage. Did she wonder if I had suggested it? If I had whispered the notion into his ear in the dark of night?

Katherine saw little sin in Henry himself. I am sure she believed he had been led into this by the Cardinal, or by me. In time, she would come to blame me for all the ills in her life. She would continue to do so even after Henry had shown his distaste and distain openly for her. She blamed *me* for everything that befell her, and who can blame her for that? It is easier to blame another, to have them shoulder the burden of our pain and suffering, than blame the one we love, or ourselves.

It was a strange world I now lived in; serving the Queen, even as I was engaged to the King. There could be no outward proclamation of his offer to me yet. It must remain a secret. Henry wanted the legality of his present marriage to be the issue called into question, and to admit me into the mixture would sour the idea that the King merely wanted to rid himself of an illegal and immoral union with his wife. Few of his advisors, even Wolsey, knew that Henry intended to marry me. I was a complication. I was a secret… The world must see that Henry wished to end his marriage for reasons of conscience and Scripture alone… not because he desired another woman.

And that was the truth… in part, at least. Henry had long considered his marriage invalid, and I believe he would have moved to rid himself of Katherine eventually even if he had never fallen for me. But he did not want people to think of him badly, and so for now, I was but another woman at court; possibly his mistress, but not his wife-in-waiting.

On the advice of his Council, Henry still came to visit Katherine, still shared her bed. To do otherwise might allow her to counter-attack him, if the case went to court, for him not keeping to the promise of their marriage vows. He came to visit her often, for Henry wanted to keep Katherine appeased, hoping to prevail on her to accept his word and enter a convent willingly. Henry was utterly convinced that his wife would listen to him, eventually, and, as is the duty of every good wife, would meekly accept his judgement. Katherine had been the very best of wives, and he respected her for her humility and graciousness. He was positive she would prove this again, by submitting to his will.

Wolsey had been working in secret to bring about a panel to decide on the validity of the royal marriage. Henry assured me that this council would find in his favour and send their judgement to the Pope. It was the only way to fix this situation. Only with the blessing and support of the Pope and his cardinals would Henry's marriage be annulled. It was the way of the world, the way it had always been done. The Church joined people in marriage and only the Church could separate them. Henry did not want a divorce, as this would not allow him to marry again. He wanted to annul his marriage, to make it as though it had never been legal, as though it had never happened. Henry told me it was simple; Wolsey would present the findings of the council to the Pope, and the Pope would decide in our favour. Katherine would then, of course, accept the Pope's judgement... and Henry and I would be free to be joined as man and wife, King and Queen... But I worried, even then, that it would not be as simple as it sounded. The Pope was still at the mercy of the Spanish Emperor, Charles. Even if the Pope viewed Katherine and Henry's marriage as immoral, would he find in favour of Henry, as his conscience ought to, or would the demands of worldly considerations tip his hand to find in favour of the aunt of the man who held him captive?

Henry believed absolutely in the goodness of the Pope; that no matter what earthly concerns weighed on him, he would decide with his conscience as the representative of God on earth... I was less certain. My passion for reform had led me to view the Church with some suspicion. A pope, after all, had joined Katherine and Henry in marriage in the first place... which clearly had been a mistake. Popes are men, like all others, and were not infallible.

And so my life was strange, disjointed, fragile and full of worries. It was also full of love and life such as I had never had before. I laughed now to think of my passion for Tom, or the soft, desperate *ideal* of love I had felt for Percy... What were such men to me now? How could I ever have thought myself in love with them? There was nothing that any man could offer that would come close to the love I had for Henry.

But it was not easy. When my love visited his wife's chambers, we would all, by necessity, pretend that nothing had changed. Ladies-in-waiting were to amuse the King when he visited the Queen and so we played music, we played games, and we played cards. But hidden under all these japes and games, the atmosphere was strained. We were all playing a part, dancing a masque about each other and sometimes our masks would slip. I remember at one point in a game of cards I had the good fortune to draw three kings; a fine hand. As I put them on the table before Katherine, having won much money of both she and Henry, Katherine smiled. "My lady Anne," she said. "You have good hap to stop at a king, but you are not like others; you will have all or none."

She smiled sweetly, but I felt the undercurrent of her dislike rush over me. It was an awkward moment. The air between us stretched and strained with tension, like a bow-string ready to be loosed. Henry ignored the comment and placed his own hand on the table. It was not as good as mine. The Queen nodded, her hanging jowls wobbling. "The money is yours, Mistress Anne," she said. "I trust you will find a valuable hood or bauble to buy with it. Maids such as you hold *such* stock in worldly adornments."

Katherine reached out to stroke Henry's strong arm with a sly look on her face. "These young ladies of the court have such desire for baubles, my lord, do you not think? Every day I see my ladies with something new... It is the flightiness of youth. That which they adore one day, they care for not at all the next." She graced me with an oily smile. "Take your winnings, Mistress Boleyn… Perhaps purchase something from the apothecary to lighten your complexion, for I believe you are becoming *most* swarthy from your time in the sunshine."

I smiled, ignoring her slight. "I had thought, Your Majesty," I replied calmly. "Rather to give the money to a trust for scholars that I and my family support." My voice was cool and light. I rebuffed her insults with calm grace. *You seek to make him believe I am naught but a silly girl, obsessed with my looks and trinkets, Katherine,* I thought as I took up the cards to shuffle them. *But there is more to me than meets the eye. That, you shall discover, if you are fool enough to set yourself against me.*

Katherine's eyes narrowed, but she said nothing. She ran a hand over the front of her purple silk gown and turned her gaze away. I saw the shine of tears in her eyes.

"A fine idea, Mistress Boleyn, it behoves us all to think of charity when we are blessed with good fortune from God," Henry said. He rose and left the table without a look at Katherine, but paused to squeeze my shoulder as he passed.

Katherine ignored it. She carried on as normal, but soon I knew I would be unable to continue in her service, and as such should find it hard to find a reason to be at court. I could not take a place in the King's household. There was no position there for a lady of my status. If Katherine dared to dismiss me, then I would find it difficult to stay near Henry … and I *needed* to be near him. But equally I knew I could not continue to serve Katherine once my true position was known. For now, all thought me but a mistress, but, as time went on, I wondered on how much Katherine suspected. I became paranoid, wondering at every move and comment she made. Could she… did she wonder if Henry's suddenly increased desire to be rid of her was due to me? The Queen was no fool. I knew that even if she did not know now, she soon would.

In my anxiety, I put pressure on Henry to talk directly to Katherine, for, to me, the proceedings of his annulment were moving like the slow creeping mists of the Low Countries. At my bidding he went to ask Katherine to enter a convent, both for the good of their souls, and for the good of England.

"It was awful!" Henry threw himself into a chair in my father's quarters after meeting with Katherine. He pulled at his jewelled collar, loosening it from about his throat. "She would not take my counsel and turned into a parrot, repeating over and over that our marriage was sanctioned by the Pope and therefore by God Himself; that our bed *had* produced children and therefore was not subject to the warnings of Leviticus; that she was my true wife and would not enter a holy order… She even had the audacity to claim that I only wanted to separate from her because I was in love with another!" He flushed, looking sheepish, for it was, in part, the truth. "She was… forceful."

I bristled. His face was no longer boyish and excited but flat and defeated. The strength that Katherine had demonstrated was clearly not met by an equal force in him; she had defeated him. I was furious.

"And you?" I cried angrily, rising from my chair, making him start. "Can you not be equally forceful? Where is the conviction I saw in you at Hever? Where is your faith in God and His will for us to be joined? Where is the strength of the man who won the Battle of the Spurs? Do not tell me that you are beaten by a woman! And not just any woman, my lord, but by an old, fat and ugly woman who has lied to you for *years* about her involvement with your brother. A woman who now refuses to see the true path opened to her by her King and by God? If you will not fight to see right prevail, my lord, then who will?"

I strode around the room. I did not see anything before me but blind red rage, mingled with fright that I would be set aside. After all, what did I have to rely on but Henry's affections? If I could not rely on Henry to fight for me, to fight for *us*, then I had nothing!

Henry sought to calm me but I shook him off. "*No!*" I protested, backing away from him. I was not about to let him kiss me and pretend this had not happened. "What have you to say to comfort me, my lord? I see that now you will go back to your wife and hide behind her skirts like a mewling child! That now you will wait for a miracle of God to bring you a son. But it will not come… God has turned his back on your marriage, Henry of England," I hissed, my black eyes flashing. "God will give you no son begot through the womb of a woman who is your *sister* in His eyes. The throne of England will be ever-cursed until you rid yourself of Katherine. Free yourself from this filthy, incestuous marriage and your false Queen! Do not let protestations of evil tempt you from the path of goodness. I want to be joined to the one I love, but how can I love him when he lingers in the bed of an unlawful wife, and refuses to strive for a union recognised by God?"

I let out a short shriek of frustrated anger and swept from the room leaving him much amazed. I amazed *myself* sometimes. Because I spent most of my time at court flattering and lying, when I was angry, I could not help but shout the truth. It was dangerous to speak so… I did not want Katherine to discover our secret, and at court, all walls have ears. But I could not allow Henry to falter.

He sought me out an hour after, and begged my forgiveness. "She has been my wife and companion for almost eighteen years, Anne," he explained, taking his hat of dark velvet from his head and running a hand through his thick red-gold hair. "And in a marriage it can be that one becomes so used to the other, that you forget who in truth is king and who is queen and instead…" he trailed off.

I shot him a sharp look. "Are you not *master* in your own house, my lord?" I asked scathingly, watching red spots of anger shoot into his cheeks.

"I am the *only* master here," he cried, his great figure advancing upon me, his eyes almost murderous with wrath. For me to question him in such a manner was humiliating, shameful, but I could not let him soften. "I am the only master here! I will have no others!" he roared.

"Then act like it, my lord!" I spat, facing down his anger with my own. "If you are the King in truth, then stand no such slight from this woman who has given you nothing but disappointment." Without warning, I walked to him and threw myself against his chest. He held me as though he was a drowning man, and I was his raft. He never knew what to expect from me... anger, hard words, warmth, love, affection... I believe, in a world where all had to bow to him, where he commanded everyone, I was exciting precisely for my unpredictability. I was the one person he could not command. I was the one person he could not control. It was a giddy feeling, for a King; an exciting voyage into unknown waters.

"I am sorry, Henry," I murmured softly, my anger fading. "It is just... I am enraged that Katherine should dare to say such things to you. You, who have granted her such grace. You raised her up from poverty. She was abandoned in this country and you made her your Queen. You honoured her throughout your marriage, you trusted her, put your faith in her... but how has she repaid your kindness? Nothing has she given you but dead baby after dead baby... And then, a living daughter ready to take the throne and plunge the kingdom into civil war." I looked up into his eyes and I saw the desperation of his own fears in them. I did not like to bring him unhappiness, but he needed to be reminded of all for which we were working. It was not just me and Henry whose futures were at stake here… it was the future of England.

"Nothing has Katherine given you, Henry, but sadness and unrest; an insecure future… and a cold bed." I reached up to stroke the soft curls at the back of his golden-red head. "And now, when shown the truth, she resists, refusing to listen to your good and kind counsel. You do not seek to dishonour her, Henry. You offer to retire her from the throne honourably, and yet *still* she defies you. She thwarts you, using the affection that you still hold for her to make you *weak* before her."

Anger flashed over his face again. "She takes advantage of your knightly chivalry, Henry," I said quietly. "She has failed in her duty to you and to England. Even now, at the end, she must have *more*; she must keep her false marriage, she must keep her throne. Katherine acts from *pride*, not from love or from duty, but from pride. That which she does to you is a sin, and that which she does to your country is wrong." I stood on my tip-toes and kissed his cheek gently. "Katherine pretends to be good… But she is wickedness itself for her selfishness, and her betrayal of your many kindnesses."

Henry was staring at me. I could see he was thinking over what I had said. *Good*, I thought. I wanted Henry to be utterly resolved to remove Katherine. Even though my words had been cruel, there could be no wavering. There could be no indecision. As much as I loved and wanted to be with Henry, I was more than aware that should this all go ill for us, then I would be bereft… and what then? My reputation would be suspect. I would not make a good marriage. Would my father marry me off to some lowly squire? Would I live out my days in the country, sitting by my hearth at night, staring into the flames, dreaming of what might have been mine, had it had a chance to be? No! I would not be cast aside… I would not!

And all that I had spoken was the truth, whether Katherine wanted to believe it or not. If she wanted what was best for

England, then she would stand down. If she could not see she was acting in a prideful and sinful manner, then she would need to be shown the error of her ways by Henry… And I would be there to make sure he did so.

Chapter Eight

Richmond Palace
Summer's End 1527

A new lady-in-waiting entered the Queen's household that season. She was a relative of mine, distantly, and although I thought little of her then, there came a time much later when I knew her as one of my greatest enemies. She sought me out when she arrived at court, as her mother had told her to, to ask for my friendship and advice, beholden through our family ties.

Jane Seymour was my cousin. Her mother was Margery Wentworth, whose mother, Anne Say, had also been the mother of Elizabeth Tilney by her first marriage. Elizabeth Tilney had been my mother's mother, making Jane my second cousin. Although Jane had served briefly in the household of the Duchess of Suffolk, she had made an impression on Katherine, and the Queen had asked Jane to enter her service.

Jane was eager to meet her relatives at court, no matter how distant, to claim kinship and gain aid in advancement. Her brother, Edward, served in the household of the young Duke of Richmond, who was Henry's bastard son by Bessie Blount, and Jane was as keen to advance as her brother. She was a plain and pale creature. Although her features were not unpleasing, she easily disappeared into the background at court. I wondered what Katherine had noted in her. Jane was like a pale shadow which seemed to vanish as soon as you tried to look directly at it; an indistinct haze hovering over cobblestones heated by the sun. Outwardly meek, quiet and demure, I thought she was not likely to shine in the brilliant Court of England. Here, it was women like me who were noticed; women who were bold, witty and talented... I could not see Jane putting herself forward, and as such, she would go unnoticed. I dismissed her as unimportant. But still, family is family, and I considered it might be helpful to gain another supporter.

"You must do your duties quietly and carefully to gain the affection of the Queen," I advised as we stood in my father's chambers at Richmond. "You seem intelligent enough, and you are humble and meek. She will like that. Do you read Latin? The Queen enjoys hearing works of devotion read aloud in her chambers."

Jane shook her head. "I do not know how to read or write much, cousin, and I do not know any Latin or French," she murmured. "I can sign my name, and read a little… but my father did not believe that reading and writing were honourable or necessary pursuits for women."

I lifted my eyebrows. "But you know your prayers and Scripture, I am sure?"

She nodded her pale face at me earnestly. "I learned by heart all that was thought appropriate for me to know."

A touch of despair fluttered in my heart. To not know how to read! What a curse! What joys my cousin was missing because of her father's antiquated belief in keeping his daughters' minds empty of thought. If I had been without literature in my life, I knew it would have been of detriment to me and to my character… And to not know the joys of reading the Word of God for oneself? I could hardly imagine such a hideous fate. For a moment I pitied the young girl. Looking on her almost translucent skin, I wondered how her father thought she was going to attract a husband. *Although*, I reasoned, *there are men who prefer a foolish wife to a clever one*… Perhaps her father could find her one of those to wed. She came from a fertile family, so perhaps she would be offered as naught but a breed-mare for some husband. That, it seemed to me then, could be her sole allure.

Jane was watching me quietly. *There is nothing in her*, I thought, *that I could ever find interesting*. I thought of my friends at court, of Mary and Bridget. They were ladies of snap and fire. They were women with whom I could talk on current events and literature, on reform and new thought. Jane was not likely to become one of my intimates… for how long can one converse on the state of the weather, even in England where the subject is so often and avidly discussed?

"The Queen will like your quietness and your virtue," I reassured her kindly, thinking that I should praise something about her. I felt sorry for the plain, simple creature. That was swiftly to change…

"Does she like *your* virtues, cousin?" Jane asked carefully. I started, suddenly unnerved by her steady blue eyes and those words, which seemed so innocent, and yet belied darker meaning underneath.

"What do you mean?" I drew her closer to the fire in my chamber, away from the ears of the servants. Perfumed juniper logs burnt hot and bright in the hearth, sending richly scented smoke out to linger in the chamber. The flames leapt as we stepped near, as though they, too, wanted to know more from this pallid girl.

Jane hesitated. "There are rumours…"

"Of what?" I grabbed her arm. My temper had been frayed of late, and it ever got the better of me even when I was not beset by such pressures and worries. She did not move from my sharp grasp, but she did wince as my fingernails dug into her arm through the velvet plush of her rather ill-fitting, russet gown. With the eye I had for clothing and design, I believed her dress had originally been made for a back other than hers.

"There are rumours that perhaps you do not love the Queen as you love the King, cousin," she said. "They say that the Queen is sad because you have taken the King's heart from her."

"*They,*" I snapped, "can say what they wish. The more time you spend at court, cousin Jane, the more you will realise that listening to rumour does not help a lady here. She is better off making her own judgements than bending to the will and gossip of others."

Jane removed her arm gently from my hold. "I shall endeavour to take your advice, cousin Anne." She folded her arms softly, tucking her hands into the folds of her over-hanging sleeves of poor, thin, furs. "I *shall* make my own judgements."

I nodded, still frowning at her. I had not expected much of such a mouse, but it seemed my colourless cousin had some mettle in her after all. "Now," I went on, attempting to ignore her last comment. "Let me show you the Queen's chambers and introduce you to your duties there. Although you are new to the court, I have been here some time and before this I was in service to Queen Claude of France and Margaret, Archduchess of Austria. I can show you how to be a good servant to the Queen."

Jane smiled without humour. "I long to benefit from your… *experience*, cousin."

I looked at her sharply, but there was nothing on her face to prove my suspicion that she was insinuating anything. I lifted my chin and she followed me from my chambers to the rich apartments of the Queen. I told her of her duties and her allowances. She was entitled to three meals per day and would receive slight wages. She had the privilege of keeping a hound, but only a small one and a maid for her own use. Jane nodded to each of these in silence, but yet I still wondered on this creature. She seemed like such a nonentity that I could hardly believe there was intelligence under her skin, and yet… her sly way of answering made me ponder. There was something underneath, I knew there was. Some measure of furtive intelligence. I could almost smell it.

But after I delivered her to the Mother of the Maids, I thought little more on her. As the days went on, it was obvious that Jane liked the Queen, and admired her. Jane's liking for Katherine was not going to make her a friend of mine. But to me, then, Jane was just another lady supporting the wrong side. Katherine had plenty of supporters and they would all be shown how wrong they were. I was determined that these insignificant people would not stop me. One day Henry and I would be together, and these people would see we were right. Although for me, the *Great Matter* was moving too slowly. Wolsey was in France, trying to secure François's support. Henry assured me that all would be well as soon as the Cardinal returned. I was unsure. Although I knew Wolsey would do anything to help please Henry, I wondered if the support of the French would do much to tip the scales unless they won the war in Italy. Would the idea of a union between France and England be enough to frighten the Emperor into releasing the Pope? I knew not. This all smelt like another chance for Wolsey to increase his personal power and prestige. My nose liked not that stench.

I also knew the Cardinal did not like me. Years had passed since Wolsey had ruined my chances with Henry Percy and shamed me, shouting at me that I was a silly girl and that I came from a family of *whores*… but I remembered it well. Wolsey was going to get an unpleasant shock when he found out about me. In some ways, I could hardly wait to surprise the great fat bat. In other ways I feared that when the Cardinal found out about Henry's intentions he would become my enemy.

The Cardinal was the most powerful and wealthiest man in England. He was Archbishop of York, Lord Chancellor of England and a Prince of the Church. He had Henry's love and he did everything for him. I did not believe, once Wolsey knew of Henry's intentions, he would work to honour them. I was troubled about the future and of what may happen to me once the Cardinal knew I could one day become his Queen.

Chapter Nine

Hever Castle
Summer's End 1527

"Katherine is not cruel to you, is she?" Henry asked worriedly.

I had decided to leave court, feeling the pressure of Katherine's dislike weighing too heavily upon my shoulders. Henry promised he would ride out to see me as soon as he could, and was sad that I was choosing to leave. "My mistress has heavy hands, my lord," I said carefully. "And she uses them to chastise me because she knows that you love me, and not her."

Henry looked angry at this, but what could he do? He could hardly demand that Katherine treat me respectfully without bringing our relationship out into the open. I suspected this was what Katherine wanted; to trick us into revealing our love and have evidence of infidelity to use against both me and Henry.

"I cannot continue to serve her, Henry." I put my hands into his. "Not only because she slaps and pinches me to try to get me to fight her, or disclose something of you and me, but because in her presence, I know how far I am from you. She stands between us."

Henry was overcome with remorse. "I will make all things right, Anne," he promised. "I will find another way for us to be together, without Katherine."

I took my leave of Katherine and she did not ask where I was going. She probably assumed that, much as he had with my sister, Henry was arranging to meet with me somewhere so that we could be together without the entire court watching.

Henry rode out to see me within a week, just as autumn came to Hever. Many of the trees were still green and lush, but the edges of their leaves had begun to show golden lights, bronzed-browns and bright yellows. Servants were working to harvest our crops, and the kitchens were busy baking, boiling and preserving late summer fruits into pies, jams and jellies. Piles of medlars sat waiting to soften and shrivel, for they were better to make into preserves when slightly turned. There was a scent of sweetness on the air from the early morn until the humid dusk. When I lifted my nose, I would smell cherry, apple, plum, quince and pear cooking in vast pots over the roaring fires of the kitchens.

Henry could only come for a day or two at the most when he visited. To tarry longer would lead Katherine to suspect he was with me. We made the most of every short visit. At night, when Henry and I finished the delicious courses the kitchens prepared for us, plates of stewed plums, juicy roasted pears and slices of poached apples would be brought in. We skewered these slices of fruit, slippery and succulent on our jewelled knives, putting them to our plate and then to our mouths. The honey-rich sweetness stole over our pink tongues and the last vestige of sourness would catch at the back of our mouths as we swallowed, making our mouths water.

I loved cherries and strawberries above all other fruit. When pies and sauces came rich and purple-red inside their golden-buttered crust, sparkling with sugar, I always had to sample them. Henry, too, loved these fruits, and when he visited I ensured the kitchens knew his favourite dishes, so they understood which ones were the most important to get right for the table. Henry was never displeased with his food in our house. I made sure of that. I was going to be a wife and a queen someday, and it was a wife's duty to ensure her husband ate well, and hearty. And besides, I loved to please him. He was charming when he was happy.

We feasted upon pottages, green with fresh summer herbs and white wine, platters of carved, roasted venison and rabbit from Hever's captive warrens. Sticky-sweet roasted hog and fried balls of mutton would grace the table next and when Henry had eaten his fill, I called for servants to bring in the carefully prepared dishes of marchpane and gingerbread carved into shapes of the Tudor rose. I made sure that there were always stocks of quince marmalade in the kitchens, for that delight was a great favourite of Henry's. It would be sliced into thick, glistening sugary slices and brought to us to eat on thin wafers. For each new visit I tried to have something new to surprise him with. I called on our kitchens to make jellies of hippocras, moulded into the shapes of animals, such as the dun cow or dragon emblems of the Tudors. Such creations were highly expensive to create, as sugar was a valuable spice, but my father's purse strings relaxed noticeably when the King came to call. The King could demand goods at a lower price for his court than any other person in the land, but the Boleyns could not... not yet, at least. Henry's visits were most testing for my father's coffers, but I assured father that the eventual rewards would outweigh any coin he spent now.

When Henry sat at the head of our table, full-bellied and content, with my mother and I sitting beside him, he would look about him and smile. His mouth stained from the rich wine, and his eyes gentle and tipsy for love of me and pleasure in all he had consumed. He was a creature of earthly delights, my Henry, for there were few things which made him happier than a fine horse to ride, and then a good meal eaten in happy company, at the day's end.

We washed our hands in silver fingerbowls, and then left to talk together at the fireside, or play at cards or chess. I never allowed him to win if I was able to beat him, and I think he enjoyed this, for when he won, he knew he had done so in truth and not for false flattery. There was a great sense of pride that he took, too, in the times when *I* won. He took this as proof of my intelligence, and rejoiced in it.

"I would not want a foolish wife," he said when I had won a small fortune from him. He lay his cards down and slid his hands across the table, claiming mine. "*My* Queen will be the cleverest *and* the most beautiful woman in the world," he continued, his eyes tender. Those blue eyes… When I wish to remember them happily, I think of such times as those. When his eyes were made soft like a warming pool between the rocks on the shore, the sun fractured over its still surface, glinting with sweet light. There were other times, much later, when I would see those eyes turn to blue fire, to frozen ice, to mirror the ocean tempests as they raged in froth and foam…

"And my husband is the only man who can beat me," I purred, lacing my long, slim fingers through his large ones. Henry chuckled, gripping my fingers possessively.

"As is the way it should be… think you not, sweetheart?" he asked merrily. "In us, there is a meeting of equals… equal minds of wit and wisdom, equal spirits of fire and courage… We were meant for each other. God has given you to me, Anne."

"And I will thank Him forever for His goodness," I murmured. Henry lowered his head, released the tops of my fingers and kissed them one by one. The sensation was alluring, teasing… I wished we could be together, alone, unheeded by the world, unseen by the court, by Katherine. Just Henry, just me…

Henry gazed at me hungrily and then he sighed. "Dance with me, Anne." He lifted his chin to the musicians at the edge of the room who were playing gently, trying to be unobtrusive. "A more rousing song!" he called, pulling my hand and leading me to the centre of the hall. "And perhaps I shall be able to dance off my desire for you, my love," he laughed quietly into my ear, "for it seems all you have to do is look at me, and I am a man who knows not if his strength can resist such a dazzling creature."

I chuckled, releasing his hand to stand opposite him. The musicians struck the first chord, and I spread my arms upwards, my hanging sleeves accentuating the slim, lithe lines of my body. Henry bowed, his eyes roaming over me. The dance began. I tripped and slipped through the elegant motions, sliding my foot to elongate my form, leaping to clap, twist and turn in perfect time with the music. Henry bounded like the most elegant of stags, alive with grace and energy. His high leaps caused servants to pause as they went from one task to another. They stopped in the corridor, their eyes fixed on Henry. They watched me too, I could see them. I made a perfect balance to Henry. As he sprang and bounded, I slipped and skipped. He danced about me as I moved slow and sensuously, each step taken as though we had trained together all our lives.

But the dance did not relieve our desire; it only increased it. We came together, his hands about my waist as he spun me, and tight on my sides as he lifted me… my body sliding down his as he brought me down from the lift… It was torture to be so close to the one whom you desired above all others in this world, and yet be allowed nothing but a kiss.

The dance ended, and as we stood from our last bow to each other, all I could see were Henry's blue eyes in the candlelight. Hunger, excitement, frustration, exhilaration… all those emotions strayed across his pupils as he watched me, flushed faced, his chest heaving. I felt consumed by his glance at times; as though I were one of the fine dishes on his table.

Talking of our *Matter* helped to cool the heat of our frustrated desire. Wolsey was due to return soon and Henry assured me the Cardinal would bring only good news. "Wolsey is my *best* man," he boasted as we stood at the fire late that night. Bess was asleep in a chair near the door, and aside from that we were alone. My mother had made herself scarce as the presence of a maid was enough to demonstrate our respectability, should we ever have the need. "Soon Wolsey shall help us to procure an annulment," Henry continued, "so that you and I can start making those sons of ours."

"Something I am looking forward to, my lord." I cast an impish look at him, my dusky lips sliding into a naughty smirk. Henry grinned, moving towards me, his hands eager and outstretched, but I moved away from him. "I think the first should be named Henry, my lord, and the second Edward," I said as I danced from his hands and chuckled throatily at his efforts to catch me. "Each will have their father's hair and build, and they will both be excellent in the joust and win every contest they enter." I ducked as he tried to grab me and pranced away, smiling at him.

Henry was watching me intently now, his keen hunter's eyes regarding the way that I teased him. He crept nearer, like a prowling cat after a mouse, and flashed forwards, trying to grab hold of me with his strong hands. But I was too quick for my hunter. I evaded his reach, my velvet slippers quick on the rushes on the floor. I turned and beckoned to him, earning a fierce grin as he stalked me.

"And we shall have a daughter or two, also, my lord," I said softly, backing to the edge of the room. "They will be fine girls with red-blond hair and blue eyes like their father. All will speak of their grace, intelligence and modesty. They will marry the greatest princes in the world. They will be mighty and well-beloved queens."

Finally he had me, cornered at the edge of the room with nowhere else to run. He pounced with a short cry of triumph. I smiled languidly and stretched my arms up and over his shoulders as I brushed his lips with mine. Henry's voice was husky when he spoke after our kiss. "I would that these children of ours should have something of their mother in them too, my love…" He took his hand from my waist and ran it gently over my face. I could feel the hard skin and rough calluses on his fingers caused by of hours practising with the sword and riding his horse. I nuzzled against his hand, pulling him closer to me as I kissed his throat.

"After all, this face and this hair I am most fond of seeing." He went on, running his fingers up through the silks which covered my long hair under my French hood. "I should like our children to have the deep dark eyes of their mother, these wise and lovely eyes."

He pressed me against the hard boards of the wall. His hands slid up from my waist so that they cupped my breasts as his lips moved on mine. Bess did not stir. For a long time we were lost in each other, oblivious to any sound or sigh the house made, to the crackling of the fire, or the sound of the servants outside.

Henry kissed me tenderly one last time, and then reached around me, putting his head on my shoulder and his face against my breasts. He sighed slightly, a sound not so much of frustration as contentment, and it made me warm to his love even more. These times, these spare moments of privacy in a world where all eyes watched us… they were precious, and all the more so because they were rare.

"I will give you fine children, Henry of England," I murmured into his ear.

He did not move his face from my breast. His words came out muffled, but strong. "You will," he said, and there was an edge of something I barely understood in his voice; a sense of certainty and resolve. For some reason, I shivered.

Chapter Ten

Richmond Palace
Autumn 1527

The smell of wood smoke and wet leaves filled the chilly air as I rode from Hever towards London. Behind me, my guards chatted and japed, enjoying their excursion. My heart was not so light. I was returning to my post at court. Even though I was troubled that Katherine might discover our secret, I knew I had to go back. Wolsey was on his return journey to England and Henry had sent word that I was to join him and hear the Cardinal's report for myself.

In the woodlands, as we rode, we heard men singing as they chopped at trees and hauled wood. The air was fresh with that frigid sharpness on the wind, letting you know summer has passed. Spider webs hung in the grasses at the edge of the forests, their silken strands glimmering with dew as they billowed like delicate sails in the breeze. Normally shy wood mice devoured the fallen, fermenting apples that lay under the branches of their wild mother-trees, growing drunk and bold on this hedgerow cider. Ivy shimmered in the dappled light, clinging fast to trees and wrapping their twisted, green-silver leaves about their trunks.

When the country roads ended, we went by barge into London. The waterways were packed with tiny boats as we reached the city. In the company of hundreds of white swans and mottled grey signets our barge sailed down the river. The young swans were now almost as large as their parents, almost ready to fly out for the winter. The wind was yet warm as I sat on the cushioned seat on deck, watching the packed streets of London from afar. The skyline was dominated by the churches of London; one hundred and twenty in all, as well as monasteries, nunneries, and abbeys. Each one displayed holy relics for those who had coin enough to see and touch them. Westminster Abbey, its spires grey against the light of the skies, possessed blood from Christ's wounds, milk of the Virgin Mary, and hair of St Peter. Although I believed that some relics of the Church might well be genuine, there were many more I knew were fakes; brought to, or made by, the Church, in order to attract wealthy pilgrims, and gain coin from those who were sick, poor, or desperate, in the hope that touching such items might help them.

As well as the churches, prisons were numerous; both those of the King, and those of the Church. At Lambeth Palace, the residence of the Archbishop of Canterbury, there was the looming Lollard's Tower; the place where suspected heretics were held, questioned, and tortured before being condemned. The Lollard movement had started several hundred years before our time. Led by John Wycliffe, they had attacked the privileged status of the clergy, and their wealth, advocated for translation of the Bible to become legal, and believed that all spiritual authority should come from the Scriptures rather than the Pope. Although widely thought of as heretics, I had much sympathy with hidden Lollards in England and beyond. They had been persecuted for years, and executed by the Church and state for heresy, but many of their thoughts had led to men like Luther, and Tyndale producing theories I now held dear. The Lollard's Tower now took in all suspected heretics. It was rumoured that within the Lollard's Tower, great walls of strong oak held iron rings, so heretics could be suspended above the floor by their arms or legs to make them talk, or to punish them for their supposed sins. I turned my eyes from the sight of that distant Tower. There were many who would call me a heretic, for some of my beliefs.

We drifted past noisy markets in which everything was sold, from bolts of cloth, to gold, to ribbons and pins for dresses made by the skilled hands of Moorish craftsmen. Men stood inside their boats along the river's slippery banks, loudly negotiating with customers for passage to the other side.

London Bridge was hectic with noise and movement. Its piled buildings frowzy and rich by turns. We sailed past whipping posts and stocks, where those condemned by the King or clergy were sent for public punishment. At Smithfield, to the north of the priory of St Bartholomew, was the meat market of London, and, perhaps fittingly, it was also the place where convicted heretics were taken to be burned. Chained to the stake, those who dared to question the Church had faggots of dry kindling and reeds put under their feet and stacked up to their waists. Crowds would gather, and men would sell hot pies and ale, as the executioner put torch to wood, and purified the condemned men's souls with bodily torment and agony. It was rare for a victim to die quickly. Sometimes it took as long as an hour for a heretic to suffer enough burns or fear to die from them. Fortunately, under Wolsey, no matter what else I might think of him, such spectacles were rare. But the threat remained for all who would question Church practises, or read banned texts, as I did. Do you wonder that I was quiet about my passion for reform? Even noble title cannot protect one the Church decides to move against.

I reached Richmond Palace and peered up at her vast towers, built by Henry's father, with satisfaction. I was never more at home anywhere than I was at court. Even with my gnawing worries about Wolsey and Katherine, I was still glad to be back.

Officially, I had returned to Katherine's service. She did not ask me where I had been, or what I had been doing, but welcomed me formally, and with a great deal of coldness. I barely cared for her displeasure. What was Katherine to me anymore? Let her manner be cold! Let her hands slap and pinch! I would ignore all such slights, and face her with the same coldness she showed to me. I felt but little pity for her anymore, for her behaviour had altered, and she was showing her true face. Margaret and Bridget were pleased to see me return, as was George, and I sought solace in the companionship of my friends. The Queen could treat me as ill as she dared. I would steadfastly refuse to rise to her. Henry was overjoyed to see me, after even such a slight break in our companionship, and he immediately took me out hunting with Margaret and some of his men. Katherine could hardly refuse. In intimate company, Henry saw no danger in showing his love for me. I rode pillion on his horse, and when the party paused to eat in the cold air of the afternoon, we sat and talked together, with barely a whisker of space between us. When I was with Henry, the shadow of Katherine's dislike could not touch me.

On a bright cold day soon after my return to court, I was seated, reading to Henry from the *Le Morte d'Arthur,* when a messenger from Cardinal Wolsey arrived. Wolsey was at last returned. The messenger requested a private audience for his master and, to my great surprise, asked where the King should *receive the Cardinal.* Anger shot through me. This upstart Cardinal! The man had been nothing but a hindrance to my family, and now here he was demanding where *he* should be received? Who was the King in England? Henry or Wolsey? It was not to be borne.

Before Henry could open his mouth, I rose suddenly, making the messenger and Henry jump with surprise. "Where else is the Cardinal to come?" I cried haughtily. "Tell him he may come *here*… where the *King* chooses to be!"

The messenger backed out of the room and left me fuming, with a baffled Henry looking on. "It is too much!" I exclaimed. "The arrogance of that man! The Cardinal asks where *he* should be received? As though you are equals? He is your *servant*, my lord! How dare he act in such a disrespectful manner?"

I glared at Henry, my fury growing, as he seemed puzzled by my behaviour. I went to a window seat and flung myself down upon it. "I do not believe that he will wish to see me married to Your Majesty…" I admitted, looking down at the floor. "I believe Wolsey would wish you married to some French princess, or to another Spanish lump, rather than to me!"

Henry knelt beside me. "You react thus because you fear his disapproval, sweetheart?" he asked gently, and I nodded. "Wolsey is *my* man," he protested. "He works for *my* interests and whatever he may think is governed by me. You and he must meet more often, for he works in our interests, my love… I would that you were good friends with those who serve me well and who are dear to my heart."

I looked at him coldly. "I do not believe he will work with *both* of our best intentions at heart, Henry." I turned my face from him as he sought to kiss me and heard his sigh of exasperation as he walked away, but I knew that he would be back, just as soon as I would let him return. We awaited the Cardinal in silence. Henry did not ask me to leave, and I did not seek to. It was time that the Cardinal knew what I was to the King. Fear made me defiant. My worries brought courage growling into my breast. Those who know no fear know no courage. The reckless are often thought of as brave, but they are not. Courage lies in knowing fear, and rising to face it despite its power.

Wolsey came to Henry, of course. What else was he to do after *that* message? The Cardinal could not quite hide his surprise as he saw me, seated, in the presence of the standing King. It was as though I were the King and Henry my subject. Before Wolsey had left for France he had assumed I was a passing fancy of no great importance. Now, however, the great Cardinal viewed me as the bear regards the dogs in the baiting pits. There was suspicion beneath the façade of politeness and amiability that this politician wore as he greeted us. He was quick enough to see that had I been just another mistress, I would have vacated the chamber upon his arrival. The fact that I remained, and was so informal with Henry, caused him great concern. He covered it well, but I saw those heavy eyes blink once with surprise as his eyes travelled swiftly over the chamber. The Cardinal was not used to surprises. He did not like them.

"How now, Thomas," Henry greeted him, throwing his arms about the Cardinal's velvet-covered shoulders with affection. "What news do you bring of France and of our *Matter*?"

Wolsey looked questioningly at Henry, and then at me. Henry gestured for him to speak, and the Cardinal decided it was obvious his King wanted me there. He ran a finger over the three chins layered beneath his first, and breathed in, making his huge belly bulge under its red robes. Wolsey started to speak of the splendour of the French Court; of his gracious welcome there, and of the never-ending love the French King had for Henry, but Henry waved a restless hand and enquired more directly.

"Will François show support for the annulment, Thomas?"

Wolsey hesitated. "The King of France loves Your Majesty like his own *brother*," he breathed, his fat face wobbling. "He says he is closer to no other man in the world, and would gladly welcome an alliance with Your Majesty against his enemy Charles of Spain, of course…"

"It sounds to me as though there is a 'but' missing at the end of that sentence, Your Eminence," I said softly from my seat in the corner. Wolsey glanced at me with his bushy eyebrow raised. "I am sure that His Majesty would know *all* that François of France had to say on this most important matter," I went on.

Henry glanced at me with warning in his eyes, but there was, too, a sparkle there. Women were not supposed to be outspoken, bold, forward… I was all of those things. Henry found it exciting, challenging, interesting… I was so very different from all the other women at court… and I was his.

Wolsey tried to hide his astonishment, but I could see his mind flopping about in horror... *What is this Boleyn girl doing here?* he was asking himself... *and why does the King allow her to speak so to me?*

Wolsey cleared his throat. "François admits he cannot risk showing *public* support for Your Majesty's *Great Matter* at this time," he went on, glancing at Henry with sad eyes. It was like the expression of a puppy caught stealing sausages, trying to escape punishment. "But he supports you in private, as one monarch and father to another. He understands your keen desire to have sons to whom you will pass your throne ... but he asks that you consider his *own* position as a father as well. Charles of Spain has François' two eldest sons in his hands. François fears that to support you openly may bring the Emperor's wrath upon them."

Henry heaved a sigh. "Of course I understand that," he murmured. "Had I a son, even *one* legitimate heir, I would protect him with all that I had... even as my father did for me."

The Cardinal was nodding furiously. He thought he had the King where he wanted him. If Henry was sympathetic to François' position, then Wolsey had not failed... But I saw this rather differently.

"François believes that in this matter, the Pope must be the leader, Your Majesty," Wolsey hurried on, sweat beads on his brow growing larger. "François believes, since the Pope is so in need of allies at this dangerous time, that Clement will be more than happy to receive Your Majesty's envoys. François continues his war against Spain and he believes victory in Italy will be his by the end of the year. François suggests sending a delegate to Rome to petition Clement for his decision. If the Pope rules in Your Majesty's favour, which *of course*, all men will see is the only true and honest choice, Charles and Katherine will have no choice but to agree to the annulment. Your Majesty will then be free to marry, and…" Wolsey stumbled at the end of this platitudinous speech and glanced at me, suddenly unsure of himself. "And François would, of course, welcome a match between Your Majesty and *une princesse de sang royal français.*"

Henry ignored the last comment. "What did François say about the idea of a trial headed by you, Thomas, overseen by the cardinals of France and England?"

Wolsey puckered his thick lips, that puppy-dog sorrow flowing into his eyes again. "None of the French cardinals would agree to the idea, Majesty," he confessed, looking uneasy. "And their King knows he has not the power to force them to do so."

My head darted up. I had not heard of this plan. I thought Henry had intended for a council to decide the *Great Matter* in England. There had been no mention of French cardinals. I gazed questioningly at Henry and he shook his head. "It was but an idea, sweetheart," he explained. "We thought that if Thomas could act in the stead of the Pope, as *de facto* Pope, then we could reach a ruling faster… Given Clement's present situation, we thought it a reasonable idea." His face darkened. "But it seems the French cardinals did not…"

"The route left to us is to apply to the Pope for a trial of Your Majesty's marriage in England," Wolsey continued. His eyes were careful now as they looked upon me. I knew he had gathered the reason why I was here… The only reason I would be in this position was if the King was considering marrying me. For what other reason would I be at this meeting? As the King's new Privy Councillor?

Henry looked deflated, and although I had not expected a great deal, I was dented, discouraged. Another delay. Envoys would have to go to the Pope, talks would go on… Wolsey's trip to France had accomplished nothing. It had been a waste of time. What did we have from it but the good wishes of the King of France, and his private support? What use was that? I exhaled heavily and stared at Henry, willing him to do more. He had told me our *Matter* was in hand and that Wolsey was the man to make our dreams reality. I did not see we were in any better position than we were when Henry proposed to me.

"I have already sent a good man of my own household to Rome," Henry said, exasperating the Cardinal's uneasiness.

"Your Majesty must of course act as you see fit," Wolsey said. "But if I am to be your good servant, I must know all that is planned... otherwise we may find ourselves at crossed purposes, Your Majesty... If you require trusted men, I have many to put at your disposal."

"Dr Knight *is* a trusted man, Thomas, fear not," Henry replied. "I have sent him to the Pope in the Castel Saint Angelo, armed with draft dispensations. I hoped that François would offer us help, but I also understand it is better to have all options covered." Henry put his hand on Wolsey's arm. "Think you I acted too hastily, Thomas?" I was unpleasantly surprised by the humble note in Henry's voice.

"Your Majesty has the energy of a *thousand* men." Wolsey smiled warmly at his master. "And it is therefore only to be expected he acts on impulse from time to time."

"I am sorry if you thought I was acting against you, Thomas. I only wish this matter to be resolved, swiftly. It presses on my conscience."

"Of course, Majesty, of course... but if I could be informed of all you intend before it is done...?"

"Naturally, Thomas, I was too hasty." Henry beamed at Wolsey. "That is why you are here, with me, is it not old friend? To make sure I always do what is right."

I watched Henry with shock throughout this exchange. I had not known of this Dr Knight either! Why was I being so kept in the dark about events that concerned me so intimately? Surely I had a right to know these things? It was my future, as well as Henry's, for which these men were playing. And what *difference* Henry showed to his servant... It was distressing to see him grovel before Wolsey... and unsettling. I made up my mind to talk sternly to my beloved when this meeting ended. I wanted to be left on the fringes no longer. I believed, then, I could do little to help, but that did not mean I did not want to know all that was going on.

Although Wolsey affected surprise at Henry's news, we later found that he had actually intercepted Knight and stalled him in his mission to reach Pope Clement. The dispensations carried by Knight stated that the King wanted dispensation to marry a woman whose sister he had known carnally. The missives did not mention me by name, but the Cardinal could not have been wholly unaware of our relationship. Wolsey had badgered the information out of Knight. He had demonstrated surprise to find me in Henry's chambers, but he had known that something was afoot before his return to England. Still, I doubt he realised how deeply Henry's affections for me ran. Wolsey knew his King, and he believed he knew his passions. He had thought them ever-changing. He thought me a new shiny toy his King wanted to play with. He was going to be proved wrong.

For now, we all agreed that the best course of action was to send envoys to Rome to request that a papal legate came to England. We would ask for a trial of the King's marriage before a Legatine Court. A papal legate would be protected by the King's forces in England, so therefore would not be under pressure to agree in Katherine's favour due to her nephew's hold over the Pope. It was the best plan... In truth, it was the *only* plan. Our hopes that the Queen would humbly step aside were fading. Henry told Wolsey that Katherine had sworn on the sanctity of her marriage, and refused to leave him. Wolsey was obviously concerned to hear this, as clearly he, too, had thought Katherine would be meek enough to step down without causing problems.

It was dawning upon me that this *Great Matter* was a most intricate business. It was no longer simply a matter of my heart and Henry's. It involved countries, politics, the Pope, and threat of invasion and war. The Emperor had not thought twice about sacking the Holy City… Would he do the same to England if his aunt was insulted? Henry sensed my rising anxiety and put his large arms around me. Wolsey watched us. His expression of barely concealed concern remained, which was somewhat soothing to my mood. It was refreshing to see a touch of fear on the face of one such as he.

"Soon, my love," Henry cooed soothingly. "Soon all this shall be over and you and I shall be the true King and Queen."

As I sunk into Henry's arms I saw the Cardinal's jaw twitch. From over Henry's shoulder I allowed myself to raise one perfectly arched eyebrow at Wolsey as though daring him to say a word. He merely dipped his head to me. It was as though he were a knight acknowledging a foe on the battlefield.

Watching this man over Henry's shoulder, I knew he was no friend to me, just as he knew I was no friend to him. But he was the best statesman in the land and we needed him. The Cardinal knew now that he would have to watch himself. He had underestimated Henry's feelings for me, and that had shaken him. The great fat bat would have to make peace with the *silly girl* he had once insulted if he wanted to keep in favour with his master. I am sure, however, even at that moment, Wolsey was considering how best to snap me away from Henry's side.

His absence during his trip to France had brought about a shift in power at court. I, not he, was now the most important person to Henry, and the great Cardinal Wolsey was aware of it. Almost immediately after his return, the Cardinal provided me with a new servant, Master Thomas Heneage, who, it seemed, was there to make my every whim reality… and, I had no doubt, was also there to spy on me. Wolsey showered me with gifts and letters, and I must say that he had excellent taste. He gave me a new illuminated book of hours, much like the one I had taken with me to France and the Low Countries, but richly decorated and much grander than my first. I thanked him graciously by letter for the book. It was beautiful and I took it with me everywhere. It was a great solace to me in the frustrating and difficult times ahead even if it was given to me by an enemy pretending to be an ally.

My father found the Cardinal's sudden humility and deference most amusing, and spent much time with Norfolk chuckling about it. I found it satisfying also, but I was under no illusions about Wolsey's motives. He wanted to keep me close, to keep an eye on me. He wanted to lull me into a false sense of security, and believed the best way to do that was to flatter me, and lavish gifts upon me. If the Cardinal thought he could buy his way into my good graces, he was much mistaken, just as he was foolish if he thought that such obsequiousness would make me trust him. But I did not dispel his illusions. If the Cardinal wanted me close to keep an eye on me, I would come close, and keep an eye on *him*.

Later that autumn, Henry and François made a great show of friendship to unsettle Charles. Henry appointed François to the Order of the Garter, and François responded in kind by granting the Order of St Michael to Henry. Neither King could leave his country to receive the honour, of course, so it was done by proxy. There was a feast at Greenwich Palace to mark the occasion. Tournaments, jousting, wrestling competitions and mock-battles went on. Cheering crowds screamed, beside themselves as they watched Henry joust, and win against every opponent. Men selling fresh-baked pies thick with gravy, pork and dried apple vied with those selling hot spice ale and wine. In the upper stalls, where the nobility was seated, all food and drinks were brought to us, provided by the King's purse.

George was riding in this joust. He cut a handsome figure in his new armour, riding out to accept a ribbon tied on his lance by a pretty girl. Jane stood near the Queen, her face resolutely turned from her husband as he begged a favour from another woman. When I glanced at Jane, I could see tears in her eyes not caused by the cold wind. She blinked them away and went on with her duties.

Katherine sat in the stalls, watching her husband compete, wearing an unreadable expression. Friendship with France was not pleasing to her, particularly at this time when she knew Henry was questioning their marriage. She cheered her husband and laughed with her ladies Marie de Salinas, Margaret Pole and her Moorish lady of the Bedchamber, Catalina de Cardones. Only a keen eye could catch the glimmer of sadness which rested about her. Mendoza regarded Henry with displeasure. Despite being an ambassador, the man was not very talented at disguising his emotions, particularly when it came to his beloved Katherine.

Henry had a great display created; two trees made from silk. One was a Tudor hawthorn, and the other, a Valois mulberry. They stood with their silks wafting in the autumn winds as celebration went on about them. That night, we danced in a masque. All the court came in disguise. Henry and I partnered each other, our masks covering our identities for the sake of propriety, as we moved together as one.

As winter approached and storms forced the court inside, I found my close proximity to Katherine unbearable. When it was fine weather there were many opportunities for us to be outside, and somehow, out in the fresh air, with space about us, my proximity to Katherine was not so claustrophobic. But as the winter came, as we spent much time in her over-heated chambers, I felt increasingly ill at ease.

I made up my mind to return to Hever. Henry was to be at Greenwich with Katherine for the Christmas celebrations, and pressed me to stay, but I was considering the notion of remaining at court dangerous. Henry was not subtle, even when he believed himself to be. It was becoming increasingly obvious to the whole court that the King loved me. When news of the envoys to Rome came out, people would question if I was really just a mistress and if the Pope heard rumours of scandal, he would never grant the annulment. Henry and I parted at Richmond. We promised to write every day, and I begged Henry to keep nothing from me.

"Please, Henry," I pleaded. "You must understand that to hear *any* news, good or bad, is imperative. Do not keep me at arm's length. You must understand this is of the utmost importance to me."

He smoothed my hair from my brow. "I promise, my love," he said, kissing my lips gently, his hand under my chin. "I only sought to keep certain things quiet until we knew more of them. I did not want to trouble you. I know this weighs as heavy on you as it does on me."

"But we are in this *together*… as one." I protested. "And so we must share *all* together." I smiled up at him, running a finger along his golden-red beard. "For better or for worse, my love," I said. "Why not start as we mean to go on?"

Henry agreed with me, moved by my desperation. As we parted, he told me he would come and see me, in secret, during the winter, and later we would find a way to be brought together again.

"It will not be long now, my love," he said. "It will not be long."

Chapter Eleven

Hever Castle
Winter 1527

That winter was bitterly cold. The Thames froze over, its lapping waters and strong currents frozen by winter's wandering hand. Its banks shone with white frost and silver ice. Along the riversides, the rotted husks of thick summer reeds stilled, petrified by the cold. A great fire was built on the deep ice of the frozen river and whole boar and mutton were roasted upon it. They say the flames of the fire could not melt that thick, frozen water. Every drip of fat from the roasted beasts fizzled into the ice only to become a part of the ice-covered expanse.

Along the coast, the sea froze where it met the shore. Waves were made immobile, stationary, as though God had brought them to an unnatural death. The white plumes of frozen waves rubbed shoulders with black rocks, sand and pebbled beaches, making it seem as though Time itself had stopped.

I awoke each morning at Hever to the sight of my breath puffing out of my mouth in white clouds. Thin ice gathered on the tops of our washing bowls, and frost covered each window in fronds shaped like fern and grapevine. Bess shook by the fire as she coaxed the sleepy embers to life in the watery light of each dawn, and often, we waited together in my bed for the fire to burn hot enough to warm to my chamber.

Each day, I would ride out over the crisp and frozen lands of the Boleyns. I rode to the hilltops and sat on my mount, looking out at the small villages and hovels of the poor, painted silver with ice and snow, wondering how they managed at such times. My mother had ever-ordered that the leavings from our tables at Hever were to be distributed amongst these villages, so that they could share in our prosperity. We gave alms at Mass each day, and I prayed for these peasants morning and evening, asking God to help them through this winter.

Sometimes, as I rode out, I would marvel at the beauty of the landscape. Cloaked in this snowy cowl of whiteness, every branch and beam, every twig and blade of frozen grass glittered with unearthly beauty. In the evening when everything was still, when I was on my return journey to Hever, I felt I might lose myself in wonder; as though Anne Boleyn may be swallowed whole by the beauty that surrounded her.

Snow fell as I rode; delicate flakes of icy crystals floated from the skies. I would catch these on my dark leather glove to admire their shapes and forms as they melted away. The sharp, crisp snap of the frozen earth under my horses' hooves was delicious and the air about me was refreshing. Being far from court irked me, but I understood I must keep some distance from the King. Henry wrote, true to his promise, every day, sending me letters, poems, and gifts. When I laid these offerings out in my chambers, I was amazed at the sheer quantity of items now in my possession. As well as all that glittered in gold and silver, there were reams of stunning cloth. There were pearls, golden rings, and small gemstones to be sewn into gowns. There were woollen blankets, linen for my table and threads of many colours for embroidery. There were books, and a fine portrait of Henry, which I hung in my room. My personal wealth was growing as the King showered me with signs of his love. But it was his letters I clung to, more than his gifts. His deep, dark scrawl on creamy parchment. His words of love and devotion. His promises that all would be well. Those were what brought me comfort that cold winter. *It will not be long…* Those words became like a prayer in those long, cold winter nights. *It will not be long…* That was how we reconciled our passion into reason... It was how we survived.

And, true also to his word, Henry came to visit. Officially, he was staying at Penshurst Place, but more often than not, he slept at Hever. My father entertained him royally when he came, and although Henry loved the feasts and the games my father put on, sometimes he found my father trying. "I think, at times, that your father wishes to keep me all to himself," Henry murmured into my hair as I sat in his lap by the fire one night.

I giggled. "Do you think you will be able to resist his charms, my lord?"

Henry's great laugh bounced about the room. "There is but one in this house I yearn for..." His hands stroked my shoulder. "One whom I long to see, every day, whether she is near me or not."

"It cannot be long now, can it?" I asked anxiously. "When will you send our delegation to the Pope?"

He sighed, pulled from his lazy lust by my demands. Henry turned mockingly irritated eyes on me. "*Other* maids would gasp and faint to hear such words of love from me, lady." He waggled his finger at me, a bright garnet ring twinkling in the firelight. "*You*, it seems, are unmoved by my declarations of love."

I jumped free of his lap. "*Other maids*?" I asked, putting my hands on my hips and tilting my head to one side with faked anger. "What other maids are these? Speak now, Henry of England, and tell me if you have played me false, or I will track these jades down and feed them to my hounds!"

He saw the teasing in my eyes and shook his head with affection. "Ah, Anne..." he said, holding out his hands to beg me back to his lap. "There is no one else in the world like you… and therefore, there will never be anyone else for me *but* you. All others become as cupboards and sideboards when you walk into a chamber… They are lifeless, solid, and graceless when compared to you. You are the only woman in the world. You are the only one for me."

I fell back into his embrace and kissed him soundly. "Good!" I cried. "For if there were others, Henry, my love would not be yours any more…" I kissed him again, putting my hands to his chin and lacing my fingers into his short red-gold beard. "If I do not fall and faint at your words, my lord, it is not because I do not love you. It is because I am hungry for this time of waiting to end. We have waited too long already. I hate the times when we are apart. I hate not being able to be at your side, where I belong. I love you, Henry… I am eager for our life together to begin."

"And I, Anne." He rested his head against my breasts. "And I…"

"So when do you send your men to Rome?"

He leapt up suddenly, with me in his arms, and bore me across the room as though I were a corn doll. "Enough woman!" he roared, laughing, bouncing me up and down. "*Enough*! I shall send them this very day if it will make your tongue stop!"

I giggled as he swept me about the chamber. "I know of other ways to ensure my silence, my lord," I whispered huskily to his ear. He dropped my feet to the floor and put his eager lips to mine. For a long time we kissed, our bodies close. Then, as always had to happen, he stopped and took my hand. We walked to the table to play at cards.

Later that night, as we sat by the fire and sipped sweet wine from Alsace, he told me that Wolsey and he were working hard on the briefs for Rome. Wolsey was insistent that they be perfected before being sent out. Whilst Henry seemed assured these delays were in our best interests, I was not so sure. I worried that Wolsey was impeding progress … I was sure he was dedicated to Henry's interests, but the problem was that Wolsey believed *his* interests were also those of his King. Wolsey viewed me as a threat. Quite apart from his dislike of my family, the Cardinal worried I would shake his hold over Henry and Wolsey did not want anyone having more power than him.

In addition to the presents sent by my often absent love, Wolsey, too, was sending me gifts. The influx and regularity of the Cardinal's presents increased noticeably each time Henry made the long trip in the dead of winter from London to Kent. Every time Henry was with me, Wolsey's servants arrived to offer me more fine goods… This pleased Henry, which I suspected was the point. The Cardinal wished to dupe the King into thinking he was honouring me. Whilst I saw through Wolsey's duplicity, I cannot but admit that the cloth and jewels he sent to me were just as fine as those that had been presented to me by the King. Wolsey was easily as rich as Henry; many suspected he was far richer. I spent much time that winter occupying myself, my mother and our maids in making clothes of my own designs, from these fine riches sent by the King and his Cardinal.

Winter is a good time for dressmaking, as long as one has a good fire to sit at. We would talk, go over my designs, try parts of the gowns on to see how they looked and note where they needed adjustment… There were merry times, but I missed Henry. I missed the court. I missed George who was still seeking to reclaim his place in the Privy Chamber by ingratiating himself with the King. I had not asked for favours for my family as yet… I was a little nervous to do so. I did not want Henry thinking that all I wanted him for was the power to elevate my family. I was considering making a few small requests, but to ask for George's restoration to the Privy Chamber would be to directly flout Wolsey, whose ordinances of the last year had taken George from his post there, along with many others. The purge had been officially intended to reduce the number of servants in the King's household and save the treasury money, but we all knew it had, in fact, been intended to reduce the number of influential men about Henry, leaving Wolsey a clear field in which to gallop with the King's love and favour by himself. I was not yet willing to go against the Cardinal in such a direct manner. But I had already had a few letters from distant cousins and courtiers. Perhaps it was time to try a small request, and see where it led.

In those hours and days, sat before the fire in the great hall at Hever, I made fine hoods, lined with pearls and gems. I designed glorious gowns of velvet and silks, with slashed skirts and striped kirtles, and long, delicate, elegant hanging sleeves. I sat embroidering grapevines and honeysuckle flowers into the gorgeous cloth I had been given, my mouth full of pins held fast by my closed lips, thinking of Henry. In my heart, every gown I made was part of my trousseau. Every stitch plunged into fabric as I imagined my life to come. Every dress worthy of a queen… and that queen would soon be I.

Despite the delays, I kept the same thought in my head. *It would not be long now…*

How little I knew, then.

Chapter Twelve

Hever Castle
Winter 1527

For days the skies had been heavy, grey and leaden. When I awoke one morning, I could smell that familiar metallic scent which told me that we would have snow before the evening came. I dressed in my warmest clothing; a good, thick kirtle of English wool under a thick velvet dress of deepest black with heavy over-sleeves of red velvet. I wrapped a fur-lined cloak about my shoulders; another present from Henry. Bess trembled with the cold even in her warm woollen dress, and I put a cloak about her shoulders, telling her to build the fire, to warm the room throughout the cold day.

In the great hall, the huge fire was roaring, and I watched maids scurrying here and there, carrying baskets of food and armfuls of wood. I heard my mother's voice calling out instructions to those who passed her in the kitchens, and went to find her. "Everyone is *most* active this morning," I observed by way of greeting as I kissed her.

The kitchens were warm and steamy. Pottage was simmering with tiny onions bobbing to its savoury surface, and a great pike was being turned on the spit, basted by one of the maids and dripping sizzling fat into the red fingers of the fire. Maids were making pastry, rolling it out in white flour and crimping the edges in pie dishes, and others were bashing and banging dough to bake bread. They sang as they worked; songs of the court. I heard a maid singing one of Henry's songs, *Pastime with Good Company*, and I smiled to hear it. Great baskets were filled with small white and lilac turnips and purple carrots, which waited to be cleaned and cooked. The steam-filled air was rich with scents of sage, thyme and rosemary; smells I have long associated with winter and the comforts of my mother's kitchens.

My mother smiled. "Your father is due to arrive this evening, and with good news, apparently. He brings George, Mary and Will with him too. We will be a full house of family come dinner time!"

She looked so pleased that I hardly wished to mention about the snow, but I knew that if I did not say, she would worry all the more when she saw it begin to fall. "We'll have snow before nightfall," I said. "Hopefully they will be here by then." She glanced worriedly out of the window and narrowed her eyes at the heavy clouds. "Does Mary bring the children?" I asked, hoping to distract her.

Mother nodded, absently. "Yes," she murmured and then tousled her head. "I should not worry," she said, still sounding anxious. "They will be here by the afternoon, and snow will not fall until the night, I am sure."

"I am sure, too." I smiled, taking off my fine cloak and finding an apron. "What can I do to help, then?"

Father arrived in the late afternoon, just ahead of the first flakes of snow, with George, Mary, Will and little Henry and Catherine. We feasted that night on pottage of carp and leek, roasted salmon and sharp-sweet pickled cowcumbers on toasted bread. Baked pike with sweet butter and onions followed, along with whiting pie, roasted eels, smoked herring and piles of shrimp. Glistening cabbage, and turnip and carrot slathered in golden olive oil and salt accompanied this feast of fish, for during Advent we did not eat meat.

Father was in an unusually good mood, and when I asked him of it, he chuckled. "Wolsey has exchanged the Bishopric of Durham for that of Winchester," he explained. "Winchester is the richest See in England, so the butcher's cur has made a goodly deal."

"Why should his better fortune make you happy, my lord father?" I asked, spearing a roasted eel its sticky sauce with my knife and placing it on my pewter plate. I cut it in half, savouring the rich scent and picked it up with my fingers, as was customary. I ate delicately, being careful not to overfill my mouth.

"Because Wolsey has decided to offer me the revenues from the See of Durham," father continued. "He offered them to the King first, of course, but as Wolsey made the offer he told Henry that he believed they *should* be mine... and the King was most happy that I be granted them." Father sat back, wiped his mouth on the linen draped over his shoulder, and then sipped at his wine. "They bring a good increase to my fortunes." He looked at me and smiled. "Your position with the King, my child, is beneficial... All will be looking at us soon to see how they can win our favour. Others will seek to offer us rich rewards in return for our support."

I disliked the gloating tone of his voice, but I could not disagree with him. My father was never one to miss an opportunity. I wondered how much he had made from this offer of Wolsey's. The Cardinal was clearly attempting to crawl into our good graces.

"On that same vein, sister," interjected Will, "there is something I was hoping you could consider petitioning the King for, for my family."

"What are you in need of Will?" I asked. "I thought the King had provided well for you and my sister?"

Will shook his head. "Not for my own, immediate, family," he explained. "The favour I wish to ask is for my sisters..." He picked up his goblet and sat back, one hand rubbing his stomach, swollen now with a great deal of good meat and wine. I had never seen any man who could eat as much as Will, aside from my own beloved Henry, of course. I wondered at times where on earth all the food they ate went.

They both ate like horses set loose in a meadow of sweet grass and buttercups, and yet never seemed to gain an ounce of fat. But then, they were both active men who enjoyed the hunt and many sports... so perhaps that was why they did not become portly as did the likes of the flabby Cardinal.

"My sisters, Eleanor and Anne, took the veil some years ago," he said, sipping his wine. "They serve at the Abbey of Wilton. There is a rumour that the Abbess there, Dame Cecily Willoughby, is sickening. My sisters say she has been growing steadily worse of late. A new Abbess must be appointed if she dies, and I was wondering..."

"If one of your sisters could gain the post?" I finished.

Will nodded. "It would be of great advantage to my own line," he admitted. "But the Abbey is also highly thought of, wealthy and well-respected. To have a member of the family installed as Abbess there would only add to your influence and supporters about the country, sister, and you know the nobles often listen to the counsel of Abbesses and Abbots. This could be of advantage to us both."

I picked up my own wine. "It sounds, as ever, Will, like a good idea."

"I am pleased you would think so." He looked warmly at Mary who gazed back with happy eyes. I wondered which of them had first had the idea. It mattered little. The Careys were a good couple, ever working together for their mutual comfort and happiness. I had no doubt that if Will had not had the idea himself, Mary would have encouraged him to ask for the favour.

"When we hear that the Abbess has indeed passed," I assured him. "I will speak to the King. And I am sure that he will be happy to listen, you are after all one of his favourites, Will... I wonder that you would not petition him yourself?"

Will regarded me with amused eyes. "There is but *one* voice His Majesty longs to hear now, Anne," he said. "And but one pair of lips from which he will grant any favour asked."

"How does the King?" I asked.

"Fractious, without you," Will sighed. "In some ways, sister, you have done a disservice to those who wait upon our King… He used to be an easy man to please, but now, he is restless and distracted. He plays at cards and loses vast sums to his men because he pays no attention to the game… We used to be able to take him out hunting or riding to calm any mood, but now, even that does not work." Will's eyes glowed in the light of the candles. "He is like every man when he falls in love, sister… He is undone, without you." I blushed rosy pink, and sipped at my wine to cover my confusion. "He sits beside Katherine like a man sitting aside his own grave," Will went on, glancing at my father who nodded in agreement. "The celebrations at court this winter have been few and far between, and at each one, Henry sits there tapping his feet impatiently on the rushes, his eyes lost to another place… All know that he is not there in spirit. Katherine knows it too. She tries to bring the King closer to her with protestations of love and devotion, but he cringes from her. The more she tries to cling to him, the more he flies from her."

"No man wishes to be clung to like a ship engulfed by a sea monster," said George, the lightness of his tone belied by poorly concealed bitterness. "When a woman clings and wails on a man's arm, he loses respect for her, and any attractions she may have had otherwise fade in the light of his disgust for her." His jaw twitched. I knew then that he was not talking of the King, but of himself and Jane. She was not here. She had been left at court for the winter. I wondered if George had even invited her, so indifferent did he seem to his wife.

"True enough, George," agreed my father, pulling another thin slice of pike from the well-carved pile on the table. He wiped its flesh in the remains of the sauce on his plate and swallowed politely before resuming his speech. "When a woman becomes as a limpet clinging to her master, he can have no respect for her any more. Women should, of course, be prepared to bow to the will of their husbands, but they should not hang off of our arms like drowning souls to a splinter of wood on the sea. We all have a dignity to maintain. Our wives should understand that..." He looked warmly at my mother who had a small frown forming between her eyes. "I am happy to see that the women of my own house are always careful of their dignity."

"Some more so than others," muttered George, draining his cup.

"Well..." said Will, looking away from George who was staring darkly ahead, lost in his thoughts. "Katherine's behaviour is certainly doing nothing to help her. He flinches from her, as he longs every day to ride to you, Anne. Strange, is it not, that when we are offered something in wild abandon it has less value to us than that which we cannot have easily?"

I shrugged. "That which we cannot have easily is more worthwhile to possess," I said. "Just as doing what is wrong is often easier than doing what is right... The Scriptures show us that more often than not, this the way of evil... that goodness is often the harder path, and evil the easy one. Perhaps, with time, Katherine will come to see this also, and agree to step down."

"I think once she realises she has lost the love of the King, and will only lose his friendship and respect if she continues, then she will give in," said Mary, washing her fingers delicately in the perfumed water of the fingerbowl. "The Queen is no dullard. She has pride and dignity. Surely, soon enough these qualities will win out and she will obey her husband, as she promised to do upon their marriage."

I lifted my goblet to Mary. "I hope so, sister." I beamed suddenly at my family. "To the Queen's dignity and pride... May they bring her to the path to goodness!"

They all laughed, even my mother, who looked slightly uncomfortable as she tittered. I drank deep and hoped that my sister was right.

Chapter Thirteen

Hever Castle
Winter 1527

Through the snows of winter, when all but my mother had returned to court, there another visitor came to Hever.

I had been reading a new book George had left for me, a French translation of the Epistles of St Paul, when the clatter of hooves sounded in the courtyard. I ran down without even looking from the window, thinking it was Henry. But when I came into the courtyard, my cheeks flushed pink with excitement, I found it was not Henry… but Tom Wyatt.

He climbed from his horse; crystals of ice frozen to his saddle fell and shattered upon the dirty snow of the cobbled ground. As he saw me standing there, looking confused, he made a short bow and smiled uncomfortably. We had little been in company with one another since his return from Italy. He had not sought me out when I had been briefly at court, and my brother brought no news of him either. In letters I had from my good friend, Margaret Wyatt, there were but spare mentions of Tom. All seemed to know that since Henry had proclaimed his love for me, there was small room in my life for this once-ardent suitor.

"Master Wyatt." My skirts brushed against the wet ground as I curtseyed. "You have come far in inclement weather to visit us."

There was a question in my tone which he did not miss, and he nodded. "There is something I would talk to you of, Anna." He brushed the earth of the road from his coat. "And I did not wish to do so by letter."

"Will you come inside?" I asked with strained formality, stretching out an arm towards the doorway that led to the warmth of the great hall. Tom followed me quietly. As we sat at the fireside, I called for refreshments. I could not meet his eyes, so uncomfortable did I feel. I called for Bess. I did not want any hint of impropriety here… and certainly not with the man who had caused such furious jealousy and anger in my now-betrothed. But Tom, as it transpired, was here to speak about something else.

He removed his cloak and gloves, took a cup of ale and then stared at the fire for a moment as I watched him. *Still as handsome as ever*, I thought. There were rumours at court that Tom had a mistress now, although I knew not her name. Perhaps this was but a polite visit, the kind made between neighbours… but then, as he turned to me, I realised it was not.

Tom frowned. "Anna," he said. "The Queen has asked a commission of me."

Whatever I was expecting to come from his mouth, it was not that. I was confused, wondering why he would ride all this way to tell me such a thing. "That is good for you, is it not?" I asked carelessly, sipping my warm, spiced ale. "A commission from the Queen can only add to your standing at court, and in scholarly circles?"

Tom's brow furrowed deeper. "She wants me to translate part of a work of Petrarch," he said. "Part of the *De Remediis Utriusque Fortunae.*"

"*Concerning the Remedy for Every Type of Fortune*," I translated. A tremor of trepidation ran through me. "I know the work, of course. I read it whilst with Princess Marguerite in France."

"Katherine wishes it known publicly that she has commissioned it from me, and she wants it to be dedicated to her," Tom continued. "She told me it was because the work spoke to her of her present misery… but there is more to it than that, as I am sure you understand."

I nodded thoughtfully. I did understand. The text he spoke of was a collection of hundreds of dialogues in Latin, written some two centuries before our time. They were highly regarded for their wisdom. Many of them showed how thought and deed could bring happiness or sorrow, advised humbleness in times of prosperity… and courage in times of adversity. The significance of Katherine's choice of commission was not lost on me; she wanted to publicly demonstrate her present distress, but also show her resolve to fight on. Nothing could have spoken more keenly of Katherine's determination not to accept Henry's judgement on his *Great Matter*. This meant trouble.

I swallowed uneasily. "And will you accept her commission, Tom?"

Tom gazed at me, and then stared into the flames of the fire, as though they held an answer. "It is a good offer," he noted quietly. "It would show that I enjoyed royal favour and that I was respected… and the money she offers is also good…" He looked back at me, the flames dancing in his eyes. For a moment I thought of our first meeting when I came to England from France… how I had been lost in the mists and winds of England, and somehow found a friend, who brought me to his fireside, and protected me from both the weather and the ills that assailed my spirits. My heart ached as I thought on the friendship I had once enjoyed with Tom… Would such grace ever be ours again?

"But I will not do this for her," he said.

"You will not?" I was surprised. It was a good offer, and an honourable one.

"The Queen seeks to *use* me, Anna," he said softly. "To use me to harm others… those who have been precious to me. And no matter what has passed between us in this difficult year, I will not turn on those I love, or have loved. I am not made of such mettle. The piece that she has chosen is on the theme of inconsolable sorrow… It speaks of how the heaviest grief is beyond reason or philosophy. Were it to be published with a dedication to her, it would engender sympathy for her of the like I can barely imagine, amongst the courts of Europe and the people of England. It is trouble she is looking for, Anna, and I will not be her agent in this. "

Colour sprang to my cheeks and my heart leapt with hope. "I would be most grateful, of course, Tom, if you chose not to take this offer from Katherine."

"Katherine wishes to use this translation as a weapon against you and the King," he said. "I will not do it, but I cannot afford to insult the Queen by refusing."

"What will you do, then?"

In his eyes I saw a touch of his old impishness. "I will accept the commission." He paused and drank from his goblet. "But once undertaken, I will present the Queen with a different work, and inform her, regrettably, the translation she asked for was beyond my skill. I will complete, instead, a translation of a work by Plutarch, *The Quiet Mind*. This text emphasises the comfort of reason and the acceptance of fate. It speaks of the futility of seeking to oppose one's destiny… I have thought long and hard on it, and have spoken to the King. We have agreed that this is the work I will dedicate to Katherine."

"You have spoken to Henry about this?" There was astonishment in my voice.

"All that I have comes from my King," Tom said. "He paid my ransom when I was captured in Italy, and since my return he has shown himself only warm and accepting, despite our past. He had good reason to act otherwise, as well you know. When Katherine asked this of me, I knew what she was up to. I went to the King, and told him my thoughts. He approves of the plan… Actually, that is why he sent me here, to you."

"Henry sent you here?" I was vaguely disappointed Tom had not come on his own stead.

Tom cleared his throat. "The King said that you should know all that was happening… He said you had insisted whether good news or bad, that you be kept informed. He sent me to explain the situation."

"But this is good news!" I exclaimed. "Do not look so dour, Tom! I am so pleased that you would decide to work for Henry and for me rather than Katherine."

He smiled softly and inclined his head. "Good news in one way, Anne, but forget not that Katherine's request spells ill for you and the King. Katherine does not wish to be set aside. She does not want to leave Henry. Every day she requests to see him, but he only appears with her when he must. Although Wolsey has men watching her, we suspect that she has got word to her nephew, Charles V, on what is occurring in England, and if she has managed that, then she may, too, have got a personal message to the Pope."

He heaved a sigh. "People constantly underestimate the Queen because she has acted with dignity and humility for so long as Henry's wife. But forget not that she comes of a dynasty that *fought* for its place on the throne. Forget not who her mother and father were. Katherine is hurt, and she is angry. She will not simply allow another to take her place." Tom stared gravely at me. "She will not go down without a fight, Anne," he warned. "And this commission is but one indication that she intends to fight for the man she loves and the position she believes she was born to hold. She says

God is on her side, Anna, and she will not be persuaded otherwise."

My blood ran cold. Although I had, of course, suspected such a thing, it was a shock to hear someone say it aloud. And Tom was right. If Katherine was attempting to spread propaganda about the King's *Great Matter* then she was preparing for war. Katherine was a popular Queen. In the past she had petitioned to stop rebels being executed and had been regent of England. Katherine had commanded forces to fight off the Scots when they invaded and she gave generously to charity and to the poor. The people loved her. And she had powerful friends in Europe, too, her nephew not the least of them. She could be a formidable opponent. Misery swept over me like a snow-storm.

Tom saw my face fall and reached forward to take my hand. His eyes were kind and sympathetic. "Do not look so downcast, Anna. Remember, whether this marriage is invalid or not is not up to Katherine. No matter what she might protest, the decision belongs to the Pope. Many at court believe the only way to bring stability to the realm is for Henry to take a new wife who can bear him children. Since it is increasingly obvious that Henry adores you, you have many supporters and you also have the love of the King firmly in your grasp. No matter if Katherine spits and hisses, if the Pope agrees with Henry, you will prevail."

"But the Pope is the prisoner of the Emperor," I whispered sadly. "And if Katherine has got word to Charles…"

"Many are the struggles in life," said Tom sagely. "But remember that once we push through our hardships and look back from the other side, our troubles seem much smaller than they did when first we faced them. He looked earnestly at me. "Thus it was in Italy, for me," he said. "When I was captured, I thought I would never see England, or my family, or my son again. And yet soon enough, I was a free man, standing on the green grass of my homeland and relishing her thick fog and endless rain."

I laughed. He had managed to tickle some humour from my breast. I squeezed his hand. "You bring me comfort, my friend."

"And know that I *am* your friend, Anna," he said in a more serious tone. "Friend to you and to the King. There was a time… a time when I thought it could never be so again. But that was another time, and another me. You have made your choice, and I… I am happy for you. Or at least I am trying to be."

"I hear that you have a mistress," I murmured.

His cheekbones kindled with a dull flame. He released my hand and sat back. "She is a good woman," he replied. "She reached into my heart when I thought that there was nothing left within but tattered scraps. She found ways to stitch those strands back together, and I find I have a heart, after all."

"I am sorry, Tom…" I said, lifting my eyes to his. "So sorry that I hurt you."

He looked away, and for a moment there was a spark of that old jealousy and anger in his face, but then it was gone. "I hurt myself, Anna," he admitted gruffly. "I heard you speak and yet did not listen. I threw myself at your feet when you were unable to be mine. I know now, looking on Henry's love for you, that I was a fool to think I could compare to him. You have made your choice. I will love and honour you as my Queen, and serve you with loyalty and devotion as a friend."

His eyes stole back to mine. I could see, despite his words, that there was still pain there. Pain he wished to hide from me, but could not. He was trying hard to put the past behind us, to become friends once more. Choosing to come to Hever, to offer his friendship and loyalty, had taken a great deal of courage and strength. Never was a better man made, than Tom Wyatt.

"I will always be your friend, Tom, if you will have me," I murmured. "But my heart was made for Henry alone. I have always loved him, although I never allowed myself to consider such a destiny could be possible. It was not that I could not have loved you. Had I been made of another spirit, I would have. But now I know that Henry is my only love." I sat back. "I will never forget this moment, Tom," I said. "I am humbled by your goodness. Many lesser men would act in spite to hurt me as I have hurt you, and yet you do not. You are a great man, Master Wyatt, and one of true nobility."

A rumble of laughter emerged from his lips. "Do not seek to make a poet into a saint, Mistress Boleyn," he chortled. "You will come up short, I assure you of that!" He breathed out through his nose. "Many were the times I considered doing otherwise," he said. "I considered being your enemy. But a better part of my conscience prevailed."

"I will be grateful, always, to that part," I said. "You have demonstrated courage and strength of character to come here today, Tom. I shall not forget this."

"Tom!" A cry from the hallway interrupted me. I twisted in my chair to see my mother striding towards us, her hands outstretched and a great smile on her beautiful face. "Why did my daughter not inform me that my favourite neighbour was here?" she scolded, kissing Tom and shaking a finger at me.

"I am sorry, my lady mother, there were things we needed to speak of together."

"And are you done now, that I might talk with Master Wyatt as well?" she jested.

I looked at Tom and our eyes met. There was warmth there, friendship. Something in me sang to know that even if all was not mended between us, we had at least begun to forge friendship once again. "Yes," I said. "I think that we have said all that needed to be said."

"Good!" my mother exclaimed, sitting herself on a stool beside Tom. "Then tell me, Master Wyatt, how does your father and sister? And when are they coming to visit us? Your father spends too much time with his cat and those brown pigeons he loves so dear. He forgets to spend time with actual *people*."

Tom laughed. It was a good sound. The sound of a friend. The sound of company and companionship. I had missed that sound.

Tom's book was presented to Katherine later that winter. She was not best pleased to find that he had changed the text, but she accepted his dedication to her. She did not, however, work to promote Tom or his work. It was obvious that the Wyatts had chosen a side, and that side was mine.

Chapter Fourteen

Hever Castle
Winter 1527-1528

That winter Henry finally sent Stephen Gardiner and Edward Foxe, both secretaries in Wolsey's pay, to the Pope to ask for a decision on his *Great Matter*. It was a mark of Henry's eagerness, and my persistent urging that Gardiner and Foxe left in the midst of that harsh winter. Henry accompanied the two men to Hever, so we could see them off together and wish them well on their mission. They had a hard task ahead of them, not only to travel through the snows and storms of winter, but also to navigate through war-torn Italy to reach Rome.

Of the two men, it was Gardiner who struck me the most. In his early thirties, he had a swarthy complexion with a long, hooked nose and brown hair. His face bore a continual expression of annoyance, as he had an almost permanent frown set between his deep-set eyes. His hands were huge, far larger than would seem necessary for this form, and he sought to hide them, which only drew attention to them more keenly. He had clever eyes, and there was a shrewd sense about him as though he missed nothing. Foxe had sandy-coloured hair and a thin beard, but he paled in comparison to his companion, and not only in his looks. There was something about Gardiner which made me pour my hopes into him. He had an air of confidence, and duplicity, both of which I believed would work well for us. In time, I was to find them both useful allies.

Although the chill, still air at Hever was calm, I doubted the passage from Dover to Calais would be tranquil. Foxe and Gardiner left loaded with Henry's gifts to the Pope and also with letters, requests, pleas and our eagerness too. As we watched them ride out, Henry put his arm about my waist.

"Soon, my love," he said with excitement. "Soon the Pope will decide in our favour and you and I shall be married." Henry grinned, his sharp blue eyes sparkling. "Soon we will be man and wife."

"I long to be your wife, Henry." I kissed him happily. We watched Foxe and Gardiner until they disappeared from sight. The afternoon air was sharp and cold. I could hear creatures rustling as they hurried to their beds in the undergrowth, and the call of robins as they sought out warm places to sleep in the branches of the trees. It was going to be a cold night, but I was warmed by hope and love.

Henry smiled indulgently. "We need also to start planning your coronation, my love."

I blinked. The thought had not occurred to me. I had been so busy thinking of marrying him, I had not had time to consider truly *becoming the Queen*; anointed in the eyes of God. Henry chortled at my expression. "You thought that the rightful Queen of England would go uncrowned?" He squeezed my hand tightly. "You are a fool for all your wisdom sometimes, my Anne." He loved to surprise me and the fact that I was humbled before his generosity pleased him.

"I had never thought I would have such a husband as you," I said. "You are the most generous lord and master I could have imagined. I had not even *thought* of a coronation."

"What *were* you thinking of, then?" he asked teasingly, his eyebrows raised as he ran one rough hand over the edge of my breasts and sought to cup my buttocks with the other.

I chuckled and cuffed him, batting his hands from me. "I was thinking of being *married*, Henry," I protested. "I was just thinking of getting married, of being married to the greatest prince in Christendom and that was quite enough to fill my mind with wonder."

He kissed me. Then, drawing me under the circle of his arm, he led me inside. The warmth of the great hall was pleasing and mulled wine was brought to us by servants. We sat by the fire through the afternoon and into the night, and he told me of the grand and stupendous plans he had for my coronation. We ate that night with Henry at the head of the table and my mother and I on either side of him, spooning delicate fish broth and baked oysters into our mouths. When we had finished eating, my mother went to speak to the kitchen servants, and Henry and I returned to the fire. I listened to him talk, lulled into a pleasant state of sleepiness by fire, food, wine and happiness.

Henry left for court the next morning, and as he rode off, my worries resurfaced. I had to convince myself not allow the dull grey light of dawn to tempt me away from the happy dreams that had so comforted my night.

Henry wrote to me often from court that winter. He sent letters written in French, sent me love poems and presents, and wrote of his ongoing work for our cause. He told me of headaches he suffered, brought on by hours of reading theology, philosophy and canon law in preparation for a trial, should it be required. Sometimes, he wrote, he was unable to do anything but lay in a darkened room to quell the ferocious pain in his head. I worried for these headaches. They had grown more frequent of late and I was sure that they were created by the worry and pressure of our situation. I wrote to him, blaming his headaches on the stubbornness of Katherine and her supporters at court, constantly barring the way to our happiness and love. A faction of supporters loyal to Katherine was growing about her as the King's *Great Matter* was increasingly whispered of at court. Her loyal servants such as Margaret Pole and others were gathering their families to aid Katherine. My furious pen wrote of my frustration and fears; that, my love, the King, would forget me and cast me aside to the ruin of our love and his realm.

Henry wrote gently to me of his never-ending love; he would never abandon me, he said.

"*There is nothing in this world that could ever take me from you*," he wrote. "*No man, no woman, no power on this earth or in heaven above. You are mine, and I will have you. Think not that I, too, do not suffer as you in our days of separation. I long for you, I dream of you… and I awake wanting to hold you in my arms. I dream of our sons, and our daughters. I dream of the day when you will stand at my side, in the sight of my country and in the eyes of God… my true and only Queen. The one and only love I have ever known.*"

I clung to those letters. They were a balm to my terrors and annoyances. At night, I dreamed of Henry. I dreamed that he came to me as a husband, as a lover, taking me into his embrace, moving against me, our heated skin finally free to take pleasure in each other's love. But each morning I awoke unsated. I went back to waiting, longing, yearning.

That February, Bishop Tunstall started an avid campaign against heretics, those who dared to read Tyndale's Bible translation, and Lollards. Ecclesiastical prisons in London swelled with suspects. Rather than burning them, which was the punishment for heresy, many were forced to repent, signing confessions and doing penance. Many had to process through London, bare-headed and bare-footed, carrying faggots upon their backs. They were made to hear Mass on their knees, and refused the Sacrament as a punishment. Some had their property seized, or were forbidden to leave their parishes, living ever after as suspected men. Thomas More, too, was increasingly vindictive in his attack on heretics and the Church was glad of his help. He had spies placed about London, ready to inform on any illicit activities and on men who met in secret to discuss Tyndale's Bible, and other works. But groups of resistance were moving in the shadows. People were leaning much the Church did not want them to know. More and his heretic-hunters were busy in that cold winter. They were after all who would dare to think for themselves.

As foxes sang their unearthly songs to vixens in the woods, as the snowdrops started to push their sword-shaped leaves through the icy ground, as the snow melted and the brown trout spawned in the rivers, I waited and I waited. Young jack pike lay like sunken ships at the bottoms of the weed beds, and men hunted them with huge barbs of treble hooks. In the frost-rimmed grass at the edge of rivers, water voles chewed on young, wild watercress, watching for young fish to pursue. As primroses came to the woodlands, spreading bright colour through the dull gloom of the forests, still I waited for news, and a chance to see my beloved once more.

Chapter Fifteen

Hever Castle
Early Spring 1528

That season, as slate-blue kestrels performed for their mates and flowers emerged from beneath frost-covered earth, I was uneasy. There had been but small news from our envoys in Rome, and no progress here in England. I was troubled that without me at Henry's side, there was less enthusiasm to hurry along the *Great Matter,* and the Cardinal appeared to be dallying too.

I mentioned absently to the ever-attentive Thomas Heneage, who rode out to see me often on Wolsey's behalf, that I felt the Cardinal seemed somewhat distracted from the proceedings of the King's *Great Matter*. We had had no news of this Legatine Court that he intended to set up to try the validity of Henry's marriage once the delegate from Rome was approved. I made it clear to Heneage that I was less than happy to think the Cardinal was not acting with all speed to ensure the King's pleasure. "The King is not a patient man," I warned Heneage who viewed me calmly. "But I am even less patient than he."

Heneage bowed. "I will inform the Cardinal that you are troubled, Mistress Boleyn," he promised, playing with his cap. "The Cardinal would not want your pretty head to be so full of worry."

What should my pretty head be full of then? I would have wagered that the Cardinal hoped it was stuffed with straw rather than with a mind… My eyes wandered thoughtfully out of the window. The world was beginning to break into new life, even as my own had grown stagnant. I wanted to see something moving for us. I wanted proof that I was not being ignored here at Hever. "It would be nice to have some good fish for Lent," I remarked. "Our ponds here at Hever are not as well-stocked, I think, as those the Cardinal owns?"

"His Eminence has a great stock of those beasts suitable for eating during holy times, it is true," Heneage agreed. I smiled. The man knew what to do should he wish to incur my favour. I wanted the Cardinal to know I was keeping an eye on him, and I wanted to see what he would do to please me.

With ridiculous speed, the Cardinal sent a gift of fresh fish to Hever. Carp arrived alive and swimming in huge barrels from his famous stock ponds, along with trout, salmon and grayling. But the Cardinal did not stop there. Huge volumes of good shrimp came from merchants who supplied his houses, along with crab, cases of smoked herrings, mackerel, mussels, winkles, oysters and ells. Groaning wagons lumbered to the castle gates and my mother was dumbfounded at the stupendous offering, wondering aloud how we were ever to eat it all. She set to work; sending servants to smoke fish, salt fish and release those we could into our own stock ponds. I walked around the barrels and cases of fish, trailing a hand over them with pleasure. Wolsey had leapt fast to try to please me. He feared my ill-will.

There was a letter that came with the generous gift, reassuring me that he was working for the annulment with the utmost urgency and diligence. He had been working both night and day, he wrote, to ensure we had the best arguments and the best case to put before the court and the papal delegate when they were assembled. The reason I had not heard from him, Wolsey wrote, was because he had hardly taken time that winter to sleep or eat, so busy was he with the King's *Great Matter*. I showed the letter to my family.

My father chuckled when he read the parchment. "To the *most* gracious lady of our Kingdom." My father grinned, laughing with pleasure when he saw my scowling face. "Oh come, Anne!" he chuckled gleefully. "I laugh not at the phrase but at the newfound humility of the writer! How the mighty can be brought to heel…" He turned the letter over in his hands. "Oh…. the little rodent will have to do a lot better than this!" He almost skipped to the fireplace where he warmed his hands whilst re-reading the letter.

"It seems the Cardinal is the second great man at court to be in your pocket, sister," said George, grinning from ear to ear. "Soon, perhaps, you will have the Pope also, and then your power in this and every other realm shall be complete!"

"Will you be serious, George?" I said waspishly. "This is not a game. The Cardinal is shaken because he did not realise how important I am to Henry and it is his business to know all that the King wants and needs, even before he knows it himself. He slipped, and now he tries to right himself. He flatters me to trick me into thinking well of him and hopes I am fool enough to be bought. He hopes I will speak well of him to Henry. He is not our friend. He is our enemy and would think nothing of crushing us if he could, most especially me. He worries that Henry will turn to me, rather than him. He seeks to placate me, that is all." I paused, running my nails down the sides of my green velvet dress. Its skirts glistened with silver thread, sewn in the shapes of rose buds, lions and dragons; Henry's emblems. "We must be careful; until the King has his annulment my position is precarious… I have only Henry's love to rely on."

"He does not seem any less in love with you, Anne," spoke my gentle sister, toying with a dark ribbon at her breast. "If anything, every day of waiting makes him only more anxious to wed you. Will says when you are not there Henry's temper is dangerous. He has never shown such emotion, nor been as unable to hide it, when he claimed to love others."

I shrugged. "But I am not others," I said coldly and saw her flinch. I *tsked* impatiently. I was not intending to hurt her. "I mean that I am seeking to be his queen, not just to catch his attention for a month." Mary cringed again, but I was growing tired of worrying about her feelings. I had enough worries of my own. This winter had not helped at all. My temper was fractious and my tongue was sharp. I nodded curtly at her. "I know the King loves me," I went on. "But Wolsey is not an opponent to dismiss. He has much power and Henry's love too. They have been close for a long time. This is the first time he has failed to immediately satisfy Henry's wishes. Henry wants to believe in him. He loves the man."

My uncle of Norfolk shifted about in the corner and groaned, rubbing his stomach. I had no doubt his digestion was paining him, for at dinner, he had eaten like a hog who had found truffles in the woods. "Then we must make sure that the King loves you *more*," he gasped. "This matter is not only important to our family, it is vital for England, for our future, that this marriage comes to pass."

He paused and pushed a hand into his side, trying to assail the cramps which gnawed at him. "But you are right to mistrust Wolsey. The Cardinal does not wish to see the headstrong daughter of a powerful family usurp his power over the King and therefore I do not believe that he will work for us, no matter what gifts he sends or flattery he uses. We shall all keep an eye on his dealings, and report on his doings. If he works for us then we shall support him. If he works against us, or stalls this annulment in any way, we will move against him. For now, Anne, take his gifts and flatter him to his face, but be wary, be watchful. If he should slip even once, mention it to the King. Last year the King accused him of being distracted on the *Great Matter* and it scared the Cardinal badly to have Henry's anger for once directed at him. Let us see if we can give the arrogant Cardinal more of a scare, shall we?"

There was venom in my uncle's voice. Who could blame him? The Cardinal had taken much from our family, and others, and had grown rich on the profits... Such a man makes enemies easily.

I agreed to keep an eye on the Cardinal, but it was almost impossible to do so at Hever. Being kept at Hever felt like a punishment, but even though I was not at court, my wishes were carried out and my pleasures were attended to. I started to ask small favours for my supporters. A kinsman, Sir Nicholas Carew, was restored to the Privy Chamber at my request. My father encouraged me in this, and convinced me that such favours would infuriate Wolsey, and so I relished the task of securing them.

I despised that red-robed rodent who flung himself arrogantly around the corridors of power with oranges stuck to his nose, waving people out of his way as though he were the King himself. I hated his greed and avarice. He often kept the wealth of monasteries dissolved for corrupt practises for himself rather than giving it to educational institutions or setting up new abbeys, as he was supposed to. He erected grand houses, some which rivalled the King's palaces, rather than using that vast wealth to bring comfort to the poor, as he should have. He accepted bribes, sold indulgences, and took pensions from countries such as France, to further their causes with the King. He wanted to become the Pope, one day, but not for the good he might do in that position, but for pride, advancement and desire for power.

I hated that he upbraided others for adultery, infidelity, or promiscuity, when he himself kept a mistress and had bastard children. He was a hypocrite, a liar, and untrue to the vows he had sworn to God. He was no man of God; he was a man of gold. I liked not his influence on Henry either. It scared me. I was nervous that, in my absence from court, he would push forward some buxom, flaxen-haired girl from another noble family to try to uproot me from the affections of the King... I was anxious, yes. But my family was my vanguard during that winter, delivering messages and extolling my virtues to the King until I was the very image of perfect womanhood. George took much time to dismiss all other women at court as being "too fair" or "too weighty" or "from a family of dullards," so that Henry should continue to believe me to be the only flawless woman. The distance between us was lessened, also, as my uncle threw gatherings which I could attend without scandal, but at which I could meet Henry, too.

Despite my fears, the distance and time apart only fired Henry's passions for me. When we met, I had difficulty in making him behave in a regal fashion in public. But there had to be some semblance of respectability, or I would be seen everywhere and by everyone as his whore, unsuited to the throne of England. But the passion in his touch and the heat between us reassured me that he was not falling out of love with me, but in love more and more deeply.

I tried to be patient. I failed.

Chapter Sixteen

Windsor Castle
Spring 1528

Unable to bear our separation any longer, Henry moved my mother and me to Windsor Castle. Windsor was a formidable fortress rumoured to be over five hundred years old in parts. Three hundred years before our time, Henry's ancestor Henry II had made it into the palace it now was, but its military bearing remained despite the lavish royal lodgings, laid out around three grand central courtyards.

Henry's father had made many improvements to Windsor, ordering a tower to be built with opulent chambers, its ceilings decorated with plaster roses painted bright red and white. There was a royal library, a great wall painting of the Knights of Malta besieging Rhodes, and in the Queen's chambers the ceiling was studded with tiny mirrors, sparkling above like all the stars in the night's sky. Henry did not like Windsor as much as some of his other palaces, as it was rather antiquated, but he had made improvements too. There was a tennis court he had added at the foot of the Round Tower, where he liked to spend time when not out hunting or riding. Windsor was usually occupied by the court in the summer months, and Henry used the castle as something akin to a giant hunting lodge. He came here to escape into the great park, and this time, to escape with me.

We would emerge from our separate chambers and meet each morning in the grey light of the dawn to hear Mass in Henry's Royal Chapel. I would close my eyes as the voices of the young boys there ripped and tore at my very soul with the beauty of their song. Henry's choir was like no other I had heard, not even in Mechelen where the beauty of music was held to be so precious. Wolsey had his own choir too, which *almost* rivalled the King's, but not quite. The music in the church made me feel closer to God, as though I stood in the presence of His own angels and heard their voices. When I struggled with my restless and changeable emotions, stepping into a church and hearing such voices, such song, brought me peace. I could lose myself for a while in listening to Henry's choir. Henry was passionate about music, and when he saw my face, overcome with bliss during Mass, he would smile lovingly; he understood my feelings well, for they echoed in him, too.

I spoke to God often as I knelt before the altar. I asked Him to bring me patience, to bring me humility and to show me my path. I asked for guidance, and for the peace of knowing that I had chosen right, in agreeing to become Henry's Queen. I asked God to care for Henry, to take pity on his headaches and the strain which beset him. *"For as he is your chosen on the throne of England, my Lord God,"* I said silently. *"Grant him the security of knowing he does your work."*

When Mass was done, we would go hunting or walking together in the gardens, and each evening played at cards or dice. Sometimes I played the virginals or lute as he sang in his fine, rich tenor, and at times he played the flute to me, or called on me to sing songs of his own composition; they were all about me. Henry was a wonderful singer, although I have to admit that I was more kind about his poetry than was deserved. But because his songs and poetry were written to me, about me, I felt they warranted flattery. I was so happy to be with him that I wanted nothing to spoil our time together, even if certain words and arrangements of his songs might have been better than they were. His tastes in composition were quite antiquated, harking back to a time long since passed. I showed him my songbook, and parchments I had been collecting since my days at Mechelen, containing my favourite melodies. Henry was fascinated to try new arrangements with me. Although he played all instruments well, he was particularly gifted on the virginals, and took to them often, to show off for me. When he looked for praise at the end of each song, as he always did, his face was so endearing. There was an innocence about Henry for all his worldly experience. He was like a lonely child at times, desperate for respect and praise. I warmed to this side of him, feeling tender and protective of him because of it.

In addition to gifts of songs written about me, Henry bought me a new saddle, shipped specially from France, crafted of black velvet over rich leather with golden trimmings. It was a work of beauty, and I gasped when he gave it to me. He chuckled, well-pleased. There were few things Henry enjoyed more than surprising someone with his munificence.

"And there is a footstool to match, my love," he said as I ran my hand over the beautiful saddle, my eyes roaming over her every lovely curve.

"You are too good to me, my lord." I breathed earnestly. "This must have cost a fortune. It is a work of art."

"There is more!" He waved a hand to the men behind him and one brought forth something large under a black silk cover, placing it before me. I drew back the cover and found a stunning yew bow, of exquisite workmanship. Its bowtips and nock were made of horn. There were fine, strong arrows, some tipped with iron and some with horn, made of aspen and birch, and waxed to hold fletching of gerfalcon and goose feathers. There were also smaller arrows, known as piles, which were blunt at the end, and made for shooting smaller game. There were two bowstrings, one of female hemp, and the other of silk, a bracer of dark, thick leather, and a pouch for holding a file to sharpen the arrow points and a cloth for wiping them clean. There was a bowcase of fine, waxy wool, to protect the bow if rain came, and a black, cylindrical quiver with gold trim to match my new saddle. Before I could thank him, Henry pulled a pair of matching gloves from his wide sleeve of golden cloth, and roared with laughter as I gaped at him. "I have pleased you then, sweetheart?" he rumbled.

I shook my head, happy and a little overcome. "You are too generous, Henry... I do not need all these gifts, although do not think that I am not grateful! I came to see you..." I turned back to the bow, picking it up and looking along its length and power with glittering eyes. "Although... I would not want to give these things up, all the same."

Henry beamed. "Although we have seen much of the park already, there is more to see. I long to show you the secret places that have long been favourites of mine."

"Katherine did not visit them with you, did she?" I asked softly, keeping my eyes on the bow.

A gentle hand fell on my shoulder. "No," he said, his breath hot against my ear. "She did not. I would share with you the places I have loved *alone*... and now they will become our special places." He turned me around and I lowered the bow. "Why do you speak of her now?"

"I am sorry, Henry... I did not want to do or say anything to ruin our time here... Perhaps it is just natural for a woman to be jealous of another who has the place that she longs for... Our situation is so strange and awkward... There are three of us in this one marriage."

His hands took hold of my waist. I felt so tiny compared to his great build. "I know, my love," he whispered. "I know how hard it is... on you and on me." He gazed into my eyes. "But here and now, I will command you as your King! Think no more on Katherine; think only on the present and our pleasures here. We will be lost in the wilderness together, my Anne... and with your new bow, you will be as Diana of the forest!"

I laughed with him. Henry was like that... choosing to concentrate on the good in life over the bad. He was boyish and eager to get out into the park and trial the bow, and I did not deter him. Sometimes I rode my own Irish palfrey, but increasingly I rode behind Henry, on a special saddle that allowed me to ride pillion. He had had this, too, made especially for the two of us to enjoy together. When we hunted for large birds such as crane or heron, we took both hawks and dogs with us. When we hunted hare or deer we would ride out flanked by large greyhounds. Henry's mews were large and well-stocked with highly trained birds like lanners, sparrow hawks, sakers and goshawks, but I always preferred falcons who were best for flying in wide open spaces, over marshland and park.

Some nights, when we were deep into the chase, accompanied by Henry's Game Masters and servants, we would stop for the night at Henry's hunting lodge, Sunninghill, in Windsor Park. It was called thus as it sat on a small hill, and caught the last of the sunshine as the wolf-light fell. On such nights we would share an intimate supper by the fireside, and then retire to our separate rooms, riding out again before the dawn the next morning.

On some of our excursions, we did not hunt at all, but merely rode out into the wild and open countryside, and practised shooting, competing against each other and wagering on who could make the best shot. But when we did hunt, I found Henry was often careful to go through the superstitious customs of old, saying prayers and reciting ancient phrases over his dogs and birds, to bring luck, and to protect against loss.

The first time this happened, I was sat on my palfrey, arranging my quiver and bow. "*In nomine Domini volatilia celi erunt sub pedibus tuis*," I heard Henry murmur over his hawk as he took her onto his thick leather glove. I looked at him and smiled softly. In so many ways, Henry was still wrapped in the superstitions of old.

"*In the name of the Lord, the birds of the heavens shall be beneath thy feet*?" I asked.

He looked sheepish, and colour sprang to his cheeks. "The old ways are often the best ways," he protested. "I have never lost a bird when I have said the old prayer to bless them before the hunt."

"Then let us hope that God sends us luck, my lord… It would be good to feast on some heron this night."

Henry chuckled, still bashful. "My father always said the same blessing over his birds," he went on. "And my mother said that her father did the same… It is not well to follow every tradition *slavishly*, but I believe these prayers have brought me good fortune."

"Then I shall say the same." I stooped my head and whispered the same words in Latin over my own falcon, who sat upon my glove in her fine hood of leather and velvet. Henry was pleased when I followed his lead, for it did not always happen, and therefore was only the more charming to him when it did occur.

When we rode out together, there was between us such a spirit of unified enjoyment in the pleasures of the hunt and the love of the countryside. We rode over the hills and through the spare woodland; tracking and flushing birds and small animals from the reeds and bushes. We ate simple fare of griddled wheat cakes, slathered in butter or melted cheese, and picking at the juicy flesh of our freshly killed prey, roasted over fires by Henry's men under the cover of obliging trees. Henry was overjoyed to find that I loved his greyhounds as much as he did, for he was fond of all the beasts in his vast collection. They wore collars made of velvet, with pearls or the King's arms upon them. They were rubbed down each night by the men who tended them, and were fed meat, unlike the lap-dogs permitted to ladies of the court who were fed only bread to discourage them from developing a taste for the hunt. Sometimes, despite his prayers, Henry's hounds and hawks would get lost on the hunt and he paid vast sums to those who found and returned them, so great was his love for these elegant and noble creatures.

When we rested on our excursions, we would sit, side by side next to the sloping, wending flames of fires made by Henry's huntsmen, and talk of the hunt, exchanging our past tales of glory in such adventures, and listening to the crisp wind as it sailed through the trees. Henry's men would bring fresh mounts to meet us at various points in the park so that we could continue to ride until dusk. In the spring sunshine and its often biting wind, even through sleet and rain, we rode, returning to the castle in the evening exhausted, but merry.

Sometimes there were problems, of course. On one occasion my greyhound, a young and over-excitable creature named Neptune, who was a gift from the King, was in pursuit of a deer I had wounded when he came across a small group of cows being tended by a young lad. In his excitement and bloodlust, Neptune fell on one of the younger animals and savaged the creature so entirely that when Henry and I reached him, Henry's men had to kill the cow there and then. The lad watching them was distraught. Although more than aware that the great giant before him was his King, he protested that he would be soundly beaten when he returned home. He was supposed to protect the animals for his stepfather, and had failed in his task.

"Fear not, lad," called Henry, leaping from his saddle and crossing to the boy who was explaining his predicament to Henry's unmoved huntsmen who had dispatched the cow. "Here!" Henry tossed him a full bag of coin, worth far more than the thin creature itself had been. "Give that to your stepfather with his King's apologies. It should allow him to buy more than one cow to replace the beast you have lost."

The boy stuttered his thanks… As well he might. For now his family not only had the flesh of this poor thin cow to use through the winter, but would have several new beasts, too. A fine present to bring home!

"Please accept my apologies, too," I said, taking a ring from my finger. It was not worth a great deal, but it was far richer than anything this peasant owned. I gave the small silver ring to the lad and his face burst into crimson flame. He bowed awkwardly.

"My thanks, my Queen," he mumbled, bowing and almost running to take the cows home so he could tell his stepfather of their newly won fortune.

As the lad ran off, Henry looked happy. "You see, my Anne?" he asked. "Even the common men see the mark of a queen in you!"

I rolled my eyes. "He believed me to be Katherine, my lord," I said and sighed. "Now that will go down as another mark of her generosity, rather than mine."

"Still," Henry said, turning his mount and indicating to one of his men to stay with the cow so that it would not be eaten by wild beasts before the lad came back with his stepfather to butcher it. "Perhaps it is better that he thinks so… We do not want the people knowing that you are at my side rather than Katherine… They would not understand, sweetheart, of the innocence of our love."

Innocence… Well it was, in one sense, and in another it was not. Hunting and riding certainly helped Henry and I tame our lust, but it never dispelled it entirely. It was always there. On days when we did not ride out, when inclement weather kept us inside, our passion inevitably escalated. One or both of us had to be stern at such times, and save us from ourselves. Even with such control, our embraces were becoming more serious, more passionate… Hands and fingers reached inside clothing, caresses grew more urgent. It was hard to bear.

My mother made herself scarce more often than not, which allowed Henry and me to physically express our love for each other in private. I am sure that the servants heard our groans and moans through the walls of his chamber and imagined me to be the greatest whore living… But we were careful never to go too far and endanger my womb with a bastard child. All our touches were kept on the surface of our clothes… or just inside them. In some ways, the cloth separating us from each other only added to the tension; smooth silk and rich velvet, soft wool and fine chemise… sensual material which was exciting to the touch. I wondered if two people had ever been as tested as we were.

Henry lavished gifts upon me as well. In many ways, I believe he hoped to please me with presents, since our *Great Matter* was far from being resolved. The Cardinal, too, continued to send me gifts when he knew I was with Henry. Wolsey was no fool. These carefully timed gifts were there to make Henry believe that Wolsey respected and loved me.

Meat and fish for my supper table arrived in plentiful amounts. Cloth for clothes, French hoods decorated with pearls, fine books and expensive trinkets all arrived at Windsor for me. When there was a surplus of food, I would send some as gifts to my family, or order it sent to near-by abbeys and monastic orders. Wolsey's plan worked. Henry was overjoyed to see his friend afford me such attention, and urged me to see that this meant the Cardinal loved me as well as my King did.

"You see, sweetheart?" he asked, turning a fine bolt of dark green velvet over in his hands, admiring it. "You see how it is? Those that I love, love you… that is the way it should be."

I agreed with Henry, but unlike him, I could see through the slippery Cardinal. He was trying to buy my complacency. It was not working.

One item Wolsey sent me that spring was a perfectly and delicately wrought golden girdle ornament. It surprised me that Wolsey was able to assess my tastes so perfectly, but then he was a great politician and flatterer. Henry encouraged me to write to the Cardinal, suggesting that we three spend time together.

"It would please me to see two of those I love most in the world to be bonded together by friendship," he said, a slither of warning in his voice. Henry was aware that I harboured suspicions about the Cardinal. I had tentatively told Henry I felt Wolsey was not fully committed to the *Great Matter*. Henry had denied this, and wanted me to be Wolsey's friend, and so I agreed, writing to the Cardinal and thanking him graciously for his generosity.

There would eventually be room for only either Cardinal or Queen on this chessboard, not both. But I was happy to bide my time for now. Even an only half-committed Wolsey was of use to us.

Chapter Seventeen

Windsor Palace
Spring 1528

Wolsey's Legatine Court had finally been assembled, and charged with investigating the validity of Henry's marriage to Katherine. Preliminary meetings had begun and the court was now preparing to sit… when, and if, the Pope could be prevailed upon to send an envoy as his representative. The Pope would have the final say on the *Great Matter*, of course, but we had hope that if Clement sent a representative he might choose to give him the power to decide in his place.

The court and their task were supposed to be a secret, but soon everyone knew. Passed by the whispers of maidens and the low voices of lords, rumours about the trial seeped through court and into London. Words crept through the walls like water, tumbled through the streets and made their way into every home in England. By now, everyone had heard a murmur of the King's *Great Matter*. Most courtiers believed Henry would marry me should the annulment take place. My position was becoming increasingly public, and however damaging that might be, there was little to be done about it. And there were benefits as well as problems as this knowledge leaked out. People started to show me more notice and asked favours of me, offering their support in return. And it was not only people of the court that saw this, but others about London. I was told of a case against a bookseller named Garrett, who had been arrested for storing and selling banned books; works of heresy, as Wolsey, More and the Church saw them. Garrett's customers had not only been private citizens, but also leading members of the Church. A monastery in Reading had bought sixty copies of one book from him, and the parson of Honey Lane, a Doctor Farham, had also purchased his wares. Farham apparently was of high interest to More and Wolsey as they thought he might be able to provide names of other suspected heretics. But the appearance of men of the Church in this affair clearly showed there were some willing to open their minds to new ideas, even within the Church itself. That brought me comfort.

Garrett and Farham wrote to Wolsey, asking to be forgiven and freed. They were not listened to and were imprisoned in a fish cellar under the Cardinal's College. Informed of this ill-treatment by George, who kept an eye on many reformists in London, I wrote to Wolsey, asking him to release them, or at least move them to better quarters. *"I beseech Your Grace with all my heart to remember the parson of Honey Lane for my sake"* I wrote, *"and to show justice and clemency to those who have already admitted their fault in this matter, and have begged for forgiveness."* Wolsey wrote back that these men were dangerous heretics, and I was wasting my compassion on them. I bristled at his dismissive tone in the letter. It was a risk to support Farham and the others, but I could not rest knowing what a pitiful state they had been reduced to, just for wanting to expand their minds. This affair dragged on for months, and I had no success in setting the men free. Poor Farham died later that year, largely for his suffering in that ill, dank cellar, but two of the men who survived I contacted in secret, and told them I would work to further their careers when I could. Although this intervention had not gone well for me, I hoped another would when my brother-in-law, Will, reminded me of a favour I had promised him.

Dame Cecily Willoughby, Abbess of St Edith's nunnery at Wilton Abbey had died and Will asked that I petition Henry for his elder sister, Eleanor, to be made Abbess. I spoke of this with Henry one evening as we dined. An embarrassed expression spread over his countenance. "What is it, my lord?" I asked, worried. Did he think I had asked too much, already? "Would you not wish to honour both my family and that of your good friend, Carey?"

Henry coughed. "I would grant you anything I could, sweetheart," he said uncomfortably, taking from the platter of spring artichokes which lay seared and tender between us on the table. "But Wolsey has already been here this morning, asking that the same post be granted to Dame Isabel Jordan, the present prioress. Technically, this is a Church matter, but Wolsey asked that I officially support his choice... And Dame Jordan *is* the prioress, and should be next in line, unless she is in some measure unsuitable."

Vexed that the great bat had got to Henry before me, I struggled to control my voice and answer calmly. "She could remain prioress, could she not?" I asked, spooning a portion of braised spring greens in oil, sugar and salt to my own plate to rest aside slices of golden-roasted capon. "It is still an honourable position in a highly regarded Abbey. Dame Eleanor Carey, I hear, is a wise and virtuous young woman. She would serve you well, my lord, and the Church."

"That may be true, sweetheart... But, you see, I have Wolsey asking for one thing, and you for another..." Henry sighed, poking at his artichokes, and glancing at me with consternation. He did not like being unable to please me.

Stay calm, Anne, I told myself. *It will do you no good to shout or accuse the Cardinal. Wolsey has been keen to demonstrate his eagerness to please you... Perhaps if he is brought before Henry, he will defer to your choice.*

"Call the Cardinal here tomorrow, my love," I said calmly, lifting a small morsel of capon to my lips. "And we can discuss this, all three of us together." I popped the flesh into my mouth and savoured the taste of the garlic and rosemary it had been roasted with. I savoured, too, the idea of playing with Wolsey.

Henry's head whipped up with surprise. I was never keen to meet the Cardinal. "A fine idea, Anne." He beamed, and stood from the table to kiss me, once on the cheek and once on the throat. We went on with our meal; Henry drawing the soft, savoury petals of the artichoke through a bowl of dark vinegar and olive oil, and me complimenting him on the skill of his kitchens.

"I have great plans to expand all my kitchens, my love," he said, evidently pleased we were no longer talking of Wolsey. "The present ones, in all my palaces, struggle somewhat with the vast number of mouths they feed. I have been down to the kitchens myself, and talked over what is needed with my men there. In Hampton Court, I am going to expand them so vastly that none will be able to say they ate as well in any other court of the world, as when they came to England!"

"There are many recipes for sauces that I know from my time in France," I mentioned, taking rich, soft flesh from a dish of smothered rabbit laced with currants and apple vinegar. "I could have them sent on from Hever if you wish, my lord? I instructed our kitchens to make dishes with them when first I arrived home from France."

"You loved France a great deal, I think," he noted. He put his knife to the black pudding made of hog liver, and set a huge portion beside the fat, roasted venison on his pewter platter. Henry ate such quantities! He could eat ten times the portions I would, and yet remain trim. I smiled to see him eat so heartily now he was happy again.

"I loved France very much, my lord," I said with a smile, picking up the large goblet we shared and wiping my mouth carefully before sipping from it. "But England is where my heart belongs." He smiled warmly, well-pleased.

When Wolsey arrived the next day, I did not attack him, but merely presented my wishes. Before Henry, the Cardinal could hardly be so bold as to refuse entirely. His eyes watched me carefully; I knew that he was sure I had invited him here so that he could capitulate to please me and therefore please Henry.

"There will have to be a decent space of mourning, of course," Wolsey said, "before the election is undertaken for a new Abbess, Your Majesty." The fat bat smiled and tilted his head towards me. "But I would assure you, Mistress Boleyn, should Dame Eleanor Carey not be elected as Abbess, I will push for her election to the position of prioress. It being the next most prestigious title in the nunnery, she would serve under the Abbess, and likely be the next elected after her... Dame Eleanor is very young to take on the post of Abbess at present, but to rise to the post of prioress would show great confidence and belief in her, and allow her to take up the post a little later in life... Would that be acceptable?"

I inclined my head. It was not the answer I had hoped for but it was beneficial enough. Wolsey was bargaining with me, like a merchant haggling over the price of meat. But since he had offered a compromise, I was willing to be magnanimous. "That sounds like a reasonable arrangement, Your Excellency."

I smiled at Henry, who was jubilant to see the Cardinal and me getting along so well. I thought back to the time when my betrothal to Percy had been quashed by the fat bat... Wolsey had not been as polite as he was now! I wondered if he remembered it too; wondered if he was hissing inside, his spine secretly curving like an angry cat's to have to be so polite and accommodating. It pleased me to think that this was so. Wolsey showed nothing on the outside, of course, but I wondered how dear it cost him to act such a role for the King. I wondered how deep and bitter were Wolsey's curses against me at night.

I nodded to the Cardinal. "Then, you will keep me informed about what occurs in this matter, Your Eminence?" Wolsey concurred. "I am most grateful to you," I purred.

I hoped Will would be satisfied; if his sister was not elected at this time, she would certainly in the future. Once the period of mourning was over, we should see if the winged rodent kept to his promises... but he had made them before the King, and to go back on them would anger Henry, and possibly make him suspect the Cardinal was not working for my interests... This was a situation worth keeping an eye on, and I was determined to do just that.

Unfortunately, some time later, it was discovered that Eleanor Carey was a woman of loose morals. Before coming to the nunnery, she had been the mistress of a priest, and bore him children. The Careys had known nothing of this, at least so Will protested to me when I confronted him. But upon hearing of these past sins, especially seeing as Eleanor's affair had been done with a priest, Henry said he could not support her election as Abbess. Eleanor's ill-reputation unfairly affected her sister, too, by association. Neither could be given the post. I had failed. I suspected Wolsey was overjoyed by the news.

"You must see that she is unsuitable, my love," he protested, glancing at me warily to try and read my temper.

I sighed. Of course I saw that Eleanor could not take the post! "I am sorry, Henry," I said, "that ever I spoke for her. I was assured that she was a young lady both of virtue and wisdom, but it seems that she not only deceived me, but her brothers as well. Will and John Carey both say they knew nothing of her past sins."

Henry nodded solemnly. "I will not have the affair investigated further, sweetheart," he promised. "To do so would bring the Carey family into disgrace, and I would not have you or my good companion Will tainted with such a stain... But we cannot support her for the post of Abbess."

"No, indeed..." I muttered, feeling defeated.

"But," Henry said, "to please you, sweetheart, I will not have Dame Jordan elected to the post either. Some other good and well-disposed woman shall take the post. If your candidate cannot take the position, then Wolsey's shall not either. Therefore, I am fair, am I not?"

I giggled at his serious face and kissed him soundly. "Always, my lord," I crowed. "You are always fair and just."

Wolsey, however, apparently did not receive Henry's order. Word reached us that Isabel Jordan had been granted the prestigious position of Abbess, on the Cardinal's recommendation. Wolsey protested that the King's missive must have gone astray, but I did not believe him. I cursed at the cunning weasel. He had tricked us! I was sure he had been planning all along to put his candidate in that position, thereby preventing my family from gaining further power. I was furious, and my anger inspired Henry to take up his quill and write personally to the Cardinal, berating him for going directly against his wishes. Wolsey came grovelling to Henry and to me, submitting his utmost apologies, and offering money and goods as a way of saying sorry.

Although the matter had not ended as I would have wished, and Wolsey got his way in the end, I was yet elated. Henry had been enraged with Wolsey, and the Cardinal knew now, more than ever, that getting on my bad side was also to fall from the graces of the King. I did not know then this would mark the start of many small, hidden and underhand battles I would fight against the Cardinal.

When our time at Windsor came to an end, I pleaded with Henry not to part us again. I did not want to spend another season shut away at Hever. I did not want to be without Henry, but my primary concern was the Cardinal. Wolsey was too dangerous, I knew, to leave alone with Henry. I could not say this to Henry, of course, for he would not believe me, but I had to convince him somehow.

"Have me installed at court where and how you wish, Henry," I begged. "But please, do not send me back to Hever. I cannot bear to be so far from you, and to hear all on our *Matter* second-hand. I suffer when I am alone, but when I am with you, I know all will be well."

"I know, my love," he murmured into my neck. "It is anguish for me also when we are not together..." He trailed off uncertainly. "But I cannot restore you to Katherine's household," he went on. "She suspects that I intend to marry you, so say Wolsey's spies. She is looking for every reason now to resist this annulment, and she may try to use you against us."

"Put me, then, in separate chambers," I said, stroking my fingers through his golden red hair. I loved to feel the curls and the thickness of it between my fingers. Henry closed his eyes as he leaned in to the touch of my fingertips. "I will be just another lady at court," I whispered. "Say that the chambers you give me are in the possession of my father, and then there is no scandal. I am just the daughter of Viscount Rochford, visiting court and staying in his rooms."

Henry nodded, pressing his head into my hands. "You have magic in those fingers," he mumbled. "Whenever I feel a headache coming, you alone have the power to drive it from me." He opened his blue eyes and stared into my dark ones. "How is it, Anne, that one person alone can so comfort and so excite me?"

"You have the same effect on me, Henry... unless you had missed the power you have to bring me joy?"

He laughed. He ran his hand, with his palm open and flat, down my neck, over my chest, with enticing slowness. "I do not miss it," he said gruffly. "And to see such passion in you only makes me want you more. I burn for you, Anne... I think of you all the time... I cannot rest, I cannot work... I cannot sleep some nights. You steal all other thoughts from me with the power of my love for you."

"Soon we will be together, my love, and all will be well," I said. "But do not send me away … I could not bear it. My heart will break."

"I could not rest easy knowing I cause you pain." He sighed. "I will find some way to resolve this. You are right… We have been apart too long already. When you are not with me, I feel as though I have lost some part of myself. I am only complete when I am with you. I will find a way for us, my love… a way that we can be together."

"Besides," I murmured, running my fingertips over the back of his hand. "It is your *present* marriage in which the sin lies. We have done no sin together. Perhaps it is time to stop acting as though it were the other way around. If people see we are resolved to be together, and that we believe this is the true and right way, then perhaps we could stop sneaking about as though we were the sinners. It is Katherine and your first marriage which should be condemned, not us."

"Perhaps you are right, Anne," Henry spoke thoughtfully. "Perhaps we should show we have nothing to be ashamed of… that we are the ones in the right, rather than hiding our love…" He kissed the top of my head, making my hood shiver at his touch. "But still, we cannot give arrows to Katherine to use against us… We must be careful, for the sake of propriety and for your honour."

Henry agreed to find a place for me at court that was not in Katherine's household. I knew my presence at court would cause gossip, but I believed it was now more important to remain with Henry and take an active part in the *Great Matter*. When I was away from court, Wolsey and his men moved at the pace of an ancient dotard. When I was here, more was done. I had remained, obediently, in the shadows until now, but I was starting to realise that if I wanted this done and done fast, then I should be present to urge Henry on, and to nudge the Cardinal along as well.

Yes, I thought, *I am no longer able to stand aside and simply watch as others decide my future.* No more would I be a shade waiting on the edge of all that went on. No more meek woman hiding in the shadows. It was time that Anne Boleyn stepped forwards, and took her destiny in her own hands.

Chapter Eighteen

Greenwich Palace
Late Spring 1528

In May, true to his word to keep us together, I was brought to Greenwich. Henry did not try to place me once more in Katherine's chambers; such a thing would have been highly uncomfortable and now inappropriate. I entered new apartments in Greenwich, ones which were officially my father's, but in truth were prepared for me alone. The chambers were located in the tiltyard gallery, surrounded by beautiful gardens, just far enough away from the palace to give us privacy, and just close enough to make visiting easy. Henry provided me with furnishings, tapestry for the walls, carpets for the floor, a magnificent bed and sumptuous covers. I even had my own flock of ladies; servants taken from Katherine and place in my service instead.

Although I was no queen as yet, I had gathered around me a small army of attendants. The court had begun to snidely call them *"the ladies-in-waiting of the queen-in-waiting"*. They were all close friends or allies of my house. Amongst them were Nan Gainsford, a beautiful and well-read young woman, and my sister Mary, who, when at court, was now by my side rather than Katherine's. Jane, my brother's wife, Margaret Wyatt and Bridget were also in attendance, along with some Howard cousins, sent by my uncle Norfolk to provide support... and, I was sure, to spy on me. My uncle did not trust me.

Henry sometimes sent his fool, Will Somers, to entertain us, and he would have us crying with laughter as he made silly faces, or passed comment on those at court. He had a small ape, which he liked to bring with him, but I asked that it come not near me, for ever since my days in Katherine's chambers I had disliked these small beasts. Like Katherine's, Somers' beast was pitiful. It wore a jewelled chain about its neck, scratched its own skin and fur off and pissed anywhere it pleased.

Somers would cackle at my aversion to the ape. "You like it not, for it hath the bearing of your own father, Mistress Boleyn," he would say, and then go into an imitation of my father that was so canny, I could not help but giggle into my lace sleeve. Somers was a humorous creature, and often a wicked one, but since the King loved him and it was the place of fools to be outrageous, he was never punished as another would be for his brilliant impersonations. He did a marvellous one of my uncle Norfolk, grabbing at his belly to groan in between words, and pulling the same sour expression that usually graced Norfolk's face.

Others, too, had started to visit me in my chambers. Courtiers came begging for me to talk to Henry for them and 'rascal' boys, lads with no true purpose at court who loitered about the halls hoping to earn a coin for delivering a message, drifted towards my rooms. I had requests for work from ambitious servants of other nobles, and from vagabonds who occasionally found their way into the court's interior. I was wary of these stragglers, for they were more often set on robbery than on providing service. I also had many noble visitors, coming to offer me their support, either openly or covertly. Many more, of course, went instead to Katherine. It was becoming clear that there were two queens in the palace; everyone was going to have to choose to which they would bow.

Henry arrived to see me each evening, and since I could not entertain him before the court, I did so in my own chambers. I put on dances and arranged games such as *Blind Man's Bluff*, *Pillar and Post* and card games, where we wagered vast sums for sport. Henry always paid my debts. He gave me spending money of my own, but would only offer a little at a time, shaking his head with a merry smile and saying, "for otherwise, my love, you would wager all the fortunes of my treasury on but one game!"

I laughed, but it was true that I was a rather reckless gambler at times. Perhaps this was even truer in life, than on the card table…

We walked through the gardens together and spent time shooting at the archery butts. I was a talented archer. My aim was true and my arm was strong. Henry was prodigiously proud of me, and often dared men to wager that they could beat "*his Diana*" as he called me, after the pagan goddess of the hunt. Henry Norris, Tom, George and others shot against me, but I was rarely beaten. Henry would bellow with mirth to see their faces as our painted arrows were checked on the butts, and mine were found to be the truest.

"You see?" he exclaimed merrily. "My *Diana*…" He would forget the need for secrecy and kiss me well and long on the mouth.

Henry and I also discovered a mutual passion for architecture. He was a passionate builder and had improved many of his palaces. When he found that I was interested, he brought drawings and plans to me so that we could go over them together. Henry was a demanding king when it came to his buildings. The men who worked for him, adding halls and galleries to his palaces, often worked through the night by candlelight, and he also had canvass tents erected so work could continue even in inclement weather. But even though he was an exacting master, Henry paid generous wages, and often sent treats such as good, hard cheese, fluffy white bread, beer and fine meats to his workmen. Men fought for positions on such projects, for Henry not only rewarded men whilst they built, but was generous after as well.

Henry was deeply influenced by Burgundian architecture. Since I had spent more than a year at the Court of

Burgundy, he respected my opinion, especially on the finer details. I told him all I could remember, and we spent many hours at night sketching and drawing. Mouldings of plaster, the arrangements of buildings, carvings in wood and marble... nothing was below his interest. Henry wanted perfection and strove hard to attain it. He loved stained glass and decorated window panes. He lingered over designs for tiles, and ornamentation. He was determined that each palace would be decorated with arms, badges, initials and mottos, made in stone, terracotta, glass or wood, and such things were also echoed in the fabrics and furnishings of the interior. He showed me sketches of his initials entwined with mine, which he intended to set everywhere as soon as we were married. I was pleased to hear this, for at the moment it was Katherine's initials and his which were everywhere. I put my ladies to making many fine cushions and hangings for Henry's new projects, and he was overjoyed to see our excellent needlework, carefully planning where each piece was to be displayed.

We kept ourselves busy, and discovered many new, shared passions. But all the time, I was wondering, when will this trial of the King's marriage begin?

Chapter Nineteen

Greenwich Palace
Late Spring 1528

One afternoon, I was sat at my window in the apartments, reading and sewing with my women. Margaret was reading aloud to us from the Epistles of St Paul and the rest of us were making a new hanging for Henry's Privy Chamber; a glorious creation with roses and honeysuckle embroidered on fine cloth with gold fringes. I was planning it as a surprise for Henry. I hoped to render him speechless with happiness when he saw what I had been hiding from him.

It was a fine afternoon at the end of May and the gardens below were bathed in light. Blossom had started to emerge, and the braver flowers were singing in the welcome of summer. Roses were getting ready to bloom, and violets, late primroses, columbines and lavender were breaking into life, making the breeze rich with floral perfume. Through the window, I could see striped green and white poles dotted through the gardens. On their tops were heraldic beasts, the sunlight winking off their snouts and heads. The knot gardens were warm, with the heat of the sun trapped within their orange terracotta tiles, reflecting onto the shrubs and flowers woven about each other into geometric shapes and symbols. An armillary sphere glinted from a small courtyard, and in the distance I could see arbours of branches and trellises of flowers set against the palace walls. Henry had started to introduce statues, like the ones I had known well in France, of classical gods and nymphs, who stood proud, shining marble-white near to the ponds. Henry loved his gardens. They were one of his favourite places to talk to his ministers, and to me.

I sighed with a languid feeling of pleasure looking on the fine gardens. Birds were winging through the air, collecting food for their offspring, and making nests in the trees. In the distance I could see captive warrens of rabbits, ringed by wattle fences, being tended to by busy maidservants. The trees bent and swayed in a balmy breeze, their leaves murmuring, and I heard the ring of a song on the air. A kitchen maid with a sweet voice was singing as she gathered herbs and wild onion leaves from the gardens at the side of the tower.

"Summer is a'coming in, summer is a'coming in. Sing good news, sing good news," she sang. Her voice was beautiful; high and sweet. I smiled at Nan Gainsford who was also listening to the melody. To the surprise of all the others in the room, who had been unaware of the music outside our four walls, I took up the tune.

"Sing good news!" I sang out of the window. The surprised maid laughed and curtseyed as she kept up the refrain with me.

"Sing good news!" sang Margaret and Bridget as they, with Nan, joined me at the window. Together with the maid, we sang the merry tune through to its end. My heart had been heavy of late, but it lifted as our voices entwined in this sweet tune of hope. That was all I longed to hear... Good news for Henry and me, good news of the annulment, news of the imprisoned Pope's support.

"Good news *will* come," my sister said as the song ended and the maid retreated to go about her business. Mary always could read my mind.

"Of course," I nodded. "I am sure. God teaches me patience every day," I smiled ruefully. "But I am a poor pupil."

"No woman is good at patience," interjected Jane. "The only time we know patience is in waiting for a child, and that is only because we know the joy that is to come at the end."

She turned her head from us and I saw her blink back tears. Jane had lost the child she was carrying a month ago. It had not gone more than two months in her womb before it died and there was not enough of the babe made to tell what sex it might have been. I rested a hand on her shoulder and she composed herself quickly. When she turned back, I could see her thrusting her feelings to the back of her soul. She went swiftly to her work again, pushing her needle through the fabric and chatting gaily to Nan.

I watched Jane continue as though nothing had happened. So often, I felt as though I hardly knew her. Jane only ever allowed glimpses of her true self to be known, but it was clear she was distressed for the loss of her child. This was not the first babe she had lost; there had been another. In one of those rare moments of honesty, Jane had confided in me when I had found her crying in private, over the death of this last child. And it seemed to me that these lost children had brought not only sorrow, but hardness to Jane's heart.

There were few she would allow to comfort her. After I had found her weeping, and she had confided in me, she had seemed suddenly uncomfortable and rushed off. I had not known what to do for her. George was no help at all. He was rarely with his wife, except in my presence. I wondered if Jane had asked become one of my women in order that she might be near George. They shared rooms at night, but apart from that he avoided her. My mother was concerned. Mary had a fine son and daughter. Although they were likely the offspring of my future husband, they were still recognised as Carey's and as such, legitimate heirs to the Boleyn fortunes. But what of George and his wife? Only two failed pregnancies in all these years was unfortunate, indeed, but then George spent more time with his mistresses than he did with his legal wife. He was growing increasingly cold towards Jane. When they were together, she fawned on him, clinging to his arm and flattering him. He did not like it.

Although I pitied Jane, I often cringed to see her so helpless and pathetic around him. George had no respect for her. He found her cloying and unpleasing when she crept about him, grovelling for his attention. But Jane had another side as well. At times, when they were alone, she screamed and shouted at him, upgrading him for his infidelity and cruelty. They had blazing arguments which were well known of at court.

It was a marriage of unrequited love; the worst possible kind. Poor Jane... In some ways, she was like Katherine, who sought to regain Henry's love by hanging on his arm whenever she was able, and reproaching him for unkindness when he rejected her. It was good for me that Katherine did not see that this combination of sticking fast to her husband and then berating him did little to help her... but Jane did not see she was doing the same to George. And just as Henry fled from Katherine, so George ran from Jane.

I wondered if I should tell Jane to act as I did with Henry. Whenever Henry was furious or disgusted with his wife, he came to me. With me he found a woman who was strong, outspoken and bold; a woman who called him to *her* with her courage and fire. But then, I was confident in Henry's love, and these two women were not. When Henry and I argued, I always waited for him to come to me. I challenged Henry. I made him work for me, rather than being a quick and easy conquest. But Katherine and Jane were not made of the same mettle. They drove the men they loved away with their desperation. I beckoned Henry with my confidence.

I was thinking on this as we returned to our work. A knock sounded on the oaken door of the chamber. One of my servants, a distant cousin on my father's side, also named Thomas Boleyn, entered bringing a great surprise, he said, from the King. Bridget looked up with expectant eyes. "See, Anne?" she said happily. "Good news perhaps comes at last!"

I smiled, expecting to see yet another brilliant jewel or fantastic piece of cloth draped over the arm of the messenger. But Thomas stepped aside and behind him was Edward Foxe, one of the two men Henry had sent to Rome that February to petition the Pope. I let out a cry of surprise and rose, rushing to greet him in a most haphazard fashion. I was overcome by impatience and demanded to know what had happened before the poor man had even got through the door.

"My lady," Foxe said, bowing. "I come with wondrous news for you and the King. The Pope has agreed that the King's *Great Matter* will be put to Wolsey's Legatine Court. Clement will send a delegate who will preside over the trial and decide on the matter in his stead, for the Pope is still held in his citadel by the Emperor Charles. But, despite this, he assures us that his delegate will decide in good and true judgement."

I was smitten with almost hysterical laughter. *At last!* My voice rang in my head, exulting. *At last!* In the excitement my ladies thronged around Foxe, twittering and flattering us both. Margaret pulled me into her arms and laughed. Bridget was smirking knowingly and I turned to her, my eyes damp with tears. "I will begin to think that you are a seer, my lady!" I crowed, as she, too, wrapped her arms about me.

"I told you all would be well, Anne," she said warmly into my ear.

I untangled myself from the many arms wrapped about me. In my excitement I forgot myself and started calling Edward Foxe, "*Master Stephens*", confusing him with his fellow envoy, Stephen Gardiner. Then, overcome, I dropped into a chair. All the pressures of the past months dropped onto my shoulders at once. All my hopes, fears, love and despair crashed upon me. I had been holding so much in and this release was almost too much. I could not speak. I was undone. For a moment, I could do nothing but gulp in air, striving to control the hammering of my heart.

"Please tell me more, Master Stephens," I breathed eventually, not noting the twitch of his jaw as I called him the wrong name. "Please tell me everything!"

Foxe knelt by my side. "Be of good cheer, madam," he said. "The waiting will soon be over and you will be our lawful queen." He spoke quietly, but there was such honest concern for me in his face that I felt suddenly supported by this man. I groped for his hand and squeezed it, laughing and weeping at the same time.

The door banged backwards, almost shattering its hinges. Henry and his attendants, including George and Tom, burst through the doors with a great shout, making us all scream with alarm. I started from my chair and Margaret even grabbed at a fire poker, wielding it like a sword. As soon as we realised who it was, everyone broke into laughter. I was a mess. I did not know whether to laugh or cry, and settled for a mixture of the two. Henry beamed at me, elated to have taken us by surprise. Obviously, he had been planning this whole scene. He roared with delighted laughter to see me thus, quite overcome with emotion. He plucked me from the ground and kissed me with vigour.

Henry dismissed my ladies who scurried from the room like mice and there was not even a second glance for my sister. I wondered later whether I *wanted* Henry to take any notice of Mary. It was callous of Henry to utterly ignore her, and yet it would be insensitive to give me any indication that he still had feelings for her. Complicated, is life, at times.

But for now there were more important matters at hand. "You are pleased with my surprise, sweetheart?" he asked. I could do nothing for a moment but nod and smile through my tears.

"It was the best of surprises, my lord!" I assured him. "But you see how you have undone me? I am all tears and laughter, my lord… I know not which to obey!"

"Obey the laughter, sister," my brother chuckled. "Always follow laughter when you are in doubt. It is the merrier companion!"

Henry clapped George on the back and George winced slightly at the power of the blow. Henry was over-exuberant when excited. "Indeed, sweetheart," Henry crowed happily. "Obey the laughter, as your brother says, for all now is well! We are at the end of our troubles!"

I saw Tom smiling at me from amongst the throng of Henry's attendants. Once there had always been want, hunger, in his eyes. Now there was friendship and courtly love in his gaze, but no longer the long look of desire that had haunted my steps when I first came to court. I dipped my head to him and he bowed. I had not time to think more on Tom, as Henry stole my attention.

Henry wanted to question Foxe about everything that had happened in Rome. I asked him to wait, for a moment, so that I could collect myself. Henry agreed and I left for the chamber where my women were, only to be called back by Henry, barely half a minute later. Henry sent his men to join my ladies so that he and I could pepper Foxe with questions.

"I may have needed a *full* minute, my love," I laughingly reproached my eager beloved as I returned. "I am hardly fit for your company." I held a gold-trimmed lace cloth to my eyes, trying to stop them from flowing like a raging river.

Henry put his hands to my face, cupping it. "You are never anything less than beautiful, Anne."

Henry fell upon Foxe, getting him to describe every meeting with the Pope, every discussion, and outlining all Clement had said about the *Great Matter*. When I was in full control of myself, I joined in.

Foxe said that when they had managed to gain an interview with the Pope, Clement had been already aware the King wanted to separate from Katherine, and had been informed this was due for his lust for "an unworthy lady". Our suspicions that Katherine had sneaked word to the Pope about the annulment were therefore confirmed. Who else would have slandered me thus? Although… it did occur to me that Wolsey could have told the Pope I was unworthy… It would have been far easier for him to get a message to Clement than for Katherine, after all. Upsetting as it was to hear this, I was warmed by the overtures our men had made on my behalf. Gardiner had defended me as a lady "animated by the noblest virtues" and said rumours had been made up about me by the Queen's supporters, who, although acting from loyalty, were wrong in their condemnation of me. They had defended both me and the King's case ably, and Clement had agreed to send a delegate to England to judge the *Great Matter* alongside Wolsey.

It took the rest of the day to satisfy Henry's curiosity. By the end of our questioning, Foxe was exhausted, but he was not allowed to rest yet. Once fortified with wine and food, Foxe was sent forthwith to Wolsey at the Cardinal's seat in London, York Place, to deliver his report. I imagine Foxe woke the fat bat from his sumptuous bed, probably stealing Wolsey from the arms of his portly mistress. The notion made me laugh. I felt as though nothing could ever make me sad again. Foxe assured us that the Pope was deeply sympathetic to Henry's plight, and understood what was needed to secure the future for England. Soon, Katherine would be no more, and Henry and I would be married! I burned with eagerness for the trial to begin.

That night, in my private chambers, I allowed Henry to unlace my gown and bury his head between my naked white breasts. As I heard his groans of pleasure and felt his tongue upon my rose-scented skin, I smiled, putting my hands to the back of his head to draw him closer. I closed my eyes and sighed happily.

There could be no harm in these small pleasures now that we were so close to becoming man and wife. As Henry's hands and tongue slipped over my supple skin, I put my head back, sighing with satisfaction and happiness. I thought all our troubles were over. I thought we had won.

I was wrong.

Chapter Twenty

Greenwich Palace
Spring-Summer 1528

The Pope's chosen envoy was a Cardinal named Lorenzo Campeggio. When Foxe returned to us in May, we thought Campeggio would follow close on his heels, but we swiftly realized this was not the case. The Pope's envoy, it seemed, was in no particular hurry to leave, and apparently required an extraordinary amount of time to prepare for the voyage. Spring turned to summer and I wrote angrily to Wolsey, asking him why Campeggio was taking so much time. Wolsey sent missives full of apology and possible reasons for the man's dawdling.

"I know Cardinal Campeggio a little, my lady," the Cardinal wrote. *"He is an old and wise Cardinal, and has visited England before, so he already knows, reveres and loves our King, as we all do. I have no doubt that when he comes, he will be the best man for this task, but some concessions must be made, for Cardinal Campeggio, although hale of mind and strong in spirit, is not a young man. He suffers vastly from bodily afflictions, and therefore may well require greater time to travel to our shores and to prepare for the long journey ahead.*

Rest, in the assurance, my lady, that if this Cardinal takes longer to arrive, he will however prove more useful to our cause once he is here. A younger man may not possess such wisdom, or take such care to honour, protect and satisfy our beloved King, as I know this Cardinal will.

Written with the hand of you most devoted servant, and friend,

Cardinal Wolsey."

I handed the letter to my father who was visiting me and he read over it with a scowl. I was frustrated again, not only with the delay of Campeggio's departure, but also with my position at court. I was almost a prisoner in this tower. I could go little about the court, as we were trying to keep me separate from Katherine. I could not attend court entertainments unless she was absent. It made me feel, for the first time, like a hidden mistress; a sin thrust into the shadows. Being cooped up, a captive bird in a gilded cage, was not pleasing. I was almost a queen and yet not quite the Queen. I was a badly kept secret. I was the other woman, the mistress who was not a mistress. I was floating in purgatory, unable to free myself.

Never had I felt this way before. My dreams were so close, and yet so far away at the same time. I was not at liberty to do as I wished. Henry had also made the suggestion that I return to Hever when the papal envoy arrived, so he would not think the King wished to be rid of his wife in order to bed me. I had rejected such a notion, saying I would leave when Campeggio actually arrived in England. That, it seemed, was not about to happen soon.

"What do you think?" I asked my father and he grunted.

"I remember Campeggio myself..." His eyes scanned the parchment as he spoke. "He came to England some years ago as a papal envoy, trying to persuade the King to join a crusade against the Turks. He is a worldly man as well as a Cardinal, for he was married before taking his orders, and has five sons." My father's lips curled. "An unusual distinction for a man of the Church... to sire sons *before* putting on his Cardinal's hat..." He grinned slyly, enjoying his own jest and shrugged. "Campeggio *was* weak and sickly, even then, so perhaps what Wolsey says is true."

"Even if it is so," I said waspishly, "I cannot believe it would take so long for the man to depart Rome. I fear, my lord father… I fear that this is a tactic they use against us. Perhaps the Pope is *not* so keen to give Henry all he wishes, despite his assurances to our envoys."

"Perhaps…" he agreed. "The Pope is in a difficult situation, of course…" He tapped the parchment against his lips. "If only Katherine would see sense," he mused. "Then, the Pope would be able to set aside his earthly concerns, and decide as he should, with the courage of his faith. If Katherine raised no objection, there would be no need for this trial at all."

"I hold small faith in the courage or the spiritual strength of the Pope," I said shortly, playing with the embroidered sleeve of my new crimson gown. "We have seen often, through the pages of history, that popes place worldly concerns before spiritual ones. I fear this will be the case now. The Emperor may not have Clement in chains, but he holds many of his lands and much of his country by force. If only the French could prevail over Spain! Then I know that we would have honest and true judgement. But with the Pope all but prisoner, I fear we will not. He will listen to the persuasions of politics rather than the passion of true faith. He will heed military might, rather than the majesty of God."

My father sniffed. "That," he said, "is true enough."

"What more can be done?" I asked, my tone pleading. I had been so happy but happiness is such a weak friend, easily stolen away by the cares of the world, by a hard word… by the resurrection of trepidation. Happiness quails and flees before such foes; a young lad pissing himself at his first sight of battle…

Father looked back at Wolsey's hand on the parchment. "If the envoy *is* delaying," he muttered, thinking aloud, "then I wonder at whose bidding he does so?"

"What do you mean?"

"I come to question whether this delay is truly as it says here… or if someone leans on Campeggio to make him dither? Either the King of England or the King of Spain will have to be disappointed. What if someone is asking Campeggio to delay?"

I lifted an eyebrow. "Do you speak of the Pope, my lord father, or of Wolsey?"

"In truth, it could be either," he stood, flapping the letter at me. "I will take this to Norfolk," he went on, "and see what he makes of it. Your uncle has men in Wolsey's household, and women about Katherine. We will see if they know whether anything has passed from either the Queen or the Cardinal to Rome about Campeggio. If we can discover that, we can use it against them."

"What good will any of this do us?" I stared helplessly at him. "All this subterfuge… I get no younger as these months pass by, father… Henry is impatient, and so am I."

"So are we all, daughter," my father said. "But if there is someone in our midst working against us, their removal will only help our cause, and speed things up for you and the King." An almost gentle light entered his eyes. If I didn't know better, I would have said he was gazing at me with affection.

"We all wish to see you married to the King and on that throne," he said. "Norfolk and I are working in every way we can to help, Anne, never believe otherwise. The King is certain that once this envoy arrives, all will be well, but we must prepare to fight our enemies, even those pretending to be our friends, as we prepare for victory. Wolsey does not want to see you on that throne. He has let that sentiment slip to his intimates on more than one occasion. We must keep an eye ever trained on him, if we are to succeed."

"I would rather that all our efforts were concentrated on the annulment," I said sullenly.

"But if Wolsey was no longer constantly in the ear of the King, daughter, and if Norfolk or I were installed there instead, do you not think our cause would move faster?"

I narrowed my eyes. "You never miss a chance for advancement, do you, father?"

He grinned tightly. "Never," he admitted. "But remember that our advancement is yours, too, Anne. And just think how satisfying it would be to bring the Cardinal down."

"Henry says he is our best chance to secure the approval of the Pope."

My father nodded. "And he may well be right, but let us not forget that the King is blind when it comes to those he loves. He sees not Wolsey's avarice and greed, nor seems to note the Cardinal's carnal adventures… The Cardinal is as corrupt as he is ungodly; he gleans money from the Church and from Henry's people. When monasteries are dissolved for poor practices or slattern ways, into whose pocket do you think that money goes? Not into the King's, that is for sure." His expression hardened. "If Wolsey stands in our way, we will remove him."

"I would not miss him."

"The King has started to doubt Wolsey, I believe," he continued. "He demanded to know why it was taking so long for Campeggio to leave for England. The Cardinal has had to do a *lot* of grovelling this week." He brandished the parchment like a sword. "If you can persuade the King that these delays stem from Wolsey, then his confidence in his chief minister will be further unsettled."

"I *do* believe that both cardinals are delaying." I shrugged. "And so will I say to the King."

"Speak kindly and *gently* to Henry, Anne," my father warned. "At times you are too passionate… He finds it refreshing, different, now… but he will tire of it eventually. He is, at heart, a conservative man of traditional values. You play the part of the bold mistress now, but in time you will have to be the obedient wife. Will you be ready to tame yourself so?"

"Henry loves me the way that I am," I bristled. "He fell in love with me for who I am, and wants to marry who I am… He does not want another Katherine." I waved a hand at my father. "What is between my future husband and me is between us, my lord father. It is I alone who has brought us to this place. Do not question the manner in which I speak to Henry. He wants an equal beside him, and it is me he loves… That is how it is."

"Well enough," he agreed with a sigh. "I cannot argue with that. The King is more in love with you every day, my love. The annulment has become his sole care and worry. I will trust in you to continue as you are, but do not be too obvious, that is all I ask. Question… Lay the seeds of doubt, speak in offhand conversation about your cares and worries. Often the more softly laid the seed, the stronger it will grow."

"I will do as you say," I agreed. "But I will not tell falsehoods to Henry, father… I will tell him what I know, or what I believe to be true, but I will not lie. I intend ours to be a match not only of love, but of honesty."

He offered me an oily smile. "And I am sure it will be… Just keep in mind that this is becoming a vast game, Anne, one of many players. I know you love the King, and he you, but in order to forward our cause, we may need, at times, to manipulate Henry as well as others."

I gaped at him but before I could protest, he made to leave. "Think on it, daughter." He kissed the top of my head. "And remember that even if such methods need to be employed, they are necessary. Sometimes... we have to do such things for the ones we love in order to show them the way. You do no ill to the King if you are acting in his best interests. If the ones we love cannot see the right path, it is up to us to guide them... to move them as pieces on a chessboard, for their own good, and for ours."

My father left me with difficult thoughts. I did not want to turn Henry into a *tool* to get what I wanted. I did not want to start our life together lying to him, manipulating him... Such thoughts were abhorrent.

I decided that I was not going to do as my father asked. I would continue as ever I had and be honest with Henry. But I did think on my father's words about the Cardinal. Was it manipulative to say what I thought about the Cardinal, but to express those concerns in ways such as my father had advised rather than blustering at the King? Would *modifying* my behaviour be manipulating my beloved? I knew not, and the notion made me uncomfortable. But I also knew that Wolsey was not about to be troubled by such questions of morality... *He* would not worry about lying to or manipulating Henry in order to remove me. I was in the midst of a dangerous game. The one strength I had was Henry's love. I had won that love by being myself, and I decided to continue as *I* thought best.

I would not lie to my beloved, but, if the need arose, I might take my father's advice, and offer Henry my concerns in a way that might sprinkle seeds of doubt more effectively. Such thoughts troubled me... but if it was the only way to win, the only way to be with Henry and to take my place as Queen, then it would have to be done. Wolsey would play any hand and use any weapon he had... I had to be prepared to do the same.

Chapter Twenty-One

Waltham Abbey
Summer 1528

In June, all my dreams were almost wrested from me. That summer arrived wet, warm and sticky. The skies were heavy both with cloud and sunshine. Rain fell often but did not cool the earth. On clear days, when cloudless skies shone glaring blue and the sun baked England, it was too hot to go outside. The palaces of court began to ripen with the stench of sweat, piss and bodies itching in the heat. Large downfalls of rain and summer storms threatened the crops of England, and many were worried that famine might come to the poor because of this. But whenever these storms erupted in the skies, they brought no relief from the heat, or the foul air.

It was the perfect weather for one thing… plague.

We began to hear rumours of deaths spreading through the towns of England. Plagues of quick-spreading illnesses were an ever-present danger during the warmer months. This was one of the reasons the court and King moved out of London in the summer, to avoid the risk of illness. Henry was horribly afraid of sickness and considered himself an expert in making cures and medicines. Some of the King's men, George especially, found Henry's obsession with sickness and its cures to be rather amusing. They laughed about it… when Henry was not there, obviously. But I understood his fixation. Henry was the last male heir of his line. His father had borne two sons, and yet Henry had only one child; a daughter. Were Henry to die, there were fears that the many distant heirs to the throne would battle for its possession, since none believed a woman, or a girl in this case, could be strong enough to hold the country together. Henry's father had brought an end to the civil war which had assailed England for so long before his rule… should it come to pass that strife would return with the death of his son? I knew such thoughts plagued Henry.

The idea that he had not yet done his duty to his country and sired a legitimate male heir was a terrible weight for him to bear. His miserly, suspicious father had succeeded where he, the young god-like giant of a son, had failed. That was why Henry was obsessed with curing disease. He delved into the subject to arm himself against his fear. He would not be taken from his destiny by a fever or die before his duty to his country was done. He would live, and he would have his heir. This passion, this drive, was as strong within him as his love for me. Henry was used to succeeding in everything he did. He was a strong, fit and healthy man. He was skilled at archery, hunting, tennis, jousting, riding and wrestling. That was why his lack of an heir was so painful. It was his one failure, in a life of success. To those who have always found achievement easy, failure is the worst of sins.

But I was going to help him. I would give him an heir. I would give him the son he so longed for.

The longing within me to have Henry's children, to see them grow and play at his knee, to hold a child of my own in my arms, was almost as strong as the desire to share Henry's bed as his wife. I wanted to be a mother. I was ready. I yearned for children. At times, the desire to be a mother was so strong in my breast that I thought I might cease to breathe. My brother and Tom might chortle quietly to see Henry with his pills and potions, but I, who understood Henry so well, understood his fears and the solution to them. When we had children, all would be well.

Even as we listened to growing reports of sickness spreading through England, we waited for Campeggio. The envoy, it seemed, was unable to travel by horse, or to walk, but had to be carried all the way to England in a litter. Needless to say, he was not making swift progress. We had reports that villagers he encountered on the way thought they were seeing a man doing penance; a shrunken, hunched and groaning figure with a long beard, travelling through the heat of summer. Some even came out to give offerings to him, thinking he was obviously on pilgrimage. The road was so painful for Campeggio, apparently, that long rests had to be taken along the way. Campeggio positively *crawled* to England. Neither Henry nor I were best pleased.

Wolsey begged for Henry's patience, citing Campeggio's age, his gout, and his many other infirmities, but assuring both Henry and me over and over that he was the best man for this task. I groaned to hear of the snail-like pace of Campeggio, but soon enough, there were other things to worry on closer to home.

The plague had begun to seep into London at the start of May, which was unusually early for Death to come pounding at our doors. In the first days of June, as the plague settled deep into the city and the pall of death hovered with the haze of heat on the cobblestones of London's streets, the court fled to Waltham Abbey in Essex. I went with them, although I am sure Katherine wished she could order that I stay behind to die. Thousands in London died of the plague they called the *sweating sickness*. People fell ill with alarming speed, looking well one hour and sick unto death the next. A raging fever, profuse sweating, troubled dreams and unconsciousness assailed the victims, and every day we heard reports of more people succumbing to the dreaded sweat. The cities were closed up, curfews were put in force and people tried desperately to avoid contact with each other.

Those who could, nobles in the main part, quickly fled the packed streets of the towns and cities. London became a ghost town. Her usually busy streets emptied and shops, churches and markets were closed. The dead were buried carefully, but quickly, and cures, charms, trinkets and amulets of protection were everywhere. People wore cloths soaked in vinegar and herbs to prevent the disease from entering their bodies through the foul air. Courtiers carried heavily scented pomanders and unicorn tusks to protect themselves, purchased from merchants and peddlers who assured their customers these items would ward off the illness. Even as Death stalked amongst us, some were willing and able to turn a tidy profit from such horror.

It was whilst we were at Waltham that several men of the King's chamber, my brother included, fell ill of the sweat. Henry forbade anyone to go near them, and took swift flight from their company, retiring to private apartments and only allowing selected courtiers near him. Those who had been out in the streets or in close contact with the sick were barred from approaching him, on pain of death. I was out of my mind with worry that George may worsen and die, but I could not go to him. Henry would not allow it.

I was also not allowed near Henry, not because he feared I might have the illness, but because it had reared its head in his household. He did not want to risk me, he wrote. *"We must be separated now, my dearest and only love, for your own safety. I cannot allow you to come near my household. I will not risk losing you, even though I will miss you every day and know myself bereft of hope until I see your beautiful eyes once again. Send messages to me, and I will do the same to you. Ensure all that comes into your chambers is rinsed or scrubbed with good vinegar or strong ale, and there will be no way for the sickness to spread and endanger you."*

Henry's letter finished with a vast list of precautions I had to take to prevent sickness. The messenger who delivered it also brought a potion Henry had made himself, to strengthen the body against the sickness. Pungent with juniper to ward off evil spirits, chicory to bestow invincibility, and feverfew to prevent fever, it was a disgusting concoction. But knowing that Henry was learned about medicine, I drank it. I almost vomited after the first mouthful, but managed to keep it down. It did not make me feel hale.

I wrote to Henry, begging that he command his messengers to bring me constant news of my brother. The thought that I might lose George consumed me. I could not rest, despite Henry's man coming with hourly messages that George still lived. Henry had sent his best doctors to tend George and put the lives of others at risk to check on the progress of my brother. Should I have worried for those I put at risk to bring these messages? Perhaps… but I could only care then for my brother, not for the lives of others. We are, all of us, selfish creatures when we fear to lose ones we love. I prayed to God each day, asking for His intervention. I pestered God, telling Him George was a man of goodness and faith, begging Him to save my brother. I could not sleep, or eat. Each day I paced my chamber. Each time the messenger came I rushed at him, searching his face for news that my brother was dead. Yet each day, George thankfully survived. My soul was desperate. I could think of little else.

One afternoon at Waltham, while I was preoccupied, worrying about my brother, I noticed Bess behaving oddly. She was ghastly pale, shivering, and pressing her head to the cool stone wall. She was not making any noise. I wondered how long she had stood thus while I failed to notice her, wrapped up as I was in my fog of fear for my brother.

"Bess?" I asked. I was most fond of her. She had been with me for many years now, since the first day I came from France to England. She had been in my service through many struggles, and had always been a loyal and good servant.

Bess looked around at me as though she barely saw me. Her eyes were glassy. Her disjointed gaze made my heart freeze. A ghostly sheen of glistening sweat covered her face.

Her skin was so pale that I could trace all the veins in her face; a translucent pallor that made me suddenly, horribly, afraid.

"Bess," I whispered, rising from my chair. Bess stood transfixed, staring, her body wavering gently as though she were a sheet drying in a light breeze. I ran three steps across the chamber and caught her just as she fell. I lowered her to the rush-mat floor where she reached a shaking, hot hand up towards me.

"The face of Death," she murmured as her fingers stroked my face, staring eerily into my dark eyes. Then she fainted. Her eyes closed and her head drooped to one side. As I held her body, staring at her in horror, I felt the raging heat of her skin through her clothes. Bess *burned*.

I ran from the room screaming for my servants to bring the doctor. As we waited, I laid cool, wet cloths on Bess' brow and opened the neck of her gown. She moaned and mumbled incoherently under the pressure of my shaking hands, but did not open her eyes. She was drenched in sweat. When the doctor arrived, his face crimson from hurrying across court, he banished me from the room, hustling me from the chamber even as I protested that I wanted to stay with my maid.

"You were a fool to stay in here when you saw she was sick!" he shouted at me. "Don't you know there have been forty thousand cases of the sweat in London alone? Don't you know what danger you have put yourself in?"

"I could not just leave her on my floor to die!" I cried into his enraged and surprised face. "She is my servant... my friend!"

"Not for much longer, my lady," he said grimly and pushed me from the door.

Chapter Twenty-Two

Waltham Abbey
Summer 1528

I was hurried away from Bess and put into different rooms. I could not rest. I scribbled a note to Henry about Bess and then I paced backwards and forwards; a restless beast in a tiny cage. Henry was aghast to learn that one of my maids was sick of the sweat and, with other cases becoming apparent in Waltham, he ordered me to my family's home in Hever.

Our parting was done by letter alone. Henry could not possibly see me now after I had been in close contact with one who presently lay fighting for her life. I was hurt, that he did not come to see me, but I understood. The threat was terrible and we were all in great peril. My packing was done hastily. My servants were pale with terror as they stuffed my gorgeous gowns, hoods and jewels haphazardly into cases.

Panic was rising in the court and in the streets beyond. I shuddered to see bodies being carried out into far off fields for burial in distant mass graves. The smell of burning vinegar and cloves filled the air, and beyond those smells, the stink of dread and the sweet, sickening odour of death lingered. I have never felt such fear before; for this was not just my fear, but the terror of an entire nation, as the sweat did its deadly work throughout the land.

Just before I left, a visitor arrived. As my servants ran, filling boxes and dismantling furniture, Tom came to the door. His face was covered with a strip of vinegar-soaked cloth. I was never so grateful to see anyone, as I knew he had been near to my brother before George had been taken ill. Tom had taken all precautions, he assured me. He had worn the cloth at all times over his mouth and nose when had spoken to

George's doctors about their patients. His pockets held oranges stuffed with cloves, sweetening and purifying the vile air that carried the sickness. He had not been in the same chamber as George, for to do so would mean he could not return to Henry's side, but he had brought news of my brother.

"He has been gravely ill these last few days," Tom said, taking me to a window seat to converse. I wrung my hands, willing him to say something to bring me hope. "But in these last few hours, the physicians who were tending him said there was an improvement in his condition. They tell us that should a victim survive the first days, there is great hope that he will recover fully." He took my hand. "I believe your brother will live, Anna."

I cried, weeping softly in relief, and he touched my shoulder gently. "I thought you would like to know." Ghosting over his face was a shadow of the great affection he had formally known for me. I clung to his hands.

"You put yourself at great risk, Tom, coming here to deliver this news," I said. "And whilst I have not always been good to you, this is the second time you have proved yourself a friend to me in a time of need."

He smiled. "I was not always so good a friend to you either, Mistress Anne, so perhaps we are even on that score. But friends do what they can for each other, do they not? Whenever there is a need, I will be with you."

I gulped through my tears. "My friend has returned, in truth," I nodded, groping at his hands and squeezing them. "And in a dark time such as this, that is a great comfort."

Tom paused. "I spoke with one of the Cardinal's servants as he was leaving the court, a Master Thomas Cromwell. He informed me that the Cardinal has spoken to the King this day just passed." He spoke hesitantly, unsure whether to reveal his findings. I looked at him questioningly, and he nodded, more to himself than to me, deciding to continue. "Wolsey said to the King that this plague… so much more virulent and aggressive than ever it has been before… could be taken as a sign that God does not approve of Henry's desire to annul his marriage."

"That *snake*!" I hissed, my tears stopping short. "He seeks to use this horror against me!"

Tom nodded. "I fear this may be the case," he agreed. "Katherine, too, has taken up such a refrain, telling the King this plague is God's judgement on his *Great Matter*… She joins her voice to Wolsey's. For once, the Queen and Cardinal are in agreement. An unusual occurrence, since they each despise the other."

"And what said Henry to this? Did Wolsey's man tell you?"

Tom grinned. "The King was enraged," he said. "He said there was none who could replace you in his heart, that he knew his *Matter* to be just. He responded to Katherine's twittering by screaming at her that he believed this was a sign of God's *disapproval* of their marriage, and the sooner he was rid of her, the better it would be for his country and for him."

I stared at Tom. Henry had rarely been so bold with Katherine. Hopefully it marked a change in him… I was more pleased than I could say to hear he had defended me against both the Queen and Cardinal. "What said the Queen?"

"Nothing. She apparently burst into tears and went to the chapel to pray," he said. "The King joined her there after an hour or so, and together they prayed, but I have no doubt both were praying for different things." Tom lifted his shoulders. "The Cardinal attempted to talk to the King again later on, but he fled when he King bellowed that he would give a thousand Wolseys for but one Anne Boleyn!" With this, Tom chortled quietly. "And Henry went on to declare that no other but God shall take you from him! *That* closed the Chancellor's mouth! Wolsey looked *assuredly* unsure of himself as he scuttled away from the King!"

"Good!" I exclaimed, squeezing Tom's fingers hard. "*Good!*"

"The King will not abandon you, Anna; not now, not ever. He is set on this, on having you." Tom sniffed. "I think he truly does believe that this plague was sent by God, to show him his path. Henry has spoken of it a few times since arguing with Wolsey, and you know what the King is like… once something is set in his mind, it cannot be undone." He pursed his lips. "You should leave as soon as possible for Hever," he said. "I will continue to send you all the news I have of George."

I swallowed. "You put yourself in danger, Tom," I whispered. "Are you sure?"

Tom kissed my brow. "Your brother is my good friend, Anne. I will remain close to him. I have faith that God is not done with me yet on this mortal plane. You go now, be safe, travel fast and stop nowhere along the road. The faster you are gone from London and this terrible plague, the better."

I nodded. "I will do as you say, Tom. And thank you. Thank you from the bottom of my heart for all you do for George. Let him know that I love him and I will pray for him."

"Of course." Tom rose and fixed the cloth about his face again. "The court will be moving once more, even as you do, Anna," his words were muffled by the cloth as he bound it to his face. The scent of vinegar washed through the air, its powerful stench nauseating. "The King's men are to accompany Henry away from all others, to try to isolate and protect him. Although such safeguards are for the King's protection, I think he also wishes to avoid Katherine."

"She goes elsewhere?"

Tom nodded, his brown eyes winking with a touch of amusement. "She goes elsewhere." He stretched his arms behind his back. "Henry will send Katherine to Hunsdon. The rest of the court will leave for their own houses and lands in the country." He looked at me, his brown eyes peeking over the top of the vinegar-soaked cloth. "The King is anxious for news that you have left, Anne," he went on. "He wants to know that you are out of danger."

"Tell him you have seen me leave this very hour," I said and paused. Although it felt strange to say this to Tom, I could not help but blurt out; "tell Henry of my love for him. Tell him that I pray for him, and for England."

Tom nodded and smiled, a little sadly, but he promised he would give Henry my message. I embraced him before he rode out. As I watched him leave, I wondered on the strength and courage of this friend of mine. And what a friend he was! To risk his own life to bring comfort and news to me! I was humbled by Tom Wyatt. I felt small compared to the greatness of his character. I made up my mind, should we all come through this awful ordeal, I would do all I could to aid him and his family. I could never repay him for this kindness, but I would try.

I was glad, too, that Katherine would no longer stay at Henry's side, poisoning his mind with her tales of superstition. She was using this horror as a weapon against me, as was the Cardinal. So, Wolsey had finally revealed his true feelings then, in the midst of all this? He had petitioned Henry to give up the *Great Matter*, proclaiming that he, the odious and corrupt Cardinal, knew the mind of God! It seemed to me that if any understood the will of God, then it was Henry rather than Katherine and Wolsey. After all, this was not the first time that plague had ravished England under Henry's rule… What, then, had brought those past outbreaks upon us? Was it not more likely the plagues that had occurred *throughout* Henry's marriage to Katherine were signs that God was displeased with their union? And this one, here and now, this virulent attack came just as there were delays from the Pope, and subterfuge from the Cardinal... I believed in Henry's theory; this was a sign that God wanted him to be rid of Katherine.

I barked orders at my servants, and helped them pack. We had to hurry. Much of my baggage was already on the carts outside by the time my father and his men came to escort me from Waltham to Hever. Like Tom, his face was bound with cloth, and he carried an apple stuffed with cloves and spices which he kept close to his face.

"The carts can come behind," he ordered my servants. "Make your way to Hever with speed, and stop at no village or town on the way. If you have to camp, do so at the roadside and let no man approach you. If you do not do as I order, we will not allow you into Hever's protection." He stopped and nodded his head at a smaller cart trundling up behind him. "There is enough food and drink here to last you until you reach Hever," he continued, staring balefully at the men in case they even considered disobeying him. "You have your orders; make sure you are, at all times, armed. *Leave!*"

"You have heard that George may be improving?" I asked him.

He nodded curtly. "I have visited him and seen it for myself," he said. "But he cannot be moved. I think he is safe, but we cannot stay here any longer. We have to get you to a place of safety, my child... You are the prime concern for our family now."

"You... went to George?" I asked.

My father's brow furrowed. "I kept the ill airs of his chambers at bay with this." He gestured to the vinegar and rose water soaked cloth. "And this." He waved the clove-studded apple at me. "Everyone knows that if you do not breathe the air near to a victim, then the sweat cannot creep inside your body."

I nodded. It was common knowledge that sickness passed through ill-smelling air. The pomander and cloth he used would have warded off the plague.

"We make for the Thames." He looked about to check everyone was obeying his commands. "We will avoid the streets, and then you and I will ride on fast horses for Kent. My men will divide; half to come with us and half to guard your carts and mine."

We did as he said, travelling down the river on a swift barge as my carts made for the nearest road headed for Hever. Then we rode fast and hard along the roads. Even with a cloth of vinegar and wormwood over my face, I could smell the scent of death on the roads. There were few towns not affected by this plague. We rode past villages where emblems of warning were hung on crude sticks, showing skulls, to demonstrate that the sweat raged within them. The sight chilled me. There were so many. Although I knew the sweat had been potent in London, I had not known it had reached so far into the countryside. I hoped it had not made it to the villages near Hever. Along the road there were also other parties of people; some poor, walking with bundles on their backs, and some, like us, riding on fast horses or oxen-pulled carts. We flashed past all of them, not stopping unless our horses needed water. Behind us my father's men pulled more horses, so we could switch to fresh mounts when our first ones tired. Every now and then, as we passed poor peasants, they would stretch their hands out, begging for alms or aid.

"Leave them!" shouted my father, veering his horse from the outstretched palms of a woman with a thin and dirty face. He cursed at her. "We cannot risk to stop!"

I felt terrible, to ride past and not offer them anything, but we were going too rapidly for me to reach my purse, and father was right, we could not stop. We had to save ourselves.

We arrived at Hever, our mounts frothing at the mouth and ready to collapse. I was sorry to have ridden them so hard, but speed was all-important. I released them to the groomsman, and asked him to look after them well. They had saved us, after all. We found my mother there already; my father had sent her ahead of him with more of our servants. She was anxious for news of George.

"We have heard but little," I said, taking my riding cloak from my back. My hot skin relished the feel of the air upon it. "But Tom Wyatt told me that he had news George was recovering. And father went to see George too. He said he believed he was improving. I believe that his constitution and his faith in God will prove him out."

"You are right," my mother said, clinging to my hand. "All sickness is in the hands of God and we are not to question His will. If George recovers then we will know he is blessed."

Her face puckered despite her brave words. "I am sure that God will not forsake us."

Chapter Twenty-Three

Hever Castle
Summer 1528

Two days later we heard from Mary; Will was sick of the sweat, and it was bad. She did not think he would recover, and she had sent her children from the house to a relative of Will's nearby. She had stayed to nurse Will and for the moment, had no signs of having contracted the sickness. *"It makes one realise,"* Mary wrote, her tear-stains marking the parchment and blurring its ink. *"How precious is our love. Should he recover, I shall never allow him to forget that I adore him and only him in this world. God grant me strength, Anne. I have never been so afraid."*

I wept for my sister, for my sick brothers, for the loneliness I felt to be away from the side of my love, for the fears of my heart and for my country. Henry wrote to me almost daily. His letters were impassioned and desperate. I was to send him word every day and was to be of good cheer, for few women had caught the disease and it seemed that I might be safe because of my sex. I was not to worry for he was shut in a small manor house far out in the country with only one servant now allowed to come to into his presence and therefore was unlikely to become ill. He wrote that he missed me, that he loved me. He sent fortifying herbs of *manus Christi*, pills of *Rasis* and instructions to eat lightly and drink wine, *"I hear that it helps to prevent the sickness,"* he wrote.

I had never felt as wretched as now, when I was apart from Henry, and peril had enveloped England. I wrote of my desire, stronger than ever, to be his wife, and that, if God should spare us, I wanted to grow old with him and our sons and daughters, happy forever in the knowledge that our marriage was meant to be. I was sick with worry for my family, for my friends and most of all for my Henry. I prayed for him at every hour, listening to fresh rain pelt the window panes. "God, in Your mercy, save our Prince," I pleaded. "There is nothing and no one in this world more precious than he. I would gladly give my life to save his. Take my life, Lord, but save our King".

I did not realise at the time that God would take my prayers so nearly literally…

That night we dined, each of us too worried to talk. We picked over the offerings prepared with haste by my mother. Pottage with fresh herbs and almonds, stewed herrings with parsley and currants, codling in green sauce of mint and garlic and roasted salmon with spinach tarts… These delights would normally have pleased us, but all food tasted bitter in my mouth. I did not even eat a great deal of the tarts, made of summer cherries and strawberries, which came later, even though these were favourite dishes of mine. I was too distracted. Mother told us that Jane had been sent to her father's house and had written to us to tell us she was safe, but out of her mind with terror for George. Jane begged for news and I wrote to her, telling her all that we knew. Her letter scared me a little, as she wrote with such vehemence and passion, saying that her father had all but imprisoned her at his house because she had tried to leave to tend to George. I did not doubt that she wanted to be with him, but her father was right to restrain her, if that was what he had done. Riding to Waltham now would be to risk death. I counselled her to wait, and told her we believed George would recover. We sat down to wait at Hever, restless and afraid. Each morning, my mother dosed us with the pills Henry had sent, hoping they would help us to ward off the sweat.

But they did not.

I was in the gardens when I began to feel unwell. I had awoken that morning with a headache. I thought I had drunk too deeply of the fine malmsey wines my father had bought with the new-found wealth the King had provided. Last night, after eating, we had sat by the fire, barely speaking. The wine had helped me to sleep, finally, when I climbed unsteadily into my bed and cried myself to sleep thinking of George, of Will, of Mary and of Henry.

But by the next afternoon I knew that there was something wrong. I was hot, and then cold, my head ached. I was trembling; inside my blood, inside my bones, as though an earthquake had awakened in my body. I could not see straight. Shadows warped and strained in the corners of my eyes. My vision seemed masked, veiled in some way. The flowers in the garden quivered before me. I was seeing double, and then hardly seeing anything at all. I staggered as I tried to get indoors. Each step I took up the stairs towards my chambers was like dragging logs. *You need to rest,* I told myself, unwilling to believe that anything more was wrong. *The flight to Hever, the worries and care of the Great Matter… This has exhausted you. That is all, Anne… that is all.*

But I knew it was not. Cold fear lurked beneath the fire of my skin. I stumbled into my room, having seen no one along the way. I stared around the chamber. I knew not where I was.

"Bess," I whispered. "Where is Bess?" I could not think why she was not there.

I sat down heavily before the mirror of highly polished copper and saw my usually pale cheeks flushed. I pressed my hands to them and then cried out as my hands burned upon my face. My eyes were bright, glassy, and strange. I stared at this face in the mirror. I was afraid, for it was not my face that stared back at me.

"The face of Death…" I whispered, reaching shaking fingers out to the vision in the mirror, echoing the words of my poor Bess.

I stared at the face in the mirror. Its skin was as white as bone and the shadows under its eyes and at its cheeks dark and deep. Its eyes blazed. Bright lights radiated from hideous black pools. The dreadful face blurred and danced as I watched it. I felt my body being sucked through the mirror and into the long, glowing dark of those eyes. I was falling, falling into the mirror.

I stumbled to my feet with a cry and flailed my hands wildly in front of me as though I could hold off the horror with but my mortal flesh. And then, then there was nothing but darkness as the strength left my body and my legs buckled. My head bounced off the wooden floor that lay beneath the rushes and scented meadowsweet strewn there. Warm blood flowed from my nose and from a gash on my head. I could smell the blood as it slipped over my face and yet I could see nothing more. My skin shivered and quaked.

The last thing I remembered was the sound of my voice. "Please God," I muttered. "Please God, save me."

Into darkness, I fell.

Chapter Twenty-Four

Hever Castle
Summer 1528

The days that followed after my collapse were nothing but a blur. Distorted faces hovered over me. I smelt the funk of roasting herbs and choked on the scent of burning vinegar. Hot urine and sweat soaked the sheets around me. I felt the smoke of the fire, the heat of the chamber, and moaned as the fire within me was already enough to set Sodom and Gomorra alight. I heard someone open the door and screamed as the stinging chill of fresh air lashed at the sweat on my body. It was like daggers piercing my skin.

I flinched from my mother's soft and firm hands as she forced bitter potions down my throat. I choked; spitting and vomiting them back up, and then was made to swallow more. I cried out in my sleep for Henry and screamed in my dreams. Demons and hungry spirits chased through the corridors of Henry's palaces and into hell.

I dreamed I saw the tower again, red with blood. I saw the walls of the castle become the hands of a scaly demon which reached out for me, ripping my flesh from my bones with its claws. I screamed out in pain as I saw the slices of my flesh and bone rupture. Gushing blood rushed from my veins. Claws sank into me, pulling, yanking my heart from its bony cage. The demon tossed my heart in its mouth and chewed, dribbling flecks of flesh and iron-scented blood as I stared at it in mute horror. It licked its scaly claws and came back for more, more of my flesh, more of my bone. Its jaws stretched into a gruesome and hungry smile as it picked me apart like a roasted capon. I screamed again, thrashing in my bed, and the vision of the demon was replaced by the ashen face of my mother, crying and dabbing my forehead with a cool cloth.

"Hush, child," she said, her voice cooing and loving through her tears. "Hush, my Anne, my love, my little girl… You are going to get well."

"Mother," I croaked. "What is happening?"

She sobbed with relief to hear my voice. "You are sick of the sweat, but you *are* going to get well. Do you hear me, Anne? You *are* going to get well. This is not the way I will lose my children."

I nodded but she disappeared again as I was flung back into the hideous nightmare world of devils and bone and blood. For more than a week I teetered on the edge of two worlds, the world of dreams and that of reality, locked in battle with the Devil Himself and unable to remember but one prayer to God through the horror and the fear.

But my mother was right. After a week I was well enough to wake one morning and see her asleep in a chair, her head nodding against her chest, clearly exhausted. The dark figure of a doctor was kneeling in prayer by the fire. The room was dark as the windows were closed and shutters were fastened over them. The air was warm, but not too hot, and its thickness smelt of the smouldering ashes of herbs and the steam of bubbling potions. Blue sage-smoke wafted above me, slowly moving streams which billowed with the draughts. About my throat, strips of parchment quivered and crunched. There were prayers written upon them, and fastened to me with string. I coughed, feeling as though I had a full-grown lad sat on my chest, and tried to sit up to lessen the pressure. As I moved, my mother and the doctor, who I now recognised as Doctor Butts of the court, rushed to the bed.

"Water," I croaked, and my mother pushed a cup of cooled water boiled with herbs to my lips. I gulped down blissfully welcome mouthfuls, cringing at the sting of the bitter herbs on my torn throat and cracked lips.

Doctor Butts felt my forehead and let out a heavy breath. "The fever has broken," he said. "It is safe to assume you are out of danger." He smiled weakly, great relief on his face. "I was worried, but it seems God has decided to keep you in this world, my lady. And now I must see my other patient." He stood up stiffly, setting his hands against his tired back and stretching it. "Who will be glad to hear that you are also on the mend."

"Other patient?" I wheezed at my mother as Butts left. My throat was dry and speaking hurt. My normal voice had been replaced by that of a dying demon. My lungs felt weak, shaky. My whole form was feebler than I had ever known. It cost me much just to talk, or sit up.

"Your father was brought to bed of the sweat the day after you," my mother said. She looked utterly exhausted. Lines I had never seen before had ploughed deep into her skin. Her face was as pale as the full moon on a clear night and dark circles hugged her eyes, giving her an almost skeletal appearance. But she was still gentle, and beautiful. She had not been strong these past years, and yet, she, the least hale of all of us, had not caught this dread sickness. "We found you in your room, collapsed on the floor, your face covered in blood and thrashing around like you were possessed." Her face puckered and tears fell from her eyes. She did not heed them. Clearly she had been crying much over the past days, and had learned to carry on regardless.

"That same night, just after he had sent word to the King to send his best doctor to you, your father fell in the hall…" My mother's face crumpled. "He did not even seem ill a minute before he collapsed, Anne, this sickness is so quick to take effect. I was so frightened. I thought I might lose you both. Many servants were taken ill on the same day and there is not a room in the house that has not been turned into a sick room… But the King sent his doctor and I had the help of the cunning woman of the village. With her herbs and the doctor's medicines we were able to save you."

My mother gestured towards another figure that I had not noticed before now; an old woman, her face crinkled and soft like a fallen crab-apple. She sat quietly in the corner near the fire. Swathed in dark brown wool, she seemed to waver in and out of the shadows. I remembered her vaguely from her visits to Hever during the time of my banishment. She lifted her aged head and nodded once in recognition. Her eyes were as dark as coal and they shone with pride. My weak eyes met her gaze, and then, with the humility expected of her rank and station, she dropped those black eyes to the fire where she stirred a pot of herbs in water.

"George… and Mary…. Will?" I asked. Each word was a stab of pain. I sipped more water, feeling it flow over every crack on my lips. I could taste blood as it washed free from where I had chewed my lips. My skin was parched and my mind was foggy, as though I had not slept in days. Everything, every bone, every muscle in me, ached.

"George is recovered and anxious for news of you, and Mary did not catch the sweat. But… Will… He died, Anne, as did many of their servants. Mary is now a widow. Her children are safe, though, the sweat did not reach Will's mother's house."

My heart tore within me. Poor Will. Poor Mary. She had loved him so, and now he was gone. "And Henry?" I asked. She poured more of the sweet water down my broken, dry throat.

"Both well and desperate for news of you," she said with a trembling smile. "It took all the force of his advisors to prevent him rushing to your side, but they convinced him it was too dangerous. He could not send his best doctor to us as he was away when the King heard of your sickness. His

Majesty did not want you to have to wait to get treatment, so he sent Dr Butts, a *fine* man." Her voice glowed with gratitude.

"The King has been sending messages daily to us, and remedies and potions, all to try to save you from the sweat, my love. He tells us that he prays hourly for your recovery and has given many great presents and promises to the Church for your recovery." She paused to give me more water. The taste of tansy, sugar and feverfew flooded my mouth and I felt my head clearing as I lapped up the water eagerly. "I will read you the letter he sent when he first heard of your illness," she said, putting down the bowl and taking up a parchment from the dark oaken cabinet at one side of the room.

"There came to be suddenly in the night the most afflicting news that could have arrived," she read aloud, her finger moving along the parchment. *"The first, to hear of the sickness of my mistress, whom I esteem more than all the world, and whose health I desire as my own, so that I would gladly bear half your illness to make you well."*

My cracked lips broke into a smile, causing the fragile, dry skin there to fracture into more tiny wounds. I winced and put a hand to my lips. When I removed it I saw spots of blood on my white fingers. "Henry has a great terror of illness, mother," I rasped. "That is a compliment above all others, if you understand his fears."

She looked up at me and pursed her lips. I knew she was thinking that he should have been willing to take *all* my illness, but I would settle for even half from a man so obsessed with avoiding sickness as my Henry.

"The second," she continued, *"from the fear that I have of being still longer harassed by my enemy, Absence, much longer, who has hitherto given me all possible uneasiness, and as far as I can judge is determined to spite me more*

because I pray to God to rid me of this troublesome tormentor. The third, because the physician in whom I have the most confidence, is absent at the very time when he might do me the greatest pleasure; for I should hope, by him and his means, to obtain one of my chief joys on this earth; that is the care of my mistress. Yet for want of him I send you my second, and I hope that he will soon make you well. I shall then love him more than ever. I beseech you to be guided by his advice in your illness. In so doing I hope to see you again, which will be to me a greater comfort than all the precious jewels in the world.

Written by that secretary, who is, and for ever will be, your loyal and most assured servant,

H. (A.B). R."

"I must write to him," I said slowly, feeling my throat burn. "He must know that I am recovered." My mother took out writing materials and gave them to me, but my hand shook so badly that I could not write and in the end I gave her the quill and dictated my response to her.

"My good lord and King,

This day has found me awakened from that fever which so threatened my life. For days now I have known nothing of this world and it was feared by my family and the great doctor that you, in your graciousness, sent to me, that I should be called forth to join God, never to see Your Majesty again.

But this day I have woken to the great relief of your great doctor and my family. It is due to the kindness and care of Your Majesty that I have recovered in body, and due to the will of God that I have recovered at all. I give thanks to both powers for my recovery. It seems that God wishes for us to be together; in preserving my life, our Holy Father hath shown His approval of our marriage. He has tested my resolve and I have come back to the world in which you live. I have been tested by God, my lord, and He has allowed me to live, to return to you. In this I take the greatest comfort.

I long to see Your Majesty, to hold you in my arms, and to see your face again. Once I am recovered I hope to be able to see you, my love, for this has been the hardest of separations we have yet endured. Yet I remain in this world and as long as I do remain, I am your servant, mistress and friend, and I send to you all my love and wishes for us to be reunited, and

I remain, as ever, your servant,

Anne Boleyn."

My mother sent the letter as soon as she could and in time, still in my sick bed, I received a reply filled with relief and gratitude. Henry's letter was almost incoherent for the joy he professed in hearing I was alive and out of danger. Over and over his words assured me of his love, and of his impatience to see me. He was giving thanks daily to God, he told me, and now nothing would stand in the way of our union. He sent me a gift of a freshly-killed buck, to replenish my health, for he had heard that good, rich meat was a helpful food for invalids.

My mother *tsked* at the venison, and only allowed me a little. She did not hold with Henry's idea that this meat was beneficial for invalids. She fed me on chicken broth with boiled rice, and pottages of the same bitter herbs I had eaten in my recovery. She gave me as much beer and ale as I could drink, also infused with those herbs, but would not allow wine, saying that it was too acidic for my fragile stomach. She smothered my lips in concoctions of clean goose fat, sanicle and parsley to heal them. She bathed my reddened skin with lemon juice, and washed my body in rose water. Once I was clean, it was remarkable how much better I felt, and, snuggling into fresh covers of cool linen, I went back to sleep. I slept with Henry's letter in my hand that night. It made me feel closer to him.

When I awoke the next morning, feeling a great deal better, Doctor Butts was at my bedside. As I opened my eyes, I saw he was leafing through a book. My heart froze. When I had fallen sick, my copy of the Tyndale translation of the New Testament had been on a table in my room. It was that book he was now holding.

I sat up quickly, and immediately felt a great pain in my head. Seeing me wince, Butts set the book on the bed and reached out to touch my head. "You still need to have a care for yourself, my lady," he said calmly. His finger reached out and tapped the book. "And if I were you, I would have more care for where you leave such books as these." He tapped the top of the book. A glimmer in his eyes and a smile on his lips told me however, he did not disapprove of the text.

"You… have read it too?" I asked warily.

He nodded. "I have found much within this book that I never knew before," he said. "When I went to Church and listened to the priests there, I never felt as inspired as when I read this work." He looked about him, even though there was no one in the room. "Although, both for my position, and for my life, my lady, I would that none knew of my evangelical sympathies."

"If you keep my secrets, Doctor," I said. "Then I shall keep yours."

He hesitated. "My lady," he said. "There are men of my acquaintance, poor scholars, but men with minds that are keen, quick and eager for new knowledge, who would greatly benefit from the patronage of one such as you, who is high in favour with the King, who understands the worth of such books, and who is in a position to aid them."

"They are reformists?" I asked.

Again he nodded. "Children of God, just as I am, and just as I suspect you are…" he trailed off. "I put myself in peril to admit these things to you, madam, but I believe you think the same way I do."

I was nervous. It could be a trap. Thomas More had many men about the country engaged in spying for him and the Church. Butts could be More's agent, or that of Wolsey, but there was something in his air and in his eyes that told me this was not so. "I would be willing to be a patroness to such scholars, Doctor, as long as they obeyed the King's law as far as is possible, and did not sanction rebellion against it." It was a careful answer, but one which opened great possibilities.

"When you return to court, my lady, may I ask permission to present some cases to you… so that you might judge each scholar's worthiness and perhaps support their educations?"

I smiled. "I have more money than I need, Doctor. If some of that can go towards the further education of worthy men, who believe in reform of the corruptions of the Church, then I would be glad to share it with them."

"Then I shall visit you often, my lady," he said and put a thick finger to his lips. "And as you say, I shall keep your secrets, as you keep mine."

Chapter Twenty-Five

Hever Castle
Summer 1528

Some days later, when my mother was by my father's bedside, I found myself alone in my room with she whom my mother had called the *cunning woman* of the village. I awoke from another deep sleep of dreamless darkness. I could sleep all the hours of the day, it seemed, and still be tired enough to sleep through the night. I awoke but for short periods to eat, drink and to hear news, and then I would sleep again. My mother assured me that my body required it, and I had not the will to resist. I dreamed of demons no more. My rest stole me away me into warm, safe, darkness free of all thought and word. That day, with my mind and eyes fogged from this deep sleep, I awoke to hear prayers being muttered in broken Latin near me and looked up into the watchful eyes of the old woman sitting by my side.

"You pray for me?" I whispered harshly. My throat was still devoid of natural wetness by the rage of the fever. I coughed, and a dry retch shuddered through me.

"I do, my lady." She helped me to sit up so that she could hand me a cup in which ground up leaves and roots bobbed in bright ale. I drank gratefully and deeply, and then made a face at the terrible taste as I swallowed. "What *is* this?" I asked.

"Eyebright and Angelica." She nodded. "They do not taste pretty, I understand, Mistress, but they will help with your breathing. Your illness has brought with it some strange complications; your father does not suffer from this wheezing as you do." She pushed the cup at me. "Drink up now, my lady. Although you may not appreciate the taste, it took me many hours to gather these herbs fresh for you this morning.

And you are lucky it was me, Mistress, and not another doing the picking, for Eyebright and Angelica are easy to confuse with dangerous plants, by those who know not what they are doing."

"My mother called you a *cunning woman*," I said, eyeing the cup hesitantly. "Does she mean you are a witch?" The woman snorted and her coal eyes crinkled as she looked closely at my face. She put the cup to one side and with a cool hand she touched my forehead, grunting with satisfaction. She did not answer me. "Am I well as yet?" I asked.

"You are one who has many questions, my lady," she said, amusement twitching at her lips. "To answer all of them may take some time, but to the last asked, yes... I believe that you are free from the sweat. It was lucky your mother called me when she did... There were many others too far gone for me to save them. My daughters have been working at all hours God sends through the village to save those they could, and help to bury those they could not. But it seems you are very valuable, not just to your mother and to your family, as a daughter should be, but to higher powers."

I sighed, sitting back on my pillows. "The King was kind to send his doctor to me."

"Indeed," agreed the old woman with a wry smile. "There were many in this land who should have been glad of the honours you received, although what they teach these *doctors* is beyond me. The man seemed to know nothing of herb lore... Still, he did his work well... with my help." The old woman breathed in deeply. "For all the fuss that was made of you, my lady, I might have thought you were the Queen... You seem to be rather important for one so young." She handed me the cup again, this time with insistent eyes.

I obediently sipped her foul potion. "You did not answer my first question," I protested. "I would know... does your wisdom come from good or from evil?"

She raised her eyebrows. "There is no wisdom, no *true* wisdom, surely, that comes from evil, Mistress."

"So you are not a witch?"

"I do God's work, as far as I am able, my lady." She brushed at her crude gown of brown, ugly wool. "All the wisdom and the power that lies in my hands is there at His will and grace and that of no other. If I was able to save you, it was because God wished you saved, my lady. He has a plan for all of us."

"Then you are a true Christian?" I asked, still suspicious.

"I am the servant of God as we all are, my lady."

"Then we think alike," I said feeling more assured. Although I did not believe that my mother would knowingly employ a servant of the Devil, she may have been deceived by one. But the crone seemed convincing in her protestations, and the Latin she had spoken over me, although uncouth and ill-said, were words of the Bible. "What is your name?"

She smiled widely, showing spare and broken stumps of blackened teeth. Her laugh was a throaty cackle, warm and amused. "When you reach my age you find you have many names, my lady," she said. "They called me Maude when I was a young maid. They called me *good mistress* when I cured them and *good mother* when I delivered their babes into the world. When I could not save them, they oftentimes called me *hag* or *crone*... But such is only to be expected. And now that I am old and have given two husbands unto Heaven and borne many children, they called me Mother Stephens, for the name of my second husband."

"You have my thanks, Mother Stephens," I said, "for saving my life and that of my father."

"I was glad to be called, Mistress." She rose with some difficulty due to her aged, stiff limbs, and hobbled to the fire, returning to my bedside with a plate of herbs and boiled roots. Her fingers were swollen and red about the joints, and she had trouble holding the plate, although she did not drop it. "As I said, it seems you are a valuable young lady, one worth saving, and I have long honoured your family who rule the lands on which I was born and on which I live now. You mother has ever been a good lady to me and my village and has offered us the generosity of her table and of her charity. If you are anything like her, then you are worth any effort that is in my power to make."

She passed me the plate. Dark green parsley and feverfew lay on it along with cool wispy strands of chamomile and fennel. There were also stripped, cooked roots and other herbs that I recognised not. "They will aid your rest, and promote healing," she advised. "And protect your sleep from nightmares of the future, or the past."

I hesitated and then started to chew the herbs as she had instructed. "You know of my dreams?"

"You were screaming in your sleep as the fever worked its way through your blood," she told me. "There were demons pursuing you, my lady; such dark spirits hunt us when we are at our most vulnerable… They come to test us when we are weak. You fought them off. I heard you struggle against them in your dreams… That is always a good sign. When I heard you fighting them I knew you were recovering."

"Do your powers reach to see the future?" I asked as the peppery taste of parsley and the fennel caused my mouth to water, painfully, for the first time since my illness. I put a hand to my jaw, cringing. She handed me ale to wash them down.

"Sometimes," she admitted cautiously. "Shadows of the future can be shown to some, by the powers of the Almighty… if He wills it, so can it be. But the future is oftentimes uncertain … and dangerous to gaze too closely upon. The future depends on our choices, and sometimes, knowing what the outcome may be, we alter what should have been… or wander right into what we wished to avoid." Her black eyes were fixed on mine and all hints of a smile had vanished from her face. "What is it you would know, Mistress?"

Tears sprang to my eyes as the silent fear that had plagued me since I woke from my fever escaped my mouth. "Shall I still be able to bear a child?" I asked. Tears slid down my pale cheeks. "This fever… You do not know of it affecting fertility?"

Her black eyes narrowed and softened; perhaps she had thought I would ask something else. She touched my face with a light hand. "You will bear children, my lady." I choked on my relief. "I see children in your future," she continued softly, her eyes far away. "Children can be a woman's greatest consolation… and sometimes they can be her greatest sorrow, too."

"What do you mean?" Her face was grave and her eyes shone no more. Her form seemed to merge with the bed hangings, with the painted cloth on the chamber walls. For a moment, I thought I saw another presence looking out at me from behind her black eyes. I shivered. "What do you mean?" I asked in little more than a whisper. "What do you know of my future? Of my children?"

Her eyes did not break from mine. Her face was a mask, unreadable and watchful. I trembled. It was as though I looked into the eyes of the last Fate, that creature whose job it was to snip the threads of mortal lives with her clever knife.

"The future is not something I would cause any to look into too deeply," she advised slowly. "We choose the paths we walk because we are the people we were born to be; the people that God made us to be. I see great extremes in you, Mistress Boleyn, great love and great passion I see but also great danger and hate. But you must tread your path yourself, not be guided by the ramblings of an old woman." She broke off and suddenly she did not seem terrible and ancient, supernatural or mystical. I blinked. My terror vanished. Perhaps in the aftermath of the fever I was imagining things.

She rose. "I must go and see my other patient. Who complains a lot more than his daughter about my herbs..." She smiled. "You chew those herbs and rest, Mistress. I have opened the window shutter to let in a little air and it will make you feel better. Some people would say that was dangerous, but I have ever believed in the benefits of clean country air."

As she rose to leave I sat forward in my bed. "Will I bear a son?" I asked her as she reached the door.

Her shoulders lifted as she inhaled deeply and without turning she replied. "You will bear a son, my lady, perhaps more than one. But they will bring you no solace, I fear." She turned her head slightly. I could see one side of her face only. "Those extremes I spoke of, my lady? Please be wary of them. You seem like a sweet child inside. Be wary of the fire that not only heats and warms, but burns and consumes. There is no escaping that once it is inside you. Learn to control the passions within you, to tame them to your will, rather than being ruled by them... and you will live to be a happy woman."

The old woman left the room. I did not see her again.

Some years later I remember my mother telling me that old Mother Stephens had died and the village had helped to pay for her burial in the churchyard at Hever. Although she was a peasant, my mother gave money for her to lie in a proper grave and gave orders that flowers were to be placed for her each summer on the anniversary of the time that she had helped our family. Her many daughters continued her work, tending to the sick and injured in the small village, using their mother's wisdom to bring comfort and promote health.

As to her warnings to me, who knew then what she meant? Once I was well enough to rise from my bed, I began to dismiss her words as the confused wonderings of an old woman, who wanted to appear important and all-knowing by muttering loose portents about the future. And yet, I drew comfort from her promise that I would bear sons. A strange mixture of scepticism and belief occupied me then. I chose that which I wanted to believe and dismissed all I did not. It is often the way; we see and believe what we wish to.

Soon enough though, as I recovered, I was thinking only of one thing. I wanted to see Henry.

Chapter Twenty-Six

Hever Castle
Summer 1528

My father recovered the same week as I, and, strong man that he was, he was up and walking before I had left my chamber. When I first saw him, he strode over, embraced me, and laughed as he held me back from him to assess me. "Still thin and pale," he said, his voice gritty.

"As you are also, father," I said, moving to a window seat. He did not remonstrate with me for my boldness.

"The fever was a terrible happening." He nodded. "But we are all through the worst now and soon enough you shall return to the King..." Pulling a rolled sheet of parchment from his sleeve, he handed it to me. "The King, who has been writing daily for news of you, demands that you go to him as soon as you are well." He smiled. "I think we should wait until you are properly recovered so he may see you at your most beautiful."

I was still thinking of something he said previously. "What of Mary?" I asked. "You say that we are *all* recovered, my lord father, but my brother Will is dead. What provision is there for Mary and her children?"

My father glanced at me with astonishment. "She will be well cared for through the provisions of Carey's will and her own dowry. Our family is not expected to take care of her or her children, although we may arrange another marriage for her when you marry the King. To marry Mary off now would be premature. There will be time enough to find Mary a useful, profitable, match once we have settled the King's *Great Matter*." His glance became stern. "There should be no thoughts in your head but the acquisition of our goals, Anne;

to see you wedded and bedded to the King of England; to see our family rise in station and title. Mary will understand, as she must, that this is our family's sole aim."

I stared at him, sadness wrenching my heart. For all the things I had thought about my father, I had never suspected he would ever abandon his own child in her time of need. "You care nothing for the suffering of your daughter..." The words came harshly from my throat. His eyes narrowed and went flat with anger.

"My sole care," he said slowly in an ominous tone, "*is* the advancement of my daughter."

He had answered my question. "I beg your leave to retire, sir," I said in a stiff tone. "I feel unwell."

He rose, turned from me, and walked off, saying nothing. Anger, and a most confusing, intense feeling of disappointment, welled up inside me. As I stalked off to my room to throw myself on the luxurious bed, padded with the rich covers and furs that Henry had sent, it occurred to me that if our father would do nothing for Mary, then perhaps I could. I sent word to her secretly so that my father would not know I was disobeying him; a letter with a costly jewel and a bag of coin enclosed. I wrote of my sorrow for the loss of Will. I could hardly believe he was no longer here. He had been a good man, and I had loved him as a brother. I told Mary I would do all I could to help her. I would see Mary was taken care of, and if I could not rely on our father to help, then I knew where to turn.

Sad news came from court later that week. Bess... my good, faithful, kindly Bess, had died of the sweat along with many others at court. The doctor who had tended to her had also died. I received the missive with dread, thinking it was ill news about George, or Henry, and was therefore almost relieved to read that it concerned them not. Feeling guilty for thinking so, I rode out to Bess' family. Her father was a tenant on our lands. The sweat had not reached their small farm, and, apart from in the larger towns and cities it was almost gone from Kent, so I believed I was safe. I took Bess' family a purse of money and consoled them, telling her wretched, sobbing mother that Bess was the best maid I had ever known. I promised to take their younger daughter named Katherine, or Kate for short, into my service in Bess' place. This would mean that the family would benefit from her wages and position.

Although they were distraught to hear of poor Bess, they were grateful for my offer and promised to send Kate to me later that month. She was no more than eleven years old, with wispy fair hair and wide, pale blue eyes. She stared up at me, bobbed a curtsey, and declared that she would do all she could to live up to her sister's reputation.

I did not tell Bess's parents that their daughter was buried in a mass grave near to the Abbey of Waltham. I could not. It was too much to see them brought so low already. I assured them that I would give money to the Church for prayers to be said in her memory. Although I had read much to make me doubt that God required prayers to be said, or bought, from the Church to allow His children into Heaven, I knew that these folk believed in such things. I wanted to bring them comfort, and so I hid my own feelings. When I rode back to Hever, my father berated me for putting myself in danger.

"But there are no new cases within our lands, my lord father." I took my riding gloves off and my hands trembled with weariness. The short ride had taken much from me. I would need to rest to recover my strength. "I promise you, there was no sign of the sweat at their farm. I *had* to go, father... Bess was my servant and my responsibility. It is better that they hear ill news from me, than never to know what became of their daughter at all."

"Send a servant next time!" he shouted, glowering at me. "We cannot risk you again! If you are gone, Anne, then so are all our plans and hopes!"

I sniffed, turning to him with my chin raised in defiance and my back straight with bristled anger. My tone was cool, even if my emotions were not. "It is pleasing, father, to hear you are so concerned for me... Although less pleasing that my value to you is measured solely by your ability to further your own ambitions through me."

I swept past him and into the house, leaving him sputtering. I was angry at him for his treatment of Mary, and I knew, now, there was nothing I could do or say that would really drive him from me. It hurt that he was not, as my mother had been, relieved to see me live merely because I was his daughter. My father was only glad of my victory over Death because of the position and prestige he would gain when I married the King. Such truths stung, even though I had known his ways all my life... When you find yourself disappointed in a parent, it is a cruel and harsh sensation. When you understand that he sees you only as a means to an end and does not cherish and love you as a parent should, the pain, and the sense of loneliness that pain brings with it, is indescribable.

But I hardened my heart. At least I had a mother, a sister and a brother yet living who loved me *for* me. My father's attitude increased my conviction that I should help Mary, if I could. If he would not do his duty to his children, then we would have to look after each other.

Tom and Margaret Wyatt wrote from Allington. Their father had refused permission for them to visit until the sweat was entirely gone from Hever's household. Some of the servants were still recovering, but in truth we had been fortunate. Many other households, who did not have the likes of Dr Butts and Mother Stephens at their service, had lost many. Of those who had sickened at Hever, we lost only two; one kitchen maid, and one young page. The sickness did seem, in general, to have carried off more men than women, and Margaret protested to her father that this meant she should be allowed to come and see me, but he refused.

"Soon enough, my dear friend," Margaret wrote, *"we will be together again. Rest in the knowledge that we pray for you every day and that we both long to see you again."*

Bridget wrote to me too. She had lost, Catherine, one of her youngest children to the sweat, but her husband, Nicholas Harvey, and the rest of her enormous brood were safe. She was distraught for the death of her daughter, and told me Catherine had been a sweet child, but she was grateful that the rest of her family had been spared. I sent a gift to Bridget of a silver ring with a skull on it, as a death memento for Catherine, and tried to console her.

Later that week, the welcome figure of my brother rode up to Hever and before he had even dismounted his horse, I was by his side, laughing and jumping up and down like a child. He leapt gamely from his horse and embraced me. I had never been so happy. This time of illness and darkness had made me realise the precious friendship I shared with my brother, and how close I had come to losing it.

We spent some time together in the great hall by the fire, in the long gallery, walking and talking and, on warm afternoons, we wandered in the gardens. The air was no longer polluted by the scent of burning vinegar. The sweat was abating all over England, although in London it was still rife. George told me that all the nobility had fled London, and were either tending their sick, or in their own homes, warding off the disease by seclusion, or use of charms, prayers and even spells.

"Tom told me he visited you." George plucked a rose from my mother's beautifully tended crop and handed it to me. "I am glad the two of you are truly friends once again."

"And I," I said, lifting the glorious bloom to my nose, inhaling the sweet scent. "Tom has been a good friend and worthy companion to all of us. He risked a great deal for us, George. I will find a way to repay him for his kindness."

George looked at me slyly. "The King has been seeking Tom's companionship also, even before this disease sent him into seclusion," he confided. "Partly for his good friendship, and partly to assure himself and others that there was never anything between the two of you."

I looked sharply at my brother. "There never *was* anything between me and Tom. Henry knows that, surely?"

"Nothing that would show now, anyway," George said, earning himself a cuff around the head.

"There was never anything between me and Tom!" I exclaimed. "He asked me to be his mistress long ago and I refused. Do you doubt me? Or do you think that I only mean what I say when a king asks me?"

George chortled. "Nay, sister. I should not doubt your word for the wide world… After all, soon I shall call you not sister first, but Queen, and I should not be foolish enough to displease my Queen for anything."

I held out my hand and laced my fingers through his. "You, above all people George, shall always call me sister first."

George smiled but it quivered into a grimace. "I thought we were lost to each other," he said seriously. "I feared for you."

"And I feared for you, George. We are a close family, but perhaps you and I are the best of friends in it."

"Then so shall it be," he nodded. "I shall protect you and your interests always."

"As I shall you and yours," I promised.

We walked into the house, and I gave the rose to one of my servants to dry and preserve. I wanted to keep this token of this day, to remind myself of all I had, and all I had nearly lost.

Chapter Twenty-Seven

Hever Castle
Summer 1528

George was with us for a week. Each day when I awoke, my first happy thought was that my brother was nearby. After so long a time of worrying for him, fearing for his life, it was glorious to know I could come downstairs to find him there. We rode out through the marshlands and hunted together in the woods and fields. We spoke on matters of religion, reform and the court. George was one of the few people I could truly unleash my heart with, and he with me. Even with Henry I had not been entirely open on my thoughts on reform. But with my brother, I could discuss anything. One day, I found him reading a pamphlet, and asked what it was.

"A report on the visions of the Holy Maid of London," he said and made a face of dissatisfaction. "She pleads with the people of England, asking that we act against the horrors that *she* believes have been brought upon England by Lutheran beliefs infiltrating into minds and thoughts. She pleads for the common people to remain within the bosom of the Church, and tells them if they hold true to their belief in the Church, in its leaders and in the Pope, then we will have no more plagues come to punish us." He tossed the paper to a sideboard and shook his head. "That woman seems to hold more authority over the minds of the people than any other."

Elizabeth Barton, known as the Holy Maid of London, or the Nun of Kent, was a serving wench who had, in recent years, risen to great prominence in the popular imagination. Born a peasant, Elizabeth had been working in a house in Aldington when she began to have visions, both of the future and of the Virgin, of Christ and of God Himself. A voice came from her which was not her own at such times. Her lips would not move, but a deep voice would speak of her visions to those who gathered to hear her.

She had grown increasingly famous and popular. The common people flocked to hear the unearthly, and some believed, divine, voice which emanated from her. Many members of the clergy supported her, and some of her prophesies had come true; she had, for example foretold the death of a child in the house in which she served. She was a staunch defender of the Church, and had urged people to look to their religious lives with more strength and honesty. Henry and Wolsey had both met with her in the past, and found her impressive. None of her visions were at odds with the Church, and so she had been largely accepted by the clergy and was well-beloved by the common people. Some at court were, however, suspicious of her predictions and her motives. Sir Thomas More had noted, at times, predictions were attributed to Elizabeth Barton that she had not actually made. He suspected this was done by her admirers, who wanted to increase the glory credited to her name. There were some who suspected she was not divine, and was merely acting a part to gain notoriety and attention.

The Nun of Kent was most outspoken on the matter of heresy, and condemned it utterly in all forms. She thought Lutherans and others who worked for Church reform were simple heretics. She would not accept the value of their theology, and condemned them. For this blindness, this lack of vision, I did not think Elizabeth was a good influence on the common people.

But Elizabeth's message was clear and simple, which appealed to many. Elizabeth's message; to obey the Church and her clergy in all matters, to trust them to know what was good for us, to never question their practises, or note their sins, was dangerous in my opinion. Elizabeth Barton and people like her would have us all acting as mindless dullards, devoid of thought or conscience. But to the Church, and to many of her followers, she was an angel who could do no wrong; a holy woman, a living saint, a soul blessed by God.

"She is supported by the Archbishop Warham and Bishop John Fisher," I said, taking up the note and glancing at it. "Henry met with her some time ago, and he found her most convincing."

"The girl is a fraud." George curled his lip derisively. "A poor servant, who seeks to make herself into a prophetess to gain wealth and acclaim!"

"She *refuses* all wealth and riches, George," I protested, putting the paper down. No matter if I did not believe in the Nun's visions, I could not allow him to speak falsehoods of her either. "She lives in a bare cell and gives her wealth to the Church. I do not believe she is truly touched with the Holy Vision, but I will not allow you to say such about her… Whatever her motives, I believe *she* has true faith in her own visions. She believes what she says is true."

"She does it, then, for notoriety," he said. "The King only likes her because she has often spoken *against* rebellion, but he will not like what she has been saying lately."

"What?" I asked, grabbing at the note again. I had only skimmed the words previously. I knew that George would find Elizabeth Barton irritating because she was so set against the works of men like Luther, and others, whom he admired. I had not thought there was something new here.

"She speaks out against the King's *Great Matter*, sister…" George said. "She opposes it, saying that the judgement of the Pope who issued the original dispensation for Henry and Katherine to marry was correct. She says that the union was honest in the eyes of God and there is no sin attached to it… *And* she has proof of this… The *Virgin Mary* came to visit her one night and told her this was truth."

I let out a snort of annoyance, and George grinned. "So…" he teased. "Not so stalwart in your defence of her now, are we, sister?"

I scowled. "I said that I believed she was not out for wealth, *brother*," I snapped. "I also said I believe that *she* believes in the truth of her visions, not that *I* believed in them!"

"To follow that line of thought, I would have to be a cleverer man than I am…" he shook his head. "But you must understand, sister… there are many who think highly of her opinion. There are those who will follow her lead. The trial of Henry's marriage inches closer, and the Nun of Kent has thrown her support behind Katherine. Another supporter for Katherine's side, and an influential one, could cause problems."

"And Wolsey will no doubt inform Henry of this with great relish," I spat bitterly. "He tried to convince the King that the sweat was an expression of God's displeasure with the annulment proceedings. Now he will have the Holy Nun on his side!" I frowned. "This is not good for us."

"So you understand my concern."

"Of course… now," I replied. "Henry is a superstitious man. He will not like this development."

"She has not openly said that the King is in the wrong," he mused. "Only that his *belief* is wrong. She does not dare to openly insult the King, but says he requires guidance."

"And how long before she starts to blame me, as all about the country seem to, brother? How long before she stirs the people up and they think to rebel?"

"She speaks often enough against rebellion, Anne," he assured me. "She promotes peace and calmness… I do not think that will become an issue."

"That is true, thank you, George," I murmured. "But still... I like not that Wolsey has another weapon to use against me. You see how clever he was when the sweat raged? He knows Henry's terror of sickness... Wolsey thought he could pounce on his master when he was at his most vulnerable. He thought if he scared him with God's displeasure then Henry would give up. He must have thought he could later convince Henry that God simply did not want him to marry *me*, and then the fat bat could place his own choice for Queen on the throne...." I let out a tense breath. My cheeks tingled. My blood was hot and irritated in my veins. "And now, Wolsey will no doubt use this peasant girl to further his own wishes. He will use the Nun against me, I know it."

"We will keep an eye on her, *and* on Wolsey, Anne," George said, standing. "I promise you."

I smiled at his concerned face. "Have you written to Jane, as yet?" I asked and was rewarded with a sour expression and a curdled sigh. "She was frantic about you, George," I said earnestly. "Her father had to restrain her from flying to your side in your sickness."

George snorted, walking away from me. "A good thing that he did!" he exclaimed. "For having her weeping and mooning over me would have surely finished the last of my strength!"

"Do not be so cruel to one who loves you," I warned. "And she does, George! More than anything."

George turned to me and glowered. "Jane loves a vision and a hope," he said unpleasantly. "She does not know or love me, sister. She looks on me and allows all her dreams flow into my skin. In truth, she knows nothing of me. She is shrill and bitter when I stay away, and when I come to her she clings, accuses and weeps. What man could stand to come home to such a creature? She has beauty a-plenty on her face and in her form, and in that alone I am blessed for at least with much wine within me I can stand to lie with her… But inside, Anne… she is a hidden and strange creature. I hate the way she treats me, as though I am her *property*, as though I can go nowhere and do nothing unless she can see me… She opens my personal letters, goes through my trunks and chests, and produces items she has stolen from me to accuse me of whatever fantasy has popped into her head that day!" He shook his head. "Accuse me not of cruelty, sister, for I am more kind to her than she deserves. Another man would have cast her off, as our father has already suggested. It is only through pity that I do not do as he has asked. I do not beat her, I do not send her away, but love her, I cannot."

I stared at him. "She goes through your things?" I asked, rather shocked.

He laughed without humour. "Aye, and reads my papers, questions my friends in her sly, jealous way, and is at times vindictive to women she thinks I have bedded about court." He ran a hand through his hair. "I do not say that I have been faithful," he admitted. "I do not say I am a saint. But I am no more a villain than other men, and I never bring my mistresses into the house to shame her. I am discreet, and so she should have no cause to be angered at me."

I sighed. "I am sorry, brother," I said. "I did not know things were so bad."

"Sometimes they are not," he admitted. "Sometimes, she can be a sweet and loving woman, and if I have enough wine or ale in me, I find her bonny." He heaved a sigh to echo mine. "But she is not what my heart wishes for, Anne." The corners of his lips lifted into a gentle, if somewhat envious smile. "I do not love her as you love Henry, or as he loves you."

I went to my brother and put my arms about him. "If you do not wish her there, then I will not bring her to my household again," I declared. "For although I pity Jane, you are my brother and I am loyal to you first."

He shook his head. "She likes being near you, Anne," he said and chuckled at the surprise on my face. Jane and I had known each other for years, but I never would have thought of us as close… I had never thought she actually enjoyed my company. "She likes being close to the intrigue," he continued, explaining himself. "It makes her happy, and occupies her so that she is not haunting me… Keep her with you."

I agreed, and we went on to talk of other matters, but I was sad. George did not recognise his own faults in this relationship. Whilst Jane, clearly, had overstepped many boundaries, I suspected that all of this bitter spite and underhandedness was born of her love for him and jealousy of others. If he would only take the time to show some kindly affection to his wife, even if he did not love her, then their marriage would likely be a happier one, and Jane would be an easier woman to live with.

Chapter Twenty-Eight

Eltham Palace
Late Summer 1528

As the fields of wheat and barley about Hever began to crackle under the hot sunshine, Henry sent a message that I should meet him at Eltham Palace. The sweat was dying down in the city, he wrote, but Eltham was far enough from the heart of London to remain protected from any lingering outbreaks. My servants took me, and my mother, as a chaperone, to meet him.

Henry had not yet arrived when we reached Eltham. I had been here with the court before, of course, as Christmas was often spent here, but in their absence the palace was more beautiful, more silent and calm than I had known. In the wake of the illness that had beset me, I relished the tranquillity of the great, empty palace.

This was an ancient palace where generations of kings had lived and held court. This was where Henry had spent his childhood. The great hall, its stupendous roof towering over all beneath it, had watched over the young Henry as he impressed the philosopher Erasmus with his intelligence. The moat stretched around the palace and made it like an island standing in the middle of the most beautiful of lush, green parks. Great gnarled oaks were dotted through open parkland and clumped here and there to form small woodlands. The inside of the palace was hung with tapestry and rich, painted cloth, and in the apartments Henry had ordered to be made ready for me, there was expensive carpet made in the Turkish fashion, hangings of velvet decorated with gold tassels, and the walls were lined with open cupboards of silver and gold plate.

When I arrived, the servants were still cleaning some of the tapestry. Such glorious and expensive items required the kindest and most delicate of care. Murk and grit were teased from them with pieces of moist bread, and then the crumbs swept away with fine horsehair brushes. The floors were made of fine oak, but had been painted to look as though they were marble, the finer work being done by teasing grey and black paint through white with the feathers of swans and geese.

Portraits of Henry's ancestors, his mother particularly prominent, were dotted throughout the palace. Henry kept many portraits of his beloved mother here, at Eltham, where he perhaps remembered her best. That great queen had died in the Tower of London, making the ultimate sacrifice for her husband and her country. When their eldest son and heir, Arthur, had died, leaving Katherine a widow, Queen Elizabeth had tried to bring forth another male heir. But she had died in the attempt, and the child, a girl, went with her to the grave.

Henry did not speak of his mother a great deal, and perhaps that silence, more than anything, told me how special she had been to him, and how much he had loved her. The pain of his grief and loss caused him to close up like a clam when it came to speaking of her... With Henry, it seemed, it was always easy to tell how much he had adored someone, by how little he talked of them when they were lost to him. I was to learn this better, over the years I spent with him.

Walking through the empty palace, the faces of Henry's mother, father, sisters and brother staring down on me, I felt as though I were standing shoulder to shoulder with Henry's family. I whispered to the portraits of Elizabeth of York, asking her to love me, as she had loved her son, and to approve of our match even from Heaven. It was not rational, I know, but more often than not we creatures of this flesh do things which are not rational, but which make sense to us all the same.

I stood in the place of Henry's childhood and breathed in the fresh, clean air that surrounded me. The servants were apologetic that they had not finished all their tasks, and scurried to complete them swiftly, but I told them it was better all was done properly, and since my apartments were ready in any case, it mattered little to me.

On the night I arrived, I sat alone by the ornate fireplace, staring into the flames. My mother was already a-bed. We were to sleep in the same bed, as much for propriety as for warmth and comfort. I watched the reflection of the flames dance over the cast iron fire dogs on either side of the hearth. A decorated screen was usually used to cover the fire in summer, but I had asked for a fire laid this night as mist had rolled in, making the air unusually chilly. The screen, set to one side, had feet fashioned in the likeness of dragons, and upon its centre was Henry's royal badge. It made me feel closer to him, being thus surrounded by his emblems.

Outside in the hallway, torches were set into iron brackets on the walls, but in my rooms Henry had paid for white wax candles set into silver candlesticks and suspended on candelabra from the ceiling. Their light was gentle, warming, and lulled me into nodding at the fireside, a goblet of wine in my hands. I sat upon one of the fine, but few, chairs in the room. Furniture was not plentiful at court; since so many people came to wait upon the King, it was more important to fit them in than it was to decorate the palace with chairs and tables. Henry had chairs of estate in various rooms, and his beds were, of course, his most expensive and highly decorated items of furniture. But aside from that, it was generally cloth and plate which made the rooms glorious.

Each room shone with cupboards and sideboards stuffed with glorious plate; cups, dishes, goblets, plates and ornate salt cellars were a true mark of wealth. A rich man could show off much of his collection thus, and still host an entertainment without using any of the plate he had on display. Being the King, Henry's collection was magnificent. Henry loved clocks, too. He had many standing clocks which chimed upon the hour or the half hour, and were adorned with rubies, diamonds and pearls set into their faces. He had smaller ones which sat amongst his collections of silver and pewter, and clocks that charted not the hours of the day, but the movements of the seas. He loved these clocks almost as much as he loved his most valuable tapestries, one set of which could cost as much as a new warship. Later, when he arrived, he spent much time showing me not only the magnificent faces of these clocks, but their inner workings, too. I was fascinated by the delicate, intricate, whirring innards, and he gloried in explaining them to me.

Henry had ordered my chambers to be adorned with scores of plump and beautifully coloured cushions, so that mother and I could sit upon them if we wanted to sew or read together. There were decorated mirrors of highly polished steel, with Venice gold set about them, fashioned into the curling fronds of grapevines. They hung beside the portraits of Henry's family, and amongst the many beautifully drawn maps of the world upon the walls.

Eventually, coaxed into sleepiness by the warmth of the fire, I went to my bed, taking with me my new maid, young Kate, to help me undress. Wiping my body with linen cloths infused in rose and lavender water, I climbed into my night gown and cloak. Kate brushed my hair, using a cloth underneath to catch any dirt or pests pulled loose by the bristles of the brush, so she would not make a mess for the other maids. If pests were found to have snuck into my tresses, then I would need to wash my hair in an infusion of lady's bedstraw, but most of the time I was free of such insects, unlike many at court. Diligent nightly brushing of a hundred strokes or more not only kept my hair free of dirt and unwelcome inhabitants, but made it shine beautifully too.

I cleaned my teeth with the silver toothpick Henry had given me, and wiped them with a small cloth covered in clean soot which Kate gathered from the wax candles by holding a polished bit of metal against them as they burned. I had learned this method in the court of Mechelen, and always held that it made the breath sweet and the teeth shine white. I would usually chew a small stem of rosemary afterwards, which, although pungent, made my breath sweet in the morning.

My mother was already deep in slumber, and barely moved when I slid underneath the covers. The scent of cloves was on her breath, as her preferred nightly routine involved a tooth powder of cloves. This sweetened her breath, but also provided relief, as her teeth sometimes pained her. I reached out for her, wanting her to take me in her arms. Everything was changing so fast, but there is something constant in the arms of a mother which never changes. Perhaps that is why we long to return to our mothers in times of trouble. They take us back to a place where we were safe, where we were innocent… the perfume of their skin and the warmth of the breath against our heads… that feeling of certainty in a world of change. I nestled against my mother, inhaling the faint rose scent wafting warm from her skin, and in her sleep she put her arms about me as though she felt my need. That night I slept like a child, wrapped in the warmth and comfort of my mother's arms.

Chapter Twenty-Nine

Eltham Palace
Late Summer 1528

Two days later, I was sitting in the gardens near the palace with a book, quietly reading, when I heard a soft footfall and turned. Henry stood with his back to the sun. I blinked; for a moment it was as though I saw a vision of Hercules, or Alexander. As though Henry were a god of old, crowned by the glory of the sun.

"Anne," Henry murmured and ran towards me. I went to rise but he was by my side before I could get up. I laughed with joy as he thumped to his knees and covered my face and neck with kisses, his hands cupping my chin and stroking my cheeks. Eventually I pushed him away and laughed.

"This is no way for a subject to greet her sovereign!" I cried. "You should have allowed me to stand and honour you, my lord."

Henry had not moved his hands from my face and he shook his head. "You rise to no one, my Anna." His hands dropped from my face and he suddenly seemed downcast and subdued.

"Henry…" I moved towards him with fear in my heart. "What is it?"

Despite his warm welcome, the manner in which he was acting was strange. I feared for a moment he had decided to abandon me, to abandon the chance of leaving Katherine. Perhaps Wolsey had got to him… burrowed into a place in his heart where his fears were deepest hidden, and hardest to remove. But, as he spoke, I found this was not the case. In fact, it was quite the opposite.

"I thought I had lost you," he muttered. There was blank desperation in his eyes. "They would not let me come to you," he said heatedly. "You must believe me, Anne, I would have been with you as soon as I heard but they would not let me. All I wanted was to ride to you and I could not. The simplest of peasants could have run to his sweetheart but I... I, the King! I could not."

He grabbed me with a violence that almost scared me and forced a kiss on my lips; it was not a kiss of love, but one of possession. When he released me there was a look in his eyes that I had never seen before, a look of determination and of defiance. I reached out and stroked his face.

"Henry," I whispered. "I would not have wished your life in peril for any comfort that I could have felt with you by my side. Your advisors were right, you cannot be put at risk; there must be an heir of your body to succeed you. God saved me because He approves of our union, of that I am sure. The humblest peasant could run to his lover because his life is of no importance. But to me, to God, and to all of this realm, *you* are the most precious person. You must not risk yourself, even for me. You are the only one in this world who matters!"

He shook his head violently. "But that is what I feel for *you,* Anne! Without you there is no world, without you there is no life and no future for Henry of England. From now on you will not linger in the confines of your parents' house as I live in the prattling court without you. We shall never be separate again. From now on there shall be Anne and Henry together. In the open! In full view of the world! What have we to be ashamed for? I will not be parted from you again. From now on you shall be recognised as the most important person in my life. All others will bow to you, or answer to me."

"We must still exercise caution, Henry," I implored, unnerved by the passion of his words. "Or we risk opening both of us to slander by those who support Katherine and the Emperor."

"*Damn them*!" he shouted, rising, blood flooding into his face. His eyes danced with blue flame and he clutched his hands into fists as he strode around me.

"*Damn all of them to hell*!" he cried. "Damn all these people who stand in *our* way, in the *true* way, in the *only* way! Damn Katherine and the Emperor and all who would stand against us! All my life I have been ordered around and told what to do by everyone and I am the King! The *King*! Shall I have nothing my way in my own kingdom? Since I was a child, I have been told what to do, first by my father...." His face twisted with scorn and derision. "... My *wise* father... who told me to marry the woman who has cursed my life and murdered my seed! And now foreign princes think they can give orders to Henry of England! I *shall* be master in my own kingdom! I shall rule where I have right and marry where I choose! You are *mine,* Anne. I will have no other. God has saved you to be my rightful wife. I know this to be the truth now! He made you sick to show me how easily I could lose the true way when I do not act fast enough. I will *not* lose you. I will have my way!"

I stood and ran to him. He held me in his arms and kissed me again. There was fire in him and passion in his eyes and in his lips. "You are mine," he said again.

"I am yours." I was crushed against his hot body. "I am yours, Henry."

"My will shall be done, Anne!" he proclaimed. "My will, and no other. I will have what I want! I will have you."

"I am yours," I whispered again, feeling as though I was placing my seal on a pact that could not be broken. "Your will be done, Henry of England."

His embrace was fierce as he held me. There was a strength, a determination within him that I had never felt before. I welcomed it… I welcomed his fire.

His will would be done. I would be his Queen, and he would be the King he had always been destined to be… A king who would rule alone, a king who did not bow and scrape to the wants and wishes of other rulers. We were joined, and there was no one who could set us apart… Not now.

"Your will be done," I said, as though Henry were God Himself.

Chapter Thirty

Eltham Palace
Late Summer 1528

We stayed together at Eltham for a week. During that time we discussed Campeggio's arrival. We were anxious for the papal legate to get to England and commence work. Henry assured me it would not be long before we were wedded, and bedded.

"This is all but a formality," he said carelessly waving his hands, causing their many rings to glitter in the hazy light from the windows. "Wolsey tells me Pope Clement has *already* decided in our favour but he must appear to investigate the matter fully."

I nodded, although my lack of faith in Wolsey's ability and in his desire to achieve this end for us must have shown on my face. Campeggio had taken England's summer plague as another excuse to pause on his journey. He was just outside France now. He sent word that he would resume his journey once it was safe to do so. Henry had written to urge him on, assuring him that the plague was abating, but I knew that Campeggio would continue to delay. There were too many considerations pressing on the Pope for me to believe that he had, indeed, *already* decided to support us. In truth, I was not sure if Campeggio's dawdling was due to the Pope, or Wolsey. Either could be working against me. My lack of faith in Wolsey had only been compounded by hearing that he had sought to use the plague as a tool to pick me from Henry's side… I had not told Henry I had heard of this, yet. But to me it was clear as ice that Wolsey was not working for us…

Henry found my lack of faith in Wolsey disappointing. He sighed and left my chambers to go to his, leaving me pensive. A glorious writing desk was placed in the room, made of dark walnut and bearing the arms of both Henry and Katherine. It seemed, even here, as though she were taunting me with her presence. When I had come here first, full of hope and happiness to see Henry, I had not noted Katherine's badges, or her initials entwined with his in wood or plaster. Now, I saw them everywhere. Perhaps my dissatisfaction had given me new eyes. I was coming to hate seeing them, these small reminders of Katherine everywhere I looked. When I mentioned this to Henry later he frowned. "When you are Queen, my love," he said, gripping my hand almost painfully in his, "I will tear them all out, and replace them with yours."

It made me feel better to know that one day my initials and symbols would sit where Katherine's did now… but still, I did not like to see them. Henry was *mine*, not hers. I wished I could have ordered them all taken out *now*, but it was not within my power to do so. Other things, however, *were* within my power. I told Henry that I was going to write to Wolsey again regarding our *Matter*.

"My Lord Cardinal,

In my most humblest wise that my heart can think, I desire you to pardon me that I am so bold to trouble you with my simple and rude writing; esteeming it to proceed from her that is much desirous to know that your grace does well, the which I pray to God long to continue. I am most bound to pray for you for I do know the great pains and troubles that you have taken for me both night and day. These are never likely to be recompensed on my part, but alonely in loving you, next to the King's grace, above all creatures living. And I do not doubt but the daily proofs of my deeds shall manifestly declare and affirm what I write here to be true. I trust that you do the same.

My lord, I do assure you, I do long to hear from you news of the legate; for I do hope, as they come from you, they shall be very good. I am sure you desire it as much as I and more, an it were possible.

And thus, remaining in steadfast hope, I make an end of my letter,

Written in the hand of her that is most bound to be,

Your humble servant,

Anne Boleyn."

Beyond all the praise and the flattery that was standard fare in letters from one noble to another, there was urging, and there were veiled warnings. The letter reminded the Cardinal I was waiting for news. It reminded him that I held the King's love and implied he did not yearn for the annulment as I did. It was subtle, but I added another element to the letter that was less so. I pressed Henry to add a note at the end. I wanted the Cardinal to know we were together, to know how close we were… to know he had failed to sever me from the King's side.

Henry took up my quill with reluctance. He hated writing. The only letters I had ever known him to write personally were either love letters to me, or angry missives scratched out when someone at court had wrought his displeasure. Still, he did as I asked. He did not like to deny me anything.

"The writer of this letter would not cease, till she had caused me likewise to set my hand, desiring you, though it be short, to take it in good part.

I ensure you that there is neither of us but greatly desireth to see you, and are joyous to hear that you have escaped this plague so well, trusting the fury thereof to be passed, especially with them that keepeth a good diet, as I trust you do.

The not hearing of the legate's arrival in France causeth somewhat to muse; notwithstanding, we trust, by your diligence and vigilancy (with the assistance of Almighty God), shortly to be eased of that trouble. No more at this time, but that I pray God send you as good heath and prosperity as the writer would.

By your loving Sovereign and Friend,

H.R."

I read over the letter, and was satisfied. It showed that Henry and I were together, were writing to the Cardinal as one, and that we were both keen to hear about the proceedings. I smiled as I sealed it with red, dripping wax and pressed my seal on it. Wolsey was about to learn I was not so easy to get rid of as he might have hoped.

Chapter Thirty-One

Eltham Palace
Summer's End 1528

I was determined to ask Henry for help for my widowed sister now that I was reunited with him. Two days into our stay, when we rode together in the great park, I raised the subject. "My lord…" We slowed our horses to a walk, turning them as we approached the edge of the deepening forest. "Would you grant me a favour?"

"You know that all you wish for you just have to ask," he declared passionately. "I will give you all that you wish for, my Anne." Henry did not like being unable to please me by hurrying on Campeggio's arrival. In the absence of being able to please me in this way, he wanted to make up for it in any other way he could.

"It is a favour… for my sister." I saw a flush parade across his cheeks. His jaw clenched.

He gazed at me steadily, a hint of warning in his eyes, as I started to speak of her. Although his relationship with Mary had been acknowledged, although not by name, in the draft dispensations that had been sent to the Pope, we had never actually spoken of her. For me there was a sense of jealousy, embarrassment, and some fear that he might remember her charms; all those paranoid feelings that love can produce in a person. For Henry, it was different. He saw himself as a knight, a true Christian knight. His affairs were kept quiet… apart from me, of course, but then he saw me now as his wife… But his affairs outside of the marriage bed *were* quiet. Mary was over for him now. He had enjoyed her once and now she was gone from his mind. That was the way, with Henry; he left behind all he did not need. It was therefore with some delicacy that I raised the subject. I was reminding him of something he did not wish to remember.

"What of Lady Carey?" he asked stiffly.

"I am sure my lord knows that William Carey, my brother by marriage, sadly died of the sickness that threatened my own life." I hoped that reminding him of how close he had come to losing me would soften his temper. "Mary is now a widow and of much diminished means. Will was a good friend to you, my lord, and his children need your help. My sister has two children to care for, and my father says he is unable to help her."

Henry stopped his horse and looked at me slowly. I had been careful. I had avoided any acknowledgement that Mary had been his lover. There was a hint of embarrassment in his expression, but he looked relieved that I was not about to say anything that should upset his private fantasy of knighthood. I loved him for the boyish look of gratitude he gave me then. With Henry, I had learned, it was often safer to avoid seeing the past truthfully, and merely presenting it to him as he would like to believe it.

"Why can your father not support his own daughter?" Henry asked, ducking under a branch as we rode about the edge of woodland on the crest of a hill.

"He says he has not the means," I lied smoothly, not wishing to say that my father considered Mary's woes of small importance at this moment. Perhaps if my father were to gain some reward, then Mary may stand a hope of benefiting also.

"The Viscount Rochford cannot support a widowed daughter?" Henry leaned back in his saddle and rubbed his hands together. His eyes narrowed as he looked out into the woods. There was good hunting to be had and he itched to do it. We had not ridden as we used to at Windsor and other places when we had met before, as I sometimes tired easily after my brush with the sweat, and he was concerned for my strength. But he longed to return to such days. Henry was always easiest to approach when in the saddle, for he wanted nothing more than to be hunting and so decisions came quickly to him here. I wondered if Wolsey knew this secret about his lord and master, as I did.

"I shall bestow another gift of land upon your father," he said, "and instruct him to use some of it to care for the widow Carey and her children." He grinned, somewhat sheepishly. "They are the cousins of the future prince of this realm... It will not do to see them in rags and tatters, will it?"

I felt so warm towards him then. He would ensure that my poor sister was cared for... I knew that he would. I smiled and leaned over, across my horse to claim a kiss from his lips. His hand grazed my breasts and his fingers crept down the centre of my gown. I pulled back to see the glazed look of desire on his face, the look I was now so used to seeing, and whispered softly, "thank you, my lord."

He removed his hands from me, his face happy and excited, but cautious. At Eltham, we had not been as intimate as we had been before, for his fear that he would tire me. But I knew he was impatient. I knew he wanted me. A touch of wickedness rose in my spirit. I would show my beloved that I was hale and strong once more! I wanted him to touch me without terror...

Without warning I kicked my horse and I flew through the woods faster even than I had intended. I heard him laugh as his horse pounded behind mine and gave chase through the trees and out into the fields, scattering hares and birds as we raced with no aim and no goal. I heard him shout with panic as my horse galloped straight for a tree in the centre of the field. I ducked under the branches of that great oak and smoothly pulled my horse to stand under the cool shade of the tree. Henry's roan stomped to my side a moment later, the rider laughing. "You ride like the Devil was behind you, Anne!" he exclaimed, gazing at me with raw admiration.

"I simply wished to show my King that I am not as fragile as he has thought me," I purred. "And then perhaps His Majesty will dare to kiss and hold me as I have so longed for him to…"

He all but flung himself from his horse and pulled me down. The strength of his arms was awe inspiring as he plucked me from my saddle and lay me on the floor, my back against the twisted oak trunk. He fell upon me and covered my body with his. He moved against me, covering my face and throat with kisses and my body with the desperate strokes of his hard hands.

We embraced with a wild and unreserved passion; my hands in his hair, his fingers tugging at the fastenings of my gown. He moved my legs apart with my gown still covering them, and lay between them. I could feel his eager hardness against my thigh and I did not care. I did not care! I was untamed and reckless. We had come so close to losing each other, and now, all the desperation and horror of that was released.

He put his head to my breasts and groaned, deep and hard, as his body rocked against mine. My body responded to his in ways I did not understand, but just seemed to know, instinctively. There was an aching in me that called out, urging me on, pushing my hips up towards his. My clothing was awry and my hood tumbled from my head, and I cared not. He put his fingers through my dark, unbound hair, kissing me so hard that I thought he would hurt me… but none of it hurt… Every sigh of pleasure that I made only excited him more. I could feel him, desperate and solid against me. He wanted me.

He moved my hand to his breeches and pushed aside the fastenings of his codpiece so that my hand was over his manhood. I felt his body quiver and he moved my hand with his, back and forth along the hard, yet silky surface as he grunted words of love and desire into my neck. "Please, Anne," he almost whimpered, his voice muffled. "Please… help me, my love… my only love... my *Diana*… My Queen."

I felt his body quake with every stroke. I was an innocent at this, but it seemed that I was pleasing him greatly. His hands rummaged up through my skirts and I felt a sudden dart of fear as I thought perhaps he might seek to take my virginity from me in this rough field. In that moment, I knew I was not ready. But that was not Henry's intent. His clever fingers sought out parts of me I barely knew existed. His fingers hunted through my skirts and into my most intimate parts. As his fingers began to stroke and move across me, tickles of pleasure ran through my skin.

Icy sparkles of frost seemed to emerge and explode on my skin. I shivered and cried out. Breathy sounds of pleasure came from my lips. I was nothing anymore. I was not a person. I was sensation alone. I washed on a wave of pleasure, my eyes closed and my head tipped backwards. He brought me to a pinnacle of pleasure where I lost myself in a silver world of bliss. I felt him stiffen. He rolled to one side, spilling his seed onto the ground.

We lay together after that, the King of England and his future wife, sprawled on the ground, half-dressed and spent on the dirt under a tree in a field. I had never known that such pleasures existed… Women at court and my sister, had spoken of the enjoyment of the wedding bed, of course… But I had never imagined it to be like this. I put my arms about him and heard his heavy breathing against my chest. He kissed me gently, his eyes closed. I could not feel bad for what we had done. For so long we had had to satisfy ourselves with but kisses and small pleasures. The force of desire had built in us for more than a year, and still we were not able to be together as man and wife. For the first time in so long, I was at peace. I felt more tranquil than I had ever been. We had not done wrong… I was still intact. We had not endangered my womb and none had seen us here. I ran my hands through his hair and smiled.

"You have been keeping things from me, my love," I muttered huskily, teasing him. "You did not tell me that there were things a man and woman may do together before marriage, things that would not make a child... I thought that we would have no secrets from each other… yet you have been keeping much quiet!"

He laughed, and the sound rumbled against me. "In some ways, my Anne, I am surprised that I should ever need to tell you anything… You seem to know all!" He lifted his head from my chest and looked at me with peaceful, lazy eyes. "And yet, I am glad that I shall be the one to teach you some things, especially about the ways in which a man and a woman may be together."

"We shall still have to be secret," I whispered, "and safe."

He took my hand and kissed it. "I would have no one doubt the validity of our marriage," he agreed, "nor the intact nature of your reputation. But if you were willing, perhaps sometimes I might… teach you, as you say, in private and without risk of a child… until we are married."

I smiled saucily. I felt naughty, and it was a surprisingly good feeling. "You know me, Henry." I twirled his hair in my fingers. "I thirst to learn new things."

He pulled me, giggling, under his eager body once more. We stayed a long time beneath that tree that afternoon, and he showed me much I had never imagined. When we returned to Eltham that night I looked into my mirror and saw a different woman there; one who understood the pleasures that my brother and sister had experienced long before me. That night, Henry came to me, and brought me to ecstasy again. He loved being my guide and finally we had found together a way to release at least a little of our tension.

But we were careful. Although I now allowed Henry to touch and to embrace me and I did the same for him, it was never to go past that point. Although at times in the heat of our passion, he begged me to let him, I did not. Although at times *I* was tempted to give in, I did not.

In the days that followed, we were alive with passion and excitement. We became mischievous and naughty. My mother made herself scarce and each night Henry taught me more. When he knew servants were in a neighbouring chamber, he would press me up against the door and we would pleasure each other; stifling our cries of enjoyment and giggling together about it afterwards. I was a quick pupil. There was a power to the art of pleasure which I enjoyed. A teasing, taunting, thrilling power. He felt it when I was at his mercy, just as I felt it when my King was within mine. I understood now why courtiers of both sexes risked so much for the act of love. I understood now the great and overwhelming pleasures that one person could take in another. But we were careful even as we were reckless; we were passionate even as we were controlled.

But all our time was not spent only in pleasure. We talked of the *Great Matter* often, I with my worries and doubts and he with his convictions and certainties. When we returned to court from Eltham, I was at his side constantly. Neither he nor I would have it any other way. Katherine was barely to be seen at court, keeping to her own chambers, but Henry and I were always together, playing at bowls, hunting, riding, playing and singing with his men and my ladies. We were a merry band at court as the last days of the summer turned to the golden warmth of early autumn. And I was becoming increasingly aware of my growing influence and power.

At my request, my cousin, Francis Bryan was appointed to the Privy Chamber to replace my dead brother Will. Mary was being supported, albeit grudgingly, by our father through the difficult time of her new widowhood. Henry commanded my father to take her in. She went to Hever with her children and there she was cared for, and looked after. Despite her duties as a chaperone, my mother went to Hever often to see her grandchildren. I had other ladies, and Kate, my maid, with me, so it was possible for my mother to take long visits home, and spend time with little Henry and Catherine. She cherished her time with them, she told me.

"You will understand when you have children and grandchildren of your own, my child," she said. "There is nothing like the feeling that either brings to you. Your children are amazing, the most astounding thing that ever happens to you. Every day is a new discovery… You see the world fresh through their eyes. And when there are grandchildren, it is as though you have all the benefits of being a parent, but with hardly any of the responsibility… The best match possible!" She laughed heartily, and I was pleased to see her so happy. Her strange illness had abated over the summer, as it always did, but she was not looking forward to winter, for in cold times she often suffered. And yet she had not caught the sweat… strange how at times the frailest of us seem to be the strongest…

I was in a strong position at court. Henry granted me anything and everything he could and there was support growing for me in many areas. Those who wanted a secure future for England, those who did not favour Spain in alliance, those who had gained through friendship with my family… Oh yes… I had supporters, and they were growing in number. Katherine did had many, of course, but when I came to court that autumn, I was bolder than ever I had been before. I was secure in Henry's love, and we told ourselves that soon, soon, Campeggio would arrive.

Everyone knew what was going on. Everyone knew everything although nothing was said out loud. Everyone knew that Henry loved me and that, if I got my way as it was whispered in the corridors of every palace and every dull hovel in the land, I should be Queen before the year was out.

But Katherine was popular about the country. Her people hated me. They thought I was an upstart. They thought I was a whore. They called me a witch and a Jezebel. They thought that my influence over Henry could never last. But they all watched me carefully, for no one had ever seen the King act like this before.

Change was coming and, like the beasts in the wood that look to the skies before a storm, all were watching to see which way they should run.

Chapter Thirty-Two

Greenwich Palace
Early Autumn 1528

"I am granting to you, my love, the wardship of your nephew," Henry said, toying with a gold button on his sleeve of purple velvet. "You will have it free of the usual charges for such a position, for I believe you can do more for Henry Carey than his mother can."

Henry had come to talk again about my sister. He had a new plan, he said, in which I was to play an intrinsic part. I had thought he meant for me to intervene with my father. Offering me the wardship of my nephew was not something I had even thought on.

It was a generous grant he was offering. Wardships were granted to courtiers by the King, making provision for fatherless children and giving the guardian custody over, and income from, the lands or other holdings of the ward. The guardian was given the responsibility of maintaining any such estates, and was also responsible for their ward's education. The guardian, also, usually arranged their ward's future marriage. Such positions were usually granted to men, who would often eventually marry their ward themselves. Henry clearly did not have this in mind, but he considered me able and better-placed than Mary to act on behalf of my nephew. Not only was my sister a widow, but she was one with a scandalous past. Mary had been Henry's mistress both before and after her marriage to Will and her time in France and activities there were also common knowledge. This would not bode well for a future match for Mary, and could also stain her son's honour. All this, of course, might be easily forgotten when I became Queen, since her close relationship to me would make her a valuable prize. But here and now, Mary was both a widow and, in many eyes, damaged goods. There were many who would shy from a union with her, because of her past. And although there were plenty of rumours about me, Henry knew my honour was intact.

It was also telling that Henry had chosen to grant this position to me rather than to my father or to George. It was unusual to grant guardianship to a woman. Perhaps he believed that I would be more likely than they to truly act in the best interests of the child, who was possibly his son. Perhaps he believed that my father would simply take the goods and wealth of the position and do little for Mary and her children. In many ways, therefore, I understood and was pleased to be appointed Henry Carey's guardian, but in other ways I knew this might cause trouble between my sister and me.

I rode down to Hever to talk with her. I had accepted the post and I knew that she would have been informed of this, but I needed to talk with her face to face. I did not want her thinking that I was stealing her rights, or her children.

"Mary," I called, finding her in the rose gardens as she played at hide and seek with Henry and his elder sister, Catherine. As she saw me a flash of anger passed over her face. She called to her maids to continue the game in her place, and she walked towards me, crossing her arms in front of her as she neared me. I sighed inwardly; this did not bode well.

The lands young Henry Carey had inherited from his father were not vast, nor was the income from them great. Despite being a favourite of Henry's, Will had not been a man of great wealth. All his offices, posts and their income had reverted to the Crown upon his death, and many had already been handed out to others. Will had held no house of his own. Mary had no right to reside at any of the houses, such as Beaulieu, where Will had acted as Henry's custodian. She had rents from manors in Essex, and a small annuity from her dowry, but these amounted to little. And with the guardianship Henry had granted me over Mary's son, Will's remaining property was now in my possession.

Mary was twenty-nine now, a widow with a past and two children to support. Our father had taken her under his roof, but only at the express command of the King. Her prospects were poor. And I, her only sister, was now the guardian of her son and heir, and the keeper of his coin. No wonder she scowled at me.

"Can we talk?" I asked quietly. Mary unbound her arms and gestured in an irritated fashion to the walled gardens. We fell into step as we walked, my gown of dark green whispering with hers of crimson.

"So, you have heard?" It was hardly a question… Of course she had heard!

"I have," she said formally. "Should I congratulate you, sister, on coming into such good fortune?"

Her tone was waspish and taut. I sighed and stopped walking. "Mary," I said, my tone gentle. "I did not go and ask for this appointment. Henry offered it to me, and I took it, as much for your good as for little Henry's."

"For *my* good?" she asked, her tone incredulous. "How is this for my good? If the wardship of my own son had been offered to me, *then* it would be for my own good. This way, you have control of all of Will's revenues and what land he had, and you have legal authority over my own son!" She tossed her golden-red head. "*Good*, you say, sister… *ill* I think of it."

"Would you rather the King had granted this post to our father?"

Her pink lips pouted. "No," she agreed in a curt tone. "I would rather he gave it to me." Her face twisted bitterly. "But then, I am a fallen woman, am I not? A widow, and one about whom men talk with free and easy japes about my past… And you, sister, are to be Queen! Obviously you are the *moral* choice to care for the son of the King!"

"I can do nothing about the things you say, Mary," I said. "You knew that there would be risks in becoming a man's lover… I am sorry that the world turns on you and judges you where it does not judge the men who were involved with you."

"Yes… Your future husband amongst them!" she spat. "And perhaps the father of the boy we talk of now! Oh, it is all very well, is it not, to give in to a man when urged to do so by your family, and by him, and then to bear all the weight of sin for the both of you once his passion is spent! No sin rides on Henry's shoulders, or those of François, or any other, for the pleasures we took together… But for me, yes! For me there *is* censure. I am judged as unfit to care for my own child, Anne! And by the man who was my partner in sin!" She turned her eyes away. They were heavy with tears.

"He does not judge you unfit," I said, wishing I could rest a hand on her shoulder, but afraid she would shrug me off. "Granting a fatherless child as a ward to another is perfectly normal in such circumstances, Mary, you know that. Henry has chosen me, as he knows that I will act for young Henry's interests first… This is why he does not grant this position to our father! And I have it in my power to release money and grants to you… You know that I am not about to take your son from you, nor am I going to leave you penniless and destitute. I promise you, Mary, I will do all I can to protect both your children, and you, and see you maintained in the estate you are used to. I am your friend, Mary, as well as your sister."

She looked out over the gardens, struggling to control her emotions. "I know that," she whispered, her tone thick with tears. "It is just…" she started and then began to cry, her cheeks reddening as she covered her face with her hands.

I reached out to her but she stiffened in my arms. I released her and stood, waiting for her to calm herself. Eventually she wiped her eyes and exhaled noisily, rubbing her arms. "It is just…" she continued, "… hard, Anne. That is all. It is hard. I had thought losing Will would be the worst thing I ever had to face, but then our father was so *cruel*, telling me I would have to learn to live within my means and find a place to live with the Careys. He did not seem to care about his own grandchildren!"

She shook her head in anger, wiping furiously at her tears. "And then, when the King ordered him to take me and the children in… Since then, our father has behaved as though we are unwelcome guests… And even mother, who I never thought of as unkind, has made plenty of remarks about how my past has come back to haunt me, and that I may never make another marriage!" Her face was ugly and ruddy with sorrow. "And then, to hear that my son had been given to you as a ward... I was almost at the edge of all that I could bear, Anne, and then this came! Surely you can understand?"

I nodded. "Of course, of course I can, Mary." I said, feeling helpless. I had not realised that fate had been so merciless to my sister… And what was this about our mother? She had never spoken such censorious words about Mary before, even though I knew she had not approved of Mary's dalliances. "But I promise you, sister, I will do all that I can for you, and for your children. I promise I will not take them from you, and when the time comes for them to serve in another house when they are older, the choice of household will be yours. I will find the best tutors I can, but you will have the final say over whether they remain in post or not. And I will release money to you, Mary, whenever you have need of it. I am their guardian, yes, but you will ever remain their mother."

Mary sighed. She appeared comforted by my words. She put a hand into mine and I clutched it. "Everyone was turning against me," she muttered, "and so everywhere I saw darkness." She offered up a watery smile. "If this is as you say, Anne, then I put all my trust in you. I should not have feared that you would turn against me as the world seems to have done. You and I have ever been good friends."

"You are my sister, and I love you," I said, taking her in my arms. "I will act in your interests, I promise you. And I have thoughts on how to do more for you… Just give me time. It is… difficult to talk of you with Henry."

She pulled back. Her mouth pouted wryly. "I am sure," she said. She looked away from me for a moment and continued. "Anne… there was another missive which came at the same time. It was from the Cardinal… asking that I come no more to court."

"What?" I exclaimed.

Mary tilted her head to one side. "Well," she said. "It did not say that *exactly*. It said that he and the King were sure that my many duties would keep me in the country from now on. But the inference was clear." Her brown eyes stared gravely into mine. "The King no longer wants reminders of his past to linger about him. He wishes to believe himself as clean and clear of sin as you are. I am a reminder of his past sins. I am the stained cloth he seeks to discard."

"I did not know."

"I wondered if you did or not," she murmured. "When I got that message, I wondered if *you* had ordered the Cardinal to banish me from court… but now I think it was done on Henry's orders."

"I knew nothing of this!" I was distraught… What must Mary have thought, getting such a message? That I was taking her son, *and* having her banished from court? "It must be one of the Cardinal's ploys… that rodent was trying to drive a wedge between us. He may well have thought that in sending such a message you would assume I *had* ordered you from court." I breathed in sharply. "In every way, Mary, the Cardinal seeks to undermine me. Even with my own family. He sneaks and schemes behind my back, trying always to weaken me. *He* most likely convinced the King to remove you, and this will therefore steal another of my supporters from court."

She squeezed my hand. "How now," she said in a motherly tone. "What is done is done… I will stay away, if that is what the King wants. But if all you say is true, and you will help to protect me and my children, Anne, then I am grateful. It seems as though you are the only one in the family who is thinking of us. Perhaps it is only to be expected… for everyone else is thinking of *you*."

Her lips twitched with a bitterness that I did not like to see. Such foul emotions did not suit my sweet sister. "Come," she said. "Catherine and Henry will be happy to see you. Catherine has been talking about the gown you wore when you last visited us as though it were the only beautiful thing in the world. She made one, in the same fashion, for her doll, and I know she will want to show it to you." Mary smiled with pride. "It is actually rather good… I think she may have inherited some of your talent for designing clothes, sister."

Mary's tone was warm now, but I was still chilled by all that had assailed her since Will's death. What horrors and fears she had faced, relentless even after she had buried her husband! I laced my fingers through hers. "I never told you in person how sorry I was to hear of Will's death, Mary," I said, sorrow catching at the back of my throat. "He was a good man. I mourned him as if I had lost a brother."

"He *was* a good man," she whispered. "I knew little how much I cared for him, and how much he had given me, until the day I lost him. It is ever the way. We do not appreciate what we have until we lose it."

Her eyes turned to the fields, gazing out. I knew she did not see the crops being gathered in, or the birds swooping through the golden stalks. She saw Will. "I had not thought, until he died, how much he protected me, Anne. My marriage made me respectable. It meant the world could not turn on me. It concealed the stains of the past, and made me a woman fit to be seen… Now, now that Will is gone, I have that protection no longer. I little thought on how much we women are in the shadows of men, absorbing not only their titles and their lands, but their standing too… Will made me acceptable to our society, and now that he is gone, I am seen as I was when first I came from France."

She sighed heavily, turning her eyes to mine. Such sadness was there. Not only for Will, but for her loss of innocence, too. Mary had come to see the world in the most harsh and stark manner. She had been stripped of her illusions. She had lost her belief in goodness. I hoped to restore some of that to her. "I thought so little of what I did then," she went on. "I was young and full of pride and pleasure. But it seems that even now, when I have lived as a wife and a mother, I will be forever judged by those wild days of my youth… and I will be called upon to shoulder the burden of sin, both for me and the men who lay with me. They escape with naught but the respect of their fellow gallants and a smile of indulgence from the Church, as I am held to be a fallen, immoral creature of frail intelligence, filled with evil…" Mary shrugged. "Perhaps you were right, all along, sister," she continued. "When you said to me all those years ago that there was danger in what I did. I have had much cause, these last months especially, to remember your words."

"The world is not fair, Mary," I said. "And yes, it appears that promiscuity is only a sin when women indulge in it. But let this not shadow your life. I will help you now. If you are let down by others, if you are judged by man and by the Church, then let me be the one who will not judge you. We will stand strong together, as ever we have. I will do my best for you and for Catherine and Henry."

She nodded and we made to walk into the house. "Just do one thing for me," I said quietly. "Do not tell our father when I release money or anything else to you. He will be tempted to take it from you, or give you less from his own pocket. If we cannot prevail on our own father to give to his daughter for love and honesty, then we will trick him into doing his part. That way, it will leave more for young Henry to inherit."

She laughed; it was a pretty sound. "Done, sister!" she chortled, happy at the idea of tricking our father. "And well it will serve the old miser too!"

"Aye," I agreed. "He has enough in his coffers to support his grandchildren and you, without us dipping too deep into the money which will be little Henry's when he grows.

"I am worried, sister..." said Mary in a rush. "Worried for Catherine and her dowry. How will I manage to provide her with one?"

"I have been thinking about that," I assured her. "Worry not. I have a plan for Catherine."

I was determined, upon entering the castle that afternoon, that I would do all I could for Mary, and I did. Although I could not ask her brought back to court, I kept her with her children and kept them in the state they were used to. Had young Henry's wardship been offered to another, they would have taken the tiny boy from his mother entirely and raised him as their own son. I had plans for Catherine too, but that would come later. Henry was generous, but I did not want to ask for too much at once. I did not want him to think that I loved his money more than I loved him, nor to give further ammunition to Katherine, who was pleased to do anything she could to paint me as a grasping and manipulative whore.

But this affair with Mary, for now at least, seemed well enough resolved. Mary was happy to find that she had a friend, *any* friend. For even within our family, Mary had lost her value, and diminished in her usefulness. Hard truths were these to swallow; that a woman suffered from blame so much more than any man ever would. How was such fair, in the eyes of the world and the Church? But of course, Eve had been the first to lead Adam into sin, and therefore women were always viewed as morally suspect, sinister creatures. And how profitable was it for men to view us as such! For then they could take all the pleasure they wanted and bear none of the sin!

This affair with Mary strengthened my resolve to wait until marriage before allowing a full union between Henry and me. I had been tempted to give in often of late. Although I trusted that he loved me, I never wanted to end up as my sister was now. She had been protected from her past sins by her husband when he lived, but as a widow, she was censured and cut off from respectable society, because she had dare to dally with pleasure in her past. The same could happen to me. I had to ensure that her fate did not become mine.

Chapter Thirty-Three

Greenwich Palace
Autumn 1528

"By the faith!" I muttered. "Why is nothing ever simple?"

I had ventured to seek Henry's favour for my supporters; but there was trouble. Earlier that year I had petitioned that a man named Sir Thomas Cheney be allowed to return to court. He had offended Cardinal Wolsey on some matter which was of small import, and had found himself banished from court. Cheney wrote to me, asking for my help, and offering his support in return. I had asked Henry to overrule the Cardinal and he had done so. That had been simple enough.

Later, however, when I was at Hever, Cheney had written to me again. He wanted to gain the wardship, and eventually the hand, of one of the two daughters of a gentleman of Wolsey's household who had died of the sweat. John Broughton's daughters were now wealthy heiresses, and their wardships had been granted to Wolsey. The family, however, wanted to retain guardianship, and had sent Sir John Russell, who had been Broughton's stepfather, to ask Wolsey that wardship of the girls be granted to him, instead. Russell was in high favour with the Cardinal, and Wolsey had valued Broughton, so the family had good hopes their wishes would be granted.

But Cheney also had an interest. He was keen to marry the younger sister, Katherine, when she came of age and his friend, Sir John Wallop, wanted to secure the elder daughter, Anne. Russell heard of Cheney's plans and brought Thomas Heneage and Thomas Arundel in to intercede on his behalf with the Cardinal. Russell insisted that the elder, Anne, was of age to marry, and therefore her wardship was not the

King's to grant. He was, in fact, lying, as both girls were not old enough to marry. It was therefore the position of the sovereign to appoint their guardian.

"Cheney and Wallop have only good intentions for these girls," I said to Henry. "They are noble lords, seeking honourable marriages." I slid my hand about his neck and kneaded the tight muscles there. "It would please me a great deal, Henry, if this should come to pass."

"Since I am displeased that Russell attempted to lie to get his own way, sweetheart, I am inclined to agree with you." Henry leaned his neck into my hand and closed his eyes, relishing the feeling of my hands. "If the agreement is that the girls will be married to their guardians when they come of age to do so, I will agree to Cheney and Wallop taking charge of them."

I was pleased to have gained such lucrative posts for two men who had promised to support my cause. It was all going well, until a blistering fight broke out between Russell and Cheney in the King's own chambers. Henry found this most distasteful, decided that Cheney had gone too far and announced that the wardships would revert to Wolsey. This then caused another argument, this time with Cheney pitted against the Cardinal, who promptly banished him from court. I called him back again. Since the man was in my household, the Cardinal should have come to me before sending him away. I knew Wolsey was only attempting to rid the court of another of my supporters and petitioned Henry for my men again. As a compromise, Wolsey gave up the wardship of Anne Broughton, who eventually became the wife of Cheney. It was agreed that the younger sister, Katherine, would remain Wolsey's ward, for the time being at least, but I assured Wallop I would do my best for him. If I could not get him this wife, I would find him an equally good match.

This rather complex affair brought me against the Cardinal again, not directly, but hardly covertly either. It seemed that wherever I tried to move, the Cardinal was there to stop me. He was clever, never allowing it to appear as though he was thwarting me on purpose, but I knew well that he was. I gained an enemy, in Russell, who was not pleased about the outcome, but I also had two more supporters in Cheney and Wallop. I asked Henry to compensate Wallop for his loss in the amount of four hundred pounds, a princely sum. It was not only these supporters I had gained of late, either. Upon my return to court, I had been busy gathering allies…

My cousin, Francis Bryan was dark of hair, quick of wit, and handsome, despite the fact he only had one eye. His black velvet eyepatch glittered with diamonds, just as his remaining eye sparkled over the court ladies. He had a wild reputation, and once in France had demanded "a soft bed and a hard harlot" from his outraged landlord. He was known about court as *"the Vicar of Hell"*, for he was religiously dedicated to sin. But for all his unruliness, he was a clever man and I was pleased when he came offering his support. He spoke his mind openly more often than not, much as I did. After Will died, I had asked that Bryan be appointed to the Privy Chamber to take his place, and that autumn I asked that Bryan be sent to meet the slow-moving Campeggio. I thought that perhaps a member of my own house could hurry the Cardinal along, but even though Bryan promised to do all he could, Campeggio still crawled towards England as though he rode a snail rather than a horse. Bryan wrote to me often, calling me "mistress" and "madam" as though I were Queen already. This pleased Henry, and I was happy that another member of my family was advancing at court.

Whilst we waited for Campeggio, a new French ambassador, Bishop Jean du Bellay, arrived at court and Henry and I were quick to engage him. The Queen and her servants looked naturally to the Emperor Charles for support and, to my delight, Henry was now considering an alliance with France.

Charles was unlikely to invade in the defence of his aunt, but it did not hurt to have powerful friends. We took du Bellay hunting and I presented him with a fine greyhound. He was charming and affable and was touched by Henry's intimate attentions. As we broke our fast before the hunt one fine morning, sat upon the earth covered in blankets, he thanked me for the fine presents I had given him.

"All I do, my lord, is at the command of the King." I spoke in French, lifted my cup of ale to him and he returned the gesture. "But I am pleased to see my country allied with France, where, as you know, I spent much of my youth. I would be loath to see England aligned with the Emperor Charles, who, as I am sure you understand, often takes as long to keep his promises as he does to wipe his chin." The ambassador guffawed. Charles V had a famously over-long chin. "The King longs for your master's friendship. In time, I hope that we will become good friends with our nearest and most sophisticated neighbours of France."

Du Bellay eyed me knowingly. "I do not think, my lady, that *all* you do is at the command of the King. In fact, and I would not wish you to pass this on to His Majesty, I feel that the situation is quite the opposite..." He smiled charmingly. "For a man, so much in love, as Henry of England is, cannot help but give way to his heart in all matters, and that makes *you*, my lady, the most interesting person I have met here at the English court."

"You flatter me, my lord." I smoothed my low-cut green gown with its long-hanging sleeves embroidered with grapevines. "Perhaps overly. The King has his own will and it is stronger than any I have ever met before."

"Which explains why you love him so, Mistress Boleyn," he said. "There is, in the two of you, a match of equals. And the fire of the English... Ah, it is in both your hearts! We French... we have not the same spirit as the English. They say there is the blood of the dragon in the blood of the King, do they not? You and I must be friends, my lady. We are united in our goal to bring England and France together as the greatest of friends. And my master was keen to hear of you, for he has retained a great affection for you and was most displeased when you left his court. I think he is jealous now to know that his brother king has won your heart, where he failed to do so."

"I had no idea that King François ever felt as you say for me." I laughed lightly. "For he was in love with every woman at court, to varying degrees! But I miss his company also. He is a refined and generous man and he once performed a service for me that I can never repay. I believe, with such a King at the head of France, England would be foolish to look anywhere else for friendship. Please tell him I remember him and his sister with the greatest affection, and I have never forgotten his many kindnesses. I was grieved to hear of Queen Claude's death, I served her for many years and she was a good woman and the best of Queens. What is your new Queen like? She cannot be happy that you are here, for is she not kin to the Emperor?"

We went on to talk of France and the new Queen. Speaking French to a Frenchman once again was wonderful, for the English could never master the lilt of the language, its beauty and depth. Du Bellay kissed my hand, made many promises and wrote favourable reports to his master. We had an ally.

It was just as well that my efforts and flattery were gaining us allies, for the King's *Great Matter* was dividing the court in two. My family stood now in undisguised opposition to Katherine and her supporters. My brother George, our father, Bryan, Norfolk, and Suffolk were merging together to form a faction, along with men like Cheney and Wallop. Suffolk had no great affection for my family, but had cast his lot in with my uncle Norfolk in order to curry favour with the King. Suffolk also saw this as an opportunity to take down his rival for the King's affections; Wolsey.

"That cow-herd has no right to the King's ear…" Suffolk sniffed. "All of us have suffered from his arrogance and greed. It is time that he left his position and that worthier men took it up."

I laughed inwardly at this, for the Duke, noble as he might be now, had hardly *always* been one of the premier peers of the realm. I could not keep a small smile from my lips, which caused my uncle Norfolk to glare at me. "Forgive me, Your Grace," I said as Suffolk looked quizzically at me. "I was just thinking of the great pleasure it would give me to see Wolsey replaced by better men, such as yourself and my uncle. The thought was a happy one." Suffolk grunted, but remained suspicious. I could see George smothering a smile, for he had known what I was thinking.

"The Staffords, the Nevilles and the Poles will stand with the Queen," Norfolk said, moving on swiftly and setting everything out like a battle plan, as was his way.

"And your wife, Your Grace…" I mentioned to my uncle thoughtfully. "She stands with the Queen, also, I believe. That could be embarrassing. Can you not persuade her to act for us instead of Katherine?"

My uncle coloured, and let out a short moan as he shifted in his chair. My father, who had sat silently listening, started up from his seat. They all stared at me. My uncle was turning various shades of red and purple.

"The King is most displeased with my aunt of Norfolk," I said calmly. It did no good for us to avoid the subject, even if it was shameful for my uncle. "He tells me that her attitude towards him borders on the disrespectful. I would not want anyone in this alliance endangered by the behaviour of rogue family members. Perhaps you should talk to her, uncle, before she embarrasses us."

"I will do as I see fit with my own wife, niece!" He hissed through gritted teeth. "And I would remind you to have a little humility. You are not the Queen yet, *my lady*." The scorn with which he said 'my lady' was evident, and I scowled.

"I shall be, soon enough," I responded stiffly. "And that is what we are all here to achieve. Remember that, uncle. Once I am married to the King and producing his heirs, the Boleyns, the Howards, the Suffolks and the Bryans will have saved this country from the brink of civil war. We will have a happy King with a brood of part-Howard princes waiting aside the throne. And who but their family and allies will these princes look to for advice and strength?"

I paused. My uncle was looking at me quite differently now, and nodding in agreement. He went to leave with Suffolk and as he did, he paused near my father. "Your daughter would have made a good general, Thomas," he said with a scowl. "Let us see if she can make as good a lady… and Queen."

Around that time, Henry Norris also threw his lot in with us. A handsome and eager young man with good intentions, Norris was the *Groom of the Stool*, the man who attended Henry in his most intimate moments upon the privy, and therefore the most important person in Henry's private household. Norris and George were great friends. George brought him out to meet with me often and as Norris usually accompanied Henry, I came to know him well.

Norris was a good friend to us, who believed Katherine should obey Henry's wishes and step aside as Queen. But Norris was not with us on all matters. He liked Wolsey, and sought to try to bring about peace between us. At present, we still needed the Cardinal and so I was happy to tell the eager Norris that I would gladly be friends with those who would be friends to me. This was enough to convince him that I meant the stinking rodent no harm, which was rather far from the truth. But there was something in Norris that made me want him to think the best of me. He had that sense of boyish innocence that I found so appealing in men. Henry was the love of my life, but I could not help but find Norris attractive. He had charm, good looks, and wit. I was drawn to him.

Since Henry loved Norris too, there was no danger. I flirted with all of Henry's retainers and then came tripping back to my love's side. It was the expected behaviour of a lady of the court, and I was to become the greatest of all ladies. I now took Katherine's place in the game of courtly love. Henry was pleased to see that other men admired me, and even more pleased I was entirely his and out of their reach.

Poets wrote about me, men sang for me and all the while Henry was at my side, claiming the most wondrous woman of the court as his alone. It tickled him to see so many fall at my feet in rapt admiration; some of it was true, but, of course, much was false. It was, really, all just part of the game we played. We needed the men of England to support us, and it did not matter if that came about through favour, true belief, or flirtation. We would use anything and everything we had and were capable of doing. There came a time, much later, when such innocent games would be used against me… but back then, I thought nothing of it. It was the way I had been taught to play my part at court, and it won us friends. It was nothing more than this.

There were many in Henry's intimate circle with whom I was great friends. These men began to treat me in the same manner that the men at the Court of Mechelan had treated Margaret. Despite my frustrations with Campeggio's slow progress, I found solace in my dancing, prancing admirers.

Henry was obsessed by the court proceedings that were soon to take place. Headaches plagued him often, and on those occasions he had to retire to a darkened room to quiet the pounding in his head. He never wanted to see me during those times, and I learned not to ask to see him. Although I wanted to care for him, he did not want me to see him during these times of infirmity.

The business of preparing for the trial took up much of our time. We had less time for hunting, less time for other pleasures. As the handsome young men who surrounded Henry pursued my hand in the dance, and flattered me as we walked out together, there arose a dark hint of jealousy in Henry's face, mingled with pride that so many should want the woman that was his alone. I liked his jealousy then. It reminded him how valuable I was, and how much he wanted me. It made me feel safe, in a strange way. But there would come a time, much later, when I understood how dangerous jealousy truly was.

Chapter Thirty-Four

Greenwich Palace
Autumn 1528

The forests burned with golden and red leaves. Fields, once lush with barley and wheat, were stripped of their crops, leaving behind newly ploughed rich, black earth. The shrieks and hoots of owls were heard in the night's skies, winging their way to feed on mice, voles and rats with bellies stuffed full of the last fruits of the year. Butterflies sat on stones warming themselves in the sun, disappearing when the long shadows of dusk fell. The wind began to blow fresh and strong, restless amongst the branches of the trees. The common people began to harvest wood from hedgerows to fuel their fires through the winter. Sweet chestnuts dropped, their sticky, spiky husks revealing tasty nuts, good for roasting and making into pottage to warm the belly. The nights stretched, long and cold, and welcoming fires blazed in each fireplace of Henry's palaces. Court maidens started to whisper how they would discover their future husband on All Soul's, by placing apple pips by the fire. Each pip held the name of a potential suitor, the first one to pop before the flames would signify whom she would wed.

I needed no such magic to discover my husband. I had already found whom I was to marry... I just could not marry him, yet.

Foul weather, a storm which blew in from the coast and ripped through London forced the court inside. For many this was frustrating, being cooped up like rabbits in the warren of the court. For me, time inside meant more time to read, a favourite activity of mine. And that autumn, my brother brought me a book which would steal all my attention, would transport me to new planes of thought, and would linger with me even when I was reading it not. It is like that with some books. They take you from the mundane and open a new world to you. They consume your thoughts, haunt your dreams and become a part of you. It was a book such as this my brother brought me that autumn.

"This present must be a secret, Anna," he said as he handed me the small leather-bound volume. "It is already banned in many countries. England included."

"What is it?" I asked.

George smiled. "Knowledge and wisdom."

"My enigmatic brother…" I said. "I take it this is not a book I should admit owning to Henry, then?"

"Certainly don't show it to Wolsey." George grinned. "The contents are radical, and the Church will view it as dangerous."

As it passed into my hands I thought little of it, despite my brother's dramatic words. George and I often exchanged books that interested us, banned or not. I owned English and French translations of the Bible, which were prohibited in England amongst other writings that spoke of reform. Marguerite had whetted my appetite for the writings of learned men when I had served in France. I thought it dangerous to ignore ideas, whether or not the Church approved. Ignorance is not a helpful state and the gaining of knowledge did not, to me, indicate one was about to sink into heresy. The Church wanted its people to follow its rules, doctrines, laws and regulations, which included not attempting to discover wisdom for themselves. The Church preferred that its priests, monks, bishops and Pope doled out knowledge of the faith in small and often confusing morsels. Many, like me, believed that it was the duty of every Christian to explore the works of the Apostles, Saints, and the Word of God for themselves.

This was how the Church controlled its worshippers; through knowledge, or rather through the lack of it. I saw this as further evidence of its corruption. Why should the Church fear its people knowing God better? Why should the Church hesitate to be made better than it was? Those who feared such changes, or gaining wise followers, were corrupt. The only reason to resist change is if one profits from stagnation. The only reason to fear wisdom is if one does not possess it.

The leather-bound volume was printed rather than hand-written. Printing had been a great advance in the manufacture of books, and printed books were spreading all over the world. Although the small volume was not beautiful, not like the hand-lettered, decorated volumes that had once been the only texts available, and only then to the very rich, the ideas in it pages were better than beautiful; they were exciting.

The book was entitled *The Obedience of a Christian Man* and was written by Master William Tyndale, that same exiled Englishman who had made such a wonderful translation of the New Testament. As I read through it, I marked passages that I thought might interest Henry, pressing my fingernail to gently indent the pages. Although the book was banned, I thought that, when presented by me and in his interests, he would not mind that I had acquired such a volume. At the whim of royalty, the nobility often lived under different laws to the common people... and I was his beloved...

As I read, I became inflamed by Tyndale's ideas and convinced by many of his arguments. It was a work of reformist philosophy. He wrote that each man needed to be obedient to God and God alone, not to the Church; that the Pope and the Church were not God's true emissaries; that the King should be the father of the Word of God in his own kingdom; that the King was the true servant of God and each of us owed our allegiance to him and God alone. Church affairs should be under the control of the King rather than the Pope, the book argued. *"One king, one law is God's ordinance in every realm."* The ideas were revolutionary, enthralling, and dangerous. I understood why George had pressed me to keep the text secret. If Wolsey, or any of Katherine's supporters, knew I held such an inflammatory book, they would use it against me. With the backing of the Church, owning this book could be seen as heresy.

To me though, it was not heresy. It was truth and it was knowledge. If God had never wished His people to possess wisdom, then why make us able to read? Of God had never wished all people to understand His will, then why did the Apostles write the Gospels at all? Knowledge was not for the Church to control and dictate; it was a gift from God. We read, we enquire, we discover... so that we might understand God better, and rejoice in our faith. *"Ask, and it shall be given you; seek, and ye shall find; knock, and it shall be opened to you"* so said Matthew... I was a seeker. I was an asker. I was a curious mind. I sought God in all I read and I was not about to be stopped in this most glorious of studies, by those who feared what others might find... by those who trembled to lose their power as the bright light of knowledge vanquished the darkness of ignorance.

Thomas More was already furiously writing a response to the book, so I heard from George. Given permission, by Bishop Tunstall, to read heretical works in order to contradict them, More was writing his first work in English, called, *A Dialogue Concerning Heresies*, or as it was later to be called by those who read it, *A Dialogue Concerning Tyndale*, for Tyndale was, in More's eyes, an agent of the Devil himself.

I cared not for men like More who fawned and grovelled before the Church. Long had I held reformist sympathies, and seeing his violent reaction to such works only confirmed the truths within them for me.

It was not only for my own studies that I found the book captivating. I was excited to think of what this might mean for our cause. The ideas it contained were revolutionary; that a king, in his own kingdom, should be the representative of God rather than the Pope. Interesting ideas indeed... No wonder the Church had banned this work! It spoke of replacing their cardinals, bishops and Pope with kings! It spoke of the ancient right of kings, as the chosen of God, to rule over matters both temporal *and* spiritual. This book was arguing to limit the power of the Church, and hand it instead to rulers. With the annulment ever on my mind, I could see that this book argued it was not up to the Pope whether Henry and Katherine's marriage was valid; the *Great Matter* was for Henry to decide.

I thought back with some wonder on the day Henry had proposed to me. I had been uneasy with how lightly he had talked of God's will; as though he understood the thoughts of the Almighty... But here, in Tyndale's text, was a vindication of this. It was clear to me that this idea was open to much abuse, as a ruler may not always act in the way God would wish, but kings *were* the chosen of God. They were placed on their thrones by God, not by man, as popes were. I thought back to Henry's impassioned words about God, fate and destiny. Was it indeed possible that God was reaching into Henry to alter the course of England's future? That He had brought me to Henry's side... Brought one who was interested in reform to the King of England, just as the King was deciding on the path England would take? Was Tyndale right? Should Henry take up the right to govern religion in England on all matters, and act as God and his conscience instructed him?

It was a radical notion. Perhaps too radical. Henry was deeply conservative and saw himself as the Pope's good servant. It would be a risk to show him Tyndale's book. He loved the Church, and believed it was a true and almost infallible institution. Whilst he and I agreed on many points of theology, I had been raised to question, rather than simply accept. Henry had not.

I read the book over and over in private, but for now I did not show it to Henry. Campeggio was at Calais, and was making ready to sail for England. If the trial went as planned, I might have no cause to show Henry this most interesting work…

But if it did not go as we wished, this book may well open another path for Henry, for England and for me.

Chapter Thirty-Five

Greenwich Palace
Autumn 1528

Finally, one grey October day as the clouds hung fat and black over England, Campeggio landed at Dover. Wolsey was sent to meet him. Our envoy, Francis Bryan, had visited Campeggio in France, met with François of France to gain his support, and had gone on to Rome, to further our case with the Pope.

Henry delegation to Rome included his Latin secretary, Peter Vannes, who was commanded to beg, cajole, and, if necessary, threaten the Pope. Vannes was instructed to say that should the Pope not give in to Henry's wishes, England's allegiance to the See of Rome would be in jeopardy. It was a heavy and extraordinary threat. But Henry was bluffing; I and all his men knew that. All the same, uprisings in the Low Countries and the Holy Roman Empire over the last years had brought mayhem and had shaken the foundations of the Church. Peasants, inspired by the works of Luther, had risen up and challenged their masters and the tyranny of the Church causing two years of chaos. But even though these rebellions had been subdued, these events had led to nobles and even princes questioning the authority and goodness of the clergy. In Sweden, King Gustav Vasa already held dominion over the Church and had sanctioned the preaching of many Lutheran ideas. Frederick I of Denmark protected reformist preachers, as did François of France. Threatening that England might take on the example of these states, and turn her back on the authority of Rome, was not as inconceivable as Pope Clement might wish to believe it to be.

Wolsey was frightened, and had warned Henry that trying to force the Holy Father into submission was not wise. But I encouraged Henry. I had not shown him the Tyndale book, but it seemed to me that Henry was starting to think as I did… If the Holy Father could not be relied upon, perhaps there were other ways to achieve our aims…

Bryan had written to me after he had met with François, and his news was not only of the annulment. Bryan wrote that the French King had questioned Wolsey's loyalty to his King, and said that such men of the Church were loyal first to Rome, and only second to their sovereign. And, given Wolsey's ambition to one day rule as Pope, François doubted that he would ever go too far against the wishes of the Holy See.

"If the Pope is not in favour of this annulment, then you can wager the Cardinal will not be either," François had said to Bryan. "I do not mean to say the Cardinal would wish to go against his King, whom I know he loves more than any prince or man in the world… but his loyalty must be questioned. How can one man serve two masters?"

I took the letter to Henry, whose face turned an unhealthy purple as he read it. "It is not so, sweetheart!" he said miserably. "Wolsey is *my* man first, and he has always acted in my interests."

I shrugged, making the dark furs upon my shoulders brush against my cheeks. "I but hand on what was reported to me, my lord." I turned my gaze to the window where rain lashed the dark panes. "But I see no reason to think that François, who has ever been your good friend, would lie to you. Perhaps they are only his suspicions, my lord, but he clearly believes Wolsey cannot serve both you and the Pope equally. His vows to the Church as Cardinal, or his oaths to you as Chancellor… Which will he obey? To whom will he stand loyal?"

Henry's face went dark. His eyes narrowed to icy shards. I had angered him greatly. Rather than discuss the subject further, he left the room abruptly. On the way from the chamber, he knocked into one of his guards and almost threw the man from his path, cursing at him. Many would fear to see their King so angry, but I did not. Henry could not stay away from me. He would always come back, even when his temper was riled. I understood why he was upset. Any king would be enraged to think his most trusted servant was not loyal, of course, but with Henry... the idea that his friends, that the ones he loved might not be true to him alone was unbearable. It undermined him, and hurt his fragile pride. It struck deep into the most vulnerable parts of Henry's heart. In many ways, my love was a most insecure man. Under all the bluster, the boasting, the active life he led, the power he exuded as King, under all that there was a young boy who knew he had never been intended for the throne. Under all of Henry's confidence, there was a fragile soul; a soul that demanded absolute love and devotion, in order to be kept alive. At heart, Henry was a frightened boy. His mother's death, and his father's preference for his brother had impacted on him deeply. That was why he wanted to be loved; to make up for her loss, and to contradict his father's belief that Arthur would have made the better king.

He came back to me later that night, his face haunted. When we dined together I did not bring it up again, and he seemed relieved. But I knew the first seeds of doubt had been sown.

There were further complications, too. Bryan wrote from the Pope's Citadel upon his arrival. His letter was bleak. He had been unable to present his credentials to the Pope, or to petition him, as Clement was suffering from ill-health and could see no one.

"I dare not write unto my cousin Anne of the truth of the matter." Bryan wrote to Henry. *"Because I do not know your grace's pleasure, whether I shall do or no; wherefore if she be angry with me, I must humbly ask your grace to make mine excuse. I have referred to her in her letter all the news*

to your grace, so your grace may use her in this as you think best."

"Why did he not write to me?" I demanded after reading the letter.

"For fear that you would react, *thus*, my love." Henry's tone was placating. I was glad he had shared this missive with me, for the letter I had received from Bryan was evasive at best. This explained the situation better.

"Do they all think I am such a dragon, Henry?" I asked plaintively. My heart was heavy. Did my cousin fear me, then? I had always thought Bryan and I got on well…

He chuckled. "Have you not noted your own fiery temper, my Anna?" he asked, gathering me up in his arms. "That fire will serve us well, but you cannot be hard on those who shy from its flames… Poor Bryan! He is such a man, and a noble lord, and yet he trembles to displease his future Queen!" Henry grinned. "It is better that our subjects hold a touch of fear for us in their hearts, my love," he consoled. "That way they always know who their betters are. But we offer them love, too. In such a way is a king and his queen made strong; through love and fear. Do not despise this knowledge. Bryan's terror shows me, yet again, how suited you are to be my Queen!"

I laughed, and allowed Henry to comfort me. But there were still more delays for Bryan in Rome and I was starting to think Campeggio meant to take up residence at Dover. Henry spoke of sending another envoy to Rome, to aid Bryan and Vannes. I agreed that if we heard of no further progress soon, then it would be a good idea to send more men. I suggested Gardiner or Foxe, since the last time they had visited a good result had come about for us. Perhaps they would be more persuasive than my wily one-eyed cousin.

Wolsey, however, was not enamoured of this plan. He was keener to wait for Campeggio to arrive in London, and for the trial to begin. Wolsey told us Campeggio was a wise man, someone he knew well, and assured us that the Italian Cardinal would be favourable to us.

"After all," the fat bat declared as we three wandered the gardens of Greenwich. The grounds were crisp with early, thin ice and bathed in the glittering light of the golden-leaved trees. "Campeggio watched the Holy City sacked by the ruthless mercenaries of the Emperor, why should he have any love for that ruler when faced with Your Majesty's friendship and peaceful nature? Campeggio is much more likely to find for us because of the Emperor's cruelty. And he assures me he will decide as is just and right. He knows England is a greater friend to Rome than Spain." We crossed ourselves for the thought of those men and women of God who had suffered at the hands of those soldiers. I shuddered in the sunshine, remembering the reports we had had of rapes, murders and rampant slaughter.

"My lady…" The nefarious rodent beamed at me, clicking his fingers to Heneage to bring forth a velvet-wrapped package. "I found this, it is but a slight trinket, unworthy of you in truth, but knowing your great eye for beauty, I thought you would like to have it."

Slight trinket? Indeed it was no such thing. Inside the layers of velvet was a necklace made of emeralds and diamonds, set into delicate gold links. A great cross was at its centre, also with diamonds and peals set into it. It was stunning. Henry drew back the edge of the wrapping, as he saw the 'trinket', his eyes bulged. "You are always so generous, Thomas," Henry breathed, drawing a finger along the folds of smooth, brilliant, yellow gold. "This is worth a prince's ransom."

"*Anything* for the Lady Anne," Wolsey said, attempting to affect humility.

"Thank you, Eminence," I said as Henry pulled it from the wrapping and slipped it about my long throat. "Although I am astounded what you consider a trinket!"

Wolsey was at his most courteous, but he fooled no one apart from Henry. He often made shows like this before Henry. But in secret, in the hidden places of the court, he was working against me. There were laundresses in my household whom I knew to be working for Wolsey. Heneage was often found loitering just outside my chamber. The Cardinal was looking for things to use against me. He was watching me closely. But I was not one to be caught out so easily. And I was making plans of my own…

Henry was becoming more reliant on the judgement of my uncle and Suffolk, and less on the great Cardinal. My love was starting to make decisions on his own. I encouraged him in this. Although Henry, of course, ruled in his kingdom, Wolsey, as Chancellor had taken much of his authority and power out of his hands. The fat bat had a hand in every matter in England. He had influenced almost every decision Henry had ever taken. But now, it seemed Henry was losing faith in Wolsey after all. In the face of all the delays, Henry was starting to believe other men might be able to help him where the Cardinal could not. And the message from France had unnerved Henry, even though he might protest it had not. His faith in Wolsey was shaken, perhaps for the first time. The seed of doubt about Wolsey's loyalty had been planted. We just had to let it grow…

I knew that he loved Wolsey, but he was wrong to do so. I was not sure François was entirely right either. I did not think Wolsey's loyalty belonged to the Pope. Wolsey looked after Wolsey: that was his first loyalty. After that… who knew whether the King or the Pope was his next concern?

But if Henry was to see this, I had to move carefully, and Wolsey was the best-placed man to advance the *Great*

Matter, so I needed him still. But he could still be of use to us even if he was reduced in the King's eyes. I had taken my father's advice; I did not berate Henry about his chief advisor, but I did not miss a chance either to point out when Wolsey delayed or did something wrong. It was time for Henry to stop putting his faith in this one man, who more often acted for his own benefit than for his King's.

We did not go too far, however. If this trial was to go ahead, then Wolsey had to be a part of it. But the Cardinal had many reasons to sweat as time dragged on and Campeggio still had not arrived in London. Henry was growing angry, and his anger came to rest on the shoulders of his most trusted advisor.

Chapter Thirty-Six

Hever Castle and Suffolk House
Autumn 1528

"You must go to Hever once more, my love, for the sake of appearances." Henry's face was a mask of suffering as he spoke to me. "But it will not be for long, and you will not be left without news…" Seeing my face fall, Henry rushed on. "Campeggio will quietly visit with you at Hever as he travels to London. I will arrange it. Then he can see you for the virtuous maiden you are, and understand my reasons for wishing you to be my wife."

Campeggio was preparing to move towards London, finally. As he did so, Henry was going to have to spend more time with Katherine and less with me. He needed to maintain the appearance of the dutiful husband. With my ladies in tow, I left court for Hever, my temper fragile and agitated.

Despite Henry's constant urging, the gout-ridden Cardinal tarried and dithered, protesting ill-health and the need for long periods of rest. Although I had expected him to stop at Hever on his way to Greenwich, Campeggio did not. An outburst of suspicion and paranoia caused me to write angrily to Henry, who replied in calm and somewhat weary language that he had spoken to Wolsey, and they both believed Campeggio could not visit me if we were to maintain our respectability. I answered his letter with humility; something that did not come easily to me in those days, may God forgive me. But I was sure Wolsey wanted me kept from Campeggio for other reasons. Perhaps he worried that my powers of persuasion, which so obviously had worked on his King, might prevail over his brother Cardinal as well. Henry, however, was delighted by my acquiescence to his request for patience and my calm in the face of this, the final challenge and barrier to our marriage.

I was too nervous, too anxious to remain at Hever. I could not bear to be so far from the proceedings. I demanded that Henry allow me to return and he agreed. I could not come to court, but was installed at Durham House on the Strand soon after Campeggio's arrival in London. I found, there, that my restless pacing and high-strung nerves were not due to Hever and her so-familiar walls. Jane, Margaret and Bridget began to grow dizzy, watching me pace about my apartments like a lioness of the Tower menagerie.

I was desperate to be near Henry, to keep him strong throughout the trial, to keep his mind set on our goal, to prevent Wolsey from poisoning his mind... After receiving an anxious and strained letter from me, Henry moved me to Suffolk House, which was closer again to him. Though it was their own house, the Duke and Duchess of Suffolk were ordered not to visit whilst I used their property. That her house had been commandeered by her brother's latest strumpet was enough to turn Mary Tudor against me for good. Although her husband supported me, Mary turned to Katherine. I cared little now for those who stood against me, and despite my foreboding about the trial, I began to hold court at Suffolk house. Courtiers arrived in droves to pay court to me. Henry ordered my rooms refurbished at great expense, and suffocated me with jewels, furs, and rich materials for gowns. I was drunk; with both new power and terror. Would this trial usher in the happiest time of my life, or would it see me fall, discarded, from the heights of royalty to disgrace where no man would ever touch me? For, after all, most people believed I was Henry's mistress. They believed that he had known me carnally. This meant I was in the same position as my sister, even though I was still a virgin. My reputation was suspect. Only Henry's love... only making an honest marriage with him would save my reputation.

I was elated by my new power and terrified by my restless imaginings and that combination brought reckless flights of fancy to my head. When Henry and I met we quarrelled often; about Wolsey, about Katherine, about Campeggio and the Pope. But, after, I would be crushed in his fervent arms as we reconciled. I felt as though I might fly apart. Never had I felt such pressure weighted upon my slim shoulders.

Henry was closeted with Campeggio and Wolsey every day. They pored over our *Matter*, and Henry sent me messages at all hours, trying to appease my changeable temper, assuring me, with obvious relief, that Campeggio was keen to keep the matter out of court if possible. Campeggio wanted to prevail upon Katherine to enter a religious order. This, Campeggio believed, would be the ideal solution for it would save public embarrassment for the King and Queen, and allow Henry to marry again swiftly.

When I saw Campeggio from afar as he travelled to Westminster Abbey one day, I was not impressed. He was an old man. A prince of the Church, he was, but still an old man, riddled by gout and infirmities. He wore a long, ratty beard, stained by his food and drink, and George informed me he complained long and often about the trials God had sent to him with his ill-health.

"It is his *favourite* subject," George said dryly one night as he visited, making me chuckle. "In all honesty, sister, I believe the man could go all night listing his many and various complaints… and then go on to say he faces them all with patience, silence and humility!" George snorted. "It is the patience of all those forced to listen to the old gouty goat which is tested!"

My brother was a balm to my fractured spirits. In his company, my heart lifted and my humour returned. But when he left me, when I was alone, I found no rest. Sometimes at night, Henry would send secretly for me and I would slip, by barge, across London, pad down dark passages by candlelight and into his chambers where we would talk. I would let him kiss and stroke my soft skin, reminding him always of the still-greater pleasures we should have together once we were man and wife. It was important, now more so than ever, that Henry keep in mind the rich rewards that would come by seeing this through. I could not let him falter.

We talked of our children, this vast brood of sons and daughters that we were both eager to meet. I took it upon myself to remind Henry of why he so desired this annulment. Henry hated open confrontation, especially with women. Battle, he could face with boyish joy. Trouble in his realm he could hand to others, such as Wolsey, to deal with. But he did not want to face Katherine in the upcoming trial. I had to keep his mind centred. We were so close now, so close to achieving everything we wanted. We had endured so much already. We both longed for the end to this suffering and limbo.

Soon, we said, *soon…* It cannot be long now.

The common people understood what was happening now, too. When I went hunting, people in villages hissed curses at me. They saw me as an evil upstart seductress who had turned their beloved King against their wonderful, saintly Queen. I was nothing but a whore leading the King astray. They did not understand, none of them, that this *had* to happen, that the marriage in which Henry was trapped was unlawful and immoral. They hated me, they blamed me for the trial, and I cannot deny that their hatred cut me. But they would understand soon enough, I hoped.

I stayed inside, hiding from the harsh words and accusing eyes of the people. For Katherine, however, there was nothing but cheers and tears. She had been their Queen for almost twenty years and they respected and adored her. But it was not only their love for Katherine that turned them against me. It was their own fears. Wives especially, hated me, for if the King set a precedence, husbands may be able to leave their wives if they tired of them. What would that spell for wives but abandonment and disaster? I knew this was not what was happening. But that was not what the people saw… They were enraged, they blamed me for all of Katherine's woes, and she was more than clever enough to play their sympathy for all it was worth. Oh yes, I was frightened then. I told Henry there was nothing in this world that could protect me but his love.

"You shall always have it," he assured me. "You and no other, Anne."

"When we are married they will all forget," I said, as much to assure myself as him. "When our sons are born, they will see God smiles on our union."

I sat on his great, strong lap and he stroked my arm. "It is true. Our sons will be the vindication of all of this, Anna," he agreed. "When you become large with my child, all will see that God smiles upon us and on England once again. We will see right prevail, my love… and the people will rejoice to see our boys! I cannot wait to see them myself!"

"I cannot wait to start making them, Henry." I giggled as he swept me onto the window seat to kiss my breasts. In amongst all my fears, when I felt him close, I knew that I could not lose him. No man had ever wanted a woman as he wanted me.

Chapter Thirty-Seven

Suffolk House
Christmas 1528

That Christmas, I held my own celebrations at Suffolk House. I ordered great entertainments for the twelve days of Christmas, to end with a most grand celebration on Twelfth Night. My servants went out into the park around Suffolk House and gathered in holly, mistletoe and branches of greenery. The scent of fresh, green leaves filled the air in Suffolk House, along with the delicious scents rising from the kitchens. On Christmas morning, my ladies and I attended Mass in the private chapel, marking the end of the fast of Advent. Henry was at Greenwich. He had to be seen with Katherine on Christmas Day, but he promised to come to me as soon as he could.

When Henry joined us on Christmas night, his face was lined with frustration. Before Mass that morning, Katherine had taken the opportunity to berate him again on his *Great Matter*, squawking on that she was his true wife and I was leading him into sin. Although he had remained dutifully at her side during the day, he was relieved to escape. The court celebrations had been uncomfortable, to say the least.

Katherine, for all her wisdom, was a fool when it came to Henry. She could not see that the way she approached and *reproached* him only drove him further from her. Henry admired women who were strong and independent. I knew that Katherine, for all her dutiful manner and loyalty, was a strong-minded and stubborn woman. Perhaps he saw the same spirit in me that once he had loved in her… But their love was done now, if ever it had truly existed. Katherine could not accept this, nor could she see that alternately screeching at Henry like a crazed harridan and then begging and weeping was not a winning combination. That night,

Henry left a wife he was starting to loathe, to join a love who welcomed him with entertainment, flirtation and wit. What would any man have chosen?

I had ordered a late feast on Christmas night, knowing that Henry would be busy during the day and early evening. The feasting would go on into the night, and then we would dance until the dawn approached. As he arrived, rubbing his head, I put my cool hands to his face and kissed his cheek. "I have missed you," I said, standing on tip toes to reach him, even though I was not a short woman. He put his huge arms about me.

"As I have missed you," he sighed. "I thought *that woman* was never going to stop. I wager I will hear her voice echoing through my mind all night."

"Then we must play the pipes, flutes and drums loudly, my lord," I smiled naughtily, "to drown out the sound of the harpy who clings by her claws to your rock."

He chuckled at that and allowed me to lead him into the great hall where my assembled supporters broke into wild cheering to see him arrive. We moved through them together, arm in arm. We sat at the head of the top table and Henry breathed in a great sigh and let it out again, as though he had finally found release from Katherine.

"You will feel better after some wine and food, my lord." I rose and poured a goblet of wine for him myself. He was touched to see me serve him. There were, after all, plenty of servants to do such tasks. I put my hands to his forehead and kneaded his brow softly. He relaxed under my hands, and then took them in his, kissing them.

"None looks to my comfort as you, Anne," he said gruffly. I sat down again, and Henry ordered that the feast be brought in.

Outside the night was already old. Stars shone in a clear sky over the icy streets of London. Everywhere people were celebrating at their firesides, or sleeping in their beds. But we had only just begun our celebrations. They were to go on through the night and into the next day.

The traditional boar's head was brought out to huge applause, decorated with bay and rosemary. The scent of its sticky, rich flesh made my tongue tingle with anticipation. We ate pottages of mary bone and carrot, French mutton pottage with herbs, almonds and winter greens, and leek and oatmeal broth. On the lower tables, the great cups of ale were passed around, each diner wiping his mouth carefully before taking a sip. At the higher tables we each had our own goblet of silver or pewter, and these were replenished with ale, beer or wine as the diner preferred.

Roasted geese, fat, golden and plump sat beside stews of mutton and onion in wine broth. Stuffed pancakes filled with kidney, ginger, saffron and cinnamon lay piled on silver trenchers. Roasted sides of venison were served in thick slices upon saffron-bright frumenty. Rump of beef stewed with cabbage and dove flesh bubbled still red-hot in its dish. Hog sausages packed with meat and pepper let out little pops as their skins were pierced by knives. Bones from the meat were placed on voider platters at the elbow of each diner, and in between serving themselves, our guests wiped their knife or spoon clean with pieces of bread which were collected by servants to give to the poor who waited at the gates of Suffolk House.

Whole roasted pig with apple preserve was carved carefully by the young lads of Henry's household, earning high acclaim from the King when they did their task well. Spit-roasted rabbits glistened in parsley and verjuice sauce and white pudding and black pudding were sliced and passed around on pewter platters. Fried mutton balls glistened in a sugar-rich sauce. Capons boiled with imported oranges were set beside pigeons in savoury rice pudding. Chicken and gooseberry stew steamed next to baked crane. Lamprey, Henry's favourite dish, was served three ways; stuffed, roasted and boiled. Whole roasted peacock, with its feathers spread out behind it, was brought in to applause from the diners. Seethed mussels with vinegar and garlic wafted delicious scents of salty, sweet flesh. Lobster was boiled and broken apart to be dipped in a simple but delicious lemon and oil sauce. Gammon was stuffed with hard boiled eggs, cloves, pepper and mace. Crayfish tarts were served alongside vinegary cod pie and roasted hare.

Pies of buttered, roasted gourd sat proud beside baked parsnips in honey and butter. Boiled and salted turnips, and cowcumbers and mushrooms potted in sweet vinegar graced our tables. Quince preserves, rich, bright marmalades and sweet pies of conserved fruits released puffing steam of overpowering sweetness. And at the banquet of sweets afterwards, I brought out a grand sculpture of the King himself, crafted from marchpane and sugar, with roses and dragons entwined at his feet. On his arm was a falcon, my own personal badge. Henry cried out with appreciation, and insisted on feeding me the falcon himself.

"None other should have it but you, my love," he said, popping another bit of sugar fondant into my already-full mouth. I put my hands to his sleeve, giggling, begging him to stop for my mouth was full, but he playfully continued.

His eyes were a bloodshot with wine and weariness, but he was so merry and playful, so different to how he had looked when first he arrived, plagued by Katherine's shadow, that I kept swallowing and opening my mouth for another morsel. By the time we finished, I felt as though I might grow wings and fly for all the sugar coursing through my blood. We danced that night with gay abandon, our feet flitting about the room, our hands clapping in time with the flute and the drum. We drank more wine, feeling it heat our senses, and eventually, as the grey dawn approached, we made for our chambers. Many of the company were unsteady on their feet and more than a few gentlemen, my brother included, had to be carried to their rooms.

That night I took Henry to my chamber, but we did little more than embrace and talk. He was exhausted by his time with Katherine, and then his exuberant celebration with me. It was past six of the clock by the time we said goodnight and went to our beds. I have to admit that rising at all the next day was hard. My head hurt and my mind was dull from the wine, food, and the small sleep I had enjoyed. But that afternoon we rode out into the country, not to hunt, but just to take the air, and that revived my spirits greatly.

I found George later, suffering greatly. He was taking a bath when I arrived in his rooms, trying to steam out the wine that festered in his blood. Then he had to take to his bed, as was necessary when one bathed in winter, lest the bather catch a wandering illness. I waited and scolded him when he emerged, ashen-faced and clutching yet more wine in a goblet in his hands. "You should have drunk more sparingly, brother." I nodded to the cup. "That will only put off the inevitable, you know."

He lifted the goblet to his lips and drained it. "It is the only thing that will revive me now, Anne," he said drolly, and then grimaced, rubbing at his belly as though he were our uncle Norfolk. "Jane was in my ear all night, gossiping. A man can only take so much before he is driven to drink."

"If you were kinder to her, she would not gabble so at you," I said, running a hand over one of the glorious tapestries with which Henry had furnished the rooms of Suffolk House. "She prattles at you because you listen so little to her, so she feels she must fill the silence." I took my hands from the tapestry and toyed with a tablet of gold with inlays of enamel which hung at my waist.

"She certainly does that." He sighed and dropped into a chair with a thump. His nightshirt fell loose about him. "Counsel me not on my wife. Not now, Anne... I have not the strength." He held out the goblet for more wine and, once filled, tilted it back and drank deeply.

Realising I was to get no sense from him that day, and sensing he would rather be alone, I rose to leave. "Try to be kinder to her, brother... for all her faults, she loves you more than anything in this world. Such a thing should not be so lightly dismissed." George groaned loudly and put a cushion over his face. I left, feeling, as always, rather sorry for my sister in law.

During the twelve nights of Christmas, my court at Sussex House revelled and celebrated just as at Greenwich all was staid and dull. At least, that is what those who travelled between the two informed me. Henry divided his time between Katherine and me, but it was far from even. Whenever there was a public event at Greenwich, he had to be there, but whenever he could, he was with me. Furious rounds of dancing, feasting, hawking, gambling and games went on at Sussex House. We danced every night until dawn, and yet still managed to rise for Mass the next morning. It was not only heady enjoyment that Christmas. I also attended Mass twice daily, read in my chambers and discussed Scripture with my ladies. But when Henry was with me I had to ensure he had a better time than with Katherine. It was not hard, of course, given Katherine's behaviour, but all the same, I knew I was not only comforting the man I loved, but was showing him the kind of court he would enjoy when I was his wife.

On Twelfth Night, before the great feast, the customary Twelfth Cake was brought in. Inside was hidden a coin; in common households, a bean. Whoever found this treasure hidden inside their portion of the rich fruitcake was made the King or Queen of the Bean, and presided over the entertainments as sovereign. That year, Norris found the coin. Laughing, Henry insisted that Norris sit upon his royal chair of estate for the night, and order the court about as though he were the King. Sweet Norris was rather overcome by this honour, blushing most becomingly as Henry commanded him to rule over us. Games, riddles and dances ensued and later, we undertook the old ceremony of drinking from the wassail cup, and crying "wassail!" to each other. It was a merry night.

My father had brought a new artist into our throng and I was pleased to introduce Master Hans Holbein to Henry. Henry loved art and was as keen as I was to make the court a glittering showcase for artistic talent. My father had shown me portraits that Holbein had done and I was amazed at his skill.

"Your subjects seem to emerge from the canvas as though they were alive," I said in wonder to Master Holbein as I introduced him to Henry. "Truly Henry, even in the works of the great masters that I saw in France, of Leonardo himself, there was never such an expression of *reality* in a painting as I have seen in yours, Master Holbein."

Holbein blushed, he was a humble man. My flattery was a bit too much for him and Henry laughed to see his modest manners. "Mistress Boleyn is ever apt to be overwhelming in praise to those she thinks well of," Henry chuckled. "As I well know, but..." He clasped my hand as I started to protest. "But, she is rarely wrong, which means I must see more of your work, Master Holbein, you will bring some examples to the palace and I will see what commissions we may give to you."

Holbein bowed, flustered, perhaps slightly overcome by the King's politeness. My father rushed in to lead him away.

"A genius," my father said later. "But not the greatest of courtiers."

"Perhaps not," I agreed. "But with such talent, he does not need to be."

Chapter Thirty-Eight

Suffolk House
Winter 1529

That winter, as gales blew and storms raged, we continued to prepare for the trial. Campeggio was, it seemed, in no particular hurry to get events on their way. He spent much time with Henry and Wolsey, but visited Katherine too, and was often closeted with her. Henry and I were tense, petitioning Wolsey almost every day, asking when the trial would begin. Wolsey spent that winter bleating like a ewe in labour, going on and on about the evidence and witnesses and protocol and any other excuse he could summon to his imagination. He wanted to call more witnesses. He wanted to go over our documentation again and again and again. I suspected neither Cardinal actually wanted the trial to go ahead. They wanted time; time to convince Katherine to leave with grace, and if that failed, time to pressure Henry to give up. In our frustration, Henry and I turned on each other. Our arguments became frequent, and heated.

"Cardinals have all the time in the world, so it seems!" I cried, gazing at him with feral, angry eyes. "And you, my lord, do *nothing* to speed them along!"

"*Nothing*?" he bellowed, pacing towards me and taking hold of my shoulders. I faced Henry icily, staring at him with cold eyes even as he shook me. "Everything I do is for the *Great Matter*! Everything I do is for you!" he yelled.

Hot rage replaced cold fury. "Then more must be done!" I shouted back. His hands gripped me painfully, but I did not wince. I stared at him, my eyes burning in their sockets. "You must *make* them hurry! You are the King, are you not?"

Henry's face was mottled purple and red. For a moment I thought he might strike me, but instead he pushed me away and stormed out, shouting he would never return to be so insulted. But I knew he would be back. I was his only comfort, and he was mine. His cardinals, his Pope, Katherine and her supporters... they were all against us. Even in his anger he knew I was not only his love, but his greatest ally. He returned later that night, contrite, begging for forgiveness. Our reconciliation was passionate. I allowed him to unlace my gown and bury his frustration in his lust. At such times, I cared not if the whole world heard us. We still had not been together as a man and wife, but of late he had shown me what joy might be brought to a woman from a man kissing her in her most secret parts. Henry was skilled at such arts, and he was teaching me well. But still, I kept the last prize from him.

"My Anne," he said as he lay upon me, his head against my bare breasts. "There is no one like you in all the world."

"Then I hope there will be none to ever take you from me, my lord."

"Never let the thought into your head," he murmured. "I am yours, and always will be." His chest was bare, his remaining clothes in disarray. I laced my fingers over his chest, stroking his hot skin and feeling the tension release from his blood.

"Still, my love," I said softly. "The Cardinals delay us... They do not wish for this trial to go ahead. Surely you see this now?"

"Campeggio is trying very hard to persuade Katherine to bow out with grace," he muttered. "It is only she who stands in our way, my love... The Cardinals, even the Pope, they are trying to convince her of what is right, but she refuses to listen." He looked up at me. "I never thought I could hate a woman as I do her."

I shivered at his malevolent expression, but at the same time, I relished it. The farther he was from loving Katherine, the better for me. "She is stubborn and sinful," I whispered. "She clings to her position for pride. Long ago she could have ended this, but she will not. I hate her too, Henry, for all she has done to you."

"She is making me sick," he said plaintively. "These headaches and pains, I never had them before, not like this. I believe truly, that she has worked some curse upon me, to torture me."

I stroked his head, listening to the winds bellow and howl outside. "You have only to come to me when the headaches assail you," I consoled.

He nodded. "You have magic in those cool little fingers," he said, kissing them. "They are the only thing that works."

We talked into the night. He fell asleep on my bed, and as he slept I looked out of the window and into the night's sky. The heavens were black, like velvet, with grey clouds obscuring the stars. Wind keened outside, wailing as it swept through London. Inside Suffolk House, floorboards creaked and whistling draughts whispered. I listened to Henry's steady breathing. In the darkness, my heart started to pound fast within my breast.

My life was racing past and I had no part to play in it. I could have been married, to another, by now and borne children. I could already have been a wife and a mother. I could have known the satisfaction of a babe in my arms. For a moment, panic assailed my spirits, but when I looked back at Henry, I knew that I would not take any of these fevered imaginings instead of him. It was him I wanted... No matter how hard all of this was... I had to keep that firm in my mind. Henry, and the throne, they would be worth the wait, worth all that I might sacrifice to gain them. I just had to hold on. I had to stay strong.

Later that week Henry came to me in high dudgeon. I hardly had time to ask him what the matter was before he started to rant in a most animated, and irritated fashion, throwing his cloak, thick with water and ice, onto a chair at the fireside. "Campeggio says the Pope will allow my daughter, Mary, and my bastard son, Fitzroy, to marry!" he exclaimed, throwing himself into a chair.

"But… they are half brother and sister," I said, astounded. "How can that be permitted by the Church? It is incest."

Henry sat forward, his shoulders hunched. "So said I to Campeggio! When I refused such an ungodly union, Campeggio said that the Pope may be prevailed upon to recognise any children that we have, Anne, as legitimate."

"Without marriage?"

"He suggests that I may be able to take two wives at the same time."

"Where has that idea sprung from?"

Henry coughed uncomfortably. "It may be that *I* suggested such a thing earlier in the year, sweetheart…" he said, and then rushed on, seeing my baleful expression. "But I only meant for as long as it would take to separate me from Katherine! Not as a permanent arrangement!"

I pushed back my shoulders, making my gown of rich damask embroidered with rosebuds rustle. "Such suggestions as these are unholy, Henry… A man cannot have two wives and you *cannot* marry your daughter to your bastard son! I will bear no children that are not born within the bounds of holy matrimony. I would never be recognised as your wife and Queen. I would only be your mistress! I will not live in such a position!"

"I said the same to the Cardinals, sweetheart," he cooed, rising and taking hold of my shoulders in an effort to calm me. "I will not have our marriage questioned. You will be my wife and Queen, not my mistress, I promise you."

"Good!" I exclaimed and then frowned as a thought swam into my mind. "Does this mean Campeggio thinks we will lose the trial?"

Henry shook his head. "He assures me that he knows our way is just. He seeks only to find a solution that will save all involved the shame of this public trial."

"Then he would better spend his time convincing Katherine that she should go to a nunnery!" I cried, frustrated.

"That *is* what he is trying to do, my love," he continued. "Wolsey has told him that without a favourable judgement, England will be no friend to the Pope. I have lectured Campeggio myself, on the themes and arguments of this matter, and he admits that I am as learned as any scholar of Church law. We cannot lose. Campeggio has shown Wolsey and me a bull he carries from the Pope. It sanctions all that we want, Anne… When the trial goes ahead, we are sure to win."

I put my head against his strong chest. The gold cloth on his tunic scratched at my cheek, but I did not care. I worried for these offers. Was it as Henry said, and Campeggio only offered such things to avoid the shame and embarrassment of a public trial? Or did he seek to appease the King with these offers, because he knew that we were going to lose?

Chapter Thirty-Nine

That winter, I asked Henry for further help for my sister Mary. I had a plan in mind, one that would provide a dowry for her daughter Catherine in the future. The Carey lands and wealth, such as they were, would be good enough for young Henry and I was going to find ways to add to his inheritance as best I could, but there was at present nothing for Catherine. The girl needed a dowry if she was to marry respectably. I had thought about it for some time, and I knew what I was going to ask. I went to Henry in his private quarters and was admitted straight away. No longer did anyone dare keep the King's beloved waiting as though she were a mere court lady. Even the Queen had to beg for admittance, but not I.

He put out his hands to me as I entered and kissed me soundly on the mouth. "Sweetheart," he cooed. "This is an unexpected pleasure. You catch me deep in reading for the trial." He indicated to the papers strewn haphazardly on the desk. "There is much to prepare."

"I am sorry, my lord, I came not to talk on the trial... for once." Henry smiled, for in truth it had been all we had spoken of for a long time. "I came to ask a favour, for my ward and his sister," I said carefully. Henry did not like to hear Mary's name spoken.

"What of them?" he asked, straightening his collar studded with rubies and diamonds.

"In the bonds of my responsibility for my ward, Henry Carey," I went on. "I have been thinking on his sister. The wealth of the Carey estates will have to provide a dowry for her when she is grown. Should Henry Carey have to bestow such a dowry, his inheritance will be much affected. I would not want my ward to be reduced in means when he becomes an adult."

"And you have an idea of how to ease this burden, sweetheart?"

"I do."

"Then ask."

The edges of my mouth quivered with mirth. Henry did so love to tease me into asking favours. He loved to please me, but he also loved that I should come to him as a supplicant... There was in him a great deal of showmanship, and when he could be the magnanimous King, he loved to play the part to its fullest. I think he also enjoyed that in such situations, for once, I was the one coming to *him*. In our relationship, I was the master in many ways, and he my servant. When our roles were reversed, even for a short time, he found it pleasurable.

"There was an annuity granted to Will Carey when he lived," I said, "of one hundred pounds per year. If this were to be granted to his widow, then she would ably be in a position to save for a dowry for her daughter."

"It would do more than that!" exclaimed Henry, twisting a golden ring fashioned into the shape of Death's head on his finger. It was the latest style, and was there to remind the wearer of his mortality; something of which Henry never really to be needed reminded. "It would be a most generous grant."

"It would, my lord... but these children are of royal blood, are they not?" I paused, just for a moment, to allow the thought that Catherine and Henry Carey could indeed be Henry's own children to sink in. "After all, William Carey *was* of the

Beaufort line, of your grandmother's own house… And they will be cousins to our children. It is fitting, therefore, that Catherine be provided for, as much for the honour of your line, as for her own dignity."

I could see both a glint of anger and a spark amusement in his eyes. He knew what I was up to, but I had presented my idea carefully, and honestly. Henry nodded. "I know the annuity of which you speak," he said. "And I think you are right, Anne, the girl should be provided for. The sums paid to her mother can also be used for your ward's future, as not all of that will be required, even for a handsome dowry!"

"You are so good to me, Henry," I said with genuine gratitude. "And to your people. Think how they will see this, as you reach out to help a fatherless daughter, one to whom the world has been cruel, and to lift her so that she stands proud, able to marry well and happily in the future. You are the best of Kings, and the most generous of men."

"How now," he blustered, becomingly pink in the cheeks. "The idea was yours, my love." He held me gently. "I will have the papers drawn up, my generous Anne, and young Catherine Carey will have all that she needs, due to the ever-watchful and kind eye of her aunt."

Mary was overjoyed when I wrote to her of the annuity, and it was implemented with immediate effect. One hundred pounds a year was a vast sum. I think Henry was pleased to grant the annuity, not only for my persuasions, but also because he knew there was a distinct possibility he was the father of Catherine Carey. She had been born when Mary was more often in the bed of the King than in the bed of her own husband, and whilst Henry might have doubts about Henry Carey being his child, we were all quite sure that Catherine was indeed his. She even looked like him, with her golden-red hair. Her eyes were like her mother's, brown and warm, but there was something of Henry in her face and in even her manners. So, yes… Henry granted me another favour, but I think he did it as much for himself and his secret conscience, as he did for me.

Mary was comfortable now, and her future was secure. Despite her troubles with our parents, she did not leave Hever. Our father had been ordered to take her under his wing, and he had done so. This arrangement allowed her to save from her annuity for her children's futures. Our father and mother were often at court in any case, so often she was there alone with her children, which I think she preferred. No one spoke of another marriage for Mary. Our father would have been quite happy to marry her off, but only once I was Queen, for then the rewards would be all the richer. I think Mary was lonely at Hever, but there was not a great deal I could do for that. I had done all that I could for her. In my role as young Henry Carey's guardian, I sought to do more; trying for estates and lands to add to his future wealth. But for my sister, I had done enough, now, I reasoned. I hoped she felt the same. But for now, I had other worries to deal with.

Chapter Forty

Suffolk House
Winter 1529

Despite continued delays, Henry clung to the belief that Wolsey and the Church were going to do all they could for us. The trial had still not begun, our ambassadors were still trying to gain access the Pope, and Campeggio was in such constant ill-health that it seemed we might never even start on this trial. By late January, as waterfowl started to return to England, I sensed Henry's trust in his chief advisor's constant promises was wavering. I called my father, George and Norfolk to Suffolk House to talk.

"I believe I have fully persuaded the Duke of Suffolk to be a friend to our cause." Norfolk pressed a hand to his side, his digestion evidently troubling him again. "Brandon is eager to be more in the ear of the King. He believes that if Wolsey is removed, he will become the King's chief advisor and even Chancellor." My uncle snorted with derision. "As if that mealy-brained, dullard donkey could take on such a post!"

"But even if we know that you are destined for that position, Your Grace," my father interjected. "We should allow Suffolk to continue in his fantasy, for now."

"Of course, Thomas." Norfolk waved a hand carelessly. "I was not about to spoil the little boy's dreams, after all."

George sat up and nodded to the servant at his side to pour wine for him. "The King examines every dispatch with keen attentiveness," he said. "He is under the impression that the Pope will capitulate, and more than that, that the Holy Father *wishes* to capitulate."

"I am not so sure," I said quietly. "Henry tells me that Campeggio has a papal bull which allows the annulment, but the Pope has not even met with our ambassadors... The Pope's illness is a feint, I am sure of it. And here, we move no faster. Henry waits for Rome, Campeggio waits for Rome, and Rome refuses to engage with us... It all feels as though they are deliberately dawdling."

"Then you must further motivate the King," said Norfolk. "Ask him to do more, to *demand* that the trial go ahead. If we cannot get an answer straight from Rome, then a decision made in England by his legate might tip the Pope's hand into a final ruling. If Campeggio *and* the Pope decide in our favour, none can disagree."

"I will, uncle," I agreed. "But you all must do the same. Let us be bound together in purpose. If we all speak as one, Henry must see that his faith in the Pope and in his cardinals is misplaced."

We agreed, and went forth to convince Henry to push for the trial to go ahead in England. But Henry was stubborn. "I believe in the goodness of the Holy Father," he protested, perhaps for the hundredth time. "Trust me, sweetheart. The Pope is a good friend to England; he gave me the title of *Defender of the Faith*, and knows I am his good soldier and loyal servant. Why else would he have sent Campeggio with a legal document allowing the annulment, if he was not on our side?"

Eventually, however, he agreed to petition the cardinals to speed things along. Henry was even more impatient than I was to be wed, and his embraces at night were becoming increasingly desperate. Part of this was because of his trysts with Katherine. The woman was proving more immovable than the white cliffs of Dover. Wolsey went to her, saying he had full proof that she had lain with Arthur as his wife. He cited the fact that all in England had thought at the time of

Arthur's death that she might be pregnant. Katherine, however, was resolute.

"Such things were said, Your Excellency," she boldly declared to Wolsey. "To provide a mask of respectability for the Prince, as he was not able to consummate the match. I never lay with Arthur as a husband. The only man I have ever lain with has been my true husband, King Henry." She went on to tell the Cardinals that she would not consider the judgement of a trial heard in England as valid. "I have many enemies here, my lords, and I will trust only in the court of the Holy Father." Katherine clearly did not trust either Wolsey or Campeggio to be neutral. She would trust only the Pope himself. As well she might since her nephew had him under his control!

They tried to reason with her, talking with her for hours on the wonders of a life lived in religious seclusion. They promised that she would keep her dowry and therefore live in comfort. Wolsey told Katherine she would retain guardianship of her daughter. The Princess Mary's legitimacy would be maintained and her place in the royal succession would be upheld. Until the King sired a son, Mary would remain England's heir. But although Katherine listened to them with good grace, her only response was to request legal counsel. Katherine also chose to confess to Campeggio, urging him to break the sacred silence of the confessional and tell not only the Pope, but whosoever he wished, that she had not slept in the same bed as Arthur for more than seven nights whilst they were wed, and that he had left her as he found her each time; a virgin. She told Campeggio that she intended to live and die in the state of matrimony, to which, she said, she had been called to by God, and that nothing could change her opinion.

Rapidly, Katherine became surrounded by supporters and those willing to give her the legal advice she craved. Bishop Fisher came forth as her representative in court. He was a clever, shrewd man, known for speaking his mind, and his appointment rattled Henry and me. Wolsey pleaded with Katherine that she should listen to the counsel of the Church, and she responded that she did listen… to Bishop Fisher, who disagreed with Wolsey and Campeggio. At one point Wolsey fell on his knees, begging with her to relent, but she would not.

Later that month, Katherine produced a new version of the original dispensation of her marriage to Henry, one which none of us had known existed. It appeared to undermine all our arguments and the bull Campeggio had from the Pope, as it stated that consummation had 'perhaps' taken place, and allowed the match between Henry and Katherine even with that in mind. Henry was livid to find Katherine had been hiding this document all this time, and demands were made that the dispensation be seized and examined to check it was not a forgery, but Katherine refused to hand it over, saying that she did not trust that it would not be conveniently lost or destroyed. Personally, I wondered why Katherine had been keeping this document a secret all these years… Had she thought that one day the King might question their marriage? Even at the time they were wed there had been objections raised due to her pervious union with Arthur. Had clever Katherine thought that she might need this secret dispensation one day, to defend herself? Therefore, to my mind, she must have always understood the possibly illegality of her match with Henry…

Wolsey and Henry were united in their annoyance at the Queen, and decided to press ahead with the trial, working on the original basis that the dispensation should not have been allowed in the first place, and that Katherine was, in the eyes of God, Henry's sister. This called into question the judgement of Pope Julius II, who had allowed the dispensation, and, in some ways, questioned the sanctity of papal authority; a dangerous path…. but one worth exploring if it brought about what we wanted.

At this time, Wolsey spoke wearily about retiring from public life, sending Henry into a panic. He summoned his minister and told him over and over how much he needed him, how he relied on him, and loved him. I knew, however, that this was a trick. Wolsey feared the King's temper. The Cardinal worried the blame for all this chaos would rest on his shoulders. He told Henry he was thinking of retiring to remind the King how much he needed him, and it worked. Henry was infatuated with Wolsey all the more for the thought he might lose him. I gritted my teeth and set my jaw. Every time he was in peril, the fat bat always had something up his costly red sleeve.

The trial approached, and it seemed that all on each side were ready to fight… to the death if need be.

.

Chapter Forty-One

Suffolk House
Spring 1529

That spring, the news from Rome was as bleak as the weather in England. Storms and tempests howled across England. Rain fell and sleet followed. The streets in London were a mess of earth, water and dirt. Every morning, when I looked from my window, all I would see was darkness.

Finally having got an interview with Pope Clement, after many months, our envoys in Rome sent word. At my urging, Gardiner had joined Vannes and Bryan in January, but even with the addition of that clever man, progress was slow and hope was spare. In late March, as downpours made the roads almost impassable in England, Gardiner wrote that they had finally met with the Pope. For months they had simply been forced to wait, presenting themselves at the papal court each morning, and waiting in the halls all day to see if the Pope was able to see them. They were put off constantly. The Pope was either too ill, too busy, too tired, too occupied, or too engrossed in constant prayer to admit them. Other envoys came and went, but ours were left there, waiting. It was months before they could even present their credentials and therefore be recognised as envoys from England according to the protocol of the papal court. It was entirely clear to me that the Pope did not want to even consider the *Great Matter*; he was too scared of the Emperor. Therefore, he stalled, just as did Campeggio here in England.

When Henry received Gardiner's missives, he had his treasurer, Tuke, send them on to Wolsey and me. After reading Gardiner's letter and one from Bryan, Henry had gone, in his fury, to play tennis and take his aggression out on the walls of the court, rather than on the heads of any he loved. Tuke was commanded to write of Henry's thoughts on the letters, as the King was, at that moment, incapable of doing anything rational.

"Master Bryan's letter, for as many clauses as the King showed me, was totally of desperation," Tuke wrote. *"Affirming plainly that he could not believe the Pope would do anything for His Grace, with these words added: 'it might well be in his paternoster, but it was nothing in his creed."*

The riddle was clear enough to me; the Pope may well *pray* that Henry would get a solution to his troubles, but he would *commit* himself to nothing. Bryan wrote further that Clement would not agree to state that the dispensation given for Henry to marry Katherine by his predecessor was invalid, and that the Pope was mightily offended that the English would simply expect this of him. Henry's tactics of threatening the Pope had only caused the Holy Father to become more set against him, and the relentless pressure our envoys were keeping up in Rome was driving the Pope further from us. What were we to do though? Give up? Henry believed that more pressure should be put on the Pope, not less.

Henry and Wolsey went to Campeggio and criticized him for the Pope's sullen stance towards our ambassadors. Campeggio, stuck in the middle of his master and the King of England, merely replied with more platitudes and half-made promises. Despite Wolsey's recent ploy to remind Henry how valuable he was by threatening to resign, in his growing irritation with the Pope, Henry was losing faith in his Chancellor. Henry wavered between wanting so desperately to believe in his friend, to doubting his motives. He could not understand why Wolsey could not just have this *done*. Every other time he had wanted something, Henry only had to turn to Wolsey and his wishes were made reality. Now, his best servant was proving as ineffectual as everyone else. Henry was disappointed in Wolsey, and his disappointment terrified the Cardinal.

Imperial envoys were pressing the Pope to decide the matter in Rome. They wanted the Pope to summon Katherine and Henry there, and have an open, public trial at the Vatican. Henry was resolute that he was not going to be dragged to Rome, and humiliated in front of the leaders of other nations. He sent letters to our envoys stating that since Campeggio was here in England he wanted the matter decided *in England*. He pressured the two cardinals to start the trial, saying that this had gone on long enough. I was beginning to suspect that the papal bull Henry had so much faith in had been provided for Campeggio to use only if Katherine agreed to the annulment.

One day, George saw Henry in his gardens at Richmond, screaming at Wolsey. My brother said that Henry seemed to grow, looming over the Cardinal like a giant. Wolsey threw himself to his knees before the King, his red robes soaked through at the knees with sodden mud, begging for Henry's patience and forgiveness. Over their heads, ravens and crows flew, attracted by the noise. They winged over the head of the Cardinal and his King, as though circling corpses on a field of battle.

"I think the time is drawing near when the Cardinal will fall from grace," said George as we sat at my card table. To please me, Henry had just made George chief steward of Beaulieu Palace, Master of the King's Buckhounds and an Esquire of the Body... which meant George had more money than ever to lose to me. We sat with cards in our hands, and fine wagers on the table, but neither of us was concentrating on the game.

"Henry loves Wolsey as no other," I disagreed despondently. "Even now, even when he knows that the Cardinal cannot get him what he wants, he does not look to others. Still he keeps faith with the Cardinal, believing that eventually the fat bat will get him what he wants."

"The King loves one more than his Cardinal." George smiled, placing his cards on the table, abandoning the game entirely. "And that is you, Anne... Wolsey is failing him. Much now depends on this trial. If Wolsey does not get the King what he wants, he will be on more dangerous ground than he has ever known."

"I don't know which outcome to wish for, in truth, George." My lips twisted. "If all goes as we wish, then I will have my crown and my place beside Henry. If we fail, then Wolsey is disgraced. I have waited long to see his face fall, to see him brought low as he has done so many times to our family... Although I want the trial to find for the King, I cannot deny that seeing Wolsey fall on his face would bring me satisfaction."

"I will pray that the outcome *is* for us..." George leaned back, stretching his arms above his head. "But remember that this cloud has a lining of sweet sunshine about it, even if we fail, sister."

From France, François wrote of his support for the trial, which bolstered Henry's spirits. But still, no date was set. We moved as though our feet were stuck in a muddy mire. But although I despaired for this, there was other news which pleased me better.

Gardiner wrote to me. I opened his letter eager for news of the annulment. He spoke of further meetings with the Pope and of their mission, to be sure, but the letter was actually written to inform me of Gardiner's transference of loyalties from his master, Wolsey, to me. He assured me of his devotion to me; his dedication to my cause, and the King's. He would work tirelessly for such a mistress, he said, "*for there is all in your being and manner that convinces me in right for your cause.*" In short, he was asking me to replace Wolsey as his patron. This was highly significant. Stephen Gardiner was one of Wolsey's best men, and a rising advisor to Henry; a man to be highly prized.

I showed my father the letter and he was pleased. "It demonstrates that people are recognising who is going to win," he said. I wrote back to Gardiner and sent assurances of my patronage as well as a gift of cramp rings for him and the other ambassadors. I had another ally, and one who was choosing to defect, secretly, from the Cardinal to me. Norfolk was also pleased to see the note.

"Gardiner is a shrewd man," he said as his stomach gurgled. "If he thinks that our side is the one to wager his career upon, this is good."

"The rest of our *Matter* does not look so promising to me, uncle," I complained. "The Pope delays, the Cardinals delay, and yet the King continues to trust in them. I wonder if there is not another path for us to take, for it seems that all we do here and now is waste precious time."

Norfolk nodded. "And you should have been married and breeding by now," he said, looking me up and down as though I were a cow brought to market. "You are not getting any younger."

I stiffened at that. It was true enough though. I was nearing twenty-seven years of age; old for a woman to be still a virgin and as yet unmarried. Most women my age had been married many years, and had a babe or two on the hip and in the cradle. My friend Bridget had a hoard of children from her two husbands. His words hurt, as I am sure was intended, but I could not argue with the truth in them. I swallowed my pain and annoyance.

"Exactly," I agreed, noting the gleam of happiness in his eye for causing me pain. "And yet I am still young enough to bear many children."

"Your mother and sister are proven fertile enough, it is true," Norfolk replied. "We must find ways to motivate the King against Wolsey. I am sure that if that worm were not forever digging into the King's ear then everything would run smoother for us."

"Then you must convince the King, uncle, that you are the best man to replace the Cardinal... You are the natural successor to the Cardinal, were he to be removed, are you not? Perhaps if the King trusted more in your counsel, then he would not mind the Cardinal's removal as much?"

Norfolk blustered at my veiled insult. To me, it was obvious Henry thought there was no one to replace Wolsey. Henry did not trust that Norfolk was as able as Wolsey, in this affair or any other of the realm, and that was causing him to hesitate. And Henry was perhaps right... the Cardinal was an extraordinary workhorse, but even if he got Katherine removed, he would not support me as Queen.

"Speak out in the Privy Council, Your Grace," I advised. "*Show* Henry he can trust your counsel and then he will turn to you more, I am sure of it."

"I speak out more than enough!" declared Norfolk angrily. "Do not presume to instruct me, niece, as though you were my better! I know well enough my place, as you should have a mind to yours!"

"My place is with the King, uncle..." I said warningly. "And soon enough, my place will be on the throne of England. It would be well that *you* remembered that."

Norfolk flushed scarlet with anger. "Never have I been so berated by such a harpy of a woman as my own niece." He raised his stick, advancing on me. "Poisonous *shrew*!" he screamed. My father leapt from his chair, catching the stick as it flew over my head. He shook his head in warning at Norfolk and the Duke backed away. I stood stock still, glaring at my uncle. Norfolk exhaled, struggling to control himself.

"Be careful of yourself, niece, you are no Queen, and I am your superior by birth, title and sex."

"But I have the love of the King, and you do not, uncle," I said coolly. "So if anyone should be careful, Your Grace, it is you. Put down that stick before I have the King break it over your neck, or have him take your head for your insolence! Shall I tell my future husband of this, my lord? It will not take much to remove you from your position *and* from the court. The King is already displeased with you… Would you like me to tell him that you raised hand and weapon against me too? You *will* learn to control yourself. I am not your wife and will take no beating from you even if you be my kinsman or my uncle."

The colour drained from Norfolk's flushed and wrinkled face. He glared at me, clutching the top of his stick as though he wanted to thrash me with it. I knew he would not dare. He might not like it but I was his best bet to destroy the Cardinal and Henry would be enraged if he touched me. Norfolk stalked off, muttering about my upstart pretensions. My father let out a great huff of breath and shook his head. "You should have more care with Norfolk, Anne," he warned. "The man might bluster and rage, but he is the most powerful magnate in England, and we need him on our side."

"He would do well to remember that I will be his Queen one day, father," I spat. "He should not insult me so, or attempt to treat me as he does his wife; with beatings and violence to keep her in line."

"As it would do you well to remember that he is rich, powerful and influential at court," he said. "Queen you will be one day, daughter, but even when you are crowned you will need supporters."

"All I need is the love of the King. When I bear him sons, I will become more precious to him than I am even now. And my son will be the future King of England. Norfolk will need to learn his place, father, and all I spoke to him were words of advice."

"And *insult*," he snapped. "You have a quick tongue, Anne, and often it serves you well, but you are apt to lash out when you are under pressure. Now is the most testing time any of us have known. Do not let it get the better of you... All those years in Burgundy and France, I sent you there to learn the art of being a courtier. The art of hiding your true feelings. Now, it is as though you have forgotten all that you once knew so well ... You are an open book for any to read, and that can be dangerous."

He kissed the top of my head. "Remember the lessons of your youth, my child," he went on. "Hide your inner thoughts and passions; it will serve you better."

Chapter Forty-Two

Suffolk House
Spring 1529

In April, as new lambs bleated in their hundreds each morning upon the still frost-laced hillsides of England, Henry wrote to our envoys in Rome, urging them to reject their desperation, and to continue to press the Pope with all energy and passion to make a decision. Henry wanted to avoid confrontation, to avoid the trial, and the best way to do that was to get the Pope to rule directly on his *Matter*. He implied that our envoys lacked zeal, and wrote ominously of his disappointment in their efforts. What our poor men in Rome made of such letters, I do not know, but it certainly frightened them into doubling their already frantic efforts on our behalf.

Henry also said that he was sure the Pope would never seriously consider dragging the King of England to Rome, as the Imperial ambassadors were pushing for, as it would be a grave insult to Henry's royal dignity to do so. François, too, wrote to the Pope, saying he supported Henry, and that he was unsure on his attendance at the conference being planned for Cambrai. There, peace between the Emperor and France was to be discussed. The prospect of continued war between France and Spain put pressure on Clement. If France brokered peace with Spain, the Pope might be freed from the Emperor as part of the negotiations. Clement wrote to Campeggio and instructed him to go ahead with the trial. A decision needed to be made.

Whilst this was encouraging, and we celebrated, letters arrived from my supporters in Rome. They hinted that Henry should not trust Wolsey. "*Whosoever made your grace believe that the Pope will do for you in this cause hath not, as I think, done your grace the best service,"* Bryan wrote, clearly implying this was Wolsey.

Henry was disturbed by these reports, but I could see he would not believe them, not without proof. In early May, Wolsey ordered his ally Sir John Russell, the same who had turned against me in the affair of the Broughton wards, to France to act as the Cardinal's representative at the French Court, petitioning François not to make peace with the Emperor, but to continue the war, and free the Pope that way. When I heard this, I went straight to Henry. "Please, Henry," I begged. "Do not send Russell to France. Not only is Russell no friend to me, but he is also Wolsey's man."

"The Cardinal has never needed my help in choosing a man to act for him, my love..." Henry gazed at me quizzically. "Why should I interfere now?"

"Do you remember what my cousin Bryan told us last autumn?" I asked. "He said that François himself suspected that Wolsey was not a good friend to you, Majesty... Although I have no proof, I fear that sending Russell, one of Wolsey's devoted servants, may only do ill for our cause." Henry's brow furrowed and a look both of anger and hurt sparked in his eyes. He hated the thought that Wolsey might be a traitor in his midst.

"Send Suffolk," I requested on impulse. "The Duke is as a brother to you, my lord, and you know he would never lie to you. He has good connections in France, through your sister, his wife." I looked up at Henry with desperate eyes. *"Please*, my lord. Although you trust Wolsey, I find myself doubting in him more and more each day. This time is so fragile. Send Suffolk, for you know without doubt that he is indeed your man... For me, Henry... Please?"

In his eyes I could see that he agreed with me. In their blue depths there was blossoming doubt on the ability and loyalty of his Cardinal. He nodded shortly. "Russell will be recalled, and I will send Suffolk in his stead." He rose from his chair, looking suddenly old and weary. "I will see you anon, sweetheart," he murmured, kissing my hand. "There are affairs I must attend to." Henry walked from that chamber as though he were an ancient soldier who had lost his last battle.

I heard later from my uncle Norfolk that Henry had gone to Suffolk himself that very hour, not only asking him to go in Russell's place to France, but ordering Suffolk to question François further about Wolsey. Suffolk was to probe about the court, and find out all he could. Although Henry had not shared this with me, perhaps feeling it was too painful to express in words to me, who had after all, long been outspoken against Wolsey, at least he was finally starting to understand he could not trust the Cardinal.

"You have done well, niece," commended Norfolk when he told me this a few days later. "The King is clearly suspicious of Wolsey, as he should be! The Cardinal will have to work a miracle now to save himself!"

"I trust Suffolk will find something incriminating in France?" I asked, lifting my eyebrows.

Norfolk nodded. A sly grin broke over his face. It was like looking at a weasel poised to rush a field mouse. "Oh," he said. "Of that I am sure…"

Chapter Forty-Three

Blackfriars Monastery
London
31st May 1529

The Legatine Court finally convened at Blackfriars Monastery to hear the case for the validity of the King's marriage. The Monastery had been used before for meetings of the Privy Council, and state occasions, and now, it would be the place where my future was decided. I could not be there. Of course I could not, for my appearance might rupture Henry's case, giving lie to his declaration that his only desire was to discover the truth about the legality of his union with Katherine. But I was there, in secret and with a deep cowl obscuring my face. I hid in an upper gallery at the back of the great hall, concealed amongst my father's servants. My father thought my actions rash, but did not manage to dissuade me from attending. I stood in the shadows, listening to these cardinals and men decide what would become of me. If they found for Katherine, I was undone. If they found for Henry, my dreams were about to become reality.

Campeggio and Wolsey, the court's two judges, processed slowly to the head of the packed hall, their scarlet robes bright even in the dull light. On their heads they wore flat red hats, proclaiming their status as Cardinals. Rings of gold and rubies, worn over the top of crimson gloves, encrusted their fingers. Blackfriars was a Dominican priory, hence the name, and the walls were covered in tapestry that depicted Biblical scenes. The floor was soft with expensive carpets. The great hall was suffocatingly hot; nobles and commoners alike had turned out to see the trial. The air was thick, cloying with the stench of mingled sweat and perfume.

Queen Katherine had eleven advocates, with Bishop Fisher and Doctor Standish at the head of them. They stood glowering at Wolsey as he approached. This would not only be a trial of the King's marriage, but a trial of Wolsey's skills and loyalty, for Wolsey had staked everything upon their trial. Wolsey had reproached Katherine before the trial for wooing the common people, "beckoning with her head and smiling," at them to win their love. Katherine had haughtily responded that it was the office of a queen, to show love to her people, and she was not about to abandon any of her duties. Outside the great hall, masses of common people had gathered, and they *all* cheered for Katherine. Her appearance on that first day was much remarked upon, as Henry was not there. He was represented by his advisors. I knew that Katherine had come to engender the support of the people, and I cursed to think Henry was not here to do the same. Although the people had no love for me, they adored their King. It might have been beneficial, in hindsight, to have him here.

The two Cardinals spoke of the reasons why the court had been convened, and asked Henry's men to speak first, and then Katherine's. Katherine, surprising everyone, chose not to let her advocates speak for her, but spoke to the court herself. She came to the front of the court leaning on the arm of her retainer, Griffith ap Rhys, and smiled for the cheers she received. She thanked the Cardinals for their introduction, but then went on to explain, in most annoyingly well-spoken words, that she believed this court held no justice for her.

"Although His Excellency, Cardinal Campeggio is a man of the cloth and the Church," she called out in a strong voice, which quite belied the feeble manner that she affected in leaning on her retainer's arm. "He is also a man *of* England! Cardinal Campeggio holds the post of Bishop of Winchester, and so he, like His Eminence, Cardinal Wolsey, is therefore a subject of my husband, the King, and is not impartial in this matter. I feel that this trial is weighted against me. I am but one poor and ignorant woman, far from her native country and home… and I am set upon by those who have a vested interest in finding for their master, and ignoring the righteousness of justice and mercy which I know would be offered to my plea were this trial held in Rome. I do not, therefore, recognise the legality of this trial, and will not accept its verdict. I ask here and now that this case be taken to the court of the Holy Father in Rome itself, and there I will accept the judgement of the Pope. He alone has the authority to decide on this matter, and to he alone will I defer."

There was much muttering at her speech. Rumbles of complaint spread through the hall. I am sure most people did not know that Campeggio held a post in England. It was a post in which he did little, although I must admit that he did take revenues from it. I looked out from under my cowl with nervous eyes. There were many heads nodding for Katherine, and I could see women wiping their eyes, pitying her. Katherine knew what she was doing; she was playing the emotions of the people for all they were worth.

"In addition," she continued, glancing about her. "I have in my possession the original dispensation of Pope Julius II. It was demanded of me by these men!" She pointed to the two Cardinals who shifted uneasily on their red cushions. "But I refused to deliver it into any hands other than my own, for fear that it may be lost or destroyed by those who seek to hide the truth… This dispensation is indisputably valid and proves that I am the King's one *true* wife. Even above this, I have been married for over twenty years to my beloved husband, and I have borne the King children, many of whom God chose to call to his kingdom, but one who remains the King's heir, the Princess Mary. If this matter is as my husband claims, that our unlawful marriage would bear no fruit, then how is it that I have borne many children, and have one precious child who is yet living? When I came to the King's bed I was a true maid. When I was married to Prince Arthur, he was a young, sick and weak boy, who was not able to consummate our union. Therefore, with this dispensation, and with the other proofs that I have spoken of, I am the King's one, only and true wife, in the eyes of God and under the laws of the Church and of England."

There was a thunder of applause as she finished, with people shouting, "God save the Queen!" and "God bless you, Your Majesty!" Katherine gazed regally about her, her expression triumphant. She leaned heavily on Rhys' arm as she went back to her seat. I gritted my teeth, grinding them against each other. Katherine was good. She should have been on the stage. She was winning approval with her deliberate combination of feminine weakness and forceful words.

Wolsey was sweating. He spoke quickly, and perhaps a touch *too* rapidly, on how this *was* a legal trial; that the Pope *had* approved for it to happen here in England and not in Rome and of how the Holy Father had appointed Campeggio and himself to this task and how there was definitely *no* cause to suspect that either of them were not impartial.

He was not believed by the gathered crowds. There may have been some doubt that Campeggio was Henry's man, but all knew that Wolsey *certainly* was. Katherine had won the first battle; there were many now who would not believe the trial was just, especially if it found for Henry.

Chapter Forty-Four

Blackfriars Monastery
Summer 1529

The proceedings went on, but the Legatine Court did not sit every day, as Campeggio often called for breaks due to his ill health. As witnesses were called, it was often necessary to wait for each to arrive. This confused me greatly, as gathering witnesses was one of the things that the Cardinals had claimed so much time for in the months preceding the trial. Why were they not already in London, and ready to testify? It was too familiar, all this postponement. But if I was dissatisfied on this count, I told myself at least the hearing was underway.

Henry appeared in person, in June, to present his case to the Cardinals, and swiftly overruled Katherine's objections. "*I will accept the verdict of this trial with all humility!*" Henry cried passionately, his deep voice booming through the sombre hall, which was as packed on that day as it had been on the day Katherine spoke. "Within the respect that *should be shown* to the Holy Father himself, who appointed these learned Princes of the Church to preside in his stead over this matter, and, as the duty of every Christian soul is to subject himself to the goodness and just nature of the Church, so shall you find your King!" Heads nodded all through the hall at his declaration. I breathed a sigh of relief. Henry was winning his people over.

He was magnificent. Strong and handsome, he stood in a doublet of purple damask and cloth of gold, his fingers glittering with diamond rings, and wearing hose of brilliant white to match his shoes. Upon his head was a cap of purple velvet topped with a long white feather. He looked so handsome, so strong and so authoritative. My heart swelled with pride and hope to see the reaction of his people. "False pride will not call *me* to question the judgement of a holy court such as this, even if it may tempt other hearts to!" Henry continued, glancing significantly at Katherine who returned his look with a steady gaze. "I am, *unlike others*, a humble penitent before God!"

"If you will speak, Your Majesty," Wolsey said, a greasy smile of satisfaction on his lips as Henry was received well by the crowds, "of what has led you to ask for this trial and for this judgement on your marriage...?"

Henry bowed his head and then looked up. On his face was genuine pain; the pain of having no son, which was his greatest desire and the agony of believing he was a sinner in the eyes of God, to whom he always looked for approval. Henry was not lying when he said his conscience troubled him about his marriage. He believed it, utterly. His marriage had troubled him for a long time. All could see the pain on his face, and many commented on it, feeling pity for their King.

"For many years, I have felt a nagging ache in my conscience, my lords," he said solemnly. "I asked myself why God had not allowed my wife and me to have living sons, heirs to this great Kingdom of England... Sons that I could cherish, nurture and love, and raise to lead this country as I have done, with strength and godly resolve." He looked at Katherine again and I saw tears in her eyes. She turned her face from him. I am sure that she was remembering the children they had lost.

"The Queen is a good woman; a woman of charity, peace and virtue," he went on. "And I am a man of God and a true knight in the cause of the faith. I was chosen by God Himself to lead England as her King. The Pope conferred upon me the title of *Defender of the Faith*, and I have ever given generously to the Church, to her men and to her scholars, for the good of my country and for the love I hold for God the Father and His son, our Lord Jesus Christ. And yet, we were denied sons, we were denied true heirs. Due to the great love I have for my Queen, I did not address this for many years, believing that in time, God would surely glance upon us with favour, but He did not. I gave more, I worked harder; to the Church I offered all that I could, and to the poor of my country I gave with generosity, seeking to do God's will upon earth. And yet still, we were offered no son to continue my line, to ensure peace in this realm. I came, reluctantly, to concede that there must be a reason for God's indifference to the fate of England. A reason why He turned his face from me, and from the Queen… and, after searching both my conscience and the Bible, I found the reason. In the Word of God Himself, in the Book of Leviticus it is written that a man shall not take the widow of his brother as his wife, for if he does so then in the eyes of God it is an unholy union, and shall not bear sons."

The passage actually said *children*, but Henry had consulted with many men who would affirm that the translation from the original mother tongue meant "heirs" and this, to him and many others, meant sons.

"It is for the good of England, which is my care above all things, and for my fear that in my great love for my wife, I am in fact keeping her in a union which brings us into sin, that I have come to this court. My conscience can no longer allow me to rest. If I lead Queen Katherine into sin because of my love for her, then I am twice a sinner. And if I leave England a poor state with no heir to pass my throne to, then I am betraying my offices as her King, turning traitor the oaths I swore before God at my coronation."

He turned to Katherine. "But should this trial find that my marriage to Queen Katherine is legal, then I will go back to her side and to her bed with joy," he lied smoothly. "For, as you know, I *chose* her to marry when I came to the throne as a youth, and were I to choose again, I would pick her from all the women of England or the world to be my wife, for I know well her value and her worth. No man has a better wife than Katherine, in all the kingdoms of the world."

Katherine's eyes were fixed on her husband as he stood and lied to the court about his feelings for her. She knew it was not so, and yet his words seemed to have touched her nonetheless. How she must have wished that such words were indeed true! How she wished he loved her still! But it was not so. Henry wanted me; he would pick *me* above all other women.

"I cannot rest with these fears and doubts upon me," Henry went on. "And I beg of you, my lords, to examine the evidence here most carefully, and judge in sober and wise consideration to release me of my fears one way or the other. I will bend to your wisdom and accept it, howsoever you decide. I most heartily urge you to ponder my mind and intent, which is to have a final end to the discharge of my conscience, for every good Christian man knows what pain and unquietness he suffers, who has a conscience grieved. I can no longer do my duty to my country, so troubled am I, and therefore I turn to the one true Church and her wisdom to aid me in this time."

As Henry finished, there was great applause, and I could see many turning to speak to each other in animated fashion about Henry's speech. I could see bitter curling lips on those who clearly did not believe him, but on other faces I could see awe and even tears. Henry had spoken with passion, and he had been believed by some; this was good. Henry sat down in his great chair of estate. But just as I thought that we were doing better than Katherine, she was called to speak.

Katherine had sat quietly as her husband had spoken; a mask of politic silence on her face. Aside from the moments in which Henry had brought tears to her eyes, she had stared him down. She was dressed in a gown of deepest black, with a few brilliant diamonds here and there, but otherwise was unadorned. On her head was an English gable hood, and dark silks covered her auburn hair. Her hands held a rosary and her fingers moved along the beads. She was praying. Her lips moved as she spoke to God, no doubt asking Him for courage in what she was about to do. What she did, however, I doubt that any could have expected…

Katherine rose, but instead of addressing the court as she was supposed to, she walked towards Henry and fell to her knees before him. There was a collective gasp from the court spectators as Katherine reached her hands out beseechingly to Henry. He looked at her with shocked eyes, wondering what to do. This was not part of the protocol of the trial. She was supposed to address the court, not him! With tears in her eyes, Katherine spoke directly to him in a tearful, yet fiercely strong voice that all the court could hear.

"Sir, I beseech you… give me peace and justice!" she called out. "Bestow your pity upon me, for I am but a poor woman and a stranger, born out of your dominion. I have no friends here and no true counsel. In what matter have I offended you? What cause hath my behaviour given to your displeasure that you should thus seek to cast me off and take your grace from mine eyes? I call God in Heaven to witness that I have these long twenty years been a true, loyal, obedient, loving wife and subject to Your Majesty. I have at all times been comfortable to your will and pleasure."

Katherine stared up at Henry who squirmed uncomfortably on his purple cushion. He frowned at her, shaking his head a little to try and make her stop, but Katherine did not heed him. She might protest that she was obedient, but she certainly was not now! Katherine was playing for pity. She wanted Henry's people to see her as vulnerable, feeble and abused. She was going to make a show and no one, not even her husband, was going to stop her. Henry stared straight ahead, his face shaking with shame and anger.

Katherine swallowed hard. "When was the hour that I ever contradicted your desire and made it not mine too, my gracious lord? I have loved all those you have loved for your sake alone, even if I knew them to be my enemies. I have forsaken those friends of mine that were not of liking to you, and have ever turned my eyes from the times you wandered, as all men must, from the bed of our marriage. You entrusted me with your kingdom whilst you fought valiant wars against the enemies of God and this land of England, and I returned her to you safe, in peace and without the threat of war. For you, I worked to vanquish your enemies, and bring harmony to England. For you, I have done all that was my natural role as a wife, a mother, and as Queen."

There was muttering at this throughout the court, for all knew that her words were true enough. When Henry had gone to war with France he had left her as his trusted Regent, and she had seen off the threat of invasion from Scotland. Silently I cursed her… Katherine was winning hearts. And she was not finished yet. Henry continued to stare ahead of him, refusing to look on her.

"I have given you many children; princes and princesses of England, my beloved," she importuned Henry, "and although it has pleased God to call them from this world for His own purposes, we are left a fine daughter, whose great talents and beauty springs from the wealth of those same attributes in her father, *you*." Katherine's eyes darted between Henry and the Cardinals as she reached the climax of her speech. "I *swear upon my everlasting soul*, before Almighty God, and to you, my lord husband, that when I came to your marriage bed I was a true maid; a pure virgin as intact as the day my mother bore me, and whether this be true or not, I put to *your* conscience." Henry narrowed his eyes, fixing them on the back of the court.

"I swear to God and upon my soul that the marriage between your brother and me was never consummated," Katherine went on. "I have these twenty years been your devoted wife, but I should never have become your wife if I was not assured by my own conscience, by the dispensation allowed by the Pope and by my true and humble obedience to God, that I *was* your lawful wife. I will go to the grave your true wife as *you* will as my husband, my lord. I call upon you, my lord, master and husband to consider my honour, as well as that of our daughter, and that which is your own, and call off this trial which so degrades your family and your own virtue."

Katherine gazed about her and I could see many heads nodding both in sympathy and agreement with her. She lifted her voice again, and it rang about the hall with courage and strength. "I ask that these *unlawful* and *cruel* proceedings be ended now and taken instead to the Holy City of Rome, for if this case is to be heard, it should be heard before the Holy Father, as God's own and only representative on earth. I say to you that as long as this is heard here, within these barren and illegal walls, I shall not stay here, for this court holds no justice for me." Katherine remained on her knees, her hands stretched out to Henry like a supplicant. He gave no answer.

There was silence. It hovered thick and immovable throughout the hall. Everyone was struck dumb at the force and power of her speech. Katherine rose and made an elegant curtsey to the Cardinals, then turned, and gazed around the court with magnificent majesty and calm. Slowly, indicating to her attendants to follow her, she walked out of the hall with dignity, leaning on Rhys's arm. Katherine walked away from the Cardinals, away from Henry, and away from the trial with her head held high. Down the wooden steps from the dais she went, down through the crowds who parted for her, taking their caps from their heads and bowing to her. Nobles stared at her, open-mouthed but all the common people gazed at her with raw admiration. She was every inch the Queen that she had been born to be, and I hated her for it.

Henry was horrified, humiliated. He sat back on his chair and closed his eyes. I knew he was trying to displace himself from this awful scene of a wife begging her husband and liege for mercy. He knew how much damage Katherine had done, and that his people would know all her words soon enough. She had not given evidence, but in speaking passionately of her devotion to him, of her obedience to the role of a true and humble wife, she had won their sympathy. And there was worse yet. Everyone knew Katherine was a devoted, pious woman. Swearing upon her *soul* before the eyes of God was not something to be taken lightly. All would now believe her, for such a devout woman would surely make no such claim as she had unless it were true.

Wolsey jumped to his feet, his chair clattering behind him, and called for Katherine to return, but his words could barely be heard over the shouts and cheers that had exploded forth for the Queen. Katherine and her servants were directly below me when I saw Rhys murmur something to Katherine. He must have been saying that she was being called back, and they should return, for she shook her head. "On, on," she insisted loudly. "It makes no matter, for this is no indifferent court for me. Therefore I will not tarry."

As Katherine left the building, we could all hear the crowds outside. Their screams of joy and shouts of "God save the Queen!" were thunderous. They believed her rapid exit meant the Cardinals had decided in her favour. Inside, the court erupted into confusion. Everyone was shouting, talking and fighting to be heard over one other. It began to get rowdy; people shoved and pushed. Everywhere I could hear voices speaking Katherine's name with reverence. Everywhere I could hear love for her. The legates tried to call Katherine back again, but she refused to come. Her representative, Bishop Fisher, sat with a small, satisfied smile on his lips as he watched the confusion. Katherine had done more for her cause in that one speech than any evidence could have done. I hated the smirk on Fisher's face and I hated it all the more for knowing that his happiness was not misplaced. By God's Holy Cross! Katherine had damaged our cause that day!

Wolsey turned to the King. "Sire," he cried desperately, trying to refute Katherine's claim that the trial was unlawful, or that this matter had been called by him to trial. "I most humbly beseech Your Highness to declare, before all this audience, whether I have been the chief inventor or first mover of this matter unto Your Majesty, for I am greatly suspected of all men herein."

Katherine's blows against the lawfulness of the trial and suspected partiality of the judges had shaken Wolsey. The Cardinal was burning under the hot glare of the crowds. Katherine's words had been taken as truth; all of them. The people suspected Wolsey and Campeggio, and they believed the Queen was in the right.

"It was I who called this trial, Your Excellency," Henry agreed, his voice a little unsteady as he tried to rally. "And of that fact, I would make it clear all men should know it."

Outside, not concealed by the shouts of "God save Queen Katherine!" and "Bless Good Queen Katherine!" there were other cries. "We'll have no Nan Boleyn as Queen!" rang out, screeched by the many women who had turned out for Katherine. "Burn the goggle-eyed whore!" came next. My heart skipped into my throat. They could not know I was here. I would be lynched. I dropped back as far as I could, gathering my hood and cloak about my face. I saw Henry look up warily from the dais. He had heard the shouting too.

Wolsey called for silence, but it took a long time to come. He ordered the proceedings to continue, stating that Fisher would stand for Queen Katherine if she refused to accept the position herself. The proceedings continued, but Henry sat slumped in his chair, looking already like a defeated man. Terror raged in my soul, not only for the threats shouted from outside, but for what Henry's expression meant. He looked ready to give up. Would he abandon me now that there was only more trouble and opposition? Would he go back to her?

Wolsey tried to continue on, but his face was ashen, and Campeggio was quiet and thoughtful. Henry was stunned. He hardly responded as he was asked questions. Seeing he was getting nowhere, and no event to follow would ever live up to the drama of that day, Wolsey called for the Legatine Court to break early. They would resume in the morning, he said, with a worried glance at his dejected King. I trembled to see Henry brought so low.

That night, Henry was quiet and sad. He seemed old, broken and lost. There was none of the boyish glee in his movements that I had come to love. I saw wrinkles beside his eyes for the first time, as though he had suddenly aged. We parted almost silently as he left my rooms to go to Katherine's, continuing the façade of their marriage.

I sat by the fire long that night, drinking wine until I became insensible. I was put to bed crying wildly and shouting. "He will set me aside and run back to her!" I shrieked, sobbing on Margaret's shoulder. "He will turn from me! I will die alone, never having known the love of a man or the joy of a child!" I stumbled against Nan, and clung to her shoulders as I stared unsteadily into her eyes. There were two of her, their faces swimming and dancing before me. "He is *weak*," I hissed, out of my mind with fear and wine. "Henry is weak. He is feeble. He will not fight for me."

I was mad to talk so, but I was distraught. I remember but splinters of the words I cried out then and they chill me now to recall them. Some of my ladies whispered they were sure I was possessed as I raged and insulted the King, Katherine, the Pope and the Cardinals. I remember my ladies pleading with me for peace, for the sake of my sanity, terror in their faces when they looked into my black, bloodshot, wild Devil's eyes. They all but dragged me to bed and heaved me onto the top of it as I wept into the cushions and covers.

My good servant, Nan, turned to them as they went to leave me. "Hush your mouths about this night if you value aught your heads," she said. "Speak of this to no one, am I rightly understood?"

I remember them nodding to her as they left, ashen-faced and full of wonder. They had watched their usually controlled mistress fall apart in her despair. But Nan and Margaret would not let me be touched by the stain of my own recklessness. Nan and Margaret sat beside me through that night, lulling me into sleep with soft words of comfort. The next morning I awoke with a raging headache. I could not move without feeling I might vomit. I lay in my bed, staring at the window and seeing nothing, my misery compounded by the poison flowing through me. Henry was busy at the court, which I was glad of, for I did not want him to see me like this.

At the end of the day I rose and dressed in my finest. I greeted him at dinner as though nothing had happened, and tried to distract him with gossip of the court. But act for Henry, though I could, I could not pretend to myself that all was well. I was sick with worry. I felt I was on a cliff edge, looking down at the rocks where I would fall and shatter to bits. I felt as though I were made of glass. As though I were a scrap of parchment tumbling in the wind. When we parted that night, I went to my bed and wept bitter tears. The only comfort I had as I doubted Henry and as I hated Katherine, was my women… my friends. They had cared for me, looked after me, when I was lost and alone.

Nan Gainsford had protected me from myself that night. Soon enough, she was to become a catalyst for something to further our cause for the better, if only by accident.

Chapter Forty-Five

Richmond Palace
Summer 1529

The trial went on, and I did not choose to go again. I was not ready, not yet, to face all my fears so closely. I stayed at my apartments in Henry's palaces, and waited for him to come to me each night with news. In the streets, even close to the palace, I could hear voices singing derogatory songs about me, calling me a 'goggle-eyed whore' and a witch. And for every ill song that was sung about me, there were more praising Katherine's grace and majesty. If it were up to the people, Henry would have been back with his wife by now.

Proceedings were, as ever, slow, and evidence was being presented by both sides. Bishop Fisher was at one point called on to give evidence for the King, but he refused and then went on to say that he would appear only for the Queen, and was willing to stake his own life on the validity of the royal marriage. With such men defending her, Katherine's case was put forward with strength and vigour. Henry was constantly in Wolsey's ear whenever there was a break in proceedings, saying he was not doing enough. My brother told me Wolsey had started to look pasty, and weight dropped from him like water. He mopped his sodden brow often in court, looking harassed and uneasy, but he quizzed Katherine's advocates with energy and cleverness.

Wolsey had asked that Henry release him from the trial as talks of peace were due to begin between France and Spain in July at Cambrai. As long as France remained at war with the Emperor, there was still hope that the Pope might be freed from Charles' hold by force. Wolsey believed it was of high importance that he attend, not only for the King's *Matter* but to sue for rights for England, and to demand the removal of Imperial troops from the Holy City. Henry refused to allow

Wolsey to leave, saying that he needed him, and prepared to send Sir Thomas More and Bishop Tunstall instead. Wolsey was distraught, not only as he believed that the future of Europe was being decided without his input, but also, I believe, because attending the negotiations would have given him ample excuse to escape from a trial that he knew we could not win.

One day as summer rain fell in sharp, cold, showers, I sat indoors reading a French translation of the Scriptures. The trial was plodding along, and I was worried about the level of support that Katherine had. I sought solace in the Word of God. As the people of England turned against me, blaming me for all that was done to Katherine, I turned to God. I begged Him to make the people of England understand. I asked Him to work on Katherine's mind and conscience. "For you of all, Lord, know what spirit and passion she would bring to any holy order she entered," I said. My prayers were genuine. Although a part of me despised Katherine, there was another part of my soul that could not but be impressed by her.

I found myself becoming introspective; beaten down by the hatred which seemed to pour from the very streets, and swelled up through the walls of the palace, threatening to consume me. I sought solace in my books and in God. I hoped that He, at least, understood my motives were pure.

It was then that Nan arrived in a flurry of panic. "It is the book, my lady," she said in a rush as she ran in through the door. I stared blankly at her, not knowing what she meant. "The book, my lady! The one that you gave me to read… the Tyndale!"

My heart froze. I had loaned Tyndale's work *Obedience of a Christian Man* to Margaret Wyatt first and then to Nan, knowing that each of them was interested in reform. I encouraged my household to open their minds to new ideas, but I had told them to keep the book hidden and secret. "What has happened, Nan?" I asked. "What is wrong?"

She wrung her hands. "I was reading the book in an alcove, my lady, when George Zouche came along." Nan blushed lightly. Zouche was her beau, and had been long courting her. Since he was also a servant in my household, and Nan liked him, I thought there was promise in such a match. "He saw me reading the book with great interest, and when I scolded him to leave me be, he plucked it from my hands and ran off with it. He thought it a game, and wanted to tease me."

"And?" I asked.

"Well, then he started to look through it, my lady… and I rushed to take it back, but several passages caught his eye. He said he was interested in the text, and had heard much about it. He begged to be allowed to keep it, only for a day or so, and he promised to be careful, so I thought there was no harm…" She lifted her eyes to mine and looked so desperate that I rose and hugged her.

"It is of no matter to me if Zouche reads it, if he is interested, Nan," I consoled. "The book is well worthy of reading, and has much value in its theories, even if the Church does not agree."

"That is not all, my lady," she continued. "He was reading it *at* church, my lady, and the dean caught him. The dean confiscated the book, admonishing Zouche for reading over a banned and salacious text within the confines of the holy church, or at all!" Nan started to cry as realisation dawned on my face. She gulped and sobbed, wiping her eyes as my arms fell from her. This was dangerous. If the dean had it, then there was only one place he was going to take a banned text; to Wolsey.

"My lady, I am so sorry, the dean insisted that Zouche tell him where he got the book from. Zouche declared that it was his, but I heard him, since I was nearby, and I insisted that the volume was mine. I said I had not realised it was banned or that it contained Lutheran influences. The dean did not believe me. He thought I was trying to protect Zouche and reprimanded me for putting carnal love above honesty. Zouche did not betray you, my lady, but the dean has passed the book to the Cardinal and Zouche was summoned to Wolsey's chambers."

I drew in a short breath. The lack of success at Blackfriars meant the Cardinal was in a delicate position. The acquisition of such a book from one of my waiting women came at a time when he needed ammunition against me the most. This needed to be handled well or the Cardinal could use the book against me. He could tell Henry I was a heretic, or was encouraging heretical disobedience amongst my household. He might use it as a reason why Henry should not marry me, or release the information to Katherine's people in secret, to defame my name further.

"You did right in coming to me, Nan." I reached out to comfort her, but my heart hammered in my chest. "You tried to protect me and I shall not forget it, but fear not, I know of people more powerful that the Cardinal to whom I may turn." I paused. "This shall be the dearest book that ever cardinal or dean took away." I comforted Nan, but left quickly. I had to get to Henry before Wolsey.

I entered his Privy Chamber and Henry was happy to see me. He cut short his embrace as he saw my grave expression. "What ails you, sweetheart?" he asked with concern. "You look as though you have the weight of the world upon those pretty shoulders."

I led him to a stool, asked him to sit down and dropped to my knees. It had been long since I had been formal when we were in private audience together and he was partly charmed and partly perturbed by this action. "Henry," I said solemnly. "It has long been my habit to read over texts and volumes that I thought may offer us comfort and help in our cause. You know what love I have for the ideas of learned men and how I have often come to you for counsel in understanding their work."

Henry nodded. He loved to be flattered in the ways of theology. I felt half entertained and half annoyed at the smug look on his face as I praised him.

"A book came into my possession that contained ideas I thought could be useful for us, my love. I read it and only later discovered that it was not a book generally allowed to the common man." I looked up into his eyes, speaking carefully. I was lying, but only to protect my brother who had imported the banned text into England.

"It was a banned book, Henry... but it contained such thoughts and ideas that I could not help but read on, even when I discovered the truth about it. I marked out many passages for you to read over and think upon as I know of your love for thought and theology. I was going to bring it to you this week, as I wanted your opinion, but one of my servants found and borrowed the book, not knowing of its unlawfulness. In his innocence, he took it to church, and was caught reading it by the dean. The book has been taken to Cardinal Wolsey. My servant told the dean that the book was his, but it was not. I fear that my loyal servant, in seeking to protect me, may have placed himself in danger and I come to ask you to intercede with the Cardinal on my behalf and beg pardon for my servant. The fault was mine, not his, and I should hate that any punishment befall my servant for my sake."

Henry narrowed his eyes. "What was the book?"

"It is called '*The Obedience of a Christian Man,*'" I said, and then rushed on. "And is a book that you should read, Henry, although your Church seeks to make sure that you never will… It is a book for kings."

"Why should I read a book that the Church has banned, my love?" he asked gently. "Surely there is something considered heretical, or immoral in it?"

"There is much in it that you will value, Henry," I replied fervently. "There is much in it that is *true*… The Church despises the book because it is written by an exiled man, and because it speaks of the rights of a king, within his own kingdom, to be lord and master over not only the worldly laws of his people, but to be their leader in matters spiritual as well. The Church sees such thoughts as a threat to their power, but I believe there is much of worth within its pages."

Henry's brow furrowed but he put his hands out to me kindly. "You know that I value your opinion, Anne," he said. "God knows… you are almost the match of me in your love for books and discussion of philosophy." A smile attempted to emerge on his lips, and failed. Henry was concerned. "But I will not see your servant suffer for his innocence. Come, we shall return the book to its owner, my love."

"And then may I show you the passages that I thought may interest you?" I asked cheekily, toying with his damask sleeve.

Henry chuckled. It was good to see him distracted from the horrors of the trial for once. "If you are ever thinking of me, my love, I am eager to listen."

We went to the Cardinal's apartments. When we arrived, we could hear Wolsey berating Zouche, shouting at him for having brought such a salacious, banned text into the confines of the church. Wolsey was demanding to know where he had got it from; who was his supplier? Who had sneaked the book into England? When Wolsey's servant admitted us, Zouche was standing in the chamber, his shoulders slumped and his face ghastly pale. I believe he thought he might be chained up in the Lollard's Tower within the hour. The Cardinal greeted us with great surprise and a lot of fawning. My lip curled to see Wolsey grovel to his master like a worm. The Cardinal was well aware that at this time he needed to please the King more than ever. The favour of princes is a dangerous thing to lose.

When Wolsey had ceased his prattling, Henry sent Zouche away and told him no harm would befall him. "You have rendered me a service in seeking to protect your mistress," he said to the astonished courtier. "And as such, you have my gratitude. It is not every man who would uphold the notions of chivalry in such a situation. You are a good man, to protect your lady mistress with such valour."

Wolsey was astonished, but as Henry explained that the book was mine and was to be returned to me with no more said, his face cleared. There was high disapproval barely concealed under Wolsey's mask of charm as he handed the volume to me. I thanked him with a clear countenance even though I thought I might laugh out loud to see his authority so undermined.

Henry and I walked back together to his apartments and I spoke to him about the book. Once inside his chambers I showed him the passages I had marked. He was immediately interested, as I had known he would be. I gave him the book and left so that he could read it for himself.

Later, when I came to dine with my beloved, I found Henry in the same chair and in the same position he had been when I left. He was utterly absorbed in the book. Henry gazed up with eyes glazed from reading all day. A small quill was poised in his fingertips with which he had marked passages himself. His fingers were stained with ink.

"This book *is* for me and *all* kings, Anne!" he said as I settled next to him in a chair. My soul hummed like a happy bee upon finding a flower fat with pollen.

Chapter Forty-Six

Richmond Palace
Summer 1529

That night, we ate distractedly as we pored over the Tyndale text together. Outside, rain fell swift and hard, battering roses and gillyflowers in the gardens, and making the trimmed hedges bounce and dance. Henry read aloud from the book set between us, quoting passages that spoke to him. "*As our strength abateth, so groweth the strength of Christ in us, when we are emptied of our own strength, then we are full of Christ's strength,*" he read, marvelling at the power of the words. "*Verily I will rejoice at my weakness, that the strength of Christ may dwell in me.*" Henry sighed. "I have felt much as he describes here, of late," he admitted. "When I have felt my spirits low, I have turned to the strength of Christ."

"I, too, pray every day for courage and strength, my lord," I said.

"I only wish I were humble enough to relish my own weaknesses." Henry turned a page, his eyes scanning the text.

"I see wisdom, here, Henry," I said, pausing in spooning carp broth to my plate as I pointed at a passage. "*That thou mayest perceive how that the scripture ought to be in the mother tongue and that the reasons which our spirits make for the contrary are but sophistry and false wiles to fear thee from the light; that thou mightest follow them blindfold and be their captive, to honour their ceremonies and to offer to their belly. First God gave the children of Israel a law by the hand of Moses in their mother tongue. And all the prophets wrote in their mother tongue. And all the Psalms were in the mother tongue… What is the cause that we may not have the Old Testament with the New also…?"*

I wiped my spoon clean with a piece of bread and then took up a spoonful of slippery leeks in melted butter. "I believe he writes well on the argument, my lord," I said carefully. "I have ever thought that the common man should be able to hear the Word of God in his native language, so he might better understand God's will. Nobles, kings and princes understand the words of the ancients, but how is the uneducated man to know what the Church or God needs of him, if he knows not the language? The Church would say that is what their priests and monks are for, but why should a man not understand the will of God for himself, *as well as* being guided when he has need? Would God wish His children to be so cut off from His truth?"

"I will admit, Anne, I have never seen the argument put so well or with such clarity before," Henry agreed, his plate of food quite forgotten as he leafed through the text, hunting for the passages that had moved him. "Truly, I had not thought of it in such a manner before, but I believe the fellow to be right! Indeed, why should the common man not hear the Scripture in English? Priests and monks would still be able to guide on points of theology which were not understood by their flock. And if God intended, as is implied here, that all men should hear the Bible in their native tongue, then there is no sin. It is taking what has been only *traditional*, and making that into canon law." He frowned. "Although I know this would take a great deal to actually bring to reality. The Church stands fast against the translation of the Bible, and More has spoken to me many times about how such an effort might be abused. He says that a translator might choose to change words, in order to strip authority from the Pope and the Church and encourage heresy… But still… there is much here to think upon."

I was more pleased than I could say. For so long I had hidden such thoughts from Henry, for I had worried he might consider my ideas on reform heretical… But now he had read the arguments of Tyndale, he was starting to think as I did, as Marguerite did, as reformers did. He was not quite as convinced as I, but it was a start. I was merry to hear his praise for the Tyndale. In his dissatisfaction with the trial and his dwindling belief in the holiness of the Pope and his clergy, Henry was opening to new ideas. He told me there were elements of the book he did not approve of, since they bordered on the heretical, but all the same, he was moved by much in the text.

"See here, Anne?" he asked, pointing at another passage. "*This seest thou, that it is the bloody doctrine of the Pope which causeth disobedience, rebellion, insurrection. For he teacheth to fight and defend his traditions and whatsoever he dreameth with fire, water and sword to disobey father, mother, master, lord, king and emperor; yea, and to invade whatsoever land or nation that will not receive and admit his doctrine.*" Henry shook his head at the revolutionary nature of the words, but he did not speak against them. I knew he believed the Pope had too much power over other nations. Were we not seeing that, now, in England?

"And here!" he exclaimed, pushing aside his plate to put the book between us. "*God therefore hath given laws unto all nations and in all lands hath put kings, governors and rulers in his own stead, to rule the world through him.*" He heaved a sigh and gazed at me with shining eyes. These words confirmed his belief that he was put upon England's throne by God. I took the book from him and read aloud from a later passage.

"*Hereby seest thou that the King is in this world without law and may at his lust do right or wrong and shall give accompts but to God only… No person may be exempt from this ordinance of God. Neither can the profession of monks and friars or anything the Pope or bishops can lay for themselves… For it is written, let every soul submit himself unto the authority of the higher powers… the higher powers are the temporal kings and princes unto whom God hath given the sword to punish whosoever sinneth… Whosoever resisteth power resisteth God; yea, though he be Pope, bishop, monk or friar. They that resist shall receive themselves into damnation.*"

I stared steadily into Henry's blue eyes. "He is saying that the King of each realm is the true servant and instrument of God, my lord," I said. "Above the Pope, above the Church, above all men. And I believe he is right."

Henry nodded, taking back the book. "*Yea and it is better to have a tyrant unto thy king than a shadow, a passive king that doth nought himself, but suffer other to do with him what they will, and to lead him where they list.*" His eyes were troubled. "Do you think I have been such a king as he speaks of here, Anne?" he asked. "That I have not led, but followed, and thereby brought the ill temper of God upon me?" The servants, unaware of this most important discussion, interrupted us, bearing platters of baked, spiced custard, and cheese tarts, placing them on the table in silence.

I reached out and put my hand into his. "No, my love," I whispered. "I do not think so. You are a strong and wise King. But I do think that you have suffered from the ill advice of others, those who would keep much hidden from you. But you see now, do you not? What other thoughts there are in this world that might aid us in our cause? If spiritual authority in this world belongs not to the Pope, but to each King in his own kingdom, then matters such as this that now tortures us should be decided by *you*! You have long known the righteousness of our cause, and our justice is delayed by the Pope who fears to make a ruling, not because he has deliberated on our arguments and weighed them in his mind, as you have, but because he fears to offend the Emperor! Such fears would not have stopped *you*, would they? And that is because *you* are the true spiritual leader of England. The Pope is corrupted… and you are not." I sat back. "Such theories as are written in this book… they bring into question the authority of the Pope to decide on the *Great Matter* at all. They say the authority is *yours*."

Henry nodded, but his eyes were uneasy. "There is certainly much to think on here," he agreed. "Not the least where Tyndale asks me to count the wealth the Church has cost me since I came to my throne…" he looked up at the ceiling. "The man estimates it may be more than fifty thousand pounds in taxes and tithes." He put the book to one side, taking up his plate and spooning flakes of white fish swimming in fresh broth to his platter. "And I *will* think on them." He toyed with the fish with his silver spoon. "Although I do not agree with him about the Seven Sacraments, Anne. There, I believe he is in error." Henry frowned. "Tyndale recognises only the Eucharist and baptism, but I believe in the holiness of the other Sacraments. Absolution through confession is a holy right and a divine comfort for the people of God."

"I believe that is the truth, also, my love," I said, for I agreed with him. "But you must admit that whilst there are errors in the book, there is much of worth too. And, should the Bible not be what leads us in our faith rather than the clergy, who, as you know, are often less well-informed about Scripture than even laymen due to the poor education of priests? Why should we fear to put ourselves in the gentle hands of God and the Holy Spirit?"

Henry nodded. "Although I see sense in your words, my love, there are many in this word not capable of understanding the Scriptures as well as you or me. But I agree that in certain circumstances, some should be allowed to trust in their own reading of the Word of God."

"Would not every man benefit from study of the Scriptures?" I asked. "Jesus commanded that his people read Scripture for themselves, so we would know false prophets when we saw them." Henry looked deeply thoughtful at that and continued to play with his food.

Since Henry had written the *Assertio Septum Sacramentorum*, *The Defense of the Seven Sacraments*, which had earned him the title *Defender of the Faith* from the Pope, I was not surprised that he would disagree with Tyndale. Tyndale said that the only Sacraments which should be upheld were the Eucharist and baptism, as Jesus Christ had performed these himself. All others, such as holy confession, confirmation, anointing of the sick, the taking of holy orders and the holy rite of matrimony, were superstitious rites of the Church, in his view. I did not agree with Tyndale on all points, and, like Henry, believed in the Sacraments, but still, Henry's enthusiasm for the rest brought me hope. There was a queer expression on his face; at once excited and troubled. "I would like to talk over this book with you more," he said. "And any others, in the same vein of thought, if they should… *happen*… into your possession."

There was a sparkle in his eyes, and I understood then I was safe to bring him other works that I had hidden in my rooms. I was so happy then! I had hidden a whole side of my own self, but now I could be honest with Henry, as I had so longed to be. Others would continue to be persecuted for possession of the Tyndale Bible, and the *Obedience* by Thomas More and the Church, but Henry would ensure I was kept safe, and more than that, he would read the works of reformers and evangelicals that I brought to him. It was a start… it was the start of something wondrous in my eyes. That one day, perhaps I could prevail upon Henry to move against the Church and prevent the persecution of those who only wanted more knowledge of God. Tyndale remained a wanted man, and his list of enemies amongst the Church was growing, but in England, the King had set his mind into the path of liberty, at last.

The book also showed us there was a radical alternative to the trials and popes and cardinals and delays we had endured. There was much in this small and innocent-looking volume that was to become important to us. But Henry was not yet ready to be so bold, so rebellious as to take up the ideas of Tyndale. For now he wished to pursue the course we were set on. The trial must proceed, we agreed. But I knew that something was lodged within Henry now, and when something took up residence in the King's mind, there was nothing that could remove it. I would not push him, not yet… but I was happy in the knowledge that he not only accepted some of the points in this book, and believed them to be true.

Zouche came to me afterwards to beg my forgiveness. He pledged his loyalty to me for my swift intervention, and swore that he would be forever grateful to me for saving him. I replied that I owed gratitude to *him*, for he had not abandoned me to save himself from the Cardinal, despite Wolsey's threats of beatings and whippings. He had showed himself to be my true servant.

"We owe much to each other, Master Zouche," I said. "Let us remember this in the future." He nodded and bowed. I had gained another ally.

Chapter Forty-Seven

Blackfriars
Summer 1529

As roses bloomed in Henry's gardens, and the skies came alive with the chirruping of baby birds, the Legatine Court dragged on, hearing evidence regarding Henry's marriage. Much of it was embarrassing… for Henry especially. Intimate details were presented, laying bare the King's private life to all and sundry. Katherine did not have to face any of this. Since her dramatic exit on the first day of proceedings, she had refused to attend. Henry gave orders that she was to restrict herself to the palace and to her quarters therein, but she found many a sly chance to escape and ride through the streets in her litter. She was cheered everywhere she went.

Henry was furious not only for her outward rebellion, but also for the secret game she was playing. Parading herself before the people only added to her popularity and increased the people's hatred for me. Songs and poems calling me a bawd, a whore, a witch and a heretic were now being secretly printed and pinned to church and market walls. Even though singing them openly in the streets would bring Henry's watchmen upon them, some people still continued. Henry ordered the printed sheets to be collected, confiscated and burned, but I heard the songs still. Every word, every verse, every slight, hurt me. These people… they knew nothing of me, and yet they judged me to be the very worst of women. The unfairness of the situation struck me hard. Katherine had lied about her virgin state when she came to Henry's bed. I actually was a virgin, and yet I was the one named *whore*, and she was the one praised for her virtue! At court, I stuck my chin out, held my head high, and tried to shrug them off. My good friends rallied about me, and other supporters flocked to me as well, but I could not ignore the pure hatred of Henry's people.

But the trial, however embarrassing, *was* going in Henry's favour. A great deal of it centred around whether or not Katherine's marriage to Henry's brother, Arthur, had been consummated. The King's arguments were founded upon the idea that *had* that union been consummated, and so Henry and Katherine were as brother and sister in the eyes of God. It was therefore critical that Henry prove consummation had indeed taken place. Proving this would also mean that Katherine had lied before her husband, before the people and in the name of God, which could only help us if we could prove it.

I was sure that Katherine *was* lying. In the months that Katherine and Arthur were man and wife, alone at Ludlow Castle, they must have shared each other's bed and known each other carnally… They had been young, and the young are often apt to give in to persuasions of passion. Also, had consummation not taken place, Katherine and Arthur would have been ignoring their royal duty, both to England and Spain. Katherine said Arthur had been too sick and weak to consummate the marriage, but there were plenty of his men who vouched that the Prince had been fit and hale. There were many who agreed with me, thinking the saintly Queen was blustering her way through this. She would not admit she had lied now, because she had so long protested to Henry that he was her first, and only.

I was again hidden at the back balcony under my vast hood when I heard evidence put forward by several of Arthur's attendants who had put the couple to bed on their wedding night, and who had been outside the door afterwards. Outside Blackfriars, thunder rumbled ominously above London. That summer had been hot and wet. Sultry days turned easily to storm and rain.

"There was enough heaving and grunting to suppose that consummation *had* taken place, my lords," announced Sir Anthony Willoughby to outbursts of laughter from commoners and nobles alike. Allowing himself a snort of mirth, he continued. "And when Prince Arthur emerged the next morning, he told us it was a *fine* thing to have a wife. Then he called to me to fetch him much wine as he was thirsty from having been *in the midst of Spain*."

The crowded courtroom roared with laughter and had to be quietened by the guards. Although Henry obviously found all this shameful, I listened with glee. Katherine could no longer pretend to be innocent!

Bishop Fisher, taking up the Queen's defence, however, I did not find so amusing. He was articulate, well-versed in cannon law and he argued well. He asked that the marriage bed sheets be brought out to show the blood stains that were created when a woman loses her virginity, and was told they had not been saved. "How are we to know for sure, then, that the *alleged* consummation took place?" he asked the crowds and the Cardinals. "All I hear is the bluster of a young Prince… a Prince who would have been mortified to have to admit that he had failed in his duty."

Many in the crowds murmured in agreement. It angered me that the people were only too willing to happily accept anything in Katherine's favour, yet they would question everything said against her! It was not fair! I hated Fisher for his calm and composed manner. He was Katherine's knight, facing down all that was brought against her with grace and courage.

Henry's face was crimson with anger as Fisher openly suggested Henry wished to separate from Katherine to satisfy his desires. "Our King has forgot that he is not above the laws of God and the jurisdiction of the Holy See of Rome!" roared Fisher with mighty boldness. "Our King would set aside a lawful, pious and good wife, who has done much for our country and her people, merely in order to satisfy his *carnal lust*!"

"Your opinion, Bishop Fisher, is but that of one man," Henry said, his face suffused with pure hatred, his eyes glittering blue against the red of his skin… But even the obvious anger of his King did not sway Fisher to desist. Even I found Henry's argument weak. He needed to speak out, to speak of his conscience, not just sit there and try to discount Fisher with feeble words!

Witnesses trundled in like deliveries of grain and meat to Henry's palaces; blushing laundresses who testified they had seen the sheets of the wedding bed ruddy and stained with blood; more men of Arthur's household who had put the Prince to bed with his wife and not only on their wedding night. Fisher stood firm, but it seemed from the amount of evidence presented that Katherine had indeed lain with her first husband. This gave me heart. We were winning.

But the dispensation in Katherine's possession was a problem. Fisher read it to the court, and it said clearly that consummation had 'perhaps' taken place, and allowed her second marriage with that consideration in mind. If this document was genuine, which we could not prove as Katherine would not give it up, then Henry's marriage *was* valid whether Katherine was lying about her virginity or not. Henry's men argued that the dispensation was given in error, and Pope Julius was wrong to have done so. But it is a hard task to convince people that the spiritual leader of the world had acted in error. The Pope was seen as infallible, as guided by God.

On the 23rd of July, after weeks of argument, shame, laughter and gravity, Henry, who by then had experienced as much as he could take, strode to the front of the court and asked for a final judgement. Just a week later, we gathered to hear the decision of the Legatine Court. It could, of course, be overturned by the Pope, if he decided so, but whichever way the verdict came, it was important.

The great hall of Blackfriars was packed to breaking point. There was not an inch of space between one body and the next. Outside, you might well have thought the whole of England had come to hear the verdict; milling masses gathered under the hot sun. Anticipation and the pungent scent of sweat filled the air, as we waited with bated breath. Courtiers, clergy, common men and women were all there. I put a hand, damp with sweat, upon the balcony's banister, willing them to decide in favour of Henry… willing there to be an end, finally an end to all of this! They must decide in favour of us… They *must*!

Wolsey started to speak about the trial as a whole, giving a round-up of all the evidence and arguments, when Campeggio rose to his feet. The gabbling murmurs of the crowds hushed. Wolsey started. It was clear he had not expected Campeggio to interrupt him. Wolsey gazed at his brother Cardinal as a starving hound looks to a juicy bone. He knew that this was his final chance to please the King and clearly hoped Campeggio was about to announce in Henry's favour, and produce the bull Clement had sent, allowing Henry to separate from Katherine.

But what he announced was not what Wolsey had expected, not what anyone expected... Campeggio looked about him solemnly, and spoke in Latin. "I have decided that no judgement will be made upon this case until I have related all that has been presented here unto my master, the Holy Father, Pope Clement. This case is too high, too notorious about the world to give any hasty judgement. I have not come so far to please any man, for fear, meed, or favour, be he king or potentate. I have no respect to the persons I may offend with my conscience. I will not ask favour of or displeasure of any high estate, or mighty prince, and will do nothing against the Law of God. I am an old man, looking daily for death. What should it then avail me to put my soul in the danger of God's displeasure? I will, therefore, God willing, wade no further in this matter, unless I have the just opinion of the Pope, as within his experience and counsel, there is great wisdom. And if I should go further than my commission doth warrant, it were vain folly, like to bring slander and blame upon us."

Continuing to speak clearly and calmly, he announced that since no cases were heard in Rome during the summer months, the case would be adjourned until October. He made no mention of actually moving the trial to Rome, but the inference was all too clear. "No more pleas will be heard on this matter," Campeggio said. "Until October, this trial is adjourned."

The trial was being postponed. And when it came to be heard again, it would be decided in Rome, not in England.

There was a moment of great silence.

I could not believe what I was hearing. This trial, this Legatine Court, *this whole thing had been a farce!* All that had been said and done here was useless. We were no closer to our goal. We had been duped.

Wolsey was staring with dumb horror at Campeggio. His mouth dropped open, like a haddock ready for the pot. His face was grey and turning white rapidly. When he dared to look at Henry, Wolsey saw his King glowering at him. Henry knew, as I did, that we had been deceived. The long journey Campeggio had made to get here, the extended delays in preparation for the trial, all the promises the Pope had made... they had all been tactics to distract us. The Pope would not decide on this matter with any fairness. No... we would not see justice from the Church.

Henry stood up, his face shocked and black with rage, his eyes flat and his hands clenched. He looked ready to tear Campeggio apart with his bare hands. Wolsey sat, still gaping with disbelief at his brother Cardinal, who sat down, apparently completely composed, writing at his desk as though nothing had happened. He ran a finger through his long beard, scribbling his notes on the parchment before him.

In the place of silence, there was sudden noise. Whispers grew, shouts were heard and people turned to each other asking what had been announced. Nobles who were versed in Latin mumbled to their servants what had been said, and this information trickled down through the crowds.

What we did not know then was that in the Italian city of Landriano, in June, the Emperor had won a crushing victory over the French, in effect bringing the war between France and Spain to an end. This had rendered the Emperor's control of Italy absolute, and Charles was now in total control of the Pope. We later heard that the Pope had said, "I have quite made up my mind to become an Imperialist and live and die as such." The Emperor and the Pope had signed the Treaty of Barcelona, whereby the Pope's stolen lands were restored to him… but which also rendered Clement nothing but Charles' puppet. Clement even offered his own nephew in marriage to Charles' bastard daughter. The Pope was now the Emperor's plaything. He was never going to decide against Charles' aunt, thus shaming his new master. We heard of these events only days later, but evidently Campeggio had already been informed, and that was why he made this ruling. When I heard the news, I wondered if Katherine had also known about it ahead of time… perhaps in a secret dispatch from her no-doubt crowing nephew.

Henry was staring at Wolsey and there was murder in his eyes. His great servant had finally, and utterly, failed him. Henry marched out of the court without speaking to anyone and suddenly there was a great noise as some people cheered and some shouted in rage. The court erupted into chaos.

Suffolk crashed his fist into the table in front of him. "By the Mass!" he cursed. "It was never merry in England while we had cardinals amongst us!"

My father and Norfolk who were seated near him rose to shout at the two Cardinals. Wolsey stared at the three of them. He had failed, and now even Rome had abandoned him to his enemies. Pale-faced and haunted-eyed, Wolsey rose and spoke, his voice shaking and breaking. "*You* of all men in this realm have least cause to be offended with cardinals," he said to Suffolk. "For if I, a cardinal, had not been, *you* should presently have no head upon your shoulders, Your Grace!"

Wolsey was reminding Suffolk that he had spoken for him when the Duke married Henry's sister and incurred his wrath. Was that old tie enough to save him now? Looking at Suffolk's face, I saw that Wolsey's words had hit a nerve, but one man, even the King's best friend, could not save Wolsey now.

Amidst the noise and chaos, one singular notion played over and over in my mind.

Wolsey had failed his master; it was time to bring him down.

Chapter Forty-Eight

Greenwich Palace
Summer 1529

The Legatine Court was dismissed by Campeggio. He could hardly be heard over the raging noise of the crowds. People were shouting, arguing and hissing. The great hall at Blackfriars had become like a cock-fight; crowds leering, roaring and screaming over each other. And amidst all of this, I could hear Katherine's name being said over and over, with love. It was dangerous to stay there any longer. I had to get out.

I was hustled from the shouting masses and bundled into a litter provided by my father. We fought through streets thick with people cheering for Katherine. Since she had said she wanted the case heard in Rome, they all believed now that the Pope agreed with her. This only made her stronger and us weaker. Inside the litter, I cringed from the stench of sweat, ripened and intensified by the heat of the summer sun. I flinched from the cries of support for Katherine. I heard shouts: "We'll have none of the Boleyn jade!" "God bless the Queen and our little Princess!" and "His Majesty will return to his godly wife!"

Would he? Would Henry capitulate and return to Katherine? The trial had not decided either way, of course, but another delay, another postponement… Henry had suffered greatly already. Would he continue to fight on, or would he abandon me now, just as Percy had done so many years ago, when obstacles were thrust in our path?

I put my head down and hid my features inside the cover of my hood. The braying screams resounded in my mind. Should I be recognised, there was a good chance the people here might tear me apart. I pulled the curtains of the litter to, hiding in the darkness. The men bearing the litter ran on through London as tears of disappointment, anger and sorrow slipped from my eyes and blossomed on the lap of my green silk gown. When we reached the palace I ran to Henry's apartments and flung myself into his arms. I wept and he held me in grim silence. We were both bitterly disappointed and I was panicked by the notion he might give up.

"The Pope does nothing but stall!" I raged. I rose from his embrace and put my hands against the fireplace. I leant against it, trying to absorb its stability. I felt I had none in my life then. "He sent Campeggio only to hold us off, my lord. He sent Campeggio to dupe us. The Pope is not concerned with whether or not our cause is just, he is only concerned with the Emperor's guards breathing down his neck. He cares not for God's law, only for the Emperor's! We will never see justice with him presiding over this the *Great Matter*."

"By God's Blood I believe you are right, Anne!" Henry stalked around the room like a man possessed. "I would never have believed it before but I think it is true. He will not give us justice."

I breathed a sigh of relief to hear his anger. Anger was good. Or at least it was better than sullen, ineffectual hopelessness. "We must find other ways, Henry… We must find other paths to lead us to justice. The Pope has shown he cannot be trusted. We cannot leave this in his hands anymore."

Henry nodded. But neither of us spoke of the other path we could take to resolve our *Matter*. The words of Tyndale echoed in my mind, calling to me… But what would it take for Henry to act on them? To become lord and master in his own kingdom? I wanted to urge him to take Tyndale's theories and make them real, but Henry was so overwhelmed with anger that he could hardly think. He left me to go to the tennis courts; the walls there held many deep impressions of the King's fury now.

George told me that Wolsey had begged Campeggio to release into his hands the papal bull which authorised the annulment, and Campeggio, not surprisingly, refused. "This will be my ruin!" Wolsey had apparently cried out as he stormed from his brother-Cardinal's rooms. Wolsey went to Katherine, pleading with her to give up her position, and again, not surprisingly, she refused. Why should she capitulate to Wolsey now? She was stronger than ever she had been before. We heard that the Pope had signed his treaty with the Emperor which assured his freedom, but one of the conditions was that Clement would never agree to the annulment unless Katherine did.

Doors were closing all around us. Our way was blocked. Every day I wondered, what could be done now?

As days passed, many at court offered their counsel. Advice from the French ambassador, du Bellay, was unhelpful at best. "Perhaps, my lady, you and the King should simply marry?" he suggested, lifting his hands into the air, because even he knew it was an outlandish suggestion, "and then the Pope will have to accept a *fait accompli*?"

I told the ambassador I would certainly consider his notion, but the desperation in his plan gave me small hope. I would not be recognised as Queen if we married whilst Henry was still joined to Katherine. My uncle Norfolk called another family meeting. It seemed all we did was get together and talk. Talk, talk, talk, words, words, words. That was all there was; words and talk and no action. But my uncle had a plan he thought would aid us. He wanted to bring Wolsey down, and end his reign of power at Henry's court and in England.

"With Wolsey out the way," Norfolk said with barely concealed relish. "We will be rid of the greatest traitor in this realm." He turned to my father. "I have called upon a scholar named John Palsgrave to write a pamphlet against Wolsey. I had it put into production even before the trial, for I knew that snake would find a way to deceive us. It demonstrates that the Cardinal's rule has been a period of waste, pride, repression and ineffective thinking, which has brought our country to its knees. When the King sees all that Wolsey has done, when it is laid bare before his eyes, we will have the power to move against Wolsey and remove him."

"But what is to be done for our *Matter*?" I asked, "I have no love for the Cardinal, but how does this help us further in my marrying the King?"

Norfolk stared at me as though I were a fool. "With Wolsey gone, niece, we have the way cleared for one loyal to you and to the King to move into his place. This trial was never going to go anywhere. We all knew that. But if we can place our faction where Wolsey stands now, we will be in a stronger position."

"You tell me now that you had no faith in this trial at all?" I asked, my voice rising. I had ceased to care what my uncle thought of me. *I* was the important one here, not him!

My uncle grunted and shifted in his seat, uncomfortable due to the boils on his bottom. I loathed him suddenly, this tired old general to whom, as a woman, I was forced to bow to in public. "There was always a *chance*, Anne," he said reasonably enough. "But it is always advisable to have a second stage of attack planned should the first fail."

"Yes, and you knew it would fail, didn't you, uncle?" My words escaped from between gritted teeth. In truth, it was not really Norfolk with whom I was angry. It was Wolsey, it was Campeggio, it was the Pope... It was everyone standing in our way.

"We are all disappointed that the trial did not go as planned, Anne." My father exhaled noisily. "Long have we waited already to see you Queen and our first prince on his way. But your uncle of Norfolk is showing us a way to bring down one of the greatest obstacles in your path. The Cardinal will not allow you to become Queen, Anne. He has set himself in the way of that ever happening. Now is the time to pluck Wolsey from the King's skin, as one would remove a tick. With him gone, your seat beside Henry will be assured."

"Much good will this seat be if it comes not with a crown," I hissed.

My uncle ignored me. "The Cardinal has held up this process at every stage and now he has failed, publicly and fully, in a way the King can no longer ignore. When he was young, the King loved the Cardinal, for Wolsey bore all the pain and toil of kingship, leaving Henry to enjoy only the pleasures. It is time our monarch had a new set of guardians to do that for him. It is our time now."

I could see the sense in my uncle's words. "My spirits fail with the waiting…" I apologised wearily. "I am eager to become Queen and to bear sons. I want to be a wife. This waiting tires me."

My uncle nodded with approval. He liked it when I was humble; that was how, he believed, women were supposed to behave. I despised him for that. "But you must stand strong, Anne. You share blood with generals and warlords. We Howards have never failed in our duty to the crown. You must keep this in mind, for it is for the good of the crown, for the good of England that we must remove the Cardinal."

My mouth twisted wryly. I thought about my uncle's father, who went to the Tower for fighting on the wrong side at Bosworth. Norfolk himself had also spent time in the Tower for treason to the crown. Oh yes, Howards were loyal… But only when the crown's desires agreed with their own.

"What can I do?" I asked.

My uncle and my father smiled at each other and then at me; two wolves baring their teeth. "Here is what you must do, Anne," my uncle counselled. "And do it carefully. Your temper gets the better of you and Henry will tire of these outbursts of yours in time."

I shrugged. "He likes my fire better than the chill of his cold wife, uncle. *Some* men are not threatened by a woman with courage and spirit."

"For now," my father warned, ignoring my emphasis on 'some' men to avoid another spat breaking out between me and Norfolk. "The King finds it different and exciting, but you must learn to read him, Anne, and know when to alter yourself to his moods."

"As every wife should," interjected my brother in a bitter tone.

"Listen carefully, Anne," my uncle went on. "And for once, do as I say."

I liked Norfolk not at all, but I listened to him and my father. I needed help, I needed advice… where was I to turn if not to them?

When I saw Henry again he was leaning with a head against a wall, cooling one of the headaches that plagued him. He was holding a letter. When he turned towards me, his face was shadowed with rage and pain. He thrust the parchment at me wordlessly. As I read, he started to pace the room.

The letter was a summons to Rome. The Pope decreed that the trial of the King's marriage would be heard in Rome. Given the distance from Rome to England, this letter must have been sent long before Campeggio had dissolved the trial here. Perhaps it had even been sent before the trial began in England! The Pope never had any intention of allowing a verdict to be reached in England. He had staged this whole farce in order to play for time. And now Henry had not only been let down by the Pope, but was summoned to Rome, as though he were a villain, to present his evidence there. Everything that had been said in England, everything that had shamed Henry and embarrassed him, would be heard again. The King of England would have to crawl on his knees before the Holy Father, begging to be heard and Clement would never rule in his favour. Henry would go to Rome only to be shamed before the world. Henry would go to Rome only to be sent back to his wife.

I glanced up. Henry was watching me. He looked ready to kill. "*I will not do it, Anne*," he bellowed, his voice shaking with anger. I had never seen him so angry. There was something predatory, something dangerous about him.

I pushed back my shoulders. "And why should you?" I said with defiance. I threw the letter across his desk, glowering at it as though I could make it burst into flames with my very thoughts. "How *dare* he? How dare the Pope command you to Rome? He knows he will only bring you all that way, away from your country, your duties, your people… and for what? To hear all the evidence and ignore it, just as Campeggio has? Just as Wolsey has? You would be *shamed* before the world, my lord, and Clement will only find for Katherine." I shook my head. "They want you to play a part for them, my lord, so that it appears they are doing their duty by God. Clement would make you a puppet, just as he is!"

Henry's face, lined deeply with disbelief, misery and anger, told me more clearly than words could ever have done that he would never go to Rome, with his tail between his legs, to face trial. Henry had reached a breaking point. I could feel him, feel him wavering on the edge of rejecting Rome's authority. His anger was intense. It radiated from him like heat from the noonday sun. But even in his rage, his shame and his wounded pride, he was not quite ready to take the last step. Not yet. He was afraid.

"We will go on progress... together." He marched to the table, snatched up the parchment and threw it into the fire. "And on progress, you shall take your rightful place."

I opened my arms and he fell to his knees and put his head against my stomach. I held him, cradling his head as though he were my child. For a long time we were silent, our mutual thoughts of disappointment and despair coursing through us. "That *bishop* of Rome has no power to command you, Henry," I said. "We will find a way to be heard. We will find another way to bring justice."

My words were empty. If the Pope would not annul Henry's marriage, then who could we turn to? Could I convince Henry that he should take this into his hands? Convince him to become as Pope in his own kingdom? I knew not. They were radical ideas, and although there was rebellion in some states of Europe against the Pope and his Church, Clement still held power over most of Christendom. If Henry defied the Pope, England could face the armies of many nations uniting against her in holy war. Clement could excommunicate Henry, setting every Christian soul in the world against him. There were paths we could take, but none were without peril. I would need to think carefully, and, at present, my head was far from clear.

We packed and made plans for progress. Henry's spirits lightened, if only a little. The thought of many months of hunting and riding brought him happiness, but the black shade of the Pope's summons hung over us. And the Cardinal was still in power.

My uncle had ordered Lord Darcy, an enemy of Wolsey's, to create a bill of *praemunire* against the Cardinal; the crime of introducing illegal foreign authority to England that undermined the power of the King. The foreign authority was, of course, that of the Pope. My uncle was sure that Henry would accept this bill, given Henry's present rage at Clement. Pamphlets against Wolsey were sent out anonymously as my uncle's men prepared the bill. My father and uncle sent it to Henry, along with a plan on how Wolsey might be arrested and held to account. The plan outlined that Wolsey would have his personal papers impounded, whilst a full investigation went ahead, but they found Henry oddly unresponsive to their badgering. Henry was not interested in moving against his old friend. He seemed to be taking on the example of the Pope, and stalling.

The *praemunire* bill held in it the very fall of the Chancellor and yet, to my chagrin, Henry received it, and did nothing. He did not speak of it and I could not question him about it, as I was supposed to know nothing of it.

My father raged at the King's inactivity in the face of such evidence. My uncle was concerned that this hesitation showed Henry's lasting affection for Wolsey. I watched, waited and planned. We could still bring the fat bat down, but it seemed to me that Henry needed further convincing. We needed Wolsey to make more mistakes and then parade them before Henry.

My anger at the Pope and at all that had thwarted us came to rest on Wolsey alone. I could do nothing against Campeggio, nothing against the Pope. But Wolsey I could work against. He had always been my foe. I would see him removed from power, and then, there would be none above me to whom Henry would ever turn again.

Chapter Forty-Nine

Greenwich Palace
Summer 1529

Before we left for progress, Suffolk met with my uncle again and found us ready and waiting to act against Wolsey. At present, with Henry unwilling to move against the Cardinal, we had limited options. But we were preparing for a secret war. Suffolk sent men to keep a watch on any communications with France, suspecting that Wolsey might try to engender support from his allies there.

Just before the end of the trial, when Suffolk had returned from France, Henry had called for him, keen to hear what the Duke had discovered about Wolsey. I had arrived in Henry's chambers just as Suffolk was leaving, and from the scowl on Henry's face I had gathered that he had heard much he did not want to about his long-trusted friend. But even with the bill, even with Suffolk's information, Henry did nothing.

It was frustrating, but in many ways I understood Henry's hesitancy. Wolsey had been his closest and most able advisor and friend, in many ways a mentor and perhaps even father-figure, since the very early days of Henry's reign. In Henry's youth, the Cardinal had taken on all of his dull tasks, saving Henry from the dire boredom that kingship can entail. Wolsey had shouldered the paperwork and the dreary meetings. He had bargained and made treaty with other nations and had entertained Henry in his own house as a friend. The Cardinal had made life easy for Henry, and therein lay his greatest power. There was a time when the fat bat's power was at such a zenith that it would have been difficult to see him and Henry as two separate people. They had worked together so closely and understood each other so well that they were almost as two sides of one coin. So now, for Henry to believe for certain that his beloved friend and advisor had not only failed him, but might have betrayed him, and may well have been lying to him for years, was not only painful, but almost unbelievable.

But we knew it was the truth. Wolsey had failed, he had lied and he had long been stuffing his own coffers with wealth that was not his. What was a man of God doing with such riches in any case? He should have been supporting paupers with it, or sending poor scholars to school and university, not lining his own coffers! I hated the grasping nature of many men of the Church, and Wolsey was one of the worst I had ever seen… Even Bishop Fisher, Katherine's own lion, though I liked him little, was a humbler and more honest man of the cloth than the flamboyant Wolsey.

What we did not realise until some time later, was that Henry did not move against Wolsey in part because his old friend had appealed to him… and bribed him. After Campeggio's announcement, Wolsey had begged for mercy from Henry, offering him many riches by way of apology. Henry was not the only one Wolsey plied with coin in light of his failure; one of our own party was on the receiving end of Wolsey's 'generosity'… as I discovered a few days after Henry received the bill. My own father had taken Wolsey's coin.

My father seemed nonplussed when he revealed what had happened to Norfolk, George and me. I was amazed. "And you took his money?" I cried, scandalised. It was hard for my father to shock me these days, but he had managed it ably this time. "Why? When you knew we were so close?"

"Wolsey will be removed in any case, Anne," my father said comfortably, stretching his arms. He did not seem in the least concerned. "The red bat is finished. I took his money because we might as well profit from this." He nodded to Norfolk. "I have a share for Your Grace as well," he added. "Wolsey has given Durham's revenues to the King and, since that income was mine, the Cardinal has compensated me. All in all, I am a richer man, and will share that wealth with my allies."

I still could not quite believe what he had done. "Wolsey is not gone *yet*, father," I warned. "The King hesitates and not only because of the coin Wolsey uses to buy him… and you! Henry loves that man… If you give him an excuse to keep hold of Wolsey, he will take it. If Wolsey remains in his position of power, then all is lost for us!"

A flicker of concern crossed my father's face. "What would you have had me do, Anne? Refuse to accept the offer? And in front of the King?"

"Yes!" I cried out, even though I knew it was irrational. "Am I the only one to ever speak my mind to Henry? What good are you as advisors, if you do not offer advice?"

"Anne, calm yourself," George said. "We will still make sure that this is the end of Wolsey. The King cannot ignore the charges against him for ever. This summer, as you and Henry are on progress, we will pry Wolsey from the King like a limpet from a rock."

"Limpets cling only harder to their rocks when they feel a knife poised to dislodge them, brother." I pursed my lips in anger and spoke commandingly to the men about me. "I want it to be clear that no one else is to take money from Wolsey for *anything*! All of you have counselled me, and now I do the same for you. If we are in this, then we are in it together. I will *not* find myself facing the wrath of the Cardinal alone if he comes to be restored fully to the King's graces!"

Norfolk seemed rather amused, and my father's eyes glinted coldly, but they agreed. As we left Norfolk turned to my father. "Your daughter will be a dreadful shrew when she is aged, Thomas," he whispered, thinking I could not hear him. I said nothing, but I took note of the insult. Norfolk was becoming more and more irritating, and less and less respectful. When I was Queen, he would have to be a great deal more careful…

We left for progress the next day, trying to forget our troubles in the wild open spaces of the country. But I had plans to make other than those for entertainment and diversion. I had to convince Henry, once and for all, to give up on the Cardinal. We were due to visit The More, a residence of Wolsey's near Rickmansworth, but when I heard that the plague had broken out nearby, it was easy to convince Henry that we should stay elsewhere. I told myself that I was not manipulating my beloved, but it was harder and harder to persuade myself that this was the truth. I consoled myself with my father's words… that I was doing this for Henry's own good. He was blinded by his love for this man. I would have my King ruled by none. Together, as a couple, as King and Queen, *we* would rule and no other would. Wolsey's time was done.

This, however, was not so easy to do. Wolsey clung like ivy to England and to the King. Wolsey communicated with Henry as usual, by letter and messenger, and he sent reports on various affairs of state. I am sure that Wolsey was often prone to exaggerate the toil he put into Henry's affairs, but Henry was, as ever, grateful. Henry's affections for the man were once again waxing. I could sense it. I had hoped that by keeping them separate, I could prise them apart, but the longer that Wolsey stayed away the more Henry softened towards him. It was troubling. If Wolsey could last out the summer, then when we returned to London in the autumn, he may well be back in favour, and I would be in danger.

Just before leaving for Cambrai, Thomas More had published his *Dialogue*, his repose to Tyndale's *Obedience*, and other works. I obtained a copy, which was not hard as the Church was busy handing them out as though they were honey tarts. I read it and was both saddened and amazed.

More was *vicious* in his attack on Tyndale, calling him an evil, pus-filled boil sure to bring about a biblical plague of heresy. More said Tyndale was *"the beast who teaches vice, a forewalker of the Antichrist, a devil's limb,"* and said he was *"so puffed up with pride, malice and evil, that it is more than a marvel his skin can hold together."*

What vile words from one who proclaimed himself to be so godly!

Having read several of Tyndale's works now, and having heard the humility of his narrative voice, I did not believe More's take on him for a moment. More cast all reformers, heretics, Lollards, evangelicals, and free thinkers into one pot, and claimed they were all agents of evil. How could a man, so praised for his intelligence, be so close-minded and easy to judge?

The work was also faintly ridiculous. Where Tyndale had put forth valid arguments and discussed his points well, More's book was a farce. The book set up a fictional discussion between More and Tyndale, and had them discussing religion and heresy in his Chelsea house. This *fictional* More easily put down Tyndale's arguments, which were, of course, *designed* to be effortlessly dismissed, and persuaded him to alter his opinion. Had this been a real discussion, and not a fictional one, I have no doubt that Tyndale would have come up with arguments that were a great deal more convincing than the ones the author *allowed* him to have! But that is the way with authors, is it not? They can pick and choose what their characters say, making them appear wise or foolish as they please.

The only saving light of the text was that More did not dismiss the worth of having an English translation of the Bible some day… as long as it was not done by Tyndale. It was clear that More despised Tyndale, and all he stood for and would ever work against him. More said that simple Christians should be protected from Tyndale's works, as they might be corrupted by them. He thought the same as the Church; that it was for the clergy to control and decide what knowledge the people of God were allowed. I would never agree with More.

But I also found myself less than pleased with Tyndale, when he wrote a pamphlet about the annulment. Saying he found no argument in Scripture for the King's belief his marriage was invalid, he stated he believed the union should continue. Tyndale wrote that as Henry claimed he loved Katherine still, he should remain with her, as marriage was a divine gift. When Henry received this, I thought he might well abandon his good opinion of the *Obedience*, in his rage. Fortunately, Henry listened to me.

"Tyndale was not correct on all his assumptions in the *Obedience*, my love," I said. "As you, yourself, rightly pointed out. It is therefore for us to read such works, and decide on their truths for ourselves. Do not abandon all that was good in one work, for his mistakes in another."

"There you speak wisdom, Anne," he said, sitting down in a chair and taking his velvet cap from his head to mop his brow. "Even learned men require guidance from men such as me… those whom God Himself has put in place to lead and guide them."

"Exactly, my lord." I breathed a sigh of relief.

Word came from the peace negotiations at Cambrai. Henry had hoped that continued cooperation between France and England might weigh on the Emperor and force him to abandon his support for Katherine in order to secure a peace. But this was but a fantasy. The French were concerned with their own affairs. Even worse, du Bellay accidentally let slip to one of Wolsey's men what Suffolk had been up to in France. Wolsey wrote to Henry, saying that Suffolk had slandered him to the French King. Henry could hardly admit that Suffolk's enquiries had been done at his bidding. Suffolk heard of this and, quite intelligently for him, announced himself indisposed, and left progress. With Suffolk out of the way, Henry wrote to Wolsey saying that it might take some time to discover the truth, but he would look into it, leaving Wolsey to sulk and mutter bitterly in private about the betrayal of the Duke.

Wolsey was beaten down, but was eager to demonstrate he still had worth. Henry believed he was the best man to continue pushing for his *Great Matter*. In a short time, my father would make it so that the King believed in Wolsey no longer.

Chapter Fifty

Waltham Abbey
Late Summer 1529

That summer's progress was to take us from London to Waltham Abbey, then on to Barnet, Tittenhanger, Windsor, Woodstock, and Reading. Perhaps trying to make up for the failure at Blackfriars, Henry stuffed my chambers with silks, furs, linen and velvet cloth. He granted me a personal allowance, and it was a very generous one. He presented me with jewel after jewel, expensive books, primers and devotional works, and smothered my coffers with coin. I was a rich woman, almost as rich as Katherine herself. Henry also made my brother the governor of Bethlehem Hospital, better known commonly as 'Bedlam' Hospital. It cared for those who were plagued by visions, evil spirits, or were unable to care for themselves due to their troubled minds.

Although none of this aided me in my goal to become Queen, I understood my love was trying to make amends. I accepted each gift with thanks, and started to set aside sums to give to nunneries, monasteries, and funds for scholars of which I approved. Doctor Butts had quietly brought several cases to me of young men who held the same sympathies as us, and I was happy to be able to support their educations. With more young men coming to Butts every month, I was supporting a new generation of reformers. Henry was aware I supported scholars, but he was not aware of *all* their leanings.

As soon as we were free of London, I felt my heart lift and my spirits soar. The air was warm and rich with the scent of ripening crops and wildflowers. Herons and cranes stood, watchful, over streams and lakes, hunting for fish, and at night bats flew from the rafters of Henry's houses, silent black shadows winging through the dim blue of the wolf-light. In the warm days, men were out in the fields, bare-backed and glistening with sweat, plunging their shining scythes, with rippled blades, through golden grasses and purple thistles to make hay for their animals in the winter. Hedges were being laid about animal pens, wrens screamed insults at sparrows, and clovers flowered, with bees bustling about them, gathering their sweet offerings to take for making honey in their globed, yellow hives.

On progress, I ruled. I stood at Henry's side. I was his constant companion. I kept ladies-in-waiting like a Queen... But I was not the true Queen yet. Katherine had been ordered to stay in London. She had accepted Henry's order by making an overly dramatic speech about her duties as a wife.

"As your good wife and Queen it is my duty and office to bend to your will, my beloved," she had said to Henry. "I will do all you ask, to please you, if this be your will.

"If you were true to that sentiment, madam," he had bellowed at her in the presence of her cringing ladies. "Then you would accept my judgement and leave your throne for a nun's cell! If you wanted to please me, you would not seek to use your nephew against me, nor turn the people of England against me! You are no *good* wife, Katherine, and you are no wife of mine!"

He had stormed out, furious with her, and we had left for progress that same day. Henry had not taken leave of the Queen. He ordered Katherine was to remain in her chambers and not go into London. Henry put men about Katherine to watch her. He trusted her no longer.

Katherine was also forbidden from corresponding with the Pope or the Emperor. Her letters were intercepted and opened, and when her ladies left her chambers, they were ordered to turn out their pockets and present any laundry or clothing for inspection. Henry now saw Katherine as a viper in his bosom. He was sure that she had heard of the

Emperor's victory in Italy before we had. He raged against her often. Katherine had surprised him, I think… for so long she had, as she herself had said, been amenable to his will. And now, she was not only against him, but had proved herself more than capable of taking him on at his own game, and winning. People forget that Katherine came from a war-like dynasty. Her father and mother had fought for their thrones, and to reclaim their country from the Nasrid dynasty. Such struggles are not won by battle and sword alone. Her father had been one the most ruthless tricksters in all of history. He had managed to deceive his own daughter, Joanna, out of her throne by announcing to the people of Castile that she was insane. He had locked her away in a nunnery, and ruled as regent until his death when Joanna's son, Charles, had inherited both Castile and Aragon. Should we have been so surprised, therefore, that Katherine came out fighting? Old, fat, weary and broken-hearted she might be, but dead in spirit, Katherine was not. Although I hated her for it, I could not help but feel a grudging kind of admiration for her too. She had prevailed over us, and she had done so with courage and dignity.

And the English adored her. They thought that now, surely, the King would return to her and all would be well. But Henry was not a man to be told he could not have something when he wanted it. He resented it, he burned, and he railed against it… for he knew that he was right! He wanted this annulment now, not only to have me and to have sons, but because everyone told him he could not.

Never, ever, say "thy cannot" to a Tudor…

Although I was still booed by the common people I was treated like a Queen by the nobles and all who supported me at court. Even those who did not like me had to show respect in public. But all the same, I did not get everything I wanted. Wolsey was in disgrace, but not gone entirely from royal favour. Henry agreed that he had failed in his task, but he wanted Wolsey kept in post. My family became obsessed with scheming against the Cardinal.

"Once he is gone," my father said as we talked on arrival at Waltham Abbey, "I think we may be able to sway the King with alternative options. We may be able to convince Henry to pursue other paths for his annulment."

I knew what he meant, my father and I, and my brother, had similar views. Perhaps a reform of faith in England would help us. We were starting to turn away from the hallowed peerage of the organised Church. People called us heretics because of it. The new Spanish ambassador Eustance Chapuys who arrived that summer would come to call the Boleyns "*more Lutheran than Luther*," but we were not Lutherans. I was never anything but a Catholic. Unlike some reformers, I believed in the Sacraments, but I wanted to see the Church as a great power bringing forth charity and goodness, and not as a snivelling and corrupt child cowering at the feet of any worldly prince. The Pope was wrong to treat Henry and England as he was so doing. I told Henry of my thoughts, but whilst he agreed with me, he was not ready to act on it. We were at a loss, that summer… The fiasco at Blackfriars had done nothing but increase Katherine's popularity. We were back where we had started.

Summer progress was a distraction for us. Henry tried to bury his disappointment and frustration in the pleasures of hunting, food and drink, but he was troubled. His headaches had become worse. We did not talk about the trial, or the *Great Matter* for a while, trying to escape them, but they hung over us every day.

We could run from our troubles, but they would only be waiting there for us when we returned.

Chapter Fifty-One

Waltham Abbey
Late Summer 1529

Whilst we progressed about England under the beautiful summer sun, negotiations for peace between France and Spain began in the border town of Cambrai. Thomas More and Bishop Tunstall wrote to Henry that their efforts to engage in negotiations were constantly ignored. Although strategically important to both empires, England was a small sprat to the great pikes of France and Spain. Wolsey had not been happy that Tunstall was sent to the talks in his place, as the Bishop was one of his most outspoken rivals on the Council, and wrote to Henry slandering his abilities. Tunstall believed Wolsey was too lenient on heretics, and saw his lack of motivation as laziness. For all Wolsey's faults, I did not see his comparatively moderate stance to be a flaw. Wolsey did not mind Thomas more attending, since he was respected throughout Europe as a scholar and philosopher. Henry had a great love for the man, and trusted his wisdom. Many times over the years, when Henry had wished to escape the court, he had gone to More's house and spent the night charting stars in the heavens. His friendship with this enemy of reform did not please me.

Wolsey had become ill in the aftermath of the trial. Although I thought this was a feint, Henry was worried. "He is an old man now, sweetheart," he pleaded. "It is easy to think of him as an active and healthy, hale man, but it is not so. He is almost sixty! We must remember that when we look at his recent failures… The Cardinal is not a youth anymore. It is only to be expected that he may trip where a younger man would leap. But I believe he still has much wisdom to offer."

I agreed, reluctantly, but Henry's words were to haunt him later as England's envoys failed in their task at Cambrai. The

Treaty of Cambrai, the so-called 'Ladies Peace' for it was largely the doing of Marguerite, her mother Louise of Savoy, and my old mistress, the Archduchess Margaret, was signed in August. The French and Spanish were now at peace, and England had all but been left out of the talks. Henry hissed sour words about François' turncoat nature, but we all knew the true issue for us was that the Pope was now the Emperor's slave. The only light on the horizon was that the Treaty of Cambrai had to be ratified by England, since Henry had loaned money to both François and to Charles in their war. François, in particular, needed England's favour, since his two eldest sons were Charles' prisoners. If England were to cause problems for the Treaty, François might never see his sons again. Wolsey wrote to Henry suggesting it might be possible to force François into continued, and public, support for the annulment, but it was not without risk. There was a possibility that causing problems could make Charles and François ratify the treaty between them instead, leaving England out entirely. But it was the best plan we had, and Wolsey set about trying to make it so.

Du Bellay started pressuring Henry to ratify the treaty, but failed over and over to give him a full copy of it. This made Henry suspicious. I urged du Bellay, as my good friend, to let Henry see a full version, for how else could he agree to it? But du Bellay deferred the matter. François was also pushing for various agreements from an earlier treaty between France and England to be upheld. Wolsey pointed out that the French were pushing for military support from England based on this earlier treaty, but said they had had omitted a stipulation he had negotiated and therefore their demands were invalid. Henry received Wolsey's letter one afternoon as we returned dirty, and hot, from a day's hunting and he frowned at the letter, handing it to me.

"The French treat me with small care and much deception," he growled. "I am much kindled and waxed warm in their hands. They mould me to what they want. Then I am discarded as though I am a lump of wax."

I sighed, reading the letter. I wanted Henry to be friends with France, for I loved that country and her people. But it was more than that. England needed allies and in the present situation, we were hardly good friends with Spain. "Are we certain that Wolsey is right about this?" I asked. "Should we not ensure that the Cardinal is correct in his assessment before attacking du Bellay and François for their demands?"

"I will ask that Wolsey's points are checked on this matter," he said. It was a strange moment, such a small thing to be said, and yet Henry would never have questioned Wolsey's judgement before this time. It showed how much his faith had been shaken in his minister.

"My father and Master Gardiner are both familiar with the treaties, and are in this building, my lord," I said. "Shall I ask that they check on these stipulations Wolsey speaks of?"

He nodded. "Send for them," he said shortly, playing with his hat as though he did not want to meet my eyes. "I will bathe and then speak to them." Henry went off to wash, and I sent for my father.

I handed him the note when he arrived. "The King wants Wolsey's assertions on the treaty to be checked," I said. My father's eyebrows shot up. He did not have to say a word to understand the implications of this. "I would like that we remain friends with France," I continued, looking at Gardiner. He had recently been appointed secretary to Henry, moving away from Wolsey's service. He had also promised to be my loyal servant, and now here was his chance to prove himself. "We need at least one friend in this world, my lords, and I would rather it was France than Spain. If we can keep François on our side, he may be able to support us more in the King's *Great Matter*. Without him, we are alone in Europe, with the Emperor against us."

Gardiner nodded, tucking his great hands behind his back. "The Cardinal allows his annoyance at the French for signing the Treaty of Cambrai to cloud his judgement." He frowned, making the indentation between his eyes deeper. "He blames the French for leaving him out in the cold by making peace and abandoning the Pope to the Emperor… thereby thwarting the King's annulment… but what could the French do for the Cardinal? He could not be their first responsibility. He is being unreasonable." Gardiner stared at me with shrewd eyes. He knew what another failure could mean for his once-master. "I will look over the treaties, with you, my lord," he said to my father. "But I believe your daughter is right. We cannot be left without friends in Europe, and France is our natural, if not *only* ally at this time. We cannot allow Wolsey's sullen anger to stand in the way of that by disputing the ratification of this treaty."

My father grinned like a slinking fox. "We will go over the papers most carefully, daughter, and counsel the King on this."

"He will meet with you when he has finished bathing," I said. "Ensure that he knows nothing of what I have said to you, other than that you are to look again at this matter. I do not want Henry knowing that I pressed for peace with France. This must appear to stem only from Wolsey's error, not from any other consideration. Henry says Wolsey still has worth. Let us prove to him this is not so."

My father nodded, and Gardiner bowed to me. As they left, my mind was plagued once again by the notion that I was manipulating Henry. *But it is for his own good,* I told myself. *And you are right, Anne, England cannot be left without friends in Europe, no matter how upset the Cardinal is with France!*

The following day, the tide had turned. My father and Gardiner had gone over the treaties through the night, and they counselled Henry that Wolsey was wrong and his recommendations should be ignored. They said they suspected he had brought these arguments up due to annoyance with François, and that his spite would bring great trouble for England. Henry wrote to Wolsey, telling him that *full* concessions would be made to the French, and ordering him to desist from allowing personal feelings to cloud his judgement. What Wolsey thought of this, I know not, but it can hardly have been easy reading. Henry was now openly distrustful of his judgement. The Cardinal was in grave danger.

I know not, in truth, if Wolsey's judgement was wrong for I did not ask, but if it was not so, my father and Gardiner made it appear convincing. We used this slip against Wolsey; another thread sewn into his winding sheet. Perhaps the fact that Gardiner had once been Wolsey's man, and owed much of his rise to power to him, made this blow against the Cardinal smart all the more harshly. Wolsey struck back by attacking Gardiner; saying that Gardiner understood such affairs not at all, and could not be trusted in his assessment. But Gardiner protested his judgement was true and honest, and accused Wolsey of wanting to stir Henry against the French. Wolsey was forced to apologise to Gardiner, by Henry, but it was clear that the Cardinal neither trusted nor liked his former servant anymore.

Du Bellay wrote to France, pleased that the English King was set to give the requested concessions to France, and thanked me for my role in preserving the peace between our two countries. "I will let my master know how much we owe to you, my lady," he said, kissing my hand. "For as long as you are here, I know we Frenchmen will always be treated well. And you see? Once again it is the great ladies of this world who strive for peace over war. You act in England as the royal ladies of the house of Valois do, in France."

"It pleases me more than you can know, my lord ambassador," I said in French, "to know that there is friendship between our countries. I will work always for brotherly love between your King and mine."

Henry smiled to see me treated as a queen by the ambassador. Henry and I were inseparable. It was rumoured that I was indeed his mistress now, even though we had still not lain together as man and wife. Du Bellay was heard saying that he expected any day to be told that I was with child, so deep and obvious was Henry's passion for me.

My father was there that summer as my supposed chaperone, but it was an empty title. Henry and I were now somewhat settled in sating our need for each other in all other ways but in actual sex, and my father was there for the sake of appearances only. He did nothing that might get between us. But his position also meant that he was around Henry a great deal. Although he said nothing, I knew he was positioning himself as a replacement for Wolsey. He was a great deal subtler than Norfolk and Suffolk who danced about Henry that summer as though he were a maypole and they the merry maids of the dance. My father simply arranged it so that he was always on hand to offer advice, and took on any work the King wanted done. All of them wanted the post of Chancellor. But that position was still not yet vacant.

At the urging of my father and uncle, I continued to shake Henry's trust in his beloved advisor. Once Wolsey was gone, we Boleyns and Howards would be the only ones he would listen to. Once Wolsey was gone, we could find another path for the annulment.

It was going to take a great deal of courage to bring down this old man... It was hard at times, when I thought of his age. But I reminded myself of all Wolsey had done, all that he was, and then it was easier to think on him not as Henry did, as a weak and old man, but as an enemy. If I merely left Wolsey wounded, he might prove all the more dangerous.

We needed to bide our time and strike when the time was right.

Chapter Fifty-Two

Grafton Lodge
Summer's End 1529

In August, Eustance Chapuys of Spain arrived to present his ambassadorial credentials to Henry. It was soon obvious that Mendoza's replacement was on the side of Katherine and her faction. Although friendly enough to my father and brother, at least at first, he refused, if at all possible, to speak with me, or even to acknowledge my presence in a room. He considered me the King's whore, this, I knew. But I was too busy with Wolsey at that time to think on the arrival of the new ambassador of Spain.

As Cambrai drew to a close, Wolsey wrote to Henry asking for an audience, so that he could impart information too sensitive to put down in a letter. Wolsey was clever, he was aware we were trying to undermine him. Henry was a deeply sentimental man and Wolsey knew that if he could get to Henry in person then he might be able to worm his way back into the King's full friendship. I asked my father to advise Henry that the Cardinal must commit all he had to say to writing.

"For what can the Cardinal have to say that he cannot write down?" my father asked as I stood next to Henry. "I believe, Majesty, he wishes to meet with you in order to discredit me and my family in Your Majesty's eyes. For all who know him well know of his resentment towards my daughter."

"He has always shown great respect to Anne," Henry protested feebly. I hated Henry in moments like this; hated to see him defend one who would see me destroyed before he would ever bow to me as Queen. It is often the strange way of the world, that those we love the most can also be those we rage against the hardest.

I sniffed. "I fear the Cardinal would prefer Your Majesty married to a foreign princess rather than to a daughter of England as myself," I said. "I wonder if he thinks that your affection could be drawn from me, like poison from a wound..."

Henry leapt to contradict me, his face distraught. "There is nothing in you of poison, Anne! And no man could take the love that I bear for you from my heart." He crushed me against his great chest and went to kiss me, but I turned my cheek away. Henry released me, sighing heavily. "The Cardinal is perhaps not as he once was, but he is an old man now and he has done good service to us in the past."

I allowed Henry to take me in his arms then, but my father and I continued to speak against the Cardinal, suggesting to Henry that his beloved Wolsey had in the past been in the pocket of Louise of Savoy, François' mother, and so who knew whose money he took now... the Emperor's? My father suggested that Wolsey had been responsible for Suffolk's failure to take Paris, oh so many years ago when we were at war with France. Suffolk was more than happy to lay this blame on Wolsey too, stating that the Cardinal, in his position as Chancellor, should have responded to his requests for more men and more money with which to take the French capital. My father had even recently intercepted a letter of Wolsey's on its way to France which clearly stated that the Cardinal thought the King should make a match with a French princess rather than with me. Henry took the letter from my father, and read it with a grim expression.

"You see, my lord?" I asked. "The Cardinal does not work for your interests, or mine."

Henry could hardly deny the truth of my words, but attempted to defend the Cardinal all the same. "Perhaps, sweetheart, it is just a feint to lure François into offering more support for the annulment."

"I would beg of you to excuse me, Your Majesty," I said, rising. "But there is a sudden pain in my heart."

"You are unwell, sweetheart?" he asked, looking up with a face full of pale concern.

"My heart is torn, Majesty, by the betrayal of your friend." I left him.

Henry was surrounded by those who urged him not to meet with the Cardinal. Distressed by the intercepted letter, he told Wolsey to put his matters into writing and send them to him at Grafton, but he was ill at ease. It was then we heard that Wolsey was coming to Grafton after all. Campeggio was due to leave the shores of England to scurry back to his master in Rome and was to come to take his leave of the King officially. He had requested, no doubt at the fat bat's urging, that Wolsey come with him.

Henry could not refuse to see Campeggio, and so it seemed Wolsey had found a way to get to Henry at last. But our faction united to ensure that when the Cardinals arrived, at least one of them would find a cold welcome waiting.

Chapter Fifty-Three

Grafton Lodge
Summer's End 1529

We had settled for some time at Grafton, a small hunting lodge in the country, far away from the summer stench of London and the pressures life had dealt us of late. The rest of Henry's court had to lodge at various houses nearby, as Grafton was so small it could only accommodate a small, intimate party. My ladies and Henry's personal servants were the only ones who stayed with us there, although my father, Norfolk, Suffolk and George rode to join us daily. It was refreshing to be not so surrounded by people all the time. Henry's nobles and the rest of the court joined us for entertainments and on the hunt, but more often we were a small party whilst there.

There was a goodly park near to Grafton and we spent much time hunting in it. There was also a new passion for bowls at court, which we played upon the green lawns at Grafton. The aim was to roll one's ball as close as possible to the jack, which was painted white, and whosoever got the closest won. I was not as good at this game as I was with many others, and Henry had to pay out large sums to cover the losses I made in wagering against his men and my ladies. He never minded though. He looked at me with indulgent eyes and motioned to his man to hand over the sums I named. Henry was a vastly generous man, and his father had left him a fortune, which he had no problem in spending. Archery butts were also set up, and Henry played against his Yeomen Guard's best archers, often besting them, for he was a superb shot. I would play against the men in Henry's retinue, and against my own ladies, and sometimes instructed them also, since it seemed I had been given more education in such arts than had many of my women. Bridget, in particular, was never an able shot, and grimaced often as her arrows bounced ineffectually from the butts, landing in the thick grass.

"You will never best my *Diana*," Henry consoled her. "But you have a good *eye*, Lady Hervey, even if you have not the same strength in your arm as my Anne. Your arrows reach to the heart of the target… they just have not the resolve to stick in!" We laughed, and Bridget took his praise and his consolation with good grace.

The days were warm and life was pleasurable for a while. We played and hunted, we distributed alms to religious houses when we rode out to visit them. We heard Mass in the morning, and abandoned ourselves to the pursuit of pleasure in the afternoon. At night we danced and talked, and tried to avoid the subject of Blackfriars, shying from the pain of that shame and misery. I was enjoying myself… until Wolsey came panting to the heel of his master, seeking titbits of favour.

Although neither Henry nor I had any wish to see the gout-ridden, long-bearded, flatulent gas-bag that was Campeggio, there was no choice. He was an ambassador of Rome and had to be afforded the dignity of such a position.

Suffolk was feeling petty, and gleefully told me that he had arranged for apartments for Campeggio, but not for Wolsey. I could not help but titter, especially when the two cardinals arrived and Wolsey had nowhere to lie down or get changed after his long and hot journey. The plan had the added advantage that Wolsey would not be able stay at Grafton and would therefore have less opportunity to work on Henry. Think ill of me, if you will, for this. It matters not. I understand well my own sins. The Cardinal was my enemy, and his fall was likely to be my salvation. I could not think badly of this treatment, this humiliation. He had oftentimes done the same to many others, and to me.

When the two men arrived, Campeggio was greeted by Suffolk's men and taken directly to his chambers where water had been prepared for him to wash. Wolsey was not even addressed. Wolsey watched as Campeggio was led away to comfortable quarters. Campeggio did not offer to share his rooms with Wolsey.

Wolsey stood helplessly in his riding habit, outraged and confused. He caught one of Suffolk's men by the sleeve as he passed, and hissed arrogantly "how can it *be* that no chambers are prepared for me?"

"I was not told to prepare any," the cheeky man answered with a shrug, and then turned his back on Wolsey and strolled away. Such a slight would have once earned him a thrashing, but now, the lower classes and the servants could join in the pleasure of defying this proud, overbearing man.

And many *were* more than happy to see the Cardinal brought low. He had lorded over England for many years with conceit and pride, taking all that he could for himself and flaunting his power over us all. However pitiful he looked on that day, standing in the courtyard, unsure of what to do, it was well to remember that in the body and mind of that old man beat the heart of a ruthless political operator. If he found a way back to Henry, he would take revenge on us all.

All the same, I gazed on him with some pity from a window. Wolsey was glancing about, perhaps for the first time in his life unsure of what to do. I steeled my heart against him. This was no time for weakness. Even now, with the evidence of that letter, it was clear he was working to remove me! We had brought him low, but he had not fallen, not yet. I could not falter now.

That afternoon, I had arranged to ride out with my ladies, but we were not to go far as I did not want Wolsey sneaking in to see Henry without me. Campeggio was due to meet with Henry later that day, and I would be there. I wrinkled my nose when the fat bat entered the hall. As I passed him, he bowed, but I did not acknowledge him. My ladies and I swept by him on our way to the horses outside.

"What a fine day to ride," I said loudly, "and to wash away the odour of whatever that unpleasant smell inside the house is." My ladies laughed cruelly with me as we gaily mounted our horses. Wolsey had worked against many members of their families too, so they had no reason to like him. Wolsey stared at us in confusion, and I gave him a triumphant glance from my horse. Now he would understand how it felt to be humiliated and put down, as he had done to me! Margaret and Nan were still giggling at Wolsey's discomfort as we rode away.

In the end, Norris offered his chamber to Wolsey so that he could change before meeting the King. I returned from my ride flushed and excited for the next battle. I washed, changed and was walking to Henry's Presence Chamber when Norris caught me on the stairs, his cheeks bright with outrage. "You and Suffolk would leave an old man out in the cold, my lady!" he said hotly as I passed.

"You forget yourself, Norris…" I looked the handsome man up and down. "And I have never left a *friend* in the cold."

"It seems to me, my lady, it is perhaps the way we treat our enemies, rather than how we treat our friends, that shows who we really are." He looked at me with censure, and under his gaze I felt ashamed.

"You are bold today, Norris," I said, my cheeks colouring to match his.

"Just making conversation, my lady."

"No, not just conversation, Norris," I said and sighed. "This world is hard for men, Norris… men must be *hard* to live at court. They must be able to make decisions and face the consequences. Sometimes it falls upon women to make those kinds of choices too." I stepped closer to him and touched his arm. His handsome face, slightly like my Henry's, was not far away from mine. For a moment, we but stared at each other. I saw his eyes trace the shape of my lips and his body soften with the closing of the distance between us. Until this moment, we had been good friends. I did not like the manner in which he had spoken to me, but I liked even less the way he was now looking at me. His gaze held censure, even if his body seemed to wish to move towards mine.

"I will not let anyone harm those I love," I said. "I will not let this man harm my family, my country or my King."

I stepped back. Norris was wearing a confused expression. I had thought in the past that he was attracted to me. There is much false play at court, but with Norris I had the sense that his words of admiration were true. There, in that hallway, my senses told me that my previous suspicions were correct. And there was a part of me that was attracted to him. I know not if it was because he reminded me of Henry in some small way, or if it was because he called upon the softer edges of my conscience to show pity, even to an enemy, which would have been the Christian way to behave. But in some way, then, I was drawn to Norris. It was not the same as the love I had for Henry, but still, it was strong.

"Do not make yourself uncomfortable, my lady, in explaining your actions to me." Norris looked at the floor, and then back at my eyes. "There is no one like you, my lady. No one can love like you and no one can hate like you either, it seems… But I would not like to see these events ruin the gentleness in you that I can see even if others do not. You are a lady, Mistress Boleyn, sometimes it would be better to be a lady, in truth, rather than having to play the part of a general."

I smiled sadly, taking my hand from his arm. "Sometimes we have no choice in what we turn out to be, Norris. Sometimes

Fortune's wheel turns and we have to find a way to stay on it."

I inclined my head by way of a dismissal, and I walked to Henry's chambers, hearing Norris's words ring in my head. I did not like that he thought badly of me, and the thought was strange, for there were so many others who thought ill of me, and I was able to bear their displeasure.

I realised that I liked Norris, as a friend, of course, and that was therefore why his censure upset me. But I had to shrug it off. There were battles to be faced, and I could not weaken now.

Chapter Fifty-Four

Grafton Lodge
Summer's End 1529

When I reached the Presence Chamber I found it packed. Even those courtiers who were lodged at far away houses had come to watch the return of the Cardinal. They wanted to see if Henry would take him back; if Wolsey's old magic would work once more on their King. Although in public nothing had been said, everyone knew that in private there was much talk and accusation against the Cardinal and they all wanted front row seats to witness either his fall or mine... Many thought my position had been weakened by the events at Blackfriars, and perhaps they were right in some ways, but I was ever assured of Henry's love. He would not abandon me... at least, I hoped he would not.

My father, brother, and Norfolk stood with Suffolk near to the dais and they bowed to me as I entered. I responded with an elegant curtsey and we settled to talking. My brother gave me wine and chatted to my ladies, now crowding near to me and giggling at my brother's tall tales. My brother had left Jane behind again. He took care to travel without her whenever possible. My father found her endlessly tedious also and so never insisted that she accompany us, even for the sake of a grandchild from George. Jane had not been able to produce another pregnancy since the last miscarriage she had suffered, and my mother was despairing of George ever producing a legitimate heir. There had been some private talk of his gaining an annulment due to Jane's infertility and marrying again, but he was in no rush to do so, being rather busy helping the King with his own marriage problems.

Campeggio and Wolsey entered after me. Campeggio walked with a stick now. His swollen, gouty limbs were infirm and he sat as soon as he could to take a goblet from his servant, staining his long ratty beard red with wine. Wolsey stood, and I watched him as I pretended to be lost in conversation with Suffolk and Norfolk. Wolsey had lost more weight. I could see the red robes of his Cardinal's attire hanging off him. It brought another stab of pity to my heart, and I tried to dismiss it, without full success.

Wolsey bowed his head to me in greeting and I inclined my head curtly to him. For a moment, I felt my heart catch as I saw the sorrow in his eyes, and at the thought of Norris calling him an 'old man'. I fought to remember all that he had done. *This man is no friend to you, Anne Boleyn!* my mind shouted at my heart. *Show him mercy now and it will be as giving up your neck to the wolf to chew upon!*

Me and Mine, I repeated that motto to myself. *Me and Mine* and no other. I could have no pity for this man.

Finally, Henry entered and called us to rise from our assorted curtseys and bows. His eyes scanned the crowd, found mine, and he hurried to my side, sweeping his arm around me, caressing my hair and kissing my cheek as he greeted me. There was murmuring from the crowds. Henry was entirely open in his affection to me in public now. He wanted all to know that he adored me above all others. He wanted, too, for all to know that no matter what came from the Pope, he was going to marry me.

Then, suddenly and much to my surprise and my family's chagrin, Henry spotted Wolsey, and went to him. Wolsey fell to his knees, causing a booming sound as he hit the floor, and wrenched his hat from his head, muttering words of supplication and greeting. Henry smiled at the Cardinal's bare head with its thin hair, and raised Wolsey to face him. He looked on Wolsey with both compassion and affection, greeted him, and made Wolsey put his hat back on his sweating head. Henry asked Wolsey in a most gentle tone if he had recovered from his recent illness. I stood amazed.

Such was the barrage of insult we had put against the Cardinal I had thought that Henry might react to his presence with anger, or distrust. It was unbelievable. Many surrounding us tittered into their starched lace sleeves to see our faces, staring at Henry and Wolsey as though we could not believe it.

I was crushed. My uncle's face went pale.

Henry drew Wolsey to a side seat near a window and the two conversed. It seemed as though they talked of friendly things, although none of us could hear their words well. I was stunned and stood gaping until my brother rapped me on the knuckles gently to remind me to keep my court mask upon my face. Too many people watched my every move and facial expression in these days to allow an unguarded look to betray my surprise and deflation. But I could hardly believe what Henry was doing! What *was* he doing? How could he make friends with my enemy? I cursed all the feelings of pity I had felt for Wolsey that day, and I threw Norris into those curses for making me ashamed of my behaviour. If Wolsey slimed his way back into Henry's graces, then would I find myself no longer welcome at court? And if this was Henry's intention, why had he greeted me and made so public his affection for me? Was he trying to keep us *both* at his side, even now? *What was going on?*

We pretended to converse, whilst all the time watching the Cardinal and Henry talk in the alcove. At one point Henry pulled out a letter and challenged the Cardinal. I had no doubt it was the letter my father had intercepted. At least in that I was pleased. "Come, Thomas," Henry said. He spoke softly. I had to crane my neck to hear him. "This is your hand is it not?"

The Cardinal's replies we could not hear, although Henry seemed worryingly reassured by them. It seemed as though, once back in his presence, Henry was as easily led by the Cardinal as he had always been. Watching this, I caught my father's eye. He had been thinking the same as I, it seemed, for he whispered under his breath, "we must needs take the hair and the head apart if we are to succeed."

I nodded. No more could we allow them to meet like this. I must put a barrier between them.

That night Henry and I supped together. The Cardinal had left Grafton to find a bed for the night, and the others of our party slipped away, too, as Henry and I went to our dinner. It was a fine feast; servants brought us pottage of summer herbs and flaked fish, fresh venison from the deer we had hunted that week and warm salads of cabbage and carrots. Baked lampreys and sops in wine were followed by peas royal, prunes in syrup and apricot marmalade. I stabbed at the lampreys, transferring them from their bright green glazed dish to Henry's silver plate, and as I did, I spoke as though I had just considered a new thought. "Is it not a marvellous thing, my lord, to consider what debt and danger the Cardinal has brought you to with all your subjects?"

Henry looked puzzled, then pursed his lips, perhaps tired of my constant wrangling about Wolsey. "How so, sweetheart?" he asked, taking up his knife and eating one of the smaller lampreys whole.

I laughed lightly, spooning some broth to my own plate. "Truly Henry, there is not a man in all your realm who is worth anything that is not indebted to you, by Wolsey, in the taxes that he has rent upon your subjects."

"Well, well," Henry tried to push the subject aside. "There is in him no blame for that, and I know that matter better than you, or any other, my love."

Katherine, or another wise woman, would have left it there, hearing his warning tone, but I hated to be pushed aside as if my opinion did not matter. "No, sire," I continued, putting my spoon into the bright green peas. "Besides all else he has done, there are many things he has wrought within this realm that give to your great slander and dishonour in the eyes of your people. Any nobleman in this realm who had done but half so much as the Cardinal has done, would be well worthy to lose his head. He is a traitor to Your Majesty, I see that clearly enough."

Henry started, his eyes opening wide. Although I had given him ample reason to suspect that I did not trust the Cardinal and believed him my enemy, I had never openly accused him of being a traitor before. "Why then!" Henry blinked with surprise. "I see that you are no friend of the Cardinal."

I looked deep into Henry's eyes. There was a moment that passed between us in which he seemed to understand me; there could only be one of us. Either the Cardinal or I, not both, could continue past this point. Henry would have to choose between us.

I spoke carefully. "I have no cause to love any man that loves not Your Grace. Nor would you, my love, if you consider well his doings." I stared unhappily at my plate for a moment, and then I rose. "I have a headache, Your Majesty." Henry stared at me as I started to leave the table.

"Anne…" he pleaded. "Stay… please."

I shook my head. Tears leapt to my eyes. In that moment my fears threatened to envelop me. "I have to go," I whispered.

I left the dinner and the diner, who sat staring after me with troubled eyes. I knew that I was causing Henry pain, but I had no choice. The time had come. Henry needed to decide which of us was more important to him.

That night, I formed a plan, and sent for Gardiner to help me. I ordered the King's servants to prepare for a day away in the countryside on the next morn, to pack food and blankets so that we might ride out into the parks at Hartwell with the dawn, and stay there all day. I then instructed Gardiner to go to Wolsey with a show of reconciliation, and to delay his arrival at Grafton the next day.

"You said that you were my man, Gardiner," I reminded him, watching his frown deepen. "So prove yourself to me now."

"I will do as you ask, my lady," he nodded. "As long as you do not forget all that I do for you."

"I forget nothing, Master Gardiner," I said softly. He went to do my bidding.

The next morning I went to Henry as though nothing had happened, and told him that I had arranged, as a surprise for him, a picnic, three miles away and we would be gone all day. This meant Henry would not have to see Wolsey again before he had to leave with Campeggio. Henry disliked having to face unpleasant situations directly and I was giving him the perfect excuse to escape from one. He accepted the invitation gladly and seemed touched that I should have thought ahead to plan a surprise for his pleasure.

Just as Wolsey arrived at Grafton, we were all mounting horses. Wolsey stood, much amazed and confused. Gardiner had visited with Wolsey the night before, and had ably delayed his leaving the house in good time as morning came. Henry gave Wolsey but a rushed greeting, and told him that we were likely to be gone for a long time. Henry knew that he was abandoning Wolsey, and he did not wish to linger to see his old friend's face as it fell. Wolsey was instructed to accompany Campeggio back to London.

As we rode off, I looked back and saw Wolsey gaping at the dust of our horses. He knew what this meant. He knew that he had lost, again. By the time we arrived back at Grafton, Wolsey and Campeggio had left. The Cardinal had lost, Henry was ours.

This was not the end of my struggles with the Cardinal, but Henry would never see Wolsey face to face again.

Chapter Fifty-Five

Greenwich Palace
Autumn 1529

Wolsey had lost, but he was not gone. He was still Chancellor and was still chairing meetings at court in London. My father wanted him entirely removed, in order to take his seat as Chancellor; a position that, after having spent the summer nestled in Henry's ear, he had high hopes of attaining. Progress was still going on, but Henry left me in the country and briefly returned to London and Greenwich to start the business of setting up a new Parliament. Wolsey, it seemed, was attempting to shrug off the events of progress, and continue on with the King's work. But Henry did not seek to see him and Wolsey knew nothing of Henry's visit to London until the King had already come and gone. Henry's avoidance of Wolsey was telling. He was closer now to making a choice than he ever had been before.

Henry was, for the first time in his reign, taking upon himself all the work that Wolsey had done before. I was more proud of him than I could say when I arrived each day to find him poring over dispatches and letters as he never had done before. I tarried with him, reading over papers with him, and offering advice where I felt able.

One of the first things Henry directly ordered was perhaps petty. He commanded that Campeggio be halted at Dover and his bags and chests be searched. This was, however, done only in part to annoy Campeggio. Norfolk had word that Wolsey was trying to sneak certain papers out of the country and send them to Rome. My uncle knew not what was in them, but a man in his pay had seen the Cardinal handing something to Campeggio in a most secretive manner when they parted in London. Norfolk suspected that Campeggio carried letters for the Pope and for the Emperor from

Wolsey, letters intended to curry their favour. Perhaps Wolsey was offering to bring about reconciliation between Katherine and Henry in return for the support of Clement and Charles? But nothing was found amongst Campeggio's belongings, and Campeggio complained bitterly to Henry about the indignity of the search.

Henry's reply was rude and offhand. *"How can we help it if the porters at the dock were rough?"* he wrote. *"You may infer from this that my subjects are not well pleased that my case has not come to a better conclusion."* Campeggio left England with his tail between his legs, and Henry and I laughed together to think of his panic when his bags were searched.

"We still do not know whether or not Wolsey has given something to Campeggio… Perhaps your men just did not find it," I warned.

Henry shrugged. "They found nothing, sweetheart, and I have done all that I could."

It was true enough, but still, I worried that Wolsey would try to make peace between himself, the Holy Roman Emperor and the Pope. He knew he had no friends left in England, but what if he could protect himself by reaching out to our enemies? I wrote an angry letter to Wolsey, showing him that I was aware he had worked for Katherine's interests over mine *"your lordship abandons my interests to work for those of the queen,"* I wrote. *"I acknowledge that I have put much confidence in your professions and promises, in which I find myself deceived. But, for the future, I shall rely on nothing but the protection of Heaven and the love of my dear King, which alone will be able to set right again those plans which you have broken and spoiled… The wrong you have done me has caused me much sorrow, but I feel infinitely more in seeing myself betrayed by a man who pretended to enter into my interests only to discover the secrets of my heart."*

I shared my letter with Henry, who whistled when he read it. "I did not know you felt this way," he said. "I am so sorry that this man has caused you pain."

After further urging, Henry finally agreed that Wolsey must be charged with *praemunire*. Henry was by now genuinely suspicious of his friend, and after all that had been presented to him that summer, and his understanding that I hated the Cardinal, he agreed to move against him. My family exulted. Norfolk even laughed; something I had rarely witnessed before. It was like watching a cat spit up a hairball. We thought this was the end of Wolsey, but we were mistaken.

As Wolsey arrived at Westminster Hall for the first day of the new legal term, he found himself alone in court. He waited for a while, wondering where everyone was, and then found himself called to the King's Bench where the charges were laid out for him. Wolsey must have known about the pamphlets that had circulated about him and his loyalties. He must have known something was coming, for he was prepared.

The charges of *praemunire* were read against Wolsey. He was accused of abusing the powers of the Legatine Court, of not acting in the interests of his sovereign, and of receiving bulls from Rome that directly opposed the wishes of his country and King. Wolsey surrendered. He decided it was wiser to throw himself on Henry's mercy and plead guilty rather than surrender to an Act of Attainder from Parliament. An Act of Attainder allowed Parliament to declare a person guilty of a crime and punish them without a trial. It nullified their common rights, their rights to property, to their wealth, and even the right to life itself. Had Wolsey declared himself innocent, he had plenty of enemies who would have used this legal right against him. Deciding that it was better to throw himself on Henry's mercy, rather than that of his enemies, Wolsey pleaded guilty, surrendered his property to

Henry, and begged for the King's leniency. He was clever, really… for Henry would have been more likely to utterly destroy Wolsey if the fat bat had chosen to defy him. After accepting the charges, Wolsey wrote to Henry,

"Most gracious and merciful sovereign lord,

Next unto God, I desire nor covet anything in this world but the attaining of your gracious favour and forgiveness of my trespasses. Grant me your grace, mercy, remission and pardon for my sins. Aside from all worldly considerations, the sharp sword of Your Majesty's displeasure in me hath penetrated my heart.

Your Grace's most prostrated, poor chaplain, creature and bedes-man,

T-Cardinalis, Ebor, Miserimus."

He said to others that it was impossible to challenge a *"continual serpentine enemy about the King,"* meaning me, presumably.

The country as a whole, and the nobility in particular, were pleased to see Wolsey tumble from grace. He had taken all of Henry's favour for himself, leaving little for others. People blamed him for their own lack of advancement and money; for the expense of the wars into which Henry had entered and for any and all ruin about the country. Since the Cardinal acted on behalf of the King, all of the failures and problems of the past years were set squarely upon his shoulders. He was censured now in public for his pride, for his carnal sins, for his avarice, and people openly mocked at the manner in which he used to ride through the streets, with his feet in golden stirrups. Ravening crows were gathering over the head of this once all-powerful Cardinal…

Wolsey was removed from his post as Chancellor, and Norfolk and Suffolk took great pride in being the ones sent to him to take the seal of office from his hands personally. Even then, though, Wolsey demanded to see Henry's signature before he would surrender his seal. Suffolk stared at Wolsey in disbelief, wondering that even now he could be so arrogant. But the two blundering Dukes had not brought Henry's signed order with them, thinking they did not need it, and Wolsey refused to give up the seal. They had to come back to his house early the next morning. Wolsey broke into tears and crashed to his knees when he saw that Henry had, indeed, signed the order.

Henry could never stand to look into the eyes of one with whom he had broken... As I was eventually to understand only too well. All that he did to Wolsey he did through other men. He never had to witness Wolsey's terror and pain... I encouraged him not to see Wolsey. Later, much later, I would come to regret this characteristic in my husband... I would come to regret that I myself taught him how to leave a loved one behind.

Wolsey retained his clerical positions, and there was nothing that Henry could do to deny him these. He was still a Cardinal, and an Archbishop, and as such held some residences and revenues in York, and in other Sees, which were beyond the reach or authority of the King. So he was far from destitute, although to a man who had lost such fabulous riches, it must have felt as though he had lost everything. Wolsey had his servants compile lists of his palaces, houses, coin and belongings, which were sent to Henry. The lists went on for page after page after page after page. The amount of goods, plate, cloth, furniture, coffers of coin, jewels, land and buildings he owned were staggering. Wolsey added a crawling note at the end of this list, saying he would have his men strip his houses, or leave the goods in place; whatever the King desired him to do would be done.

Wolsey was to move to a small house in Esher, which belonged to the See of Winchester. A new Chancellor was needed, and Henry favoured Suffolk for the post, but Norfolk protested to me, saying that it would give Suffolk too much power. I agreed, and asked Henry to choose another, recommending my father. Henry wished to please me, but he said that if Suffolk was not to my liking then he wanted Sir Thomas More in the post. My father was disappointed, but I could not argue that More was qualified for the position, despite my dislike of him.

More took the post with reluctance. Although he was on Katherine's side in the *Great Matter*, he had promised Henry, as a friend, that he would not involve himself with it, nor would he speak against Henry… But he did, however, make it clear that he thought the King's marriage was valid. More worried that in taking this post he would be unable to fulfil his promise to Henry. As Chancellor, would he not be asked to take on Wolsey's responsibility, and find a way for the King to legally separate from his wife?

Henry went to More's house to persuade him to take the post, saying that he wanted him as Chancellor *because* he was impartial, and because he had great faith in his honesty and virtue. I am not sure why Henry thought he was impartial, for More had made his views on the annulment clear. More finally accepted, believing Henry would value his opinion, and perhaps also believing that the King himself was becoming unsure in his previous convictions about the illegality of his marriage. My family were not best pleased, for More despised people like us. He was determined to use his new position, even though he had not wanted it, to stamp out heresy in England. We were going to have to be careful with the new Chancellor.

With Henry, however, I was jubilant. I had won! We had *won*! Finally, Henry was free of Wolsey's poison!

They say that when Wolsey came to leave London, he stood on the banks of the river at York Place, waiting for his barge to take him to Esher. An early autumn mist was rising over the river, hazy in the light of the dawn. The Cardinal stood looking back at his palace, swathed in swirling grey fog. A huge mass of people had turned out to watch him depart; both crowds along the banks and crowded in boats along the river. Some had come because they loved him, but many more were there to witness his disgrace. Many of them expected he would be taken to the Tower, but Henry was satisfied with confiscating the majority of Wolsey's holdings. Wolsey was, in effect, going into exile. Any other man who had acted as he had would have gone to the block. Henry loved Wolsey too much to allow that to happen.

Wolsey looked back at what had been his rich palace, now being picked over, inventoried and confiscated by the King's men. Already Wolsey's emblems were being taken down and replaced with Henry's. George Cavendish, a retainer of Wolsey's turned to his master, putting a hand on his arm and said, "I cannot but see that it is the inclination and natural disposition of Englishmen to desire change in men of authority, most of all where such men have administered justice impartially."

Wolsey nodded his head sadly, and replied ruefully, drawing on the bull emblem of the Boleyns, and the dun cow of the Tudor line to make a point. "When the cow doth ride the bull, then priest, beware thy skull."

When I heard of this, I shook my head. *Cow* was not the worst name he had called me. *Night crow* was his favourite name for me, or *serpentine witch*. I wondered if he knew I called him the *fat bat*?

But just as Wolsey despaired, he was offered a ray of hope. Unbeknownst to our faction, Henry was not done with his former friend. As Wolsey stood at the riverside, Norris was secretly sent to him with a note and a small golden ring from Henry. The message assured Wolsey that he could not be arrested without the King's express authority. Henry wrote to Wolsey that he had been brought low *"only to satisfy more* the minds of some, which I knoweth be not your friends, rather than through any perceived indignation of mine own." Henry went on to say that should the chance present itself, then he would restore Wolsey to his former position and wealth, *"in better estate than ere you were."*

Wolsey knelt on the dirty riverbank, to give thanks to the Lord God and to the King. He gave Norris a golden crucifix, which he said contained a part of the true cross, and furthermore instructed his fool, Patch, to enter Henry's service. The fool put up a great show of not wanting to leave his master, and six Yeomen Guards carried him off to be presented to Henry. I doubt that Patch was genuinely so downcast to be leaving the service of a disgraced master, entering instead the service of the King of England. He would have been well aware of the rewards of such a position. Fools were canny mortals. Patch knew that in entering Henry's service he would be richly rewarded if he pleased his master, and the position, too, gave him greater scope for his audacious announcements, than even the Cardinal's service might have brought to him. He howled as his master stepped onto his barge and sailed down the river. Many watching Wolsey from the boats and on the river banks jeered and insulted the Cardinal, happy to see him leave.

Wolsey was fallen, but not forgotten.

We Boleyns and Howards rejoiced. We believed then that Henry might order Wolsey's arrest rather than simple exile. But we were fools. Henry was just waiting for a chance to save his friend. He was waiting for a time to bring him back. My father was right. Henry did not know what was good for him.

Chapter Fifty-Six

York Place
Autumn 1529

When the Cardinal had departed for Esher, Henry and I went to see his new property of York Place, which had been surrendered by Wolsey. It was stunningly beautiful. The Cardinal had such expensive tastes. Even Henry's palaces and castle paled in comparison to the richness within York Place.

At York Place, there were no chambers for the Queen. Wolsey had built York Place for himself, as his personal seat in London. It was a house that had known only one, unmarried, male owner, and so there had never been a need to construct a second, equally grand set of chambers for a wife. This pleased me for although, whilst Henry was on progress, Katherine had been forced to stay at Greenwich, now she seemed determined to follow him, and to set up her household in opposition to mine at every turn, often forcing me to take lesser apartments with my ladies. Like a fawning lapdog, she panted at Henry's heel. It made life in London more and more uncomfortable. Katherine seemed to believe that now the King's *Great Matter* was in peril, and Henry had been called to Rome, he would go back to her. When they were in the same palace, she would ask daily for audiences with him, which were usually denied. She sent word to Henry that he might visit her at night, if he pleased, and arranged feasts for him in her chambers, and diverse entertainments. She was trying to woo him back, trying to emulate me. Henry did not attend. He tried to avoid her at all costs. But at York Place, there was nowhere for her to stay, which made me happy.

Katherine was acting as though the events of the past few years had not happened. But, smarting from the humiliation at Blackfriars, and finding himself bogged down by all the work that Wolsey had once performed for him, he was in no temper to pander to Katherine. Her unvarying protestations of love and adoration fell upon deaf ears. Although, at the time, I revelled in his coldness towards her, I would one day come to understand the pain she suffered then.

Although, on that summer's progress, I had been as Queen in my own right, in the real world Katherine still held on to that title with her fat, stubby hands and would not let go. Worst of all, the common people loved her for it. When they saw the crests and emblems of the Boleyns on litters or carts, they threw stones and mouldy bread. My father's men were repeatedly accosted in the streets by screaming commoners, and even when the King's guards, or my father's men, saw them off, they persisted in their hatred. Their voices were raw, ragged with disgust and revulsion. It made me nervous to travel through London. I took to travelling by barge when I could, and at less busy times of the day or night, but still, I heard their words. They scared me, I do not deny it. They were turning Katherine into a martyr, and people are not swift to give up their heroes once they are made.

But when I was about court, I pretended I was oblivious to their hatred. I could not face this persecution like a wounded lamb. Any hint of weakness was enough for many at court to pounce. I laughed off people's hatred in public, claiming that I cared not. But I did. It would have taken a much harder heart than mine to stand before such censure and not be affected. Supporters and friends at court, I had many, and yet their numbers seemed small when I gazed from my window to see how many hundreds and thousands of people hated me in England, and throughout other courts of the world.

In my braver times, I spoke sternly to myself. I *would* be Queen. They would forget this hatred. I would show them, when I was Queen, how good I meant to be. They would see how I meant to use my power to support universities, scholars, and reform the corruption of the Church. One day, they would cheer me as they once had Katherine. The time would come. *My* time would come.

To some it seemed I was there already, for du Bellay noted in his dispatches to his master in France that my uncle Norfolk was now the King's chief advisor, and More his Chancellor, but, *"above all others, the Lady Anne"* was truly in charge. I smiled when I read the stolen papers that my father acquired… *Above all others*. I liked the sound of that. Perhaps it was true enough as well, for as Henry gathered new men to give him counsel in Wolsey's absence, he also often turned to me.

With Wolsey gone, Henry and I entered a period of peace. He had finally taken action against my greatest enemy, and I knew how much it had cost him. I was unaware, then, of the messages of support he had sent to the Cardinal, and, in my innocence, I felt only closer to Henry. I believed he had made the ultimate sacrifice for me.

I was kind to Henry, shying away from arguments, and seeking only to soothe him. We played at cards, went out for long hunting trips, and I played on the virginals or lute at night to calm his mood. He loved to hear me sing, for I had a good voice, and often when we sat together, after he had read through state papers, or had attended meetings all day, I sang him to sleep, with his tired head upon my lap. He grieved for the Cardinal as though Wolsey had died, and I made it my task to try and comfort him. Henry was pleased by this. Although I think he enjoyed the stormy parts of our relationship as much as he feared them, there were many times when we were not a raging, passionate couple, but a pair of friends, looking after each other. It was a side of us that many people did not see. Our arguments were famous, but there were other sides to our story; times when we were gentle and calm together. This time after Wolsey's fall was one of those.

Whilst Henry sorrowed for the loss of Wolsey, he could not but be amazed at the fabulous riches that had come into his pocket through the fall of the richest man in England. As the properties and goods that Wolsey had surrendered to him came into his possession, Henry was astounded by the volumes of riches that he now controlled. Gold and silver plate and ornaments were piled in front of him like apples at a market. Jewels, coin, rings, bracelets, and necklaces sat in heaps in coffers. Tapestry, carpet and painted hangings were lain out for Henry to view. Furs, cloth, velvet gloves, leather hunting gear, saddles, footstools and richly decorated reins were like mountains in the great hall. In the mews there were hordes of falcons, sakers, and hawks, and Wolsey's hounds were plentiful in number too. Although Henry may have suspected it often enough before, it was now obvious Wolsey had been even richer than the King himself. The Cardinal had spent a lifetime acquiring goods and money, and had hoarded much wealth not only from his own revenues, not only from dissolved monasteries but also from Henry's pocket. He had received rich bribes from those currying his favour, and had taken money from pensions from France as well. His lands had been numerous, and all the rents, taxes and tithes from those had flowed into his coffers too. Oh yes… there was more wealth than a man could imagine here. The riches of princes… The riches of the people… The riches of the Church. Even I, who had known much of Wolsey's corruption, could hardly believe my eyes.

"How *has* this man *so much*?" Henry asked in wonder, eyeing the trunks, chests and piles of tapestry that continually arrived at his feet. Wagons had creaked along the streets for days, depositing load after load of goods, fabric, coin and jewels.

"From *you*, my lord," I said calmly, fingering a section of gorgeous embroidered cloth. "From revenues and from incomes that should have been yours, always. From your people and from those who wanted to buy Wolsey's loyalty."

Henry glanced at me with an uneasy face, but he nodded slowly in agreement. He looked around him and in a sudden change of topic, typical of Henry when he wished to avoid a painful subject, he went on. "This palace, Anne, this shall be yours and mine."

"What do you mean?"

He turned to me and his blue eyes were sparked with the fire of his imagination. "This shall be our palace. We will design and build upon it. We will make it our own," he said, opening his arms. "Here, we shall make our mark, together… Your ideas and mine will be made into physical form, here for our sons and daughters and all of our line to see. They will view York Place, and they will remember us here. They will honour the start of the dynasty that continued to rule for a thousand years!"

He laughed suddenly and crossed the room, putting my arm through his and marching off through the palace. Henry started to talk rapidly about his ideas, and I added my thoughts to his. Even before we had walked about the whole place, he was sending messengers for his workmen to come to him. He wanted to expand the palace, and there was land about it to do so. It was grand and vast already, but Henry wanted it to be awe-inspiring. And he wanted to undertake this project with me.

In truth, Henry was speaking too rapidly and too excitedly for me to believe that he was actually so overcome by this new idea that he had forgotten Wolsey. Henry often sought to forget the painful past and smother it with his future plans. He was seeking, in that exuberant display, to force Wolsey from his mind and concentrate on the future, with me. I did not try to wrestle him from his dreams. I entered into the performance, and we wandered about the palace making plans for expansion and change. In time, York Place would be known as Whitehall Palace, and it would become the greatest, and largest of all of Henry's creations.

Chapter Fifty-Seven

Greenwich Palace
Autumn 1529

One afternoon I was walking to Henry's Presence Chamber from my apartments in Greenwich. A page in Katherine's colours stepped out of the King's rooms as I approached, holding a pile of fine linen shirts. "What are these?" I demanded, stopping him. I put a hand to the linen, which clearly belonged to the King and touched the shirts with a horrible suspicion growing in my mind. The page was wearing Katherine's pomegranate emblem upon the traditional colours of red of a servant of the royal apartments.

"The King's shirts, my lady," he said. Although he bowed, he also, just perceptively, curled his lip. Katherine's servants hated me, as well they might, although about the court they could show only small signs of their disdain. The page made to leave, thinking that since he had answered, I would let him go, but I stopped him.

"Where are you taking them?"

"To Queen Katherine…" He shied back as my face darkened with anger.

"What do you mean? *Why* do you take the King's shirts to her?"

He coughed uncomfortably. "I take the King's shirts to the Queen so that she may mend them and make him more, my lady… As she has always done, as part of her wifely duty to the King."

I whipped him a look of sheer malevolence and he shrank from me as though I were the Devil. "I wish to see the King,"

I said coldly, as though this page was the guard on Henry's door, and then I pushed past him with my ladies following me in a scampering, whispering flock. The page fled.

I marched past the Yeomen Guard who stood at the door of Henry's private chambers. They nodded at me. Their gilt halberds, swords and silver breastplates glittering in the light that shone through the windows. Their tunics were of green and white velvet, embroidered back and front with the Tudor rose and decorations of gold and silver. They were all giants of men, standing tall, head and shoulders above the other men of the court, but even they moved aside when they saw me coming. One of them banged on the door, and Norris came to unlock it, as only he, aside from the King and the Queen, held a set of keys to that inner sanctum.

Henry called me in and before he could stand and utter his customary, "sweetheart…" I marched in as though I were on my way to battle. "It is a matter of shirts," I announced coldly, my black eyes snapping with anger and my hands resolutely by my side, clutching into fists as I faced my sovereign as though I should murder him then and there.

He stepped back and, noting my white face and clutched fists, spoke slowly, clearly baffled. "A matter of shirts…?"

Anger swelled inside me like a storm's wave. He nodded to his men who left the chamber, looking in astonishment at their king who seemed to accept the arrival of a Fury in his house with the greatest calm. "Those shirts that your *wife* still makes for you, Henry!" I cried.

Henry rubbed a hand over his short beard. "I know not what you mean, Anna…" He sounded genuinely confused.

"*Pah!*" I threw my hands in the air. "Those shirts that your wife makes, sews and mends for your body, my lord! Those shirts that you wear on your back even now as you say to me you know not of what I talk! *That* shirt, my lord, *those* shirts that she sews for you as her *wifely* duty!" I stood stock still, glowering at him. "Those shirts that she still makes for you even though *you* say she is no true wife! Even as you pledge yourself to me you still wear her shirts!"

Henry looked both amazed and angry. "I had little thought of it," he said, trying to restrain his temper. "She has always sewn them for me. I considered it of no importance... I do not *hand* the shirts to her men, Anne. Servants have their tasks, many of which have been in place for a long time... If they still come and take my shirts to Katherine, it is not by my daily and direct order, but only by tradition! Of that I assure you..." He scowled. "I have not time for these... women's matters," he mumbled into his short beard.

"*Women's matters!*" I exclaimed. "Women's matters? They are none such! These are *your* matters, Henry, yours and mine! How can I be a wife to you when you have another already? How can I fulfil my role in your life when another grabs it from me? There is *no* task that Katherine should now do for you! Every time you allow her such an office, she finds a way to creep back into your life. Every time you allow her a *wifely duty* you maintain the fiction that she is indeed your wife! You complain mightily about her resistance to leave, my lord, but you do not push her from you, do you? And every time you go to dine with her or sit with her, or talk about your child... you break my heart!"

My lip curled and my nostrils flared like those of an angry horse. He stared at me in naked astonishment, as though none of what I was saying had ever occurred to him. "No! No matter, Henry, that your *wife* still makes your clothes, no matter that she still performs each *wifely duty* for you as though you were truly married. No matter that each and every one of those duties keeps me from you. No matter that the two of you are still in this marriage and I am kept out by the laws of men and Popes and by your failure to make true effort to rid yourself of her!"

He went to speak but I railed over his mumbled words. "Perhaps you still hope that sooner rather than later I shall give in and be your happy *whore*, bear your bastards and suffer Katherine's glory as you continue with that Spanish crone as your Queen! Soon enough, perhaps, you think that all this will come to nothing, and so you keep her as your true wife as I live in the shadows! 'Tis but a shirt you say…!"

I drew myself up, beautiful and mighty before him in my anger. "…'Tis the sign of your *failure,* I say!"

I was angry, hurt… I wanted to shame him. I succeeded.

He seemed to grow larger, towering over me, his nostrils flaring and face scarlet with wrath. His blue eyes were as cold as the ice on the Thames and his cheeks were almost black with fury. "You have said enough, Mistress!" he said in the most terrible voice I had ever heard. He looked set to strangle me.

"*Mistress* is all I am to you, my lord," I cried boldly. I was afraid of him then, terribly afraid, but I had always the spirit of a lioness when I was frightened. I faced him with every scrap of courage I had. He had to *see*, to see that this was but another way for Katherine to hang on to her place at his side.

"It… is not so," he growled from behind gritted teeth.

"How can I believe in your words, when your actions show them to be lies?" I walked away from him.

"Do not turn your back on me… I am the *King*!" he shouted, slamming his hand upon the back of a chair. I turned my head to him as I reached the door.

"If it were not for your cruelty, your indifference, then I should never think of turning from you, Henry. But you are *not* my husband and so you do *not* control me, my lord. *Go back to your wife!*" I laughed bitterly and my lip curled. I hated him in that moment. He could see the revulsion in my face, and amidst the anger there in his face, there was also fear; fear that he would lose me. It was my greatest weapon. "Go to your wife, Henry of England," I repeated, my voice shrill. "For I am not she, am I?" I swept from the room, scattering servants from before me like the winds scatter the chaff.

Henry went to see Katherine that very day, and told her that no more would she make or mend his shirts, nor do any of the tasks she had performed in the past. Katherine protested, asking why, since she was his wife, should she give up such things? "You have always loved the clothes I made for you, my beloved," she cooed, trying to take his arm. "Why should I not continue to please you?"

"Nothing that you do pleases me!" he screamed at her. "I would that I could cast you into the seas and never have to look on your face again!" He stalked from her rooms and made sure that all her servants and his understood the new arrangements.

From then on, his shirts and any other items were to be delivered to me. From that day onwards, until the very day before my arrest, I made Henry's shirts.

Chapter Fifty-Eight

York Place
Autumn 1529

Parliament opened that year in early November, and although Henry was still in secret communication with Wolsey, he allowed many of his subjects to speak of the man with braying insult, setting free years of pent up envy, jealousy and hatred. Even the *saintly* Sir Thomas More, whose friends would have described as a moderate and sweet-tempered man, went about the business of picking Wolsey's flesh from his bones with zeal.

More's opening speech compared Henry to a good shepherd who had seen that his flock contained those that were "rotten" and had to be removed. More went on to say that Wolsey had "so craftily, so scabbedly, yea, and so untruly juggled the King that men must surely think he was so unable to see his wrongdoing or had counted on his master's ignorance." More censured Wolsey for all the troubles that had occurred in Henry's reign, and was as outspoken as any on his fall being for the better. More ended by saying that Henry had seen through Wolsey's wiles, and that the Cardinal was now being offered a "most gentle correction," by his master.

For those who loved More, and there are many more of them now than there ever were when he was alive, it would have seemed impossible that such a modest, righteous man could have made such a speech about one he had apparently considered a friend. Oftentimes at court, More and Wolsey had been seen together and noted as friends and allies. But More had privately despised Wolsey for his avarice, much as I had, and was not at all sad to see the Cardinal disgraced.

More was an oddity to many. He hated wearing the golden chain of his office and seemed more at ease with peasants than at court. Norfolk once went out to meet with him, and found the Chancellor wearing a plain gown and singing with a local choir in the church. "God's Body, my Lord Chancellor!" he exclaimed to More when he emerged to greet him. "You are the Chancellor of England, man! And yet you behave like a parish clerk!"

But, for all his supposedly humble ways, More was a dangerous creature. Luther once called More "the most cruel enemy of truth" and he was not far wrong. Whilst Henry gloried that such a man of eminently regarded wisdom should become his Chancellor, many had good reason to be troubled by his appointment. One of his first acts as Chancellor was in direct opposition to the charity and goodwill he had written about in his published work *Utopia*. In that text, his fictional account of a perfect state, he had called for love and charity to be shown to the poor. As Chancellor, one of his first proclamations was to condemn beggars and vagrants, instructing that should any man or woman be found outside their native parish without money to support themselves, they would be arrested, stripped naked, tied to a cart and whipped through the streets until their bodies were bloody and raw.

There are many who claim Thomas More was a good man of noble virtue. He was nothing of the kind.

He rapidly extended powers to punish and detain those who dared to read Tyndale or Luther, and leaned on Henry to increase the punishment of heretics. Henry's belief in this man was misplaced, in my view, and his being Chancellor was going to help neither the people of England, nor our cause, one bit.

In that Parliament, a bill was brought forth containing forty-four articles of Wolsey's corruption and treason. The signatories on the bill were all men whom Wolsey had harmed at some stage in his career; my father, Norfolk and Suffolk's names amongst them, of course. Henry did nothing to stop it, despite his covert support for the Cardinal. Perhaps Henry was truly in two minds about what to do with Wolsey, not knowing whether he was guilty of all that was set against him, or if the charges had been made up or exaggerated by Wolsey's enemies. Perhaps he also felt as though, having given up everything and gone into exile, Wolsey had suffered enough. But for whatever reason, Henry sat in silence, and allowed them to continue.

The Cardinal was accused of much ill. He was charged of granting appointments in return for favours, depriving monasteries of free elections and impeding bishops attempting to stamp out heresy. He was accused of embezzling goods, pillaging the wealth of the Church, concluding secret treaties with France and Spain and using the expression "the King and I," thus showing undue familiarity and lack of respect. The bill said Wolsey treated the King more like a subject than a master and had endangered the King's health by bringing the pox into his presence, contracted from his mistress. It also censured him for having a mistress and bastard children, thus betraying his vows of chastity and celibacy... The list went on and on.

Henry said nothing to these charges, but he did not move to help the Cardinal either. Henry remained silent. My father told me however, that Henry's face had blanched at the idea that Wolsey had the pox, for all knew his hideous fear of sickness.

The articles were presented to the King, and then sent to the Commons. The bill asked that Wolsey never again be given power or authority in the realm, but Henry did not agree to this. Again, he remained quiet and in that weighted silence there was worry for many, for we knew not what he was thinking. The bill, however, did provide a platform from which Wolsey's enemies could publicly bring all they had hated about the man to the eyes and ears of England. Wolsey was utterly disgraced, and everyone was now aware not only of their suspicions about him, but of his many true crimes. There were, of course, many false and exaggerated accusations in the bill, too, put there because Wolsey's enemies did not want this worm to rise into a phoenix from the ashes of his past.

There was only one man who seemed able and willing to defend Wolsey in his absence, and that was Master Thomas Cromwell. Cromwell was Wolsey's servant, and a loyal one at that, for at every condemnation and charge given against the Cardinal, Cromwell answered with calm and dignified responses, attempting to clear his master's name. I wondered if his desire to protect this master was solely for devotion to Wolsey, for when Wolsey fell, Cromwell had been heard to say, "I am like to lose all that I have ever laboured for," so perhaps some of his defence for his master came from self-interest as well as sympathy.

Cromwell was an interesting character. There were rumours that he had been a mercenary in the wars in Italy before entering the Cardinal's household. Cromwell had eyes of warm brown, with flecks of green at their centres and dark hair. He was strongly built, much like Henry, but a slight heaviness lay under his chin, softening the lines of his jaw. He had quick, keen eyes, and, as I was later to find, a fine sense of mirth and humour. His tongue and mind were swift and strong, and he was wry and dry in company. Henry was moved by his defence of his master, as many were, even Wolsey's enemies, and asked Cromwell to come to court, to see what he might do for him. "For, in showing such loyalty to your old master," Henry said to Cromwell, "I see in you virtues that I like."

Wolsey charged Cromwell to seek the best possible outcome on his behalf, writing to him that he was his only friend left in the world. Wolsey had already attempted to offer bribes in order to be absolved of the charges of treason brought against him, sending my brother a grant of two hundred pounds per year from his revenues at St Alban's; a vast sum, and one that showed clearly, despite being much reduced, Wolsey was not destitute. And my brother was not the only one Wolsey tried to bribe. Wolsey granted Thomas More a house, which More accepted, despite his protestations about the Cardinal's corruption... How ironic that More should rail against Wolsey's avarice and yet take bribes from his hands! Even Thomas Winter, Wolsey's bastard son, gave up lands and money to buy his father friends and allies.

Wolsey invited both friends and enemies to dine with him at Esher, including my uncle Norfolk, who refused. Henry continued to offer secret messages of comfort to Wolsey, sending John Russell, my old enemy, with further gifts. I did not hear of this at the time. Henry was careful. He did not want to offend me as he attempted to cling to the Cardinal's red robes.

Wolsey, however, was perhaps handing out too much too fast, as he informed Henry that he could not pay his servants, and even lacked normal everyday goods such as linen for his bed and plate from which to eat. Whether this was true or an exaggeration, I was unsure. I suspected that he wanted to play on Henry's compassion... But it was true his servants were leaving his service in droves. Whether this was due to non-payment of wages, or just that they believed they had a better chance of more gainful employment elsewhere, I know not. His servant George Cavendish was one of the few who did not leave him, but he was one of very few...

Henry, however, had other thoughts in his mind. Even this brief interlude during which Henry had taken the reins of his country for once into his own hands had shown him that Wolsey had been invaluable. Norfolk was supposed to be Wolsey's replacement as chief advisor, but he was arrogant, self-motivated, and, compared to Wolsey, a dullard... and Henry knew it. Suffolk, he loved like a brother, but he was no scholar. More he trusted, and appreciated for his intelligence, and yet he knew full well the man was not with him on his *Great Matter*. My father was keen and clever, but Henry knew that he, too, had much self-interest and would always work for his own best outcome first and foremost. This left Henry with a problem, for who could step into Wolsey's shoes and do the job as well as he? I, who was most often at Henry's side, could tell you that despite all his flaws, Wolsey was the most able servant Henry ever had… My enemy, yes… but as the happiness of his fall dissipated, we became aware that we had lost a valuable tool. Henry did not believe in throwing the old tool away. My thought was that we needed to find a new shiny implement to do our work.

We needed a new man to take Wolsey's place, and my keen eye was busy searching for the right one.

Chapter Fifty-Nine

Greenwich Palace
Autumn 1529

With one enemy out of sight, if not out of mind, it seemed that the other was primed and ready to give as much trouble as she could.

The three of us residing at court was a constant jest, I am sure, to everyone who was not one of us. The King, the Queen and the... other. The courts of other lands rocked with mirth when they thought of all of us holed up together, with me pretending to be Queen, and Henry trying to ignore his present wife. I did not laugh. It was a vastly uncomfortable situation and one that was causing us many problems.

Where Katherine was, I could not be Queen, so I began to spend a lot of time still at York Place with Henry, poring over our ideas and plans late into the night and talking with his workmen on our expansions and changes. I kept a court all my own, and it was bigger than Katherine's. We played at bowls in the alleys that Henry constructed. We wagered at cards and on games of tennis in which Henry played against my brother and other men. We danced late into the night, and I put on hunting trips and excursions, always being careful to avoid coming into close contact with the common people who still despised me. Henry was at my side at all times... when he was not with his wife.

In public, he still had to maintain his relationship with Katherine in order to pacify the Pope. It was she who presided at court, she who greeted and hosted when ambassadors and dignitaries visited. Henry could not send her away, for he feared what the Emperor, the Pope, and even his own people, might do. We had reached a stalemate. There were no moves either side could make. And so we rubbed together, and became irritated and raw.

I could only grit my teeth and wait until Henry would visit me, frustrated with Katherine's martyrdom. She still protested her love for him, invited him to her bed and talked constantly of their daughter and her accomplishments. Katherine made snide comments on my "*fabled virginity*", as she called it. She refused to acknowledge me as anything but his mistress, and told him of how so many disapproved of me, his "*whore*". It did not matter how many times he protested that we had not slept together, Katherine did not believe it. She did not see how I could have kept him this long if I were not the wild seductress many accused me of being.

Henry still had men gathering evidence on his *Great Matter*, and hoped to resolve it in England. Whilst I encouraged this, I was becoming increasingly aware this line of attack was getting us nowhere. We were stuck, in a kind of limbo, with even less hope of achieving our goals than we'd had before. We needed fresh blood and fresh ideas, but for all my searching, I could not see a way to turn.

Katherine kept up her barrage against Henry. She more often than not got the upper hand in their arguments. I told him to cease arguing with Katherine, for she managed to bring his spirits so low with her continual courage and spirit. Fear was increasing in me that he would cast me off, thinking all this too much trouble. But whilst he assured me this would never happen, he did not listen to me about Katherine. When Katherine started bleating, Henry could not stop himself from shouting back at her. Henry was used to getting his own way. He was used to his being the voice that was heard. His only reaction to being defied was to scream and shout like a spoilt child.

At times, I despised him. At other times, I pitied and loved him so deeply I thought I might drown in my feelings.

One day, as she reproached him for unkindness and neglect, he told her that the decision about the legality of their marriage must go in his favour, or he would "denounce the Pope as a heretic and marry whom he pleased." Katherine went wild, slashing his fragile confidence with her tongue. When he came to me that night, whining that Katherine had crushed his arguments, my temper snapped. I leapt out of my chair, making him stumble backwards.

"Did I not tell you that whenever you disputed with the Queen she was sure to have the upper hand? I see that some fine morning you will succumb to her reasoning and that you will cast me off! I have been waiting long, and might in the meantime have contracted some advantageous marriage, out of which I might have had issue, which is the greatest consolation to a woman in this world. But *no*! Farewell to my time and youth spent to no purpose at all!"

I glowered at his stunned and miserable face. "I shall not see you, for all I can think is that you are planning to leave me, planning to remain in sin with that cold Spanish fish! You will leave me and my reputation spent and sore for your love! You are not true, my lord, *you do not love me*!"

I tried to run from the room but he grabbed me roughly, covered my face in kisses and begged me to stay. "It is not true, sweetheart," he protested. "I *will* make you my Queen." He could not bear to see me like this; it hurt his heart.

I allowed him to comfort me, but I felt like a hare cornered by a hound, unable to find an escape. No matter what Henry said, we were stuck and we had nowhere to go. I could not see how he could make me his Queen… The Pope was no friend to our cause, and Henry was simply not ready to join the movement of reform sweeping over Europe and act as King and Pope in his own Kingdom. I hung in his arms, feeling helpless. But Henry was determined.

"I will not be told what I can and cannot do," he muttered over my head as he stroked my hair that night. "I will be King in my own Kingdom, and none shall tell me otherwise!"

There was something in his tone that I recognised. This cause, his *Great Matter*, this quest to marry me was not only about his love for me anymore, it was about the question of his kingship altogether.

His authority as King had been called into question; by Katherine, by the Charles of Spain, by Pope Clement; even by his own people. Although his love for me had sparked these events, it was, by now about much more than the two of us. He did not like being told he could not do as he wished, and he saw it as a direct challenge to his authority; the authority placed upon him by God Himself. If Henry could not act as he wished to, then he was not the King in truth. That notion scared him more than anything else.

If Henry was not King, then he was nothing. And there was nothing, not even me, not even the prospect of a son, more important to Henry than his God-given position as sovereign.

He would find a way for us. I comforted myself with the thought. But although I understood his zeal, I found myself uneasy to think that the *Great Matter* was now less of an issue of love for Henry, but one of pride.

Chapter Sixty

Greenwich Palace
Winter 1529

In early December, perhaps to appease me following our argument, my father was made twice an Earl. Henry granted him not only the long-coveted Earldom of Ormonde, that very title for which my hand had once been offered, as a bargaining chip, to James Butler for, but also the Earldom of Wiltshire. Thus, my father became one of the premier nobles of the realm, and a very rich man. George, too, was knighted that winter, and in respect of our father's new titles, he became Lord Rochford, and I became one of four Lady Rochfords, along with my mother, my sister, and Jane. At the same time, George won back his lost position in the Privy Chamber, and became one of Henry's most intimate companions.

Henry put on a grand celebration to mark the occasion, inviting all at court to come and rejoice with the Boleyns. Katherine was obviously not invited and did not seek to attend. Before the revelries, Henry presented me with a new gown of purple velvet trimmed with ermine; a colour of cloth and a fur that only royalty may wear by law.

When I arrived in my stunning gown there were many gasps, but I held my head high and processed with Henry to the head of the table. There was no public sign he could have given that more ably showed his intention to marry me. His will was as strong as ever, and in that show, using but cloth and stitch, I was confirmed as his *only* true Queen.

Henry's sister Mary, and my aunt by marriage, the Duchess of Norfolk, stood open-mouthed and horrified. Both were close to Katherine, despite the Duchess of Norfolk's connection to my own house. They were disgusted to see me paraded so, not only usurping Katherine's place, but raised above them in precedence. As the dancing began, Mary caught her brother's sleeve and I heard her admonish him for his cruelty towards Katherine, and for his faith in me. "You do not see, do you, brother, how she *uses* you? The people of England are revolted at this behaviour... Do you not see where that goggle-eyed snake and her poisonous family are leading you?"

Henry scowled at his sister, pulled his coat from her grip and walked away from her without a word. Mary stood staring at him in amazement. He had never treated her thusly before; when she had eloped with Suffolk, he had raged at her. Now, she was met with cold indifference. Later, Suffolk was told angrily by Henry that if he could not restrain his wife and her mouth, she would find herself banished from court. This was highly shameful for Suffolk, as he was part of our faction. But it was even more shameful for, in so many ways, Mary was his superior in station and rank. His wife she might be, but she was also a princess of England and the dowager Queen of France. She outranked him. I doubted that the Duke would to be able to do much to curtail his wife's behaviour, and Henry was only going to grow angrier at him if he failed.

Norfolk, too, was having problems with his wife. He had not liked either than I should take precedence over her at the feast, no matter if I was his niece and would one day be his Queen. He was the highest noble in the land, and to have his wife disgraced brought shame upon him, too. Don't think that he cared for his Duchess... Oh no... Norfolk and his wife were not on good terms. Norfolk had, a few years previously, moved his mistress into his house and set her above his wife. There were rumours, too, that when the Duchess protested about this "low whore" residing in her own home, Norfolk and his mistress, Bess Holland, had pinned the screaming Duchess to the floor and beaten her. The Duchess had complained of this to any and all she could, but it made no difference. A man was allowed to beat his wife if she did not obey, as she had promised to upon marriage. It was sanctioned by law, and encouraged by the Church. Only extreme cruelty was ever acted upon, and even then it was rare. But even if he hated his wife and thrashed her in private, in public, Norfolk wanted her to be shown the respect to which his position entitled her. It was his own wounded pride which moved him to anger that night, not love, affection or respect for his wife.

That night we feasted on all manner of fine fish and beasts of the seas. It was Advent, and so we were not permitted to consume flesh. But it mattered little for the fish served at court was every bit as fine as the flesh. We ate of sallats of imported olives and capers and Alexander buds cut long and cooked with whelks. There were stews of seethed shrimp in ale and pottage of ray and plaice. Then came baked oysters in their shells served with lemon juice and salt and boiled cockles in beer and pepper. Sturgeon, the fish of royalty, was served in aysell to the top table alone. Roasted salmon with cinnamon and ginger was brought out along with pike in mustard sauce, skirrets with vinegar and oil and bream in white wine. Trout pâté, baked porpoise, stewed herrings with onion and sugar and pies of whiting emerged from the kitchens. Laver bread shone purple-black and was served with cockles. Tarts of winter greens and warm sallats of purple and white carrots sat happily next to golden fritters of gourd and apple. Baked artichokes were served in slices, beside buttered greens on diced bread. Apple tarts, poached pears in red wine, walnut comfits and wobbling quince jellies were served last, alongside great pies of preserved cherries. Chapuys mentioned sardonically to Norris that it was as though the celebration were a wedding feast for Henry and me.

I cared not for his sarcasm. I was happy. Happy to see me and mine honoured. Happy to sit beside Henry in my rightful place. I ate, I laughed, I danced through the night in the purple gown that had caused so much gossip, and all the time Henry was at my elbow; flattering me, praising me and showing his love for me to all. Although we were no nearer to our goal, his open devotion and love for me made me feel as though we were.

After the feast, Henry led the members of my family and his own personal friends to a banqueting room, where we continued to drink wine and eat from dishes of sweet confection. The tasty treats were taken from the sideboards at the edge of the room, as the servants had been dismissed for the night. Suckets of fruit in syrup were eaten with sucket spoons of pewter and silver. Marchpane, jellies and biscuits were plucked at with eager fingers. Henry fed me kissing comfits of sugar fondant with his own fingers, and mounds of syllabub naughtily called 'Spanish paps' by the court, wobbled on their plates. The white flesh of highly expensive imported nuts of India was flaked so that we could pluck at the dry, sweet and creamy morsels. Comfits of pippin and caraway seed were passed around informally, as we jested and chattered. At the end of the evening I was presented with a golden cup of hippocras, as though I were the Queen in truth. Much of the food offered at such events were intended as aphrodisiacs, and when the other company parted from us, Henry and I made our way to my chambers, where he lifted my skirts and made me breathless with the magic of his gentle kisses and clever fingers. Later, somehow hungry again, we sat together, eating from a plate of aleberry pudding made of bread soaked in ale and baked with melted, salted butter and sugar, exhausted and content in each other's company.

When Henry wanted a dish such as this in the middle of the night, whole rooms of his kitchen servants had to be roused from their beds and ordered to produce whatever tempted him. To Henry, who was so used to such things, this was but normal, but to me it was always amazing. He was kind and gracious to them when they arrived from the kitchens, bleary-eyed with tiredness, carrying his food. Henry always thanked them handsomely, often offering them a coin in reward. They never seemed unhappy in their task, and the fact that Henry remembered most of them by name and asked after their families always made them feel special. They loved their King for these small attentions. It was not only because he paid their wages and gave them lodgings that they adored him; he was interested in them and often spoke to them informally. It gave them a chance to touch the hand of the power that ruled them; a time to know that he was also their friend. He could make anyone feel like that, Henry... it was one of his powers. Be in his company for a short while, and you felt as though you had known him all his life. And to be wooed by him, as I was, was often to feel as though you had been enchanted by magic.

Just before Christmas, Wolsey fell ill at his house in Esher, and his doctor asked Henry to send his own physicians to the Cardinal. Hearing this, and fearing for the man, Henry agreed to do so. "God forbid that he should die!" Henry said to the whole court as he received the news. "I would not lose him for twenty thousand pounds!"

I was less than pleased at this public statement and it set off rumours that Henry was going to reinstate Wolsey. Doctor Butts wrote to Henry saying that he thought Wolsey's illness was, in part, produced by his mind and the troubles which he faced. He urged his King to write to the Cardinal. *"If you would have him dead,"* he wrote, *"I warrant he will be within these four days if he receive not comfort from you, and Mistress Anne."*

I was sure that the Cardinal was faking illness in order to attract Henry's sympathy, but Henry was bowled over with concern. He asked me to write to Wolsey, with him, and to send a token to him, so that he might rest.

"He is but a sick, old man, Anne," Henry pleaded. I saw the pale concern on his face, and quietly, I took a tablet from my waist; a jewelled ornament of gold and rubies, which Henry had given me some time ago and Wolsey would recognise. I unhooked its chain, and handed it to Henry.

Henry was so pleased with me that he was for a moment rendered speechless, and I put my quill to the letter Henry was preparing for the Cardinal, assuring Wolsey in the usual flowery language of court that I prayed for his recovery. Henry set down words, in his own hand, telling Wolsey of his concern and love, and the messenger rode for Esher that night. But Henry was not done, for he sent cartloads of furnishings, plate, linen and furs to Wolsey. Henry also sent items of food, such as a deer he had killed himself. It seemed to me that the Cardinal's little ploy to engender the King's sympathy had worked only too well.

After several days of treatment, and being leeched by the King's doctors, Wolsey rallied. Soon after, I received a letter from the Cardinal, expressing his delight in my gift and wishing to be of service to me. *"As the full favour of our lord the King rests in your hands,"* he wrote. *"And his happiness doth also abide with you, Lady Anne, it is my duty and greatest wish to be of service in all matters."*

I wasn't fooled. The old bat just wanted another way to wing back into the arms of the master he had lost. I was not about to offer him a roost.

Henry did not think the same as I, however. Although Wolsey was officially still in disgrace, there were many hints that Henry might soon welcome him back into favour. Henry made ominous remarks; the Councillors he had now were not "the best he had had," and, "there were others who understood the will of the country better than those now advising him."

It was obvious he was referring to Norfolk, who was woefully inadequate for the task of replacing Wolsey. Henry did not know whom to turn to. More was opposed to the annulment, Norfolk was useless, my father was so busy he had little time to take on anything else, and Suffolk was a beautiful, but brainless, boy masquerading as a grown man. Henry was starting to think the only course of action was to recall Wolsey. He never said such a thing to me, but I could see it in his eyes.

It was around this time that I learned of the secret gifts and messages Henry had sent to Wolsey upon his fall, and after. It was George who discovered this, after talking to Norris. I was horrified. It seemed that all along, Henry had been planning to one day reinstate his chief advisor. Wolsey had fallen, but apparently not far enough. I had not ever wanted to move against him unto death, his disgrace had been enough for me… But that winter I worried and I wondered. Was simply removing Wolsey enough to make me safe? Would I have to go further? To bring Wolsey to death, in order to be secure in my position beside the King?

Chapter Sixty-One

York Place
Winter 1529-1530

At Christmas, I declined to attend celebrations at court since Katherine was there, and took to York Place, which was becoming my own centre within London. Henry dutifully celebrated Christmas with his wife, but on New Year's Day he sent me many gifts, including over one hundred pounds in spending money for my games over Christmas.

I put on a pageant for Henry on one of the nights he could escape his wife. It was an allegorical piece and I designed all the costumes and constructions myself. Brave knights dressed in white robes fought for the possession of a castle called *"Good Justice"* from satyrs. The satyrs wore mottos such as *"False Hope"*, *"Bad Religion"* and *"Deception"*. The knights wore ribbons that said *"True Faith"*, *"Ardent Loyalty"* and *"England's Pride"*.

Watching from tiered benches, the audience was offered a show which represented the struggles between Henry and me, and Pope Clement. When the knights won the castle of *Good Justice*, they took hands with beautiful ladies from my household and brought them out to dance. Upon the breasts of my women were mottos of *"Joyous Marriage"*, *"Mother to True Heirs"*, *"Peace"* and *"Unity"*.

Henry applauded the pageant loudly, and came to dance with Nan, who was playing *"Mother of True Heirs"*, saying to me after, that this was the figure he was most drawn to. I pressed my hand into his. "Our sons will be magnificent creatures, Henry," I whispered. "I dream of them when I rest in my bed. I long to carry them beneath my heart, and to know the weight of them in my arms."

His eyes became haunted, looking on my natural and growing desire to be both a wife and a mother. He squeezed my fingers painfully. "You shall hold them in your arms soon, my Anna, I promise you. I forget, sometimes, in my own desire to have a son, that you, too, long for children."

"Every day, the yearning is stronger," I said.

"I will not let you down, my love," Henry replied. "One day, you will have all you want."

"And what of you?" I asked, smiling. "Should you not have all you want too?"

"You are all I want." He lifted my hand and kissed it gently.

We rose to join all the court in a brawl; a round dance that had originated in the peasantry, but had become popular at court. Then, Henry and I danced a *passamezzo* together, a more lively version of the stately *pavane*. Then followed a *saltarello*, a dance in which we pranced and tripped about one another, with Henry lifting me, almost flying through the air at times, through the leaps and jumps. There was none at court who could best me for the agility of my body and the nimbleness of my feet. When the dances began and ended, all at York Place curtseyed and bowed to Henry and me... in reverence to their King and Queen...

In the New Year, Henry again added to my father's titles. He was made Lord Privy Seal, making him England's third highest-ranking officer of state. My father wanted further recognition of our family's new status and George was made the English Ambassador to France, a most advantageous placement for such a young man! Our family resided now amongst the highest powers in England. George was also made a member of the Privy Council; possibly the youngest man to have ever sat upon it. Boleyns now surrounded Henry. My father, George and I were now his closest friends and advisors. Erasmus himself sent his portrait to Henry

Norris, whom he knew to be our friend, and dedicated a book to my father.

George was immensely proud of his new titles, and before he left for France to present his new credentials, many at court started to complain that of all the haughty Boleyns, George was the one most affected by the sin of pride. Tom spoke to me, concerned that George's new attitude was hardly winning hearts. "He roams about with such a look on his face, Anne, that all would think he was the King himself!" He shook his head and glanced at me worriedly.

"He feels pride where pride is due, Tom," I replied, pulling a golden stitch through a piece of cloth. I was embroidering a cushion for Henry's bed with our emblems of the falcon and the rose shown together. "The King shows trust and honours my family. I would hope that you were pleased to see us rise."

"I am pleased for you, in some ways, Anne," he said, looking uneasy. "But in others… I know not…"

"What do you mean?" I looked up as I pulled another stitch through the cloth.

"You have become so… hard…" He bit his lip as he finished speaking.

"I have had to grow a thick skin about me, Tom; such may make any woman less yielding than she was before." I glanced at him and sighed, putting my embroidery aside. "I am ever as I have been," I told him. "But this *Matter* of the King's marriage, it has taken more from me than I could ever tell you. Perhaps God seeks to test me, test my patience and my resolve."

"Perhaps…" he said softly. "But I would not that in all of this you become something you are not, Anne." He shook his head, and went to leave, but at the door he turned back. "Perhaps it was all ordained, Anna," he said.

"What do you mean?" I asked again.

"The *Chateau Vert*... do you remember? That pageant when you first came to court? Do you remember the role you played then?"

"*Perseverance*," I said and then laughed as I understood his meaning. He grinned to see me smile.

"That is a sound I hear not enough of these days, Anna... your laugh... I would that we heard it more."

"As would I, Tom," I said. "As would I." I stood from my chair and crossed to him, taking his arm. "Do not think that I have changed so much as to forget your good friendship to me. I am still a friend to those I love well, and I am gentle with them... But to my enemies, Tom, I cannot afford such grace."

"I know, Anna," he said, stroking a hand on mine. "Just try to remember the love of life that ere you enjoyed, and to try to remove some of the disdain from your face when you come to court."

"My face but mirrors what I am shown," I murmured sadly.

He took hold of my chin and lifted it to face him. "Then look more upon the faces of friends, my Anna, and all will be well." He kissed my hand and took his leave. My visits with Tom were all too rare these days, but I treasured each of them.

By February, Henry was spending all his time at York Place with me. We spent day after day reviewing the renovations and embellishments we had initiated in the palace. The Boleyn emblems, and my own, were painted, carved and moulded onto every available space next to Henry's own heraldic symbols. We also, of course, talked about the *Great Matter*.

Henry had begun, publicly, to question the Pope's authority. He was frustrated at Clement, but recent struggles aside, Henry had long resented the authority of the Church over certain issues in his realm. Early in his reign, Henry had supported a ruling that the decrees of the Church and Rome were admissible in England only with his express approval. He had never denied the spiritual authority of the Pope, but had said even then that the kings of England were appointed by God, and therefore had no superior but God within their realm. These events came back to him now, and added to his growing belief that Clement was not the one who should decide on his *Great Matter*.

Henry was becoming increasingly bold. Whilst most people held that papal authority was granted by God and therefore immovable, Henry was heard arguing that *his* authority was *also* granted by God. Who, therefore should decide but the King, on what was right in his own kingdom? The Pope ruled in Rome, but Henry ruled in England. He began leaning further towards the ideas that we reformers held dear.

To him, Henry's *Great Matter* became primarily about his right, as King, to do as he willed. To me, it was about the change that we could set forth in England; a chance to establish a reformed Church, free of corruption, existing only for the service of God. Encapsulated within our desire to be married, we had each found our higher mission.

Clement believed that Henry was blustering when he spoke bitterly of removing Rome's authority for good from England, but many of us were most interested in Henry's new leanings. Perhaps there were other ways for us to achieve what we wanted here... Perhaps if Henry could be persuaded, then another path would be opened to take us to our goal.

But it seemed to me that many in our faction, Suffolk and Norfolk most notably, had small interest now in pushing for the annulment. They had achieved the removal of Wolsey, and their own ascent to power. Now that they were each in their own position, they were not overly keen to place me on the throne. Norfolk especially did not like me; he hated the way I talked to him, the lack of respect I showed to him, and he was having trouble convincing Henry that he was competent to replace Wolsey. Why should he trouble himself much with my cares? It became obvious that Norfolk had had no real intention of seeing me placed on the throne. Although I had never harboured a great deal of trust in my slippery uncle, it was a surprise to find that he so quickly took off the mask that had concealed his true intentions.

"Norfolk shows but small interest in the King's *Matter* lately, my lord father," I complained as he visited my chambers. "I thought that he was as set on Katherine's removal as are the rest of us, but it seems that all he said, of the Scriptures and all else, was but a feint to enlist our help in removing Wolsey. He has used us as his soldiers, father... as his pawns."

My father snorted. "Norfolk knows *nothing* of Scripture," he said dismissively. "The man has never read the Bible... He picks up what he knows from others and uses their words as his own. It is how he appears cleverer than he is. This I have learnt well enough of late, struggling aside him on the Council to cover his blunders."

My father took a long breath in through his nose and huffed it out the same way. "Nor is Suffolk interested in pursuing the annulment now. It seems that his wife may have moved him to pity Katherine, for he speaks less and less warmly of the annulment each day. If the King wishes it, Suffolk will continue to seek a way. But Suffolk has less between his ears even than Norfolk, and I am carrying them both on the Council." He frowned. "I have also wondered, of late, if

Suffolk may have finally realised that helping the King to get a new wife might threaten the position of his heir. If Henry has no son, then Henry Brandon may well rise to the throne. He is placed behind the children of Margaret Tudor, at present, but that could change. The King has no wish to hand his kingdom to the Scots, and he disapproves of his elder sister's divorce from her second husband. He has passed comment about placing Mary of Suffolk's children above those of Margaret in the succession. Suffolk's son could become a king, if Henry never has an heir."

"What can be done?"

"I know not, daughter... we are stuck, and Henry complains daily that his present ministers are not up to the standard that Wolsey set. I fear that the Cardinal will return, and, possibly, stronger than before. Norfolk and Suffolk are too blinded by their present glee at their positions to realise their ineptitude is causing the King to yearn for Wolsey. I do my best, of that I assure you, but carrying the weight of the two Dukes, and all my own work, is no easy task."

I was troubled, and rapidly it seemed that my father was right.

In early February, Wolsey was given the lodge in Richmond Park in which recover fully from his illness. This edged him closer to Henry. Wolsey sent overtures of love and friendship to me, to George, to my father and all of our faction, hoping to worm his way into our teeth and have us speak for him to Henry. Despite my father's doubts about Norfolk's intelligence, the Duke did finally seem to realise that there was a real chance that Wolsey could return to favour. He worked avidly to keep Henry and Wolsey apart, but the numbers of Wolsey's supporters at court were increasing. Enemies of the Boleyns and Howards, and friends of Katherine, knew Wolsey was their best bet to remove us. There were calls from most unexpected quarters for his restoration. As his terror grew, Norfolk suddenly became attentive towards me again.

"The King would not turn so, to our old enemy, if he thought his counsel from you was good enough, Your Grace," I snapped as he arrived, as though on a whim, with a gift of fine pike and carp for my table. Norfolk was such an arrogant dullard that he thought he could just turn up with presents and I would fawn at his feet, but I saw through him. He was angry, abashed, and left muttering about this *unnatural* creature that was related to him by blood.

Both Charles and Clement voiced support for Wolsey's return. In truth, they harboured little affection for the Cardinal. They meant only to irritate us and make us uneasy and knew, as others did, that Wolsey's return could mean my removal. Henry was not of a mind to listen to men who had opposed and humiliated him, but he still loved Wolsey and was deeply unhappy with his present Council. He heard all the petitions for Wolsey's reinstatement, and eventually, frustrated by Suffolk, Norfolk, and even my father, he made a choice.

Gardiner was sent to make an arrangement with Wolsey. The Cardinal would be based in York, far from London, in order to satisfy Norfolk and others, but he would be absolved of the charges which had precipitated his downfall. The Cardinal had been complaining he had not enough to live on. He stated he required no less than four thousand pounds a year to maintain his household; a sum worthy of an Emperor. Whilst many bristled at the idea of handing out so much money to the Cardinal, Norfolk and my father hoped, if he was offered enough coin, he might well capitulate, agree to advise the Council from a distance, and desist in trying to sneak closer to Henry, or London.

"I fear this father..." I said to him in my chambers one day, watching ravens croak and spiral over the high tops of the trees in the gardens. "Norfolk has shown his colours, and

Suffolk leans each day more towards Katherine. We are losing allies just as we send our greatest enemy off to the north!"

"Then we must enlist new ones," he said. "What think you of Gardiner?"

I shrugged. "I trust him. He has worked for me and for this cause on more than one occasion. I believe he is on our side."

"Be careful in whom you trust, Anne," said my mother from her chair. "There are many who flock to those they think will bring them privilege and power and retract their loyalty easily enough when their needs are served."

"As we have seen, most unfortunately, with your own brother, my lady mother," I snapped, and then, when her face fell, went to embrace her. "I am sorry," I said. "I did not mean to cause you grief."

She patted my arm. "I know, child… in truth I am as disappointed in him as you are."

"Then we seek out new friends," I said. "You will go to Gardiner and ask for his ideas, father?"

He nodded. "It is time for new ideas, and new minds. Worry not, my child… Soon enough we will have what we want."

As he left, I turned to my mother. "How is Mary?" I asked. "I hear from her so rarely."

She smiled. "She complains the same about you."

I frowned. "You are… kind to each other, are you not?" I asked. "Mary said some things to me that made me think you two were not the best of friends."

My mother flushed. "I have, it is true, told her of her present situation in this world," she said curtly. "And I was only honest, Anne. Mary has to see that she is not a great prize for another match in marriage now. I but told her the truth. Mary is fortunate that you were made guardian of her children, for if the King decided otherwise then she could have lost them for her past sins."

"The King had a hand in those sins as well, my lady mother," I reminded her.

"Anne! Do not speak so! What if someone heard you?"

I sighed. "Be gentle with her, mother, for my sake if you cannot manage it for hers. I wish her to be brought to court when I am made Queen, *if* I am ever made Queen, for I miss her company. Be gentler to her than the world has been, mother. This world is not a fair place for women; it aids us not at all to turn on each other as well."

"I am her mother," she reprimanded. "As I am yours, and will ever offer my advice when I feel it is fit." Her face softened. "But I will do as you ask, Anne." She started coughing. Her long weakness in the winter months had come to her again this year, and she had spent most of the season at Hever, recovering. Although even Henry's skilled doctors had attended her, no one seemed able to cure what ailed her. They bled her, they fed her pills, they put leeches upon her, and nothing worked. She grew thinner every year, and clumps of her hair had started to fall out. She wore false sections in amongst her tresses now to plump them out. Her teeth troubled her much as well, and she had had many removed over the winter. This caused her some trouble with eating, and she had taken to smiling in a tight-lipped fashion in order to hide her affliction. But even losing teeth and hair, my mother was a charming looking woman. Her high cheekbones and bright eyes gave her face elegance, and she would always be the most beautiful woman in the world to me.

"Here," I passed her some ale. "If you were not fully recovered, you should not have come back to court."

She snorted. "I am well enough, to do all I can to help you," she said sullenly. "I would that my children would stop treating me as though I were a child when I have been grown and a woman longer than any of you!"

I laughed and promised to leave her be. But amongst my other fears, I worried for her. I little wanted to think that one day I could lose her.

Chapter Sixty-Two

York Place
Winter 1530

On the 10th of February, Henry issued a general pardon for Wolsey. A few days later, all of the property Wolsey had granted the King from the archbishopric of York was returned to him, excluding York Place, which Henry was never going to give up, since he and I liked it too much. Wolsey was given three thousand pounds, and a pension of six hundred and sixty-six pounds. Another three hundred was granted for clothing, and he was given enough livestock to feed his household for months. For a man who had, only a few months previously, complained he had no linen for his bed, this was a quick and profitable turnabout.

The generous offer was made and approved by Wolsey's enemies on the Council. They hoped it would keep Wolsey away from London and from Henry, enabling our faction to work on undermining the Cardinal once again. But to Henry, it was the start of reinstatement for his old friend. He tried to avoid the subject with me at all costs, and in that silence I knew that he would one day bring Wolsey back. No matter what pain it would cause Henry, I could not let that happen. I had to do as my father had said, and work to remove Wolsey for the good of us all. One day, Henry would see that I was right.

Around this time, Henry started to draw Master Cromwell, that avid advocate of Wolsey's, more closely into his service. He had found Cromwell's loyal dedication to Wolsey charming, and liked the quick mind he saw in Cromwell's defence of his master. Whilst I liked not Cromwell's love for the fat bat, I saw much usefulness in the man, as did Henry. I suspected that the leniency being shown to Wolsey was, at least in part, due to Cromwell. That he so well understood

Henry's love and sympathy for his former minister, and was able to play on it, was disturbing. My father believed that we should move against Cromwell's further promotion at court, but, when I saw Henry turn to him in the same manner he had once done with Wolsey, I began to think along different lines.

Henry admired men like Cromwell and Wolsey. They had both risen from humble stock as Wolsey had been the son of an innkeeper and butcher, and Cromwell's father was a blacksmith and innkeeper. There was a subtle difference between them in this, however. Wolsey never mentioned his family or origins, whereas Cromwell was open about them; he was curiously honest about his past, which I found striking. Many courtiers would seek to hide such humble origins, particularly from the King... but Cromwell did not. He had, in fact, pride in the manner of his rise, and people knew of it. Henry liked men who had worth beyond the nobility of their blood, and was never ill at ease as some of noble blood were with the common man. Henry was interested in people, a valuable trait for a King. But it also gave him a capability that others, like Norfolk, did not have... the ability to see men for their worth, not just for their blood.

"I think," I said to my father, "that we should enlist Master Cromwell for our side." He stared at me in disbelief.

"But he advocates for Wolsey..." he said, glancing at me quizzically.

"The King begins to love Master Cromwell," I replied, gazing on the window through which I could see late snow starting to fall. "And he starts to lean on his judgement. Henry trusts that Cromwell is a man of deep loyalties, for his support of Wolsey... As the King draws him close, why not take him under the shelter of our arms too?"

"He *is* clever," my father grudgingly admitted.

"And witty," I added. "He may be on our enemy's side at present, my lord father... But what if he were to join ours instead?" I watched my father with thoughtful eyes. "He must have incurred debts to further Wolsey's cause, must he not? Bribes about the court do not come cheap, and I doubt very much that the flying rodent would have offered him much of his own wealth to Cromwell... Wolsey would just *expect* his help, would he not?"

My father narrowed his eyes. "So... what say you on this?" he asked.

"Merely that if Cromwell has debts for standing so loyal to his master, then it may be that eventually he will see this as a lost cause, not only for the Cardinal, but for himself. Perhaps there are ways, then, that we might help him... Men are loyal to they who support them. Why should it not be the Boleyns who support this most able man, who is growing every day higher in Henry's estimations?"

My father nodded thoughtfully. "He is shrewd," he admitted. "And he has a far better mind behind that dark head of hair than Norfolk or Suffolk."

"And the King loves him... Those whom the King loves should be our friends if we can make it so."

"I will inquire into the costs Cromwell has incurred in supporting his master," my father promised. "And I will invite him to dine with me... This is a dangerous path though, Anne... If Cromwell chooses to remain loyal to Wolsey then this may not go well for us."

"If we replace his master's patronage with a patronage of our own, I think he will come around," I purred. "And besides, the King is not *so* attached to Cromwell as yet... A word or two from me could dislodge him. But I have been looking, father, since Wolsey fell, for a new tool to use in our cause, and I wonder if Cromwell is not that implement. You, despite your cleverness, cannot possibly fulfil all roles for the King. We need more men, men like you rather than like Norfolk or Suffolk… Men who have brains and know how to use them. Better yet, men who will show loyalty to us, not only for what they may gain, but for Henry's *Matter*… And let us see how loyal he is willing to be to his former master in truth, when we offer him more rewards than Wolsey ever could. I will be his Queen one day… A canny man such as Cromwell will come to see that supporting a rising star is better than remaining loyal to a falling one…"

My father nodded. "You have become like a commander, Anne," he noted with admiration. "You would have made a great general, had you been a boy."

"Do I not command and move my troops even now, father, even though I be a woman?" I asked. "This war is not fought with sword or blade, but we have troops, we have manoeuvres, we have battles… Perhaps I *am* a commander in war… with a fight for the love of my King, and the future of the true faith in England at stake."

I looked out at the snow once more. Swans and geese were alighting the choppy surface of the Thames, whooping loudly as they landed. In those waters, salmon were starting their February run.

It felt as though as winter would soon be ended, that spring drew near, that everything was in motion. There was a sense of expectation. We had to move too… We had to move swiftly to strike our enemies before they came for us.

Chapter Sixty-Three

York Place
Winter 1530

Soon after my father began to enlist fresh blood for our cause, I had a visit from Stephen Gardiner and Edward Foxe. Ever since going to Rome on our behalf, the two had often been in company with each other. My father wanted new ideas, and when they came to me, I could see a sly look on Gardiner's swarthy face. My maid Kate took their cloaks, and left batting them with her hand and shaking her head for the cold water upon them. I offered them ale, and we sat down at the fireside, for it was a cold morning. Rain and wind whipped about the outside streets, sending merchants' goods sailing through the air. People hurried through the city, their clothes and coats clenched about them. Inside York Place, it was warm and comfortable. The fireplaces, many of which still bore Wolsey's emblems, were fine, large and well-stocked with expensive sea-coal.

"My father sent you to me?" I asked as we all sat down on the cushions I had made. I had been embroidering many fine cushions for my apartments, all bearing the Tudor rose and my own emblems; the leopard of the Rochfords and my own personal falcon. They were beautiful creations and I was proud of them. There was something in embroidery that allowed my mind, so often troubled, to calm. It was good to have something to occupy the fingers and yet still leave the mind free to think. In my days of exile at Hever, so long ago when I had been banished from court for daring to become engaged to Henry Percy, I had come to despise embroidery. But now, I turned to it, even as I turned to the works of Tyndale, Lefevre and Luther and to the Scriptures, seeking peace and calm in a world in which life often spiralled wildly out of my control.

"Your father came to us, my lady," said Gardiner, resting his goblet of ale in his hands, "and asked us for fresh ideas on the King's *Great Matter*."

"And know you of anything that might help us?"

Foxe and Gardiner looked at each other, and Gardiner nodded slightly to Foxe. "My lady," Foxe said, his face open and excited. "When you and our royal lord were at Grafton last summer, Master Gardiner and I were put up at a house nearby belonging to a Master Cressey. When we came to dine that night with his family, we found that his sons were being tutored by an old university acquaintance of ours; the scholar and theologian Doctor Thomas Cranmer of Jesus College. Master Cressey is a great advocate of yours, my lady, and he and Cranmer had already talked much on the subject of the King's *Great Matter*."

"And... Master Cressey had something to add to the discussion?" I asked, sipping my ale.

Foxe grinned. "Not he, so much, my lady... but Doctor Cranmer did."

"And what had he to say on this?"

"He listened patiently to us discussing the trial and its poor outcome, my lady, and then, as we came to talk on what the King would do now, he spoke up." Foxe paused and looked at Gardiner.

"Master Cranmer is a rather reserved man, my lady... He listens much and speaks only when he feels there is a need." Gardiner explained.

I arched my eyebrow. "A rare virtue, indeed, in this noisy world we live in," I said, smiling.

"Indeed, my lady!" Foxe chuckled. "But when he does speak, it is always worth listening to. I remember him well from our school days together, and he was ever given to sharp insights."

"And what were these insights?"

Foxe set his ale aside and leaned forward. "Cranmer said that canon law would not get His Majesty anywhere," he explained. "He said that the *Great Matter* was not an issue of law so much as it was of *theology*, and theologians would give him the true answer. He pointed out that opinion on the *Great Matter* could be canvassed in all the universities of Europe, and that such opinions would not be hard to get, or take long to put together, to see which side they came out on. He said that collecting opinion would in fact take only a matter of months, as many would be happy to converse on the subject, it being so current and interesting a subject. Then, Cranmer went on to say that once the *Matter* was therefore resolved by this canvassing of opinion, His Majesty could finally put his conscience to rest on the subject, one way or another. If he wished to present the evidence to the Pope, then he could, and if he simply wished to use it within England, he could do so."

I blinked. "A matter of *months*!" I marvelled. "For this all to be resolved so swiftly... How would I like to believe this were possible!"

"Once the universities in Europe had decided in His Majesty's favour," Gardiner continued, "there would be a public weight of evidence in favour of the annulment... and then, if the King chose to try... other ways to gain separation from his unlawful union, he would have evidence to support his cause for doing so."

I put my goblet to one side and rose. "You must go to the King with this, immediately!" I commanded, and the men rose, looking rather pleased with themselves. "Say that you have been sent directly from me, and they will allow you in without having to wait. I want the King to hear this now, today!"

They left me and I wandered restlessly, excitedly, through York Place's long gallery, with Margaret and Bridget silent at my side. Rain battered on the panes and the wind screamed about the walls, and I heard it not. I thought through Cranmer's idea from all angles … What an idea, to canvass opinion outside of the clergy… in the universities of Europe! Surely they would find for us! *Well*, I bit my lip as I thought, *all but those in Spain, of course*… But if the English and French universities, those of the Holy Roman Empire, and perhaps the Low Countries, too, even though they were under Hapsburg control… if they would find for us, then all would know that educated opinion was on our side.

And perhaps, just perhaps, I could use that to convince Henry to be strong, to take on the role of King as envisaged by Tyndale… A King who was both Emperor and Pope… A King who could decide on the *Great Matter* for himself.

Chapter Sixty-Four

York Place
Winter 1530

When Henry received Foxe and Gardiner, which he did immediately since they came from me, he was excited about what they told him. "Has not the problem in our matter always been that canon law speaks of one thing, and yet divine disclosure speaks another?" he asked. "This man hath the sow by the right ear!"

Henry peppered them with questions on this Master Cranmer, this obscure cleric who somehow had seen straight to the heart of our problem where none of his own advisors had. Foxe and Gardiner answered their excitable King as best they could, and Henry asked that they seek Cranmer out and invite him to court; he wanted to meet with him as soon as possible.

Even before meeting Cranmer, however, Henry asked du Bellay to send men to France, men who would begin canvassing opinion there as swiftly as possible! Henry sent for me and as I entered, he bounded towards me, wrapped his hands about my waist and swung me up and into the air. Over and over he twirled me about, as I shrieked and giggled helplessly.

"My lord is a happy man this day!" I panted as he set me down and re-arranged my French hood which he had knocked loose of its pins. I turned my head sharply to the window as a clatter of rain and ice hit the panes. The storm outside was growing, and all in London were fleeing to their homes to take shelter.

"*Finally*, Anne!" he cried exuberantly, walking to the window, sitting in a seat and gazing at me with a pink and happy face. "Oh!" he cried as though a great weight had been taken from him. "All has been so heavy of late… I have felt as though my shoulders might never rest for all the troubles upon them… and then, then you send me such messengers!"

"Foxe and Gardiner are good friends to us, my lord. I should like to reward them for their efforts on our behalf."

"Give them whatever gold and silver you want, my Anne." He beamed at me. "I would empty my treasury this day if one man alone would say that we could be together!"

I knelt at his side. "This man, Cranmer, Henry… he said that opinion could be gathered in a matter of months… think on that! A matter of months, after all the time that we have waited!"

He put a hand against my cheek. "A matter of months… It is almost unbelievable. I think of the beginning so often now, Anne… Do you remember? How I chased you and you held me off! How you teased me and danced about me and I came to you, seeking you as a mistress! How could I have treated you so? You have been, through all of this, as a lioness at my side, never weakening, never giving up… You alone held your nerve better than any of your family or my advisors. So often have people told me to go back to my sinful bed with Katherine, but not you… You are my rock, Anne, you are my safe harbour… and now… Perhaps now we are almost at an end!" He sighed, his eyes shining with warmth and love.

I put my hands into his. "I was sustained by the constancy of your love, Henry," I whispered. "And I will always be here, in whatever form you need me to be, to help you, aid you and protect you, as best I can. I was not as strong as you thought… all these months, there were many times when I was afraid. But as I knew I loved you with all my heart, so I also knew that you loved me. It is our love that gives me strength. Even if all of the world were to turn on us, even if all of the people of the earth were to turn their faces from me, I would have you, and that would be enough."

Tears came to his eyes at my words and he slipped from the window seat to the floor beside me. He pulled me into his arms and kissed me, long and hard. His hands moved, pulling my hood from my head, so that he could run his fingers through my dark tresses. Then he pulled me to him so that my head rested on his chest. "I would give up the world and all in it, for you, Anne," he whispered.

"Many in this world despise me, sire, for my love for you… But I care not for them. I have put myself into your hands entirely. As long as I have your love, I have all I will ever need."

He gripped me closer. "When you are Queen, Anne, they will love you… It is Katherine… She tricks them." He pulled back and put his hand to my chin, lifting my eyes to his. "But when they have a chance to know you, when they see past Katherine's sinful wickedness, they will love you, as I do."

"You will always be enough for me, Henry," I murmured. "As long as I have you, I fear nothing."

He set his lips to mine, kissing me with passion. Outside, the wind blew and the rain fell. Voices seemed to scream in the storm, begging, demanding and pleading for things that we could not understand. We sat in each other's arms, listening to nothing but the sound of the storm and the thoughts in our heads.

Later that day, in his own excitement as well as at my urging, Henry sent once more for Gardiner and Foxe. They were to find Cranmer personally, Henry said, and give him a message: *The King not only wants to meet with him, but wishes him to put together a proposal for the universities of Europe.* We wanted to meet with him, and if Cranmer proved suitable then he was going to be invested as a royal agent in order to solicit the views of the theologians of the world on our behalves.

Chapter Sixty-Five

York Place
Spring 1530

Wolsey took a long time to leave Esher. He dithered and hesitated, not wanting to head towards the lonely north to York. He protested that the roads were still bad in this cold spring, that his wagons would get stuck in the mire and mud. The next week he said he had not enough servants to aid him in packing. Wolsey's excuses grew like weeds. Despite his many new riches, Wolsey asked Gardiner to obtain *more* money from Henry for his journey, but Gardiner reproved the greedy Cardinal, saying if he had not money enough then that was his own fault, and that he ought to be grateful the King had offered him as much as he had. The man had a point.

Norfolk complained to Cromwell that his master was delaying. Wolsey even took a trip to the Carthusian Monastery in Richmond and, it was said, had started to wear a hair shirt in order to atone for his sins; something that Henry took as a true mark of a recovering faith and goodness. It seems to me, however, that when such a thing is done, and it *is made known* that it is done, it loses the benefit of true and honest spirituality. It becomes, rather, a pretence, a show designed to tell the world just how very good that person is... Eventually Norfolk lost his patience. "Tell Wolsey," he hissed at Cromwell. "If he goes not away, and tarries longer, I shall tear at him with my own teeth!"

Cromwell was growing weary with his erstwhile master, my father informed me, and he had, as I had suspected, run up great debts in attempting to clear Wolsey's name. Cromwell was ripe, father said, for plucking off of Wolsey's branch and transferring to our waiting basket. Cromwell had recently been appointed secretary to the King, and my father invited

Cromwell to dine with him, pointing out what we Boleyns could do for his career at court. At the time, I do not think Cromwell was entirely persuaded to turn on his old master. But there soon came opportunities for me to lean on him further…

Cromwell was often with Henry. The two were growing close, not only in matters of work and state affairs, for which Henry increasingly relied on Cromwell, but a true friendship was also budding between the two men. I would invite Cromwell to York Place, to walk in the gardens with Henry and me, and dine with us. Since he had been a mercenary, Cromwell talked with Henry often about war, battle and tactics; all subjects the King loved. He had worked as a lawyer when returned from his adventures abroad, and was thick with the merchants of London as well. He had a good eye for figures and money, and had trained under the Cardinal on how to best line his pocket… something at which Wolsey had been ever so talented as well.

Despite the fact that he was still working for the fat bat of the North, I liked Cromwell. It was hard not to. He had charm… When first you met him, he seemed to fade against the cloth on the chamber walls. One got the impression that he would never bring himself to your attention, but would wait until called on by you. When he had worked for Wolsey, I had barely noticed him. But once noted, you would never forget him. He had an air about him of confidence and security. He had charisma and intelligence. It only took one conversation to understand that Cromwell was an unusual and astute soul. It was difficult to get close to him, since he was, after all, still Wolsey's agent. But at times it did seem that he was coming to regard me and my family as allies. This was the impression when we met with Master Cranmer….

The gentle-mannered Thomas Cranmer was most interesting. He was not of noble birth, but had been born into a family of modest wealth and standing. He had large blue-grey eyes and thick brown hair. His nose was rather long, and his lips small, but he seemed wise and gentle, and was clearly rather overwhelmed by the sudden interest that Henry had shown in him. He was about forty years of age when first I met him, and all about him there hung an air of modesty… almost innocence, which charmed me. I had made it my business to find out more about this man, and I was not disappointed in what I had uncovered.

At the age of fourteen, Cranmer had been sent by his father at great expense to Jesus College, Cambridge, and had taken rather a long time to achieve his degree. It was said this was due to his tendency to constantly read subjects other than those he was meant to be studying. He had studied politics, logic, classical literature and philosophy, and was a great collector of books, on which he spent more coin than his sparsely filled purse could perhaps afford. What interested me the most about the days of his scholarship was that he had chosen to concentrate on the works of humanist, and one might say reformist, scholars, such as Jacques Lefevre and Erasmus; men I also greatly admired.

When he had finished his schooling, he had rebelliously married a woman called Joan. Since fellows of the college were not supposed to wed, this had lost him his fellowship, and he had taken a post as a reader at Buckingham Hall instead. Joan had died in childbed, and took their child with her to the grave. Cranmer returned to Jesus College, where he continued to study theology and philosophy. He seemed to have many reformist leanings. A few years after Joan's death, he had been ordained by the Church, and became a Doctor of Divinity only two years before coming to Henry's attention.

Cranmer had previously worked for Wolsey in a minor role, as part of an envoy to Spain, and Henry had met him once before. Henry, however, met so many people in passing that, he admitted, he remembered this humble man not. But now he was interested in Cranmer… Most interested.

"Your thoughts bring fresh hope to me and to my *Great Matter*, Master Cranmer," Henry said after we had greeted the man. "I would like you to work for our cause, setting forth our arguments for annulment in order to present them to the universities of Christendom, so that their scholars may rightly understand all the issues involved and deliberate in good conscience. When we have their opinions, we may find a new path for England."

"I… would be honoured to work for you, Your Majesty," Cranmer stuttered, earning a look of pleasure from Henry who always appreciated humility in his subjects. "I will put myself to work with all haste."

"I am told, Master Cranmer, that you are a scholar of the works of Jacques Lefevre?" I asked. "In his works I have found great wisdom on the many corruptions of the Church and on how it may yet be redeemed."

He blinked at me with a touch of surprise. "Indeed, my lady?" His eyes lit up with the enjoyment that comes when one soul recognises a shared pleasure with another. I liked his expression. I saw within him that same spark I had experienced upon reading the works of such a master of reformist thought.

"I have shown the King many of his good works," I continued, glancing at Henry with affection. "And he agrees with me that Lefevre's ideas are most interesting… no matter what Bishop Fisher has to say against them."

"Bishop Fisher is a man ever apt to back the wrong cause…" Henry added.

Cranmer's lips twitched. I believed there was a chuckle hidden under his solemn appearance. "I admire the works of Lefevre greatly, my lady," he said. "It is unusual to find a woman of the court so interested in such matters."

"Lady Rochford is a scholar of some renown herself, Master Cranmer… In my eyes at least," Henry said. "You should meet with her and talk, for she is almost the match for me in her love for the Church, and in seeking always to better it… She has introduced me to many works, which we discuss together, and I have found her influence in such affairs to be to my betterment. So should all women serve their husbands and betrothed lords."

I blushed. "My gracious King flatters me overly, Master Cranmer," I said. "But it is true that I have a great passion for those who speak of how to better the Church, to remove corruption and to work always to better our understanding of God."

"A cause also dear to my heart, my lady," Cranmer replied, the warmth in his voice growing.

"And such is the case with my *Great Matter*," interjected Henry, rising from his chair of estate and throwing an arm about Cranmer, which surprised the man greatly. "Come, and I will talk to you." Henry led Cranmer off and as they walked about the chamber I could hear him speaking of his arguments, and present disappointment with the Pope.

I stepped from my chair and walked to the fireplace where a softly spoken voice made me turn. "It is interesting to me, my lady," said the voice, "that you should indeed profess such an avid interest in the works of reformers… Many would call them heretical."

I turned towards the voice to find Cromwell standing nearby, his soft brown eyes gazing at me quizzically. Did I not say he had a talent for merging with the shadows? He had managed to emerge without me noticing.

"When I was a young maid in the service of Queen Claude of France, Master Cromwell," I replied. "I learned much from the great Princess Marguerite, a known patron of Catholic scholarship and thought." I held my chin high and then smiled. "I learned that to love something is to question it... to be allowed to discuss it, and to only fall the more in love with greater knowledge." I breathed in. "Many in the Church would say that some of the works I have come to know and appreciate are works of scandal," I said boldly, "but I disagree. We come to the Church as those who love it, and only want to see it bettered for the glory of God. Such is my faith in this that I would gladly stake my life on the truth of my words." I smiled more widely. "And besides, sir, were you not involved in the dissolution of certain monasteries under the command of the Cardinal Wolsey and the Pope? So you must have seen with your own eyes that there is much in the practises of the Church requiring correction?"

He nodded his dark head, brown hair peeping out from beneath his black cap. "It is true," he admitted. "There is much I have seen over the past few years that would lead me to believe that many Church institutions require correction from time to time."

"And so we sift the chaff from the wheat and make the bread pure," I smiled. "I have heard, Master Cromwell that you chose to educate your daughters along with your son... A noble choice, and one that mirrors the upbringing my father offered to me."

He cocked his head. "I have ever believed in humanist principles, my lady," he said. "I wished my daughters, may God rest their souls, to become useful to their future families. They were bright girls. I miss them more than I can say. Some say that women should not be taught so, for it is not their place, but I still believe otherwise. Had they lived, they would have been intelligent and useful women."

"I understand your loss, Master Cromwell," I said. "In the same epidemic which took your wife and daughters, I lost my brother-in-law and almost my own life. It was only my faith in

God and the King which kept me clinging to life. But others were not as fortunate as I."

"Thank you, my lady," he said. "Many people try to avoid the subject of loss. They shy from it, believing we should leave the past behind us. I prefer to remember my daughters, and speak of the grace they brought to my life."

"I feel the same, Master Cromwell. The dead never truly leave us; they are carried within our hearts and souls. When we speak their names, they come alive once again."

"My feelings exactly." He smiled and looked down at his shoes. "Many criticized me for educating my daughters," he said. "But Grace and Anne… they deserved the best I could afford to give them."

"And those same people who criticized your beliefs and called them unnatural, good Master Cromwell, may well call me heretic for merely believing in the necessary act of reform?" I grinned as his face broke into a smile.

"Perhaps we each have had undeserved criticism directed at us, my lady?" he asked with a cheeky twitch to his lips.

"Perhaps it is so, Master Cromwell," I replied.

Chapter Sixty-Six

York Place
Spring 1530

That spring, armed with the arguments Cranmer had prepared for our case, Foxe and Gardiner went to Cambridge University. They gave Cranmer's arguments for the King's *Great Matter* to the scholars for them to read, deliberate over, and then discuss. At the same time, my father and Cranmer went to tackle the Emperor and the Pope. Henry was sending diplomats out all over the world for an answer to his riddle.

My father and Cranmer did not, however, get far. In March they attended a meeting where the Emperor and the Pope were both present. Clement reiterated that the annulment would only be discussed when Henry came himself to Rome. He prohibited Henry in the strongest terms from marrying again, believing that this rebellious King may well take matters into his own hands. Many in Europe believed that Henry and I would simply marry, and face the consequences, if there were any, later. This was not the case, but I was beginning to suspect that Henry was considering it. I did not want to marry whilst everyone believed him still wed to Katherine. I would be his only true wife.

It was not all bad news for Cranmer and my father, however. Whilst in Rome, Cranmer was given the Rectory of Bredon in Wiltshire by Jerome Ghinucci, Henry's ambassador and advisor in Rome. It was a distinguished post, and one which had been linked to the office of Archbishop of Canterbury. Whilst in Rome, Cranmer and my father set about gathering opinion from the universities. There was a great deal of discussion and debate… but there was also a great deal of money offered by my father for favourable opinions from the scholars. My father tried to keep this quiet, and did not succeed. In hindsight, I believe it was a mistake for Henry to send my father to fulfil this task, despite his many skills in diplomacy. The Emperor was hardly going to look with kind eyes on the father of the woman about to displace his own aunt, and he controlled the Pope. After canvassing the universities, my father returned home, leaving Cranmer and the other envoys in Rome to continue their work. I prayed that the scholars and theologians would find in our favour; bribes, after all, do not work as well as a conscience for settling the minds of all men.

Finally, in April, Wolsey left Esher for York. He took with him one hundred and sixty attendants and twelve carts loaded down with his baggage. Much more had to be brought up by sea. Whilst Wolsey now owned nothing like his previous riches, he was hardly a pauper. He wrote to Henry upon arrival at Southwell, in Nottinghamshire, complaining that his residence there was full of leaks, and was heavily decayed, and so he had been forced to take refuge at the cannon's house instead. He made no further move to proceed to York itself, and lingered at Southwell instead. Many believed he was waiting for Henry to recall him.

"Poor old Wolsey," I laughed, reading the latest letter he had sent to the King to my mother and George, freshly returned from France. Wolsey was complaining in it that he had not been able to procure what he wanted for his dinner. "The man acts as though not finding quail for his table makes him comparable to St. Francis for all his lack of wealth and present *poverty*!" I curled my lip. "The amounts given to that weasel were enough to sustain a Prince and his household, and yet the Cardinal acts as though he is a beggar on the street! We must keep an eye on him in York. I believe he will get up to much behind our backs."

"I have a man already in place, sister," George assured me, taking the missive and reading it over himself with a snort.

"The butcher's cur thinks himself hard done by, despite all his returned riches."

"And Henry still thinks he has value left to give," I warned.

That May, I often invited Cromwell to join Henry and me. He and I began to converse almost, but not quite, as though we were friends. I believe he was starting to see the benefits that might come from being a part of our faction. Yet still, he was not quite convinced to give up on his former master. Henry had been entrusting him with a great deal of state work, and Cromwell was rising high in royal estimation. Just as Wolsey had once shouldered the burden of Henry's rule, so now Cromwell was often being sent to take his place. He was still known merely as one of the King's men, yet at the same time, everyone could see he was in favour. Henry's daughter, Princess Mary, even wrote to Cromwell, asking him to speak to her father on her behalf. Henry had seen little of his daughter in the past months, finding her devotion to her beloved mother hard to deal with. But the fact that even she, estranged from Henry's love, could see Cromwell's position of influence with her father, was something of note.

Cromwell was suspicious of me, I believe... at least at first. But we found that we had things in common apart from the love of our King. I loaned him books that I had read avidly, although I did not share banned works with him, worrying that they might be used against me, by Wolsey, should Cromwell pass such information on. But I also sent books for his son and he thanked me for my personal interest in his son's education. What Cromwell had achieved in such a short space of time was remarkable. He had risen from the ashes of a fallen master, to a new and prosperous position. He had won the admiration and affection of his King, had the support of notables at court and demonstrated aptly that he had the skill to take on much, if not all of the work his former master had performed.

I had long believed Cromwell was the new tool we required to complete our cause. If only I could persuade him to join us, and abandon Wolsey for good, I felt there was a chance we could succeed.

Chapter Sixty-Seven

That spring I was sent a pamphlet. It came directly to me by messenger, and was one of the first of a great number which were to flood through London that year. The author was an English exile named Simon Fish. He had left England under threat from Wolsey when, some years earlier, he had satirized the Cardinal in a play he had written, performed at Gray's Inn one Christmas. Fish was known to run a trade in banned books. I believe my brother had received volumes from him in the past; works by Luther, Tyndale and other theologians on corruptions of the Church.

Fish's sent the pamphlet to me himself. It was called *A Supplication for the Beggars*, and it was a petition, written with excellent clarity, to Henry, on matters of the immorality and greed of the Church in England. Fish wrote passionately that the people of England were reduced to the state of paupers by the clergy. He made the case that the Church was sucking all wealth from Henry's people, and he asked the King to rise up and stand against such corruption, as the leader and good master of his people.

Fish argued that clerical arrogance made a mockery of the King's own justice, and that, in order to be a good master and loyal servant of God, Henry must take a stand against this, and lead his people into glory, with himself standing in authority over the clergy in England. The work was avidly anti-clerical, and I knew that the Church would move against him as a heretic for it. But I saw much truth in the pamphlet, and it addressed many of my own long-held beliefs about the vice of the Church.

Fish was presently in the Low Countries, in Antwerp, but had sent his work to me as it was well-rumoured that I held evangelical and reformist sympathies. Fish's text was already under investigation in England, after having been discredited in the Low Countries as heretical. But he was about to have more copies smuggled in, he wrote, and wanted me to read the work first. I knew that he was hoping I would take it to Henry. And I would do so, but first I called George to me to talk it over.

I handed the pamphlet to George, and allowed him to sit and leaf through it before I spoke. "Fish calls upon Henry to deliver his people from misery," I said softly.

"He argues well," George noted with approval, turning the pages and then looking up. "Will you show it to Henry?"

I nodded. "I believe that he will take much from it at the present time," I said. "Fish points out that the Church holds a most disproportionate share of the riches of England, and Henry has only to look at Wolsey's confiscated goods to know this is the truth."

"And he argues that the monasteries compound the Church's corruption by taxing the poor rather than aiding them." George ran a finger along the page. "His calculations are rather shocking if they are correct... That the clergy own one third of the land and one tenth of all produce, live-stock and wages of servants... He shows clearly here that the Church is indeed bleeding England dry."

"Henry has already been, with Wolsey, investigating and dissolving certain corrupt monasteries and Master Cromwell played an active part in this," I mused. "But here, it shows that there is a need for a true reform of the whole! Think of what this money could do, George, for the poor, for orphans left upon the mercy of the parish... Think of what it could do if it was re-allocated to the promotion of scholars or as aid for good monasteries rather than kept by men such as Wolsey who have no care for their flock!"

"He speaks, too, against indulgences."

"Which even the King, in his most conservative faith, judges to be works of corruption," I snorted. "As all should see that they are! How can a man *buy* his way into Heaven? Did not Jesus himself say that it would be easier for a camel to fit through the eye of a needle? The sale of indulgences is an antiquated evil; a way of feathering the beds of the Church, whilst offering naught to those who purchase them... Through true faith alone, a man gains entrance to Heaven... not through bartering with God!"

"But he also speaks against purgatory, sister," he warned. "Which, you know, Henry believes in."

"Fish says but little on that subject," I replied. "Apart from saying that we have no cause to pray for the dead to gain them entrance to Heaven faster, and again, he is right, is he not? *Faith* takes us to God, not the pleading voices of those who loved us in life... It should be for every man to live as well as he is able, and to have pure faith in the Almighty, not to live in sin and then rely on the well-wishes of loved ones once he passes!" I paused. "But I think the most important argument here, for us, is that Fish points out that the clergy undermines the power of the state, of the King. Fish says the Church has surpassed the King, and set up their own subversive state against his power. He says, here... do you see?"

I leaned over my brother's shoulder and flicked through the book in George's hand until I found the passage for which I was searching. "*Here...* that the ancient Kings of Briton were never subjugated by the clergy, nor did they assent to the imposition of taxes on their people, to be paid and then stolen away by Rome! Those kings of old had a firm hand on external powers and did not allow the clergy to overreach their authority. And Fish warns, too, that should Henry not act for his people, then there is risk of rebellion."

"The King will not like that," George noted, staring at the page. "He believes his people love him with all their hearts and many of them do… They prefer to blame…" he trailed off and looked at me with a touch of pink in his cheeks.

"To blame me," I finished for him, and even smiled. "Yes, I know that well enough, George. I am the King's whipping boy. His people blame me for every ill in this land… If the winds howl, then it is my fault. If the sun does not shine, it is because of me. If their wonderful Katherine is cast down, it is my fault alone. If the crops fail, if the fields flood, if the night is cold or the day is too hot… All is my fault in England!" I stood back and laughed bitterly. "They would make me the mistress of magic and smoke," I said sadly. "So much do they hate me."

"The common people know not the truth," George consoled, closing the text. "In time, they will come to know you better. It is just that Katherine is now their martyred Queen, and they have known her longer." He stood and took my hands, holding them out before me. "Besides," he smiled, "whom have you ever known who has not fallen for you, my sister *spirit*? When men come to know you, they adore you."

"That is not true of even half the court, I believe, brother." I smiled. "But I thank you for your pretty lies."

"Now," he said, shaking my arms in his hands once, "what will you do about this warning of rebellion? The King will not take kindly to it, and you know that his resentment is dangerous."

I tilted my head to one side. "I will say to him that it is a warning only," I said, "and that, truly, if the people were to rise against him then it would not be for lack of love for *him*, but for hatred of the clergy. I will say we often lash out at the ones we love the most when we are angered by others."

George shook his head in wonder. "You understand him well," he marvelled.

"I love him, George," I reminded my brother. "And when we love someone, we know all their virtues and all their vices. I will find a way to present this to Henry so that he understands it for what it is… a call, a plea from his people. And it can only aid our cause. I see not now why we need the Pope to smear his dirty little hand over the *Great Matter* any more… It is shown that a king should be as Pope and Emperor in his own realm. If Henry can be persuaded to believe this too, then we shall not only have our marriage, but he will be the leader of the faith in England. Think on it George! We could have the Bible translated to the mother tongue for all the people of England! We could have the Scripture plain for all to understand! We could do away with indulgences, and root out dishonesty … We could have, as we have always dreamed of having, a good and righteous Church in England, freed of the corruption and superstition of the past!"

"Tread with care, Anne," George warned. "Henry is a most conservative man in his faith, and he does not like all reforms of which you and I speak… He thinks many are heretical."

I tossed my head. "I have already opened his mind to many new ideas," I sniffed. "And he has all but agreed with me that his people would benefit from understanding the Bible in their mother tongue. I speak not of outlandish reform, or of rejecting the Sacraments or the transubstantiation of the host as some reformers do; such things I do not hold with… But there is much here that we could do, for the betterment of the people of England, and for us… if Henry could but be persuaded to see this… do you not think?"

George nodded thoughtfully. "I have thought for some time that the path of reform might take us to a place where you could have your crown at last, sister," he agreed. "And you are right; there are many benefits that could come, and not just for our family... But tread carefully, as I have warned. You know that many are rising in opposition to us... That fraud, the Holy Nun of Kent, has made many dire prophesises on the King's *Matter* and you know how superstitious Henry is at times."

"We just need the right men to show Henry the true way..." I said. "For it must be done with care. Throwing the whole idea at him at once would be too much, but showing him a little at a time, so that he has time to ponder and think upon the righteousness of the matter, that will do well. I know him; batter him with such things and he will turn away, but speak to him little and often, and he will thirst only to know more." I took the pamphlet from George. "I will give this to Henry, in my office as his true Queen," I said. "And I will ask him to go through it as I have found much of interest there. I will try to deflect the things that may annoy him, so that he might see the good in all of it."

My brother was looking at me with amused admiration. "What?" I asked, batting him playfully with the pamphlet.

"Perhaps when you are Queen, my dear sister," he said ruefully, "you could instruct all your ladies on how to manage their husbands, for I think it would make England a land of happier men, if they all had wives like you who understood them and took care of them so well."

I laughed and took his arm. We went straight to Henry, and I showed him the pamphlet.

Chapter Sixty-Eight

Greenwich Palace
Spring 1530

Henry was struck by Fish's work, and after reading it, called me to dine with him so that we could speak on it. I was nervous that he might have responded to some of it, as my brother had said, with resentment, but this did not seem to be the case. Henry took Fish's warnings of rebellion as the logical end result of the clergy's repression of his people, and he agreed with much that Fish had to say.

"*So captive are your laws unto them that no man that they list to excommunicate maybe admitted to sue any action of your courts,*" he read aloud as we sat, side by side, dining privately. "*If any man in your sessions dare to be so hardy to indict a priest of any such crime, he hath, ere the year go out, such a yoke of heresy laid upon his neck that it maketh him wish he had not done it.*" Henry shook his head, taking from the bowl of purple grapes on the table and then wiping his hands on the linen napkin that was draped over his shoulder. "The man speaks of such vice..." he said, "and such power of the Church over my own people!"

"And he cries out to you, my lord, to make things right, as his good and honourable master."

Henry nodded, his eyes still moving over the text. "He speaks of the Hunne case..." he muttered broodingly. "Wolsey asked me to pardon the Bishop of London, and I granted it, hardly thinking more about it..." He trailed off uneasily and I put a hand on his arm.

"Here is another occasion when you were deceived by Wolsey, my lord," I consoled. "It was not your fault, Henry. You trusted his judgement. It was his error, not yours."

He nodded, but I could see he was still uneasy. Hunne had been a rich tailor of London. His son had died, at the age of five months, and the local priest wanted to charge Hunne for the burial of his child. This was known as a *mortuary*; a payment demanded for performing the service of burial. This was another ill-practise of the Church that I found abhorrent. Some money is needed to inter the dead for the cost of breaking the ground or for a plaque to mark the site, but many priests chose to milk exorbitant sums directly from the sorrow of their people. The priest who was to serve Hunne had demanded the embroidered bearing sheet in which Hunne's son had been wrapped for his christening as payment. This was too much for Hunne, and he had refused to give up the precious cloth.

The priest had brought suit against Hunne in an ecclesiastical court. Hunne counter-sued, insisting that the case was one of common, rather than ecclesiastical law. The Church had taken this as a direct challenge to their authority. If Hunne kept his son's christening blanket, then common law would have vanquished ecclesiastical law. The case was heard and the judge ruled in favour of the Church, but Hunne had still refused to give up the christening blanket.

As a result, Hunne had been arrested on charges of heresy, for daring to challenge the Church, and sent to the Bishop of London's prison. He had been excommunicated. In response, Hunne had accused the priesthood of *praemunire*, recognising the authority of a foreign power over that of the King of England, and of acting against common English law. Thomas More had been convinced that Hunne was a Lollard sympathiser. More despised Lollards, along with anyone else he considered heretical. He had accused Hunne of seeking fame, and the case had been widely talked of about London.

Two days later Hunne had been found dead in his cell, hanging from the ceiling by his own belt. The clergy insisted that Hunne had taken his own life, but his widow had objected violently, saying that he had ever been a man of God, and knew full well that to do so would be to condemn his everlasting soul to the fires of eternal torment. The coroner investigated, and foul play had been suspected. It was found that Hunne's wrists had been bound, and it was suspected he could not have inserted his neck into the noose, for the only stool in the cell was found too far from the body to have been used by Hunne. Finger marks had also been discovered on his neck, suggesting he had been strangled before being put into the noose. It was thought that the Bishop of London's doctor, a Master Horsey, was responsible. But despite this evidence, the Church had continued to act against Hunne for the charge of heresy. It was claimed that an English translation of the Bible had been found amongst his papers. Thomas More declared he had seen it, and vouched that Hunne had written notes about the "heresies" contained therein. What heresies could the Bible contain? The Church had charged Hunne's corpse with calling the Pope "Satan" and with condemning papal indulgences. More was one of those who had stood for the Church during the trial. Hunne had been condemned, and his property declared forfeit to the crown. His wife and remaining children had been left with nothing. Some days later, Hunne's corpse had been burned at Smithfield.

But the coroners who had attended to Hunne were not frightened of the Church. They found the jailor who had attended him that night, and the man confessed that he and another had strangled Hunne in his bed. No matter Hunne's crimes against the Church, murder is murder. A jury had brought three of the Bishop of London's men to answer the charge. But through Wolsey's good graces, Henry had pardoned the Bishop and his men... No man ever stood trial for the suspected murder. Hunne's remains were not allowed to be buried on consecrated ground. Not only had his life been taken, but his soul was lost, bereft of Heaven and the saving light of God. Thomas More insisted, despite all the evidence to the contrary, that Hunne had committed suicide, and continued to believe the punishment, which had been carried out upon not only Hunne, but on his wife and children, had been justified in the war against heresy.

Fish used this shocking tale to illustrate the clergy's abuse of the charge of heresy. They would levy such charges against any who opposed them and were not above murder to remove those who stood against them.

"It was not your fault if you were taken in by Wolsey, my lord," I said, and then added, "and perhaps Wolsey *himself* was taken in as well... The Bishop of London may only have told him the barest facts of the case in order to gain his pardon. He could have deceived Wolsey and you."

Henry squeezed my hand gratefully. He liked more the idea that both he *and* Wolsey had been deceived. I put my knife to the imported figs in syrup and speared them to my pewter plate, carving them into delicate sections. I then took from the plate of rich venison which had been ably carved by Norris, and ate, using my clean fingers to lift the delicate morsels to my mouth as Henry read on.

"He says here..." Henry pointed at the page. "... That Hunne was murdered because he recognised the authority of *my* courts above those of the clergy." He pressed a grape into some new, white cheese with his fingers and chewed contemplatively as he thought. He swallowed and wiped his mouth. "I have often thought that the ecclesiastical courts interfere much in affairs which should be for the state alone to decide."

"The clergy have placed themselves above the law of the realm, my love," I said, slicing through another plump, sticky fig. "They should not be allowed to interfere so. The Church should be for the faith and spiritual guidance of the people, and it should be the state alone that upholds common law and seeks your justice. It does not hold that the two should overlap, or that the clergy should interfere in matters of state.

Do they not have enough work to do in tending to the spiritual welfare of the people?"

"It seems to me that the Church in England requires much work to make it as it should be," I continued. "And if the willingness to root out corruption comes not from within the Church, then surely, it should come from the King... You are, after all, the *Defender of the Faith*, my lord."

"He speaks much of the corruptions of the flesh amongst the clergy, also," pondered Henry. "For a long time I have had my own men, such as Cromwell and Wolsey, seeking out those institutions in which avarice, lust and greed have overtaken the men of the Church... but I believe that more might be done."

"When I was in France, my lord," I continued. "King François' sister, Princess Marguerite, was an outspoken reformer of Church institutions that had fallen into sin. I have always believed it is the duty of the royal line of any country to ensure that the spiritual welfare of their people is taken care of properly."

He nodded. "I will speak to my men," he said. "Master Cromwell was ever his master's good servant in such affairs, I will ask his opinion, and see what is to be done."

"I think that is well, my lord, for I come to trust the word of Cromwell more and more as I meet with him." Henry smiled at me, well pleased to know that I, too, held the man in high esteem. "And what of Fish, my lord?" I asked carefully, laying my jewelled knife at the side of my plate and washing my hands. The water had petals of roses floating in it, along with tiny purple fronds of lavender. They bobbed and swam out of the way of my fingers, like boats on a tiny sea. "The poor man but seeks your love, and assurance for your people. I believe he speaks not heresy here, but only good sense. The Church would move against him, but does he not speak the truth? Some of his beliefs are more outlandish, I admit... but, with the right prince guiding him, such a man might see where his errors lie. And even if he requires guidance in some areas of theology, this does not detract from the truths held in his works."

Henry inclined his head. "I will issue a pardon for the man," he said, and then scowled. "Chancellor More will like it not at all... But I would like to meet with this Master Fish, and hear his views in person."

"You are the greatest of Kings, my lord," I said warmly. I meant it truly. "To listen to the pleas of your people, even those exiled and banished, and take their words into your heart. You are a generous prince, Henry; the wisest I have ever met."

Henry's cheeks coloured a touch as he pushed his great hands into the fingerbowl and cleaned them carefully, then dried them on a linen with golden embroidery, handed to him by Norris. Henry looked up at his friend with affection. Since Henry loved Norris so well, he was often called to serve at dinner. Henry believed that Norris carved meat, a refined skill of gentlemen and nobles, better than any other.

Henry put his hand over mine and patted it. "How, now," he blushed, although looking pleased by my compliment. "Leave this paper with me, Anne, for I wish to study it more."

"And I would love to talk of it with you more, too, my love. I do so enjoy hearing your thoughts. In listening to you, I understand my own thoughts only the clearer." This was also true. Although my thoughts were often clear enough, discussing them with Henry helped me to fine-tune them, to express them with clarity. Sometimes I struggled, when I was passionate, to make myself rightly understood. Henry made me slow down my thought process and approach each argument logically. In return, I opened his mind to new ideas. We matched well.

"I feel the same, my love." He reached across the table and traced a finger down the side of my jaw. I kissed it as it reached my mouth. "What a Queen you will make, my Anne," he said tenderly. "As wise as you are beautiful."

Henry's support of Fish did not go down at all well with More, as Henry had predicted. More was presently engaged with Archbishop Warham in condemning Tyndale as a heretic, for his *Obedience*, for his translation of the New Testament and for his new translation of the Old Testament. He hardly wanted the King to become enamoured with other men he considered heretics.

Despite Henry's acceptance of many points in the *Obedience*, he was pressured by More to condemn both translations of the Bible as heretical. Henry had also decided that Tyndale needed to be arrested. Although he agreed with much of his arguments, Tyndale's stance against the annulment had angered Henry. He believed Tyndale was dangerous, and needed to be stopped. What was I to say? To outwardly defend someone Henry hated was perilous. I hoped to persuade him in time that Tyndale was not a threat, to England, to him, or to the faith.

More had already started up the fires of Smithfield in his zeal to rid the world of heretics, making it clear he thought his predecessor, Wolsey, had been too lenient. The fires started that spring, and over the summer a pall of smoke made from the body and blood of reformers and free thinkers would come to float over London.

More was also suppressing the legal rights that suspected heretics had when arrested. They were not supposed to be held for longer than three months without trial. They could not be accused of the same crime if acquitted and could not be held if their trials were postponed. More ignored all these rights. He was relentless, and his interrogations did not only go on in the Lollard's Tower of Lambeth Palace, nor in the ecclesiastical prisons... No... there were reports that More liked to take such men to his own house in Chelsea, and torture them there. There was a tree in his garden which he called "The Tree of Truth" where he whipped and flogged men he had arrested. His gatehouse was fitted out with stocks and chains so he could hold men fast as he interrogated them. More was breaking the law. As Chancellor, he was duty-bound to uphold it. He was obsessed with heresy, and determined to use his new-found power to destroy it.

That May, a conclave of bishops and clergy met at Westminster. More went along as the only layman. The conclave discussed the translation of the Bible into English, and although one or two spoke out in favour, the Church re-issued its ban on such works, and issued a Public Instrument for "The abolishing of the Scripture and other books to be read in English." The Church did not want to loosen its grip on the people of God.

More was a keen advocate for keeping the ban in place, and even keener to press for severe measures for those found defying the Church. Under More's influence, Henry was persuaded that heresy and treason were almost the same creature; that those who disobeyed the Church were likely to rebel against him. Whilst Henry understood the sense in Tyndale's works, and others I had brought to him, he did not believe that *all* people should read them. Much like the Church, in this way, he believed that some books, some knowledge, was dangerous and could not be understood by all.

I was bitterly disappointed in Henry. Although he said he would allow a translation of the Bible to be made by a learned scholar, at some stage, which went against the conclave, he also ordered that all translated works of Scripture be handed in, so they could be destroyed by More and his minions.

He did not, of course, include my books or his in this purge. Henry kept hold of his own copies of the Tyndale works, just as many other rebellious Londoners and people of England did. That is the nice thing about books. They are easy to hide, if one has the will, and if only shared with those who are seekers of knowledge, have the power to seed fresh ideas, and new ways of thinking.

But this proclamation, linking heresy to treason, gave More new powers. He could call suspects now to the Star Court at Westminster, and try them without having to go through the Bishop's courts. He arrested a great many booksellers, increased his spies about London, and created a fog of fear about the city and beyond that was hideous to behold.

More was dangerous. Not only to all those who wished to explore their religion, not only to reformers, evangelicals and actual heretics, but to the very ideas I was trying to get Henry to accept. My love was still wavering in his beliefs. I had to find a way to convince him of the truth.

Chapter Sixty-Nine

Richmond Palace
Late Spring 1530

Despite all that I was bringing to him on the matter of reform and new thoughts, Henry still wished to pursue the Pope for an annulment. He still believed it to be the quickest and easiest path. I did not agree, but Henry was King, and therefore he usually had his way. I *was* pleased, however, that he was also pursuing other methods, such as using Cranmer's work to gather theological opinion on the *Great Matter*. Henry believed that once presented with the findings of the universities, the Pope would have to capitulate. Henry was, at this time, teetering between his old beliefs and new ones. It would not do to pressure him too much, for then he would resist. I had to lace his dinner with a tiny bit of new sauce each time he dined, in order for him to develop a taste for it. In doing so, I assured myself I was working for his good and the good of England. The voice inside my head, which whispered such excuses to me, sounded remarkably like my father's.

Since Henry was still in favour of prevailing upon the Pope, my father revisited a plan that had been brought up two years ago; a petition, signed by all the nobles in England, asking the Pope to rid Henry of his unlawful Queen, and to allow him to take me as his wife instead. A draft was made, but upon its first reading at the Council, Henry declared it "too anti-papal" to believe that it would hold much weight with Clement. It was taken back, modified and agreed by the King and Council, but the final draft remained heavy with threat towards Clement.

The petition warned that if Henry was not given his annulment, it would make his subjects miserable, but, "*not wholly desperate, since it is possible to find relief some other way.*" It was a veiled threat; should the Pope fail Henry again, then perhaps he would take matters into his own hands and turn to the new ideas of reform sweeping through parts of the Holy Roman Empire and the Low Countries... perhaps Henry would turn his back on the authority of Rome as other states were, and decide upon the *Great Matter* himself.

It was, in truth, what I wanted him to do. Not only for us, not only so that we could finally be together... but also for his people, for the faith. Henry was poised on the cliff edge of possibility. But he was still not ready, not yet, to be the King I knew he could be.

The amended petition was taken about the country by a man named William Brereton, a groom of the Privy Chamber. Brereton was a bit of a rogue. He was an older man with a colourful past who had once been suspected of piracy. But he was a good friend to our cause and was eager to help. My father liked him and found him amusing company. They often jousted together. Assisting Brereton was a young man named Thomas Wriothesley. This man was a servant of Gardiner's, but he owed his education at Cambridge to my father and the money that we Boleyns had given towards helping young scholars who had not the funds to be educated themselves. The two rode up and down the country in the summer sun, the air about them humming with the sound of dragonflies, bees, and flies, as swift-winged flycatchers and skylarks hunted through the insect-rich air. And as bugs and bees buzzed about their heads, so they did the same to the nobles of England.

All adult peers visited by Brereton and Wriothesley signed, along with twenty-two abbots, and all the senior members of the royal household, including Henry's personal clergy and lay preachers. Six bishops also put their name to the document. Those bishops and other clergy who we knew would refuse, were simply not asked. "Even if the petition has no effect on the Pope," my father said as he listened to reports on its progress about the country. "Then at least we know well enough now who Katherine's people are, don't we?"

It was remarkable that my father could still take me by surprise after all this time, for in truth I had not even thought of something so devious, but he was right. We knew who some of our enemies were, but we did not know them all. Men who had wavered, who we were unsure of, would now be called on to make a choice. We would finally see who was with us and who was against through this petition. There were other suspect elements about the petition, too. George had apparently signed, which was impossible seeing as he was in France continuing to petition François for help, and aiding Henry's envoys as they presented our arguments to universities. When I questioned my father, he flicked his hand airily, saying that George had signed before he left... but I was not entirely convinced this was true.

Henry's impatience with the Pope became unquestioningly apparent that summer. He asked his Council whether, in their opinion, he could disregard the Pope in his *Great Matter* if it became clear he had the support of scholars, universities and theologians. Henry was running out of patience. His Council received the question in stunned silence. My father soon found his voice, and declared that, in his opinion, Henry was free to ignore Rome, but the Marquis of Exeter dropped to his knees before Henry. "Majesty," he begged in a quiet voice. "Please, if you are to do such a thing, wait at least until the winter, for then the cold and wet will discourage those who might raise their hand in rebellion at such an act."

Henry blinked as though he had not considered that his people might rise against him, but the Marquis went on. "We all know of Your Majesty's impatience and frustration at the slowness of this matter," he said, holding out his hands to Henry. "But perhaps it would be better to allow the canvassing of support to continue, so that we knew where and how strong we stood in public opinion on the matter. I speak only out of love for Your Majesty, and to keep our sovereign safe upon his throne."

Henry came to me that night, and I spoke warmly of Cranmer's work. Henry huffed sullenly at me that he wondered if the evidence of the universities could ever stand up to the authority of the Pope. "You should have more faith in your own servants and your own self, Henry," I scolded. "Have I not held that same faith in you all this time?"

"And there is much I have done for you, madam, that I would remind you of!" He glared at me, drinking heavily from his goblet. His cheeks were puffed and paunchy. Of late, he had taken more often to reading and attending to matters of state, than to riding, hunting or playing tennis. Henry was becoming heavier, thicker, softer, for his appetite for meat and wine had not diminished as his sporting activities had. I knew Henry was angered that another barrier had been put in his way and sought to take it out on me. "I would remind you," he continued darkly, "that you owe me much, and you have made many enemies at court and beyond."

"Any enemies I have were made in my love for you," I replied. "And it matters not. Gossip tells me that there is a prophesy told that a Queen shall die at this time, burnt in flame. But even if I were to suffer a thousand deaths, my love for you will not abate one jolt."

Henry stared at me and then set his wine to one side. He embraced me. "My Anna," he whispered lovingly. "I am sorry, my love. I spoke like a beast. What would I do without you?"

"That is something you will never have to find out, my lord," I said, stretching my arms up and drawing his head down to kiss. Our kiss grew hungrier. He pushed me to the fireside, and there pulled at my gown until he had my breasts free. He pushed his face into them, cupping his hands under them. I took my hand down to his breeches and pushed my way inside until I had him in my hands. Against the fireplace, with my King's head nestled in my naked breasts, I brought him to ecstasy.

Afterwards he picked me up and carried me to my bed where he put me down, taking my gown from my body. He traced a light finger over my shivering, naked flesh, and then he lowered himself to put his head between my thighs. I clung to the back of the bed, letting out breathy gasps and cries of joy. As he brought me to my own climax, I screamed out, unable to resist the power that moved within me, and then we lay by each other's sides, with his hands about my breasts.

"Henry," I murmured, hearing his breathing slow as he drifted towards slumber.

"My love…" he murmured.

"Is the full act of love… like this?" I asked.

"Better," he murmured and then looked up at me with a wicked little grin. "Better even than this."

"I cannot wait to try it, my love," I whispered.

"Nor I, Anne," he sighed, putting his head back against my skin. "Nor I…"

Chapter Seventy

Greenwich Palace
Late Spring 1530

One day, Henry came to visit with me in my new apartments at Greenwich. They were the finest I could ever imagine, with tapestries lining all the walls, Turkish carpets on much of the bedchamber floor, and rushing mats strewn with sweet-scented herbs covering the rest. Mulberry branches to ward off pests lay under my bed, and dark oaken cupboards filled with my own plate lined the walls. Henry had given me gifts of standing clocks, maps, and portraits to hang upon the walls, and there was a writing desk decorated with the arms of the Rochford leopard and my white falcon. I had servants to bring me anything I wanted, and my own kitchens prepared to make me whatever I fancied. Henry's fool, Patch, who had been given to him by the Cardinal, was entertaining us merrily as Henry and his men arrived.

Henry was announced just as we were all doubled up with laughter at a jest Master Patch had made about Norfolk, and we all struggled to contain ourselves even as Henry walked in. He looked at our faces, flushed with laughter and our twitching lips, and asked us what the jest was. Patch leapt in before I could say anything, and with the usual daring boldness of a court fool, he simpered before Henry in his fool's tunic of many colours, and horned hat. He waved his staff, topped with a jester's head in Henry's face. "Sire!" he exclaimed, "how does your fat face this fine day?"

Henry laughed with good humour, for it was the place of the fools to be rude and outlandish. Although it was a jest, there was a ring of truth to it. Henry was gaining weight. He waved Patch away. "Sweetheart," he said lovingly. "How are you this day?"

"Recovering from the mirth that your fool inspires, Henry!" I giggled, watching Patch scamper about the room, insulting Henry's men.

"It is good to see you merry, my love," he noted.

"I have much to be merry for, Henry," I smiled at him. "Master Cranmer is working hard on our case, so he writes to me. I feel as though we are finally reaching a point at which we may be able to act as we should do!" I grinned wickedly at him and indicated to Bridget to bring a deck of cards over.

"You wish to lose *more* money to me, sweetheart?" Henry teased.

"I have a new game for Your Majesty," I told him, taking him over to the table and shuffling the cards.

"And where has this game come from?" he asked, sitting down as Nan brought us wine.

"It is a variation on an old game, Your Majesty," I said, a teasing smile playing on my lips. "Brought forth by my imagination."

"And its name?" he asked as we waved Norris and Tom over to join us at the card table. Margaret and Bridget took seats too, and Nan poured out the wine.

"Pope Julius." My lips sprang up in a cheeky grin. Pope Julius II was the man who had allowed the marriage between Katherine and Henry.

Henry glanced at me with a startled expression and then chuckled. "And what are the rules of this game, my love?"

I explained the game. It was quite simple. Players took four cards each. The player with the highest in the suit was in the best position. Hearts was the best suit, followed by Clubs, Diamonds and then Spades. The King of Hearts was the highest card one could draw, the Ace being low in this game. Players would bet on their first hand and then be allowed to swap a card at each round as wagering continued. There was a rebel card; the Knave of clubs, who represented the Pope. This card could be used to best any King when the cards were called. If a player therefore put down the King of Hearts, another player with the Knave of Clubs could put his hand down, and win. The way to flummox this rogue hand was to play the Queen of Hearts, who could best the Knave, but not the King. Should someone put down the Queen of Hearts, the player with the King would win after all. If you had both the King and Queen of Hearts, victory was certain.

Henry rumbled with mirth as I explained the game, and we started slowly. Within no time at all, wagering was growing wild, and Margaret and Bridget were overtaken with giggles as Henry handed them money with which to bet. I had the rebel Knave in the first game, and laid it down to beat Bridget who had the King of Clubs, but Tom bested me with the Queen of Hearts. Henry clapped him on the back in approval. Then he laid down his cards, which included the King of Hearts, winning the game.

"A fine game, Anne." He chortled with approval as the money on the table was taken by one of his men and put into a pouch. "We must play this often."

"But, as you see, Majesty," I purred. "The King will *always* win, as long as he has his Queen of Hearts to best the Knavish Pope."

"Let us hope that this happens in our own lives, my sweet," he said, and then Henry called for another round of my new game, as he had so enjoyed the first.

Chapter Seventy-One

York Place and Woodstock Palace
Summer 1530

In June, as the marbled, fluffy chicks of lapwings ran between the forest-like stems of grass in the fields, my father had word that the Cardinal was sending messages to Chapuys, the Imperial ambassador. Although my father's spies in Wolsey's household knew not what these messages contained, we were advised that the Cardinal had sent his physician to Chapuys and had been closeted with him for some time. It was enough to suggest that the fat bat, who would not find support for his return to favour amongst the Boleyns, was instead attempting to gain help from our enemies. Apparently, the Cardinal had first approached the French ambassador, who had turned Wolsey's man away, saying that all favour the French were shown in England was due to the good offices of the Lady Anne.

I smiled when I heard this. "At least du Bellay is a good friend to me..." I tapped my fingers on the top of the fireplace.

"We will keep a closer eye on the Cardinal, and on Katherine too," said my father. "If he is indeed conspiring with her then we will take it to the King with all speed."

I paused in thought. "No," I said quietly. "You will not." I fixed my eyes upon his. "You will wait until there is *full* proof of the Cardinal's treason," I said. My heart hammered within me for I knew I was laying a trap. "Only then will we take it to the King."

He let out a low, quiet whistle. "You mean when there is enough proof that the Cardinal has betrayed his master," he said thoughtfully.

"I mean when there is enough proof so that Henry knows beyond doubt that he can trust in Wolsey no longer. This must be *the last time* that the Cardinal rears his head, father… I want you to make sure of that."

"Trust in me," he said softly, kissing my hand.

Soon after that conversation, another bout of sickness broke out in London. Summer was all but another word for pestilence in the cities. Henry moved us out into the country, where we settled at Eltham Palace together. Katherine, with her daughter Mary, were sent to Windsor. Henry would have sent them further away, but he feared what his people's response to this might be. I worried more about them being kept together.

Princess Mary was now fourteen years old, and was aware that her father wished to rid himself of her mother. She was utterly devoted to Katherine. Henry visited Mary but little, for he knew that her mother poured poison into Mary's ear, and most especially about me. Despite his frustrations with Katherine, he still loved his talented daughter a great deal. I did not like this, for it gnawed at my old fear that Katherine would prevail against me. She was not above using any weapon, even her own daughter, to get her way, and I was worried that spending time with Mary would distract Henry from keeping his eye set on *our* goal. Since Mary was often in her mother's company, however, when he came to call on her, this was not so much of an issue, as Henry tried to avoid Katherine at all costs. I suspected Mary was so often with her mother so that she and Katherine could, together, attempt to force Henry into spending more time with Katherine through her. It did not work as they would have wished; it meant only that he spent less time with the both of them.

When he went to tell Katherine she was to be moved, the Queen took the opportunity to reprimand him. "I call upon you to be a good prince once again to me, to your daughter and to your people," she said. "Set aside this evil life, Henry, and set a good example for your people as once you always did." Katherine went on to say that even if he did not respect her as his true wife and Queen, "you should at least respect God and your conscience." She urged him to listen to the Pope, and to set me aside.

Henry replied that the Pope's opinion meant little to him, and he *was* acting upon his conscience in the *Great Matter*. "There are plenty of people in this world who agree with me, Katherine," he said. "And fewer and fewer who take side with you and the Pope." He had left the room without saying another word, and had her quickly dispatched to Windsor.

After spending a week or so at Eltham we travelled north and spent time at Woodstock. I loved that old palace. Many parts of it were in sad decline, and I said to Henry that here, we should establish yet another building project. Work was progressing to expand and improve York Place, and at Hampton Court Henry was having his own private tower built, with hot and cold running water, and a whole floor built to hold part of his vast personal library. But Woodstock seemed to speak to me. Its rambling corridors, beautiful, almost wild gardens and magnificent, ancient great hall had romance about them, and the walls echoed with stories and voices of the past.

Here, legend said, Alfred the Great, the saviour of England against the Danes, had once held court. Henry I had built a hunting lodge here, and many kings had followed after, adding to the building and making it into a great manor house. There were acres of parkland and woodland surrounding it. Henry II had kept his fair mistress, Rosamund de Clifford, in this place, and it was rumoured that his Queen had come to Woodstock, offering the mistress either a knife or bowl of poison with which to die. Rosamund's Well still stood within the grounds, and Henry and I spent much time sitting there, near to the great ponds, poring over the texts on reform I had given him. Perhaps because Woodstock had also witnessed the great clash between Henry II and his former friend, Thomas Becket, Archbishop of Canterbury, this place moved me all the more, for it I believed we were coming, in our own time, to another conflict between state and Church... Although this time the King was clearly in the right.

It was said, too, that Edward IV had brought his love Elizabeth Woodville to this place whilst they were secretly married, and that they spent much time here together. For a woman who was in almost the same position as that earlier Queen, Henry's own grandmother, Woodstock seemed to me to sing to me through its walls, telling me that it was a place for love and for lovers. *All would be well,* it whispered to me as I walked through its halls and corridors, *all will be well...*

All was not well all the time though. Once, on a rare break from spending time with me, Henry was out riding near Woodstock, a man yelled out, "Back to your wife!" and it was only because the guards were too late to catch him that he escaped Henry's fury. He returned that night with a dark and angry face. It took a while for me to tease this information from him. When I did, I tried to laugh it off, but in my bed, in the dark of night, I was troubled and restless.

My father, Foxe and Gardiner came out to Woodstock with something new for Henry. It was a set of papers which became known as the *Collectanea satis copisoa.* Henry had not commissioned it. It had been worked on for some months that year by Fox, Cranmer, Gardiner and others. We hoped it would convince Henry to finally take on the role for which he was destined.

The *Collectanea* demonstrated the ancient assumption that the Pope was supreme in spiritual matters was erroneous. The work was full of scriptural and historical arguments that proved the King was the true leader of all matters, both temporal and spiritual, within his own Kingdom. This first draft of the text made clear that in the early days of the Church, each kingdom had its own jurisdiction, independent of the Pope. Since each kingdom had the right to decide its own laws and systems of justice, the true body that should decide on Henry's marriage was therefore the Church of England. Another part of its argument said that all authority was the King's in his own kingdom, and was given to the King by God Himself, therefore, there was no reason for the Pope to be involved at all.

Foxe pointed out that Henry's authority in this matter *already* existed; he had, after all, been chosen by God for the throne, and therefore had no need to even vindicate his rights. It was the Church, and the Pope especially, who were the interlopers here… they were usurping power from Henry that was his God-given right. The works of Tyndale had called upon the King to act against previously sacrosanct law, but Foxe pointed out that Henry was already in possession of such authority. He was answerable only to God. He should be the head of the Church in England.

It felt then as though I was standing on the edge of something remarkable; a new time, a new way for the Church to be governed and ruled. Not by some corrupt and far-off entity like the Pope, but by my own King, a man I knew was most given to goodness and reason when guided well. With Henry at the forefront of this movement, we could bring England to a place of glory, and true faith. For me, this was like a light shining through the darkness of our troubles. Henry was *already in possession* of all he required to act for our own good, and for that of England. The only thing he seemed to lack was the confidence to do so.

Henry read over the document carefully, and we went over many points together, but he was still not fully convinced he could act in such a way and that it would be accepted, not only by his people, but by the rest of Europe as well. He feared war and invasion. Henry was happier to wait for

Cranmer and his other envoys to bring back opinions from overseas, to give more weight to his case. But he allowed the distribution of the first draft of the *Collectanea*. And this soon caused a mighty noise all through Europe and beyond.

Chapter Seventy-Two

Greenwich Palace
Summer's End 1530

In August, as Henry and I returned to London, I received further information from my father's spies in Wolsey's house. The Cardinal was now sending messages almost daily to Chapuys. We had managed to intercept some of the letters and the contents were shocking, even to me.

The Cardinal suggested to Chapuys that strong action on behalf of the Emperor and Pope should be taken to support Katherine; that the King should be *ordered* to put me aside, and return to his wife, upon threat of invasion or excommunication. Wolsey proposed that a papal envoy could arrive in the autumn, signalling the start of a *coup* that would remove the Boleyns from our posts. Henry would be forced to see reason; he would be made to reinstate Wolsey, and return to his wife, as a dutiful subject of the Pope. Wolsey implied that Chapuys should take his letter to Katherine, and gain her support.

What Katherine thought of all this, I know not, for she had made no attempt to answer the Cardinal, as far as we could see. I suspect that she was, in fact, reluctant to put quill to parchment, as she could see how very dangerous Wolsey's suggested plan was. Katherine had no love for Wolsey, and she would not be sorry to see him ousted for good. He had worked against her in the matter of the annulment, and now he was trying to be her friend? Katherine was no fool. She knew this was perilous ground. She did not write to Wolsey herself, and any messages that were passed along were made clear that they were from Chapuys alone.

It was a shame for us, that Katherine was so cautious, for if Katherine were conspiring with Wolsey to bring her nephew, the Holy Roman Emperor and King of Spain to our shores in a show of force, then she would have been guilty of high treason, and the king would have an excuse to arrest her. But Katherine was cleverer even than the mighty Wolsey. We had damning evidence against him now. It was time to move once and for all against the Cardinal. It was time to take this to Henry.

George took the letters we had intercepted to Henry. That night Henry came to my chambers, pressing his sore head with his hands, his face grim.

"My brother has shown you the truth, my lord." It did no good to pretend that I knew not what assailed him. I poured wine into fine goblets as I spoke. "Now you know what I have said for so long is true; the Cardinal is no friend either to you or to me. And more even than this! He is an enemy to England for he works to bring the horror invasion upon your people."

"I am so tired, Anne," he said weakly. A stab of annoyance hit me in the gut for his feebleness. How many times did he have to be proved that Wolsey was a traitor? Once? Twice? A thousand times?

Henry took the goblet from me and sat down. "I thought Wolsey was *my* man, my friend… and yet it seems that he works against me. Whom can I trust when my own friends turn against me?"

"Trust in me and mine," I said. "For have not we always worked to satisfy your conscience and desires? Perhaps you wish the Cardinal to have his way? To see me sent from court? To put me aside and return to the sinful bed with your brother's wife? To have peace with the Emperor and the Pope, who stand against the wishes of God and against what you know to be true and right?" I sat down next to him, and his face that told me this was not so. "If you want not this, Henry," I said, sipping my wine, "then you must take action against the Cardinal. He has proved himself a traitor… Not only once before when he failed you, but again when you forgave him! You cannot afford to be so gentle with those who work evil against you, my love."

"He is but a weak old man," Henry protested. "He has lost his head in his desire to return to my love."

I set my goblet to the table at my elbow and tried hard to hold on to the frayed edges of my temper. "A weak old man?" I asked, my jaw twitching. *"A weak old man?"* I stood up and walked to the fire, staring balefully into it. "This man makes pacts with your enemies, Henry. *He has sent letters asking the Emperor and the Pope to order you back to Katherine! Asking that direct action be taken by a foreign prince against England!"* I turned to him, my eyes wild. "Are you the King in this country?"

"I am the King," he said coldly, taking a large gulp of his wine and sulking like a sullen child. A second chin was growing under his first and he was coming to look more aged in these days of such struggle and trial. I still thought him handsome though, in those times when he was not frustrating me…

"Then for the love of God, Henry!" I cried. "Open your eyes! The Cardinal has betrayed you. He means to separate us! He seeks to send me from your side and ruin me! And more than that, he asks that the Emperor and the Pope offer *force* to reinstate Katherine! Wolsey would bring war upon your country, invasion! He is no friend to you, to me or to England and if you are too weak to see that and do something about it…"

Henry leapt from his chair, spilling wine all over the floor as he grasped me by the shoulders. He shook me, my teeth rattling in my head. *"I am not weak!"* he bellowed into my face. I stared back at him with icy eyes.

"I should have married another whilst I was still young," I said coldly. "I see now that I was right; you will pardon mine enemies and leave me in the cold. You will bow to the wills of other Kings rather than face them in pride and glory! You *will* leave me… You will cast me aside and see my good name disgraced… You have no care for me. You do not love me."

I was desperate. How could I make him finally understand what had to happen here? If Wolsey came back, or even was allowed to live, then he would undo me, and Henry was doing nothing to stop it!

Henry stared at me, and shook his head. There was anger in his expression, but beneath that there was weariness. He hated to hear me speak so. "It is not so, Anne… All that I do, I do for you… How can you not see that?"

"What is easier? To walk beside me, or face my enemies?" I asked. "If you will not move against the Cardinal now then you are no friend to me. If you would work against me and befriend my enemies then I see you are not my love and my husband, you are an enemy to me too!"

He tried to hold me, but I struggled, wild in his arms. As I broke free I stared at him with a contemptuous gaze. "I thought that I had the best man in all the world ready to make me his wife," I whispered harshly. "But I see now that I have none such. There is no love in your heart. You must *want* me taken from you! That is the only reason for this betrayal! I have *wasted* my youth waiting for you… By now I might have been married to another and borne sons… But I see now that I am never to have such a blessing. For when you throw me away, no man will come near to me again. The people will rip me into pieces, for I suffer all their hate for my love for you… And you? You will suffer nothing, other than the return to the cold bed of your infertile Queen… And I will suffer *all*, for having loved you! For having given up my life and my honour for love!"

Henry stared at me, dumbfounded. I could see the horror in his face... the thought of losing me... the thought of my disgrace... He went to speak, but could not find the words to comfort me.

Tears came to my eyes. I chased them back and bit my lip to stop from crying. "You have *ruined* me, my lord," I whispered. "Despoiled my honour, and stolen my life from me. I have waited in vain, like a fool, believing in a love that does not exist. I have wasted all this time, blinded by my love for you, and it is all for nothing. All will fall to dust and ash about me. You have undone me... You have ruined me..."

Tears flooded Henry's eyes. He looked helpless, and distraught. He walked towards me, opening his arms, as though an embrace would set all this right. I put up a hand, stopping him. "No," I whispered, staring at him blankly. I felt empty... hollowed out. "Come not near me... I cannot be held in your arms even once more if you are to take me from them forever..."

My hand shook. "How can you do this?" I asked, breaking into tears. "How can you do this to us?"

Henry rushed forward, but I fought him off and ran from the chamber. I heard him call my name but I fled. I went that very night to the stables, took a horse and two guards and rode for the river. The city was dangerous at night, and as we clattered through the dark streets, torches blazing in my guard's hands, shadows of thieves and murderers moved in the alleyways.

I spent an ill night on a freezing barge down the Thames, and then made for Hever across country. It took me another day, riding on hired horse with my men to reach home. Rain fell as we rode and I did not even put up my hood to protect myself, so lost in misery was I. My mother and Mary took me in, sodden wet and weeping, and they took me, shivering, to the chambers I had shared with Mary as a girl to wrench the dirty, wet clothes from me and wrap me in wool to make me warm again.

Henry was frantic. He did not know where I had gone, and he made a desperate search through the palace, then about London for me before sending messengers to the homes of my friends and to Hever. The note we received urged my mother to send word if I was there, and to beg for my return to London. He promised that he would never cast me off; that he loved me, and that if it was my will, he would move against my enemies.

Wrapped in blankets, shivering at the fireside and sneezing mightily, I was warmed only by his letter. My mother wrote to Henry on my behalf, saying that I was here, and that I had received the message. She promised him that I would be back at court in a week's time, for my flight had made me ill. The day after he got the note, Henry sent his doctors to me, four of them, out of his mind with terror that I might die of this small cold I had contracted. But at least his panic was a measure of his love.

The next morning I sat still wrapped in blankets, cupping ale warmed with hot ginger and lemon in my hands as I looked from the window at ploughmen urging their heavy horses over the last of the fields they had to tend. I thought on my flight, on Henry's promises, and wondered if this time he would be true to his word.

Henry sent another missive.

The Cardinal was to be arrested for High Treason, a crime punishable by death.

I returned to court a week later, and Henry was overcome with relief and joy. He assured me that he was not going to let me down. That he had been brought low by all that I had said to him. That he was dedicated to me, and only me.

I was victorious. No more Cardinal... No more fat old bat, wrapped in red silk and encrusted with riches he had stolen from his King, from the poor and from God. Soon, I would be at Henry's side, as his chief advisor, as his wife and as his equal. I would have my way. I would be Queen, and no one would stop me.

Chapter Seventy-Three

Greenwich Palace
Autumn 1530

In September, Cromwell came seeking an audience. He had been working on an issue Henry wanted resolved. Wolsey had granted certain Church lands to Henry in St Albans and Winchester as well as lands belonging to colleges Wolsey patronised. Henry was able to take revenues and give grants from these lands, but only whilst Wolsey lived. If the Cardinal died, ownership would revert to the Church, or to the colleges and universities. Henry wanted full possession for the Crown, and had enlisted canny Cromwell to ensure this came to pass. Courtiers who wanted to receive grants from these lands sought Cromwell's favour. The King's new favourite was making a tidy profit in his new line of work. Many gifts of money, property and goods were coming his way to ensure he suggested the right names for the grants.

Wolsey, however, unaware Henry was preparing to move against him, had been grieved to hear that the King wanted to seize his lands for good, and had written to Cromwell asking him to do all he could to save them. When the Cardinal received no answer, for Cromwell was, in fact working to achieve just the opposite outcome for his King, the Cardinal's letters became increasingly aggressive towards his former servant. Wolsey learned that Cromwell was doing well out of the situation, and the two began to argue via letter. This friction troubled Cromwell, but not enough to desist in working for Henry.

"And you tell me of this for what reason, Master Cromwell?" I inquired smoothly as he told me of the rift between himself and his erstwhile master.

He regarded me with those light brown eyes and shrugged. "I perhaps wished for some advice, my lady," he said. "The Cardinal appears to be unable to accept the reality of his present position. He seems to think that all is as it was in the old days; that he has only to lift a hand and all will scramble to do his will. He does not seem to appreciate that I am now, first and foremost, the King's servant. The Cardinal believes that any who have *once* been his servants, are *always* his servants." He paused and his eyes narrowed. "I know also there is much being spoken of at court about him. Much that implies trouble."

"Then you must also know that the Cardinal continues to meddle where he should not," I said warningly. "The time is coming, Master Cromwell, as I think you have long known, when you will have to choose which master to serve... Will it be the Cardinal, who now does not now note the many services you have done for him in the past? Or will it be the King, who loves you as his own brother?"

Cromwell started at that and I smiled. "Do you not know the heart of your own King, Master Cromwell?" I asked. "For I, who have had the privilege of being loved by such a man, can see well when he offers affection to another." I breathed in and let the air out though my nose. "Choose well," I advised. "And let me give you fair warning and prove that I am your friend in truth. To be associated with Cardinal Wolsey will become imminently most dangerous. As a friend, I would advise you to cease communicating with the Cardinal, and to instead work with all your passion for the King."

He watched me steadily. I could almost hear his mind ticking away like one of Henry's clocks. He knew I was taking a risk in warning him, for if he proved loyal indeed to Wolsey, then such an admission could forewarn the Cardinal that he was in grave danger. But it was a wager I was willing to make, for if it won me into the trust of Henry's newest favourite, it was worth taking.

"I will take your advice, my lady," Cromwell said eventually. "And I thank you for offering it to me."

"The King's true friends are *my* true friends," I said. "And I think that there is much that you and I might do for one another, Master Cromwell, if we put our heads together."

He did as I had advised, and distanced himself from Wolsey. He must have known that I had taken a risk, but perhaps the fact that I had done so convinced him that I intended to be his friend and ally. He was not one to miss anything, Cromwell.

Later in September, I obtained a copy of Tyndale's newest work, *The Practise of Prelates*, which had a subtitle most interesting to me: *Whether the King's grace may be separated from his queen because she was his brother's wife*.

I am sure you can see why I was interested.

Upon reading it, however, I was less than pleased. Tyndale said he had still found no argument within the Bible that would allow the King to leave his present wife. In saying this, I knew he would anger Henry, and there was worse to come. Tyndale criticized Henry for his condemnation of Luther for marrying a former nun, saying Henry's disgrace was far worse than Luther's. Since the King had argued he would return to Katherine, if it was found she was his true wife, and had not, Tyndale thought him shameful. Tyndale's work, however, pleased Thomas More. Copies smuggled into the country did not seem as hindered by More's men as other works were… strangely enough.

Henry was enraged. He told me he would have Tyndale found, arrested and executed. Tyndale's brother, John, was arrested, tried in the Star Chamber, and flogged through London for having passed money to Tyndale. To me, it seemed that More had won on two counts, for not only did Tyndale's work advocate for the Queen, a cause dear to his heart, but also, this new work had angered the King, and perhaps turned him against Tyndale for good.

It took a lot of effort on my part to try and uphold the arguments we had been working for, for so long, in Henry's mind. "You should invite him here, my love," I said calmly as Henry raged. "You have admitted that some of his notions are erroneous, and that he requires guidance, why not have him brought to England, and talk with him?"

Henry stared at me, dumbfounded, and then left to go riding. I hoped that, in leaving the thought within his mind, it might take seed and grow. Tyndale was not lately proving a lot of help in my cause, but luckily, I had other men to help.

One of those arrived back in England that October. Cranmer was set to work immediately after Henry had hammered him with questions about the universities of Italy and what their findings were for our cause. Most, it seemed, were for us, with some against, but we were hopeful that with the French universities generally finding in our favour, and all of the English ones doing the same, that we would have enough scholarly opinion to out-weigh the universities of Spain, who, of course, were all for Katherine.

Cranmer was staying at Durham House as the honoured guest of my father, who had recently made him his personal chaplain. Whilst there, he was working on perfecting the *Collectanea,* and on collating the responses of the universities in a document that would be published in the next year called *The Determinations of the most excellent universities of Italy and France, that it is unlawful for a man to marry his brother's wife; that the Pope hath no power to dispense therewith.* Although not exactly a catchy title, it stated what it was about in no uncertain terms. Cranmer had some opinions already from the universities, and set about collating, translating and describing their discussions and arguments, whilst adding his own opinion to them as well. An English version of the draft work was published late that year, and Cranmer went on to add to it after that. The work was remarkable in one sense that it never once mentioned that the persons involved were Henry and Katherine, as the question had been put to the universities without names, although everyone knew who it was they were talking about, of course.

Cranmer met with me upon his return and I knelt before him, offering congratulations on his new post in the Rectory of Bredon. "It is so good to see a man such as you take this position," I said, "for in you I feel there is all the goodness that our Church so desperately requires."

Cranmer flushed and looked down at his hands. "I hope to live up to your expectations of me, my lady," he said gently. I put my hand to his.

"I know that you will, my gentle friend." I smiled softly at his burning cheeks. I genuinely believed that I could love a man such as Cranmer. Not in a romantic sense, but in one of true friendship. His humility touched my heart, and we had found much in common through our letters to each other. "For a man of faith, you have all too little in yourself." I said warmly. "But take from the strength of God, as I have all these years, and you will see how He sees you… then will you know your own worth."

He smiled shyly. "You should have been born a man and made a Bishop, my lady," he murmured. "Then God would have had a true advocate within the Church."

"God chose me for a different path, Master Cranmer," I replied. "But I assure you, I will do all I can as Henry's wife and Queen, to bring him to see the light of reform and the good that may be done for his people."

"You are a child of God, my lady," he whispered, looking at me with shining eyes. "A leader... like Esther, who delivered her people from persecution by intervening with her King, or the prophet and judge, Deborah, who led her people to freedom. And yet, there is within you the gentleness of Mother Mary. I see both strength and compassion in you, my lady. England is blessed to have you."

"I will do all that I can to live up to your faith in me, Master Cranmer," I said, a little overwhelmed by his vision of me.

"As I will, in your belief in me, my lady," he said.

That month, the draft of the *Collectanea* reached Europe, and the Pope and Emperor were disgusted by the ideas it contained. Henry went to a gathering of lawyers and clerics and proposed that, on the weight of the evidence in the *Collectanea,* he could empower Parliament to grant the Archbishop of Canterbury the power to decide the *Great Matter.* The gathering were shocked, and told the King outright that Parliament could not act in such a way. Henry reacted with anger, stalking from the chamber and postponing Parliament until the New Year. As he left, he shouted that the Pope's power was nothing but "usurpation and tyranny."

At court, my father and I, along with our allies, spoke openly about our lack of faith in the Pope's goodness and honesty. Sometimes, I admit, we got carried away, and managed to shock Chapuys so entirely with our anti-papal talk that we drove him to Katherine, saying that we would alienate England from the Holy See, if we had our way.

All were not, obviously, on our side. One such was of course Thomas More, who came to Henry often; speaking with him carefully on the radical suggestions and texts he was being shown. More had not been at all happy that Henry had pardoned Simon Fish, the reformer, and was at this time actually writing a book in answer, and against, Fish's arguments. Henry was not about to stop More replying to Fish's text, but, he told him more than once that he was not convinced that the Pope had the authority to decide on his *Matter*, and he believed the Pope was being influenced by the Emperor to stand against him.

"How can the Pope be true and just in any decision, when he is led so fully by the desires and wishes of another, Thomas?" Henry pleaded with More. I am sure that More believed Henry was also being led by another…

In late October, a papal bull reached Henry, absolutely forbidding him to marry again whilst his annulment was still under consideration. Whilst clearly a reaction to the *Collectanea* it also seemed to finally confirm, in Henry's eyes, the evidence we had brought against Wolsey, for there were further rumours that the Pope intended to excommunicate Henry if he did not obey, and order me to be banished from court. Such rumours echoed the schemes of Wolsey too boldly to be ignored.

Around this time, Wolsey summoned many of the northern men of the Church to him to prepare for his enthronement as Bishop at York. Wolsey had long held that title, but now had decided to honour the north with a celebration and formal enthronement. Norfolk was sure Wolsey was hiding something, and Henry became convinced that the Cardinal was in truth working against him. Henry believed that the enthronement was to be the stage from which the Pope would launch his excommunication of the King, and banishment of me.

It was the final push Henry required. There were simply too many small things that Wolsey was doing in the north for Henry to judge him still honest and true. Henry knew that Wolsey had been attempting to communicate with the Emperor and Katherine, and now, in light of the Pope's threats, he believed Clement had indeed received Wolsey's communications and they were both plotting against him. A threat of excommunication was no light matter, and Henry feared it greatly. Excommunication would not only endanger his immortal soul, but it would allow all Christians to lawfully rise against him, including his own people. Such a thing could bring his country to invasion, or rebellion. If this was what Wolsey was up to then he had to be stopped. Henry's horror made him defiant; another aspect of character we held in common.

I watched Henry's face closely as the warrant for Wolsey's arrest was, at last, brought to him. He stared at the parchment on the table. His face was blank, bereft of joy, but his eyes were harrowing to look upon. In them I could see emotions fighting each other; love, friendship, disbelief, anger, sorrow and hatred. Even now, at the end, he could not believe the Cardinal would have defied him. Even now, as his quill was poised over the parchment, he hesitated.

"It falls to the Earl of Northumberland to arrest the Cardinal," I said. "He is the greatest magnate of the north. It should be he who confronts the Cardinal."

Henry looked up sharply, a dangerous glimmer in his eyes. The Earl of Northumberland was none other than Henry Percy, the man with whom I once thought myself in love with, and who I had been engaged to marry. Was Henry suspicious that in asking that Percy be sent to arrest Wolsey I was trying to obtain a special favour for him? Or that I still had feelings for him? It was not so. The Earl was the greatest noble of the north and one most suited in position and standing to arrest a Cardinal, a Prince of the Church. I had no feelings for Percy now but those of derision, but I knew, too, that sending him would remind Wolsey of the time he had chastised and humiliated me, and that thought was satisfying. In sending Percy, Wolsey would know it was me who had brought about his downfall. It was spiteful, but there was a hungry part of my soul that wanted that satisfaction. God forgive my sins. We do not always act as we should when facing down our enemies.

Henry's gaze lingered on me for a moment, and then he dropped his eyes. "It will be done," he said, dipping his quill in ink. He went to sign his name to the warrant, but paused over the parchment again. Ink dripped from the swan-feather quill, dropping onto the creamy parchment, blossoming like a flower.

"Have it done. Have this finished, my love…" I said smoothly. "I am sorry to cause you pain, Henry, but you have been deceived by a friend, by a man you loved. The sin here is not yours, it is his. Have it done. We will hear what the Cardinal has to say for himself when he faces trial."

He did not look up. "That is true enough," he said sadly. He put his pen to the paper, and quickly scrawled his signature. He stared at it for a moment. "I will go for a walk," he said, trying not to look at the paper. Even now, he could not stand to act against Wolsey.

"I will see the papers are sent out," I assured him, and, with a sigh, watched him leave. His shoulders were hunched with misery. He looked smaller, somehow. I was pained to see his sorrow, but this was for the best. Wolsey was too dangerous to be left at liberty.

Just after Henry issued the order for Wolsey's arrest, Wolsey's doctor was arrested as he visited with Chapuys again at court, and under interrogation, and, I have no doubt, torture, he confessed. The doctor admitted he had been ordered to take messages to ambassadors of both France and Spain, and a number of letters, written in cipher, were discovered on him. He confirmed all the charges against Wolsey.

Henry heard all of this and then looked away with the eyes of a broken man. He could not deny any more, even to himself, that Wolsey was a traitor.

Chapter Seventy-Four

York
November 1530

The day before Wolsey's arrest, it was said that he had a premonition of his fate. Whilst finishing dinner with his men, one of his physicians rose from his seat and accidentally swept his coat against the giant silver cross of York, which stood on the cupboard beside them. The cross fell, and, with an almighty crack, bounced harshly off of the head of Edmund Bonner, Wolsey's personal chaplain. The diners sat stunned, even as Wolsey's retainer, Cavendish, hurried to tend to Bonner.

"Hath it drawn blood?" the Cardinal asked, staring in horror at the fallen cross on the floor.

"Yes, my lord," replied Cavendish, grabbing at linen on the table to stem the flow from Bonner's head. The Cardinal stared at Bonner, and then at the cross. All who saw him that night said that he went deathly pale, and his hand shook as he spoke.

"*Malum omen*," said Wolsey, *evil portent.*

Hardly checking that Bonner was well, Wolsey made for his chambers to pray. Cavendish reported later that he was struck by the seriousness with which Wolsey seemed to take the event. The Cardinal, it seemed, had sensed something in the air, some portent of doom.

On the evening of the 4th of November, Wolsey was once again dining with his men. They had eaten well, and were savouring sugared slices of imported orange, peeled grapes and figs in syrup. A hurried messenger entered the chamber and whispered in the Cardinal's ear. The Earl of

Northumberland and a large group of his men had come to call upon him. Wolsey was happy to hear that his old servant Henry Percy had finally come to see him. Wolsey had been inviting all and sundry to his house in hopes of regaining favour and influence, but the Earl had thus far resisted his calls. He bade them to enter the house, and warm themselves at the fire in the great hall. He left his other guests, and went out to meet Percy.

"I regret, my lord, that we have already dined," he cooed to Percy, not noting the pallor of Northumberland's face. He led Percy towards the roaring fire, and gazed over at his men. "I am pleased to see that you have done as I suggested when you were in my service, my lord, and kept about you many of your father's loyal men. I recognise many in this throng," Wolsey went to greet the retainers he recognized, but stopped when Percy's hand fell firmly on his shoulder.

"My lord," Percy intoned darkly, "I arrest you of High Treason."

Wolsey gaped at Percy, and then flinched, as just for a moment he saw a hint of satisfaction in the man's face. If Wolsey remembered Percy with affection, the same was not true for the Earl. Since his forced marriage to Mary Talbot, he had known only strife and misery. Mary despised her husband and made no secret of it. Wolsey had been the one to take me from him, to publicly humiliate him and to shame him before his father. He had no love for his former master.

"I… I demand that you produce the seal of the King to prove this is true," Wolsey stuttered, for Henry had promised him that only with his express order could the Cardinal ever be arrested. Wolsey glanced again at the men who had accompanied Percy, and recognised several members of Henry's Privy Council. Wolsey understood then that he was being arrested in Henry's name.

"Even the lowliest subjects of the King may come to arrest the greatest peer of the realm," he said, insulting Percy, who ignored him, and demanded the keys to his coffers. Percy knew if Wolsey had access to his money, he might be able to bribe servants to help him escape. Wolsey stared at him for a moment, wondering at the hand fate had dealt him. Silently, he unhooked the keys from his belt, and handed them to the Earl.

"Am I to leave now, even in the dead of night?" he asked Percy.

"We will leave with the dawn. For tonight, your bedchamber will be locked, and my men will stand watch to ensure you do not escape."

"Where would I go, my lord?" Wolsey asked. "And why would I flee? Only the guilty run. I, an innocent soul, have no cause to fear." Percy said nothing to Wolsey, but gave the keys to one of his captains, and started barking orders to others to secure the house. "May I not even know of what I am accused?" Wolsey asked.

"You are accused of high treason, of conspiring with enemies of England and the King. You are accused of attempting to bring foreign influence and armies to bear upon the fate of England." Percy's lip curled. "You are accused, Your Eminence, of betraying the King, your good and loyal friend."

"The accusations against me are false," Wolsey said. "But I know I can expect no indifferent justice in this. I am left here bare, wretched, and without help or succour."

Wolsey put up no fight when Percy's men took him to his chamber and locked him inside. But his men attempted to protest his innocence. They were told sharply they had better watch their tongues, lest they incriminate themselves along with their master. Quickly, they fell silent.

The next day, the day before his planned enthronement as Bishop of York, Wolsey left the north. He was taken under guard to Pontefract, and it was said that many people turned out to cheer him, for since his arrival in the north he had made it his mission to win the support of the common people, about whom he had but little cared before. He took five retainers with him, Cavendish amongst them. He feared the destination, for at Pontefract Castle, Richard II had been murdered. Wolsey feared the same was to happen to him. He broke into grateful tears when he was told they were not to lodge at the Castle, but at the Abbey. He wore a hair shirt that night, for penance for his many sins, but still he protested that he was innocent of all he was accused.

From Pontefract he was taken to Doncaster, and then Sheffield Park, where he stayed and was treated well for three weeks, even taken hunting by his host, the Earl of Shrewsbury. Whilst there, however, Wolsey was taken with pains of the stomach, which turned serious. He passed blood and foul stools. He feared to take the potions and powders offered by Shrewsbury's physicians, as he thought they might be poisoned, but after Cavendish tried them first, Wolsey agreed to take them. But even with such medicine, the Cardinal sickened only more.

Master Kingston, the Constable of the Tower of London, rode out to meet him with many guards. "Master Kingston, Master Kingston," Wolsey said, mewing piteously, "I am a wretch replete with misery, and hope has left me bereft." Kingston said Wolsey was grey of face, and seemed like a lost soul wafting through purgatory. Kingston tried to comfort him, but Wolsey dismissed him. "Your words are but a fool's paradise, Master Kingston," he whimpered. "I know what awaits me."

In the night, the bloody flux grew worse. Cavendish later reported that Wolsey passed blood and liquid through his rear over fifty times in but one night and one day. The matter that came pouring from him was black and vile smelling. By dawn, his blood raged with fever. He was white and shaking, unable to even sip at water. Kingston decided that he could not charge Wolsey to mount a horse, or be carried in a litter in such a state. They would wait, he said, until the Cardinal recovered to bring him to the Tower.

After two days, Wolsey seemed to rally, and they brought him by litter to Hardwick Hall, and then to Leicester Abbey, which he reached on the 26th of November. Carried staggering into the Abbey, Wolsey gazed glassily at the face of the horrified Abbot. "Father Abbot," he whispered, his face pale as death. "I have come hither to leave my bones amongst you."

Three days later, and the Cardinal still lingered. He took some broth from Cavendish, before recognising the taste of chicken and refusing to take more, as it was a fast day, on which he should only eat fish. But later, he knew that his time had come. He received absolution from his confessor amidst the howling screams of a great storm which swept over the whole country. The tempest raged as Wolsey fought for life. Rain hammered England, winds swept roofs from houses, and cattle in their pens screamed in terror. Later, people would say that this was the coming of the Prince of Darkness himself, to take the soul of his most precious servant from the earth and into hell.

As rain lashed the window panes, and the howling wind shrieked outside the Abbey, Wolsey turned to his men, and the Abbot and spoke calmly. "If I had served God as diligently as I have done the King," he said calmly. "He would not have given me over in my grey hairs." He spoke of Henry with affection, saying that he was a gentle and noble prince, but one who would "hazard the loss of one half his realm to have his will done." He smiled gently and said to Kingston, "I assure you, I have often kneeled before him in the Privy Chamber for the space of an hour or two, to try and persuade him from his will and appetite, but I could never dissuade him when his heart was fixed on some matter." Wolsey nodded feebly. "When I am dead and gone, Master Kingston, you will remember well my words."

As the clock struck eight in the night, Thomas Wolsey, Archbishop of York, Cardinal of the Catholic Church, and once-Chancellor of England, died. He was fifty-seven years old.

His last words whispered of his love for the King.

His body was laid out in state as the people of Leicester came to view the corpse dressed in its cardinal's robes, and lying on a coffin of boards. Wolsey was carried to the Lady Chapel where he lay for some days as people came to see him. Throughout the day and the night, wax tapers burned around him, gently covering the old man's face with dappled light. Some days later, he was taken to his final rest, and put into the ground not far from the grave that held the bones of Richard II.

Some came to grieve at his graveside, but others, including myself, called that place "the tyrant's sepulchre."

Chapter Seventy-Five

Greenwich Palace
Autumn 1530

Henry was told of Wolsey's death by George Cavendish whilst he was at archery practise in the grounds of Greenwich Palace. The King said little when he heard of the death of his oldest friend, but gave Cavendish a coin and thanked him quietly for caring for the Cardinal in his last hours. Then he put his bow down and went to walk alone in the gardens, telling his men he wanted to be alone.

George came to tell me the news and I went to find Henry. He turned as he heard my step upon the path, and looked down at the floor, waiting for me to come to him. I put my hand to his purple sleeve and he glanced up. Grief was all I saw in his face.

"I know that you loved him, Henry," I said gently. "And despite all that happened, I know he loved you, too." He stared out at the horizon, tears gathering in his eyes. I knew he saw nothing there but the Cardinal's face. "Perhaps it is better this way," I consoled. "In dying before he had to face trial, Wolsey does not go to the grave with the stain of treason on his name. Now, you can remember the Cardinal as wish to, as a friend whom you loved, not as a traitor to the crown."

Henry's eyes were haunted, hollow as they met mine. "He has done me a final service there," he whispered.

"The Cardinal was not a young man, Henry," I continued, tucking my arm through his. "His death was bound to come and it was not done by your hand. You were ever a gentle master, and forgave him more than he deserved. I hear that he spoke on you with affection at his end, and called you a generous and merciful prince. Such things, when spoken at the end of a life, hold truth within them."

Henry nodded, accepting all I said, absolutely. "I was. It is true, sweetheart, sometimes the love I bear to others means I am overly gentle in my kingship."

"All of which speaks only of your greatness, Henry," I assured him. "You are the most gentle and Christian of princes, qualities that I should learn to emulate more."

Henry laughed shortly. "Nay, sweetheart… you are perfect as you are. Your passion for me is what causes you to rush to my defence, I know this well enough." He smiled indulgently, a flicker of his old humour returning. "You are, after all, of your sex, and apt to be ruled by your heart. I would not have you any other way."

I tried very hard not to show how vexing I found that comment. "Remember Wolsey as he was once to you, Henry," I urged, leading him along the little path and through the chilly knot gardens. A sparkle of frost was still upon the branches in the shade, and they glittered at us; diamonds in the shadows. Jackdaws and rooks cawed and croaked in the trees above us and bright-chested robins flittered through the skies. "Remember him as a friend, and as a man dear to your heart. There is no cause now to discredit his memory. Let him lie as he is, and remember him with love." Henry hung on to my hand, tears in his eyes. He tried to shake them away, but more only came to surface in their place.

"Come, my lord," I said. "We shall talk no more, unless you wish, but know that my heart grieves with you to see your once-friend gone from this life. I shall be with you always, now and forever, to take your sorrows as my own, and to comfort you."

The King of England's hand wrapped itself about mine as we walked through the gardens in silence that day, together.

Chapter Seventy-Six

York Place
Autumn 1530

Two days later, as the winds of the winter began to nip at the heels of autumn, Cranmer came to visit. I called for him to come in as I finished reading a letter Cromwell had sent me.

"I end," he wrote, *"by thanking you most graciously for the advice you offered me freely these months just passed. I believe that I had already decided on the choice I was to make, that is to give all my attention and love to the King, but it was your counsel that helped me to take that final step to this path I now walk. I know that you had no need to advise me with such honesty and goodness, my lady, and yet you did. Be assured therefore that I am, and always will be,*

Your servant and good friend,

Thomas Cromwell."

I smiled to read such. With Wolsey gone, for good this time, Cromwell knew where his best chance for the future lay. Henry, it seemed, could not do without him, and spoke of his great skill and wisdom with earnest admiration. I was glad Wolsey was now gone for good, not only because my enemy had been removed, but because this also removed the barrier that had until then remained between Cromwell and me. We could become close allies now, now that Wolsey was no longer between us. I folded the note and placed it in the little bag I wore on my hip, thinking well of the path I had taken with Cromwell. With such a man at my side, working for Henry's cause, I believed there was a time of new hope coming to us. And the man approaching my chambers, too, offered me even more hope.

"How goes your work, Master Cranmer?" I asked after offering him wine and bringing him to the fire to warm up. I had Kate take his cloak, for he was soaking after riding through London in the pouring rain.

That charming, shy smile broke across his face like the gentle dawn on the horizon. "I struggle with it daily, madam," he admitted softly. "Although I will confide this to you alone, if I may, and not to my master the King! I do not wish to disappoint his Majesty, but with you, I feel I have to be honest in all matters." His cheeks turned pink. "You tease such truths out of me, my lady," he confessed.

I laughed. "I will take that as a sign of the good friendship between us, Master Cranmer, and not as one of fear."

"I do not fear you, my lady," he said warmly. "Although I admit that before I met you, I did."

"I am sure many people feel the same when they hear what is said of me. The way I am spoken of about England is not the way I am truly, Cranmer," I said sadly. "I hope one day to show the people of England that I am better than they believe me to be."

He looked concerned, thinking he had hurt my feelings. "Do not despair, my lady," he consoled. "For as soon as I met you I saw in you a true and godly soul, and a brave one, fighting only for the salvation of the people... In time, the English people will see this, and they will adore you for it."

I thought my heart might burst for the swelling of affection therein. Cranmer was so open, so honest, so very good. He saw good qualities in everyone and everything because they were so generously strewn in his heart. "With all that is within my heart and soul, I hope that is indeed true, Master Cranmer... Now, please do tell me of your work."

"I try to make it the best I have written, and to make it engaging even if the subject matter is scholarly." He held his hands out to the blazing fire and frowned. "I admit there are times when I sit with my head in my hands for sorrow at my poor sentences, and other times I sit back and stare at what I have written and wonder who it was who wrote something so well and so prettily." He exhaled noisily. "I suffer the sin of pride and fall to the blankness of disbelief in myself over and over."

"I have felt that way often in the trials of the *Great Matter*, my friend," I admitted, pulling my chair closer to the fire. "Oftentimes I have lost my faith, and then found it once more that same day. I have struggled through fire and torment, and the King and I have been ever-tested in our virtue… And yet there is much to sustain me in my struggles. The King's love, the words of God… the friendships I have made with remarkable men and women."

I gazed up at him, the warmth from the fire reflecting on my face. "And all the while I think that there was a purpose in all this… When first the King admitted his love for me and his desire to be separated from Katherine, he told me that it was the will of God that I was brought into his life, that it was the will of God that I refuse him, for pride in my maidenly virtue… That it was the will of God that we be together. At the time, I wondered, for even though my beloved is the King, it seemed like arrogance to believe that one knows the will and wishes of God with such ease. And yet, after all I have been shown in these years since, I believe now that Henry *is* the chosen of God, placed here to rule over us, answerable to God alone. So perhaps, even then, he heard the voice of God sound within him, calling him to take this matter into his hands, and act upon it."

Cranmer returned my steady gaze. "I believe that is the case, my lady," he agreed. "I know that this has not been easy for you." The red glowing light of the fire danced against the shadows on his face. His expression was gentle, and affectionate. I felt so at peace when I was with Cranmer; he calmed me and brought clarity to my thoughts. I knew that he thought highly of me for my reformist ideas and the information I had brought to Henry. Cranmer and I had very similar beliefs and were fast becoming close friends.

"But sometimes," the good man continued, "it happens that what will, in the end, bring the most good takes the most work. The delays and the trials you have suffered... resent them not, my lady, for they only make you stronger. Our Lord Jesus suffered death for the salvation of the whole world, but we ask you only to suffer in life a while longer, so that this country and her people may be turned from the darkness of ignorance and into the light of truth. Keep in mind that you suffer, not only for yourself and for the King, but for the people of this realm. They will benefit more than we can imagine, when Katherine is finally replaced, and you are made Queen. Then they shall have not only a gracious and goodly woman of true virtue ruling over them, but a King set free from the slavery of the tyranny of Rome. It will take time; all things that bring goodness do... There are barriers to break and hearts to win, but in time, my lady, right will prevail, and God will look on you with a kind eye and a warm heart... I promise you."

"The people do not see me as such now, Master Cranmer," I said with sorrow. "They revile my name and call me things that cause me grief. They love Katherine, and they see me as a usurper."

"Our Lord Jesus was also hated, if you remember, my lady?" he said. "The saints, the apostles, many of them died for their faith at the hands of those who understood not their goodness. You will not have to die for your matter... But keep in mind their strength and their courage as you battle through your own trials. And when you are Queen, the people will see the charity and bounty that I know live in your heart. It may not seem humble to do so, but I would suggest that you make known the support you offer to scholars, and the largesse you distribute to the poor and the Church... Such things are not done by you, I know, to win hearts, but the people should see that you do just as much, if not more, for them, than Katherine."

I blushed. "I am no saint, Master Cranmer... but if any man could make me into one, I believe it would be you."

He leaned forward and pressed his hand into mine. "Be of good cheer, madam," he said. "We are, all of us, not as perfect as we would like, but in you I see great strength, courage and true faith. Those are the virtues that mark out the true children of God, and I am honoured to serve you."

"You flatter me too much," I protested. "There are many times when I fall into sin... spite, fury, rage... I promise you, I am not as good as you think me."

Cranmer grinned. "Those who can see their faults and put them to mending, are those who are blessed before God, my lady. Do not be so hard on yourself. These years would have tried the patience of any... Keep faith, in God, in yourself, in the King and in your friends, and you will have all you need."

I sighed, but it was a happy sigh. There was something so honest and good in Cranmer that I felt as though I had come home after a long time away whenever he was near. "You give me the strength to hope, my friend," I said, looking into the flames. "And I hope that soon there will be a resolution to our *Matter*." I paused. "I have asked the King again to pardon Master Tyndale and bring him to England. Although our King is most displeased with the scholar, I believe Tyndale may aid us, if he can be persuaded to abandon his arguments for the Queen."

"A bold request, madam, and one that once again demonstrates your strength of character... Has the King said he will consider it?"

"He has," I said. "He is ready to listen to much, now." I glanced up at Cranmer. "I hope, I hope so much, my friend, that all of this struggle will lead on to greater good. Henry is becoming open to new ideas and thoughts. It is as though he has awoken from a deep sleep, and begins to see the world anew."

"Let us hope that is indeed the case, my lady."

As he left me that evening, I sat by the fire by myself, letting my ladies play at cards together at the table. They asked if I wished to join them, but I did not. Kate offered me wine, but I set it to one side. My eyes were stolen by the flames, leaping and prancing about each other, stroking and whirling in their beautiful dance. Outside, the night was clear and the stars were bright.

I thought on all that Cranmer had said, and drew comfort from his words. He was right; faith in God, in Henry, in myself and in my friends... this was all I needed to succeed. *And soon*, I thought, *soon we would.* We had the opinions of the universities, we had Cranmer and other scholars, we had the quick mind of Cromwell... And my great enemy Wolsey was no more.

Above all others, that was what du Bellay wrote about me... *Above all others, the Lady Anne.* And it was true now... there was no one above me in Henry's heart, estimations or friendship. Any who opposed me would be cast down. And soon enough I would find a way to persuade Henry that the words of Cranmer and the *Collectanea* were true... He would become the King I knew he could be.

I sat for a long time that night, thinking of all that had passed since Henry asked me to be his Queen. It felt finally as though we were standing at the edge of something, something vast and unimagined before in England. A time in which we would break free of the oppression of Rome and her corruption, but also a time of fresh hope, when the new learning could be brought to the people, and set them and us free.

I was at the edge of something wondrous and beautiful, teetering at the cliff tops of this possibility and change, so vast, that I could not see all that lay ahead. But I was excited, elated... I felt as though if I but put out my arms then wings would grow from them, and I would fly free. I knew too that there were many miles left to go for us, but with the strength of the people who believed in me, such as Cranmer, I felt as though I could flow over those miles, wending my wings through the skies, and coming to rest only when our great task was done.

This was no longer only the King's *Great Matter*, it was all of England's and I was the force, the power and the will that seemed to drive it.

One day, we would have all that we dreamed of, I thought... for Henry, for me, and for England.

Epilogue

The Tower of London
The Afternoon of the 18th May, 1536

Shadows have started to appear in the corners of the room; they stretch long in the afternoon light. The ghosts of my past have returned to stare at me through the whitewashed walls. Master Kingston left me many hours ago, and I have prayed, and remembered the past all this time…. All this time I thought not on my present misery, and it has done me good. I have barely noted the hours pass, so deep and long have been my reflections.

Those men who came to us then, Cranmer; Cromwell; Gardiner; Foxe… Each had his part to play in our story. I thought them all friends and allies then, but I did not know I had already met and befriended the man who would one day spell my doom.

But how could I have known, then, that one of these men would topple me from the precarious seat of power so many years later? Should I have seen such a thing, somehow, and prevailed against it? Should I, too, have noted the changes in Henry, and feared them rather than welcoming them? I did not see that my greatest enemy would rise one day from the heart of my greatest love… and that he, and the powers of the court, would one day remove me, just as I had done so with Wolsey.

I did not consider then, what I had done. I did not think that one day I would face the same charges as Wolsey. I did not understand I had shown Henry how to remove a loved one, how to leave one behind. I did not know I had given a sketch of my own fate, to my enemies.

But on that night as I sat before the fire, I knew not what was to come. I knew only that I was at the edge of something great, something momentous, not only for me, but for the faith I turned to so often and so desperate in those years to console me. I had risen higher than any could imagine, but there was still further to go... and but two barriers to overcome; Katherine and her daughter Mary. In those years that would come to pass after, I would come to know things about myself that I had never known before. I came to face aspects of my character I had hardly known existed. I was tested in those years. Tested more than I had ever imagined possible. And yet, in all the ill I did to Katherine and her daughter, I sought to do much good for my country, for my King, and for my friends...

We are none of us, perfect creatures. There are many who come much closer than I to the mark of sainthood. I know this. I have asked God to forgive me of my sins, and I hope He will.

It is past noon. The morning wanes to afternoon. I have but what hours of this day are left, and one more night before I face death.

Cranmer has asked to come to me once more. I will be glad of his company, for he always managed to bring me peace, and peace is what I need now, as I prepare for the end.

My story is not yet done. I have to face memories of the time when my greatest sins were done. I will have to face Katherine's ghost, and Mary's memory. Now, as I sit awaiting death, I know what I did to Katherine and her daughter. It is only now that I come to fully understand the pain she endured. Perhaps this, then, is God's way of making me understand all that I did. Sinners find ways to repent... I have found mine. This story is my penance. My way of explaining to God all that I did, and why I did it. My way of confessing my sins, and trying to uphold all the good I did amidst the evil.

And yes. I know I did wrong by many. I do not seek to excuse myself of such sins. Tomorrow morning, I will meet God. I must do so with a clear conscience. I must explain myself to my maker.

I wonder if I will get the chance to speak to Katherine in Heaven. If we walk under the light of God together, I will tell her much… And perhaps she will forgive me… for she was always a stronger woman than I…

There are voices outside the door. I turn, waiting to see who has come to see me on this, the last full day of my life.

Here ends *Above all Others*. In book four, *The Scandal of Christendom*, Anne works to remove Katherine and her daughter Mary from their royal titles as Henry's men work hard on the King's *Great Matter*. In her quest to become Queen, Anne will find ways to persuade Henry that he can rule as Pope and Emperor… changing the course of British history, and shaking the foundations of the Church….

About the Author

I find people talking about themselves in the third person to be entirely unsettling, so, since this section is written by me, I will use my own voice rather than try to make you believe that another person is writing about me to make me sound terribly important.

I am an independent author, publishing my books by myself, with the help of my lovely editor. I write in all the spare time I have. I briefly tried entering into the realm of 'traditional' publishing but, to be honest, found the process so time consuming and convoluted that I quickly decided to go it alone and self-publish.

My passion for history, in particular perhaps the era of the Tudors, began early in life. As a child I lived in Croydon, near London, and my schools were lucky enough to be close to such glorious places as Hampton Court and the Tower of London to mean that field trips often took us to those castles. I think it is hard not to find the Tudors infectious when you hear their stories, especially when surrounded by the bricks and mortar they built their reigns within. There is heroism and scandal, betrayal and belief, politics and passion and a seemingly never-ending cast list of truly fascinating people. So when I sat down to start writing, I could think of no better place to start than somewhere and sometime I loved and was slightly obsessed with.

Expect *many* books from me, but do not necessarily expect them all to be of the Tudor era. I write as many of you read, I suspect; in many genres. My own bookshelves are weighted down with historical volumes and biographies, but they also contain dystopias, sci-fi, horror, humour, children's books, fairy tales, romance and adventure. I can't promise I'll manage to write in *all* the areas I've mentioned there, but I'd love to give it a go. If anything I've published isn't your thing, that's fine, I just hope you like the ones I write which *are* your thing!

The majority of my books *are* historical fiction however, so I hope that if you liked this volume you will give the others in this series (and perhaps not in this series), a look. I want to divert you as readers, to please you with my writing and to have you join me on these adventures.

A book is nothing without a reader.

As to the rest of me; I am in my thirties and live in Cornwall with a rescued dog, a rescued cat and my partner (who wasn't rescued, but may well have rescued me). I studied Literature at University after I fell in love with books as a small child. When I was little I could often be found nestled half-way up the stairs with a pile of books and my head lost in another world between the pages. There is nothing more satisfying to me than finding a new book I adore, to place next to the multitudes I own and love… and nothing more disappointing to me to find a book I am willing to never open again. I do hope that this book was not a disappointment to you; I loved writing it and I hope that showed through the pages.

This is only one in a large selection of titles coming to you on Amazon. I hope you will try the others.

If you would like to contact me, please do so.

On twitter, I am @TudorTweep and am more than happy to follow back and reply to any and all messages. I may avoid you if you decide to say anything worrying or anything abusive, but I figure that's acceptable.

Via email, I am tudortweep@gmail.com a dedicated email account for my readers to reach me on. I'll try and reply within a few days.

I publish some first drafts and short stories on Wattpad where I can be found at www.wattpad.com/user/GemmaLawrence31 . Wattpad was the first place I ever showed my stories, *to anyone*, and in many ways its readers and their response to my works were the influence which pushed me into self-publishing. If you have never been on the site I recommend you try it out. Its free, its fun and its chock-full of real emerging talent. I love Wattpad because its members and their encouragement gave me the boost I needed as a fearful waif to get some confidence in myself and make a go of a life as a real, published writer.

Thank you for taking a risk with an unknown author and reading my book. I do hope now that you've read one you'll want to read more. If you'd like to leave me a review, that would be very much appreciated also!

Gemma Lawrence
Cornwall
2017

Thank You

…to so many people for helping me make this book possible… to my editor Brooke who entered into this with me and gave me her time, her wonderful guidance and also her encouragement. To my partner Matthew, who will be the first to admit that history is not his thing, and yet is willing to listen to me extol the virtues and vices of the Tudors and every other time period, repeatedly, to him and pushed me to publish even when I feared to. To my family for their ongoing love and support; this includes not only my own blood in my mother and father, sister and brother, but also their families, their partners and all my nieces who I am sure are set to take the world by storm as they grow. To Matthew's family, for their support, and for the extended family I have found myself welcomed to within them. To my friend Petra who took a tour of Tudor palaces and places with me back in 2010 which helped me to prepare for this book and others; her enthusiasm for that strange but amazing holiday brought an early ally to the idea I could actually write a book… And lastly, to the people who wrote all the books I read in order to write this book… all the historical biographers and masters of their craft who brought Elizabeth, and her times, to life in my head.

Thank you to all of you; you'll never know how much you've helped me, but I know what I owe to you.

Gemma
Cornwall
2017